Finding Rachel Davenport

Finding Rachel Davenport

MICHAEL HARLING

Published 2012 by Opis,
an imprint of Prospera Publishing

Published 2015 by Lindenwald Press

© Copyright 2012 Michael Harling

ISBN-13: 979-8-9907389-0-4

vi

Lindenwald **LP** Press

For Rachel Davenport:
Thanks for giving me the business card that
started all of this

Also by Michael Harling

The Postcards Trilogy

Postcards From Across the Pond
More Postcards From Across the Pond
Postcards From Ireland

The Talisman Series

The Magic Cloak
The Roman Villa
The Sacred Tor
The Bard of Tilbury
The Crystal Palace
The White Feather
The Isle of Avalon
The Talisman

Chapter 1

IF I HADN'T ACCIDENTALLY blown up Keymer View Court, things might have turned out differently. I knew being a real-life crime fighter meant accepting disadvantages that a comic book super hero wouldn't have to contend with, but those details didn't trouble me; I had a calling, I felt destined for great things, but right now I was in Burgess Hill watching two men dig a hole.

They were obscured by darkness and the riot of weeds that infested the land behind Keymer View Court, an aging block of flats in what had once been an affluent part of town but which had, in recent years, slipped into the "relatively safe" category. There were no security lights and the glow from the street lamps couldn't penetrate the tangle of trees and shrubs along the walled boundary of the estate. No light came from the flats, either. Many of the windows were unadorned black squares fronting empty rooms, and most of the flats that were occupied were also dark; only a handful emitted muted light from behind drawn curtains. I peered around a forsythia bush for a better view of the two shadowy figures.

"I think we missed it," the tall one said.

"No, it's here," said his shorter, rounder companion. "I'm sure of it."

"Then you dig."

Their whispers stopped. The scrape of shovel against soil resumed. I crouched behind the bush, waiting and assessing.

Considering I had come expecting to surprise a gang of teenage vandals, I regarded this development as a step up. True, I didn't know what they were up to, but I knew it wasn't legal. Legal enjoyed daylight; legal wasn't furtive; legal would have brought a torch.

I crept away from the bush for an unobstructed view. Dressed in black, I would be invisible to them, so long as I moved with caution and remained silent.

I held my breath, listening, nodding to the rhythm of the shovel. When it next struck the earth, I slid the camera from my utility belt. At the next stroke, I turned it on. It was already set for infrared mode and had all of its blips, beeps and flashing

1

lights turned off but there was nothing I could do about the whirr of the telescopic lens.

I waited, listening for a break in the digger's cadence. They gave no sign of having heard me, so I unclipped my infrared beaming device. Balanced in a semi-crouch, the camera in my right hand and the IRB in my left, I flicked the 'on' switch. Nothing changed; the men remained hidden in shadows. I aimed the IRB and camera in what I hoped to be the right direction and snapped three photos in time to the beat of the shovel.

What I was taking pictures of, I couldn't guess.

I waited, wondering how to proceed. I'd been prowling Keymer View Court for three nights now and had found nothing out of the ordinary. About an hour ago, I had decided to call the mission a success—assuming the objective had been to work the kinks out of my identity-swapping routine and field-test my crime fighting equipment—and go home to catch up on my sleep. But then I had stumbled upon the Laurel and Hardy lookalikes creeping around the perimeter and had followed them here, where they had begun their surreptitious nocturnal digging; I wasn't sure if I felt elated or disappointed.

A clank of metal on metal made the digger lose his rhythm.

"That's it. Here, let me."

The shorter man sank low and merged into the shadows on the ground.

"I've found the bolt. Gimme the spanner. We'll put the block here."

More scraping and a few whispered curses. I snapped a few more photos.

"That's got it. I'll take this from here, you find the other hatch."

The shadows moved a few feet closer to the building. The taller one picked up the shovel, the short one pointed. "Dig here."

"You know, you're making an awful lot of work out of something so simple."

The taller man's voice, even as a whisper, sounded deep and gruff compared to the high-pitched excitement of his partner. "Trust me; this is going to be worth it."

The tall man grunted and resumed digging. The short one fumbled in the darkness with something I couldn't see. I heard gurgling and caught a strong whiff of kitchen drain. After another minute of scrabbling around, the shorter one began filling in the first hole. "That should do it. You find the pipe yet?"

2

The tall man grunted again.

"We've got about fifteen minutes before the block sets. Just keep digging."

I thought I might put the time to better use than continuing to crouch in the dark watching them; they had brought a lot of gear and I hadn't heard any vehicles drive in since I had arrived, so the odds were that they had started out from somewhere within the complex. I secured the camera and IRB device to my utility belt and backed away, keeping the bush between us, taking slow, deliberate steps. The air was sharp and still, a ready amplifier for any snapped twig or rustling leaf. It was also cold, but inside my outfit a slick of sweat rolled down my back. After twenty yards, I judged I was far enough away. I turned and walked in a low, silent crouch to the edge the building, cutting around to the front courtyard where dim yellow circles glowed at irregular intervals from the few working lights.

Keymer View Court was built when people still cared about where they lived, and had the misfortune of surviving into a time when they no longer do. In front of me, a network of pathways crisscrossed what used to be a manicured, oval garden separating the north and south blocks. It was now so overgrown with brambles and thistles that only the main paths were navigable. I crossed the stretch of tarmac, using the parked cars for cover, and headed towards the path that cut diagonally to the far side of the court where I had first picked up their trail. The mass of weeds and feral bushes had been hacked back just enough to allow single-file access. I slipped into the shadows and stood upright, the relief of stretching my muscles overshadowing the need for secrecy. If anyone was watching, they had seen me already and would no doubt be phoning the authorities to report a sighting of a ninja or an escaped panther.

I followed the path, walking as fast as I dared in the darkness, my hands held in front of me like a sleepwalker to ward off the brambles. My gloves were thin but the Kevlar-lined palms kept any thorns from poking through. The path led to the back of the complex, where the two facing blocks of flats ended and the wild scrubland of neglected gardens began. Ahead of me, the boundary wall separating the flats from the railway line angled away from where it hugged the edge of the north block, carving out a wedge of woodland as it surrounded a double row of garages at the end of the south block. A single light glowed from a lamp post near the entrance.

Like the flats, the garage area consisted of two long brick structures facing each another. They were separated by a wide strip of tarmac cluttered with litter and parked cars, some with their bonnets open and resting on breezeblocks above ancient oil stains.

The men had come from this direction, most logically from one of the empty garages. I entered the cluttered canyon and pushed on the first unlocked door I came to. The metal squealed in protest. If they had come from a garage, I would have heard them, even on the far side of the complex. I pulled out my torch and moved further into the shadows.

At the far end, the boundary wall cut close to the side of one block, the narrow opening choked with holly bushes and decorated with empty beer cans. On the other side the gap was wider, leaving room for a dirt path and access to the wooded area beyond. I followed the path a short distance to the back corner of the property, where the boundary wall took a sharp left and angled towards the street. The path continued through a gap in the wall that looked as if it had once contained a gate.

Outside the complex, built up against the exterior wall and hidden in the patch of wood between the complex and the rail tracks, sat a squat brick hut. The windows were dark, the door closed but unlocked. I went inside.

It was definitely their lair; a fug of cigarette smoke hung in the air, mingled with the smell of old oil, new sawdust and a hint of the kitchen drain smell I had whiffed earlier. I shone the torch around, found a light switch and turned it on, blinking against the sudden fluorescent brightness.

The building was long and low, roomier than it looked from the outside, and appeared to be part caretaker's shack, part workshop and part playroom. Unused rakes, hedge trimmers, spades and other gardening bric-a-brac hung from one wall. A large wooden workbench covered in electrical bits and bobs and pieces of wire took up much of the near end of the room. At the far end, amid a scattering of old heating units, sat a battered fridge, two chairs and a table—made from a sheet of plywood and two sawhorses—where one of the heating units was undergoing surgery. The unit lay open, like a patient in a primitive operating theatre, surrounded by empty bottles of Newcastle Brown ale and crumpled cans of Scrumpy Jack.

There were no signs of what they might be up to, but I wasn't ready to give up; this was where they had come from so the answer was here somewhere. While waiting for inspiration to strike, I pulled out my camera, put it on normal mode and took flash pictures of the workbench, empty bottles, garden tools, everything. Then I reviewed the photos I had taken earlier. The

IR photos were off centre and out of focus, but they showed the figures of two men digging a hole. Behind them I could make out the gallon jugs, bucket, shovel and various other tools they had brought with them. Also in the frame, and out of context given their furtive work, was a traffic cone. It wasn't there to warn pedestrians of a potential hazard. Then I remembered the sloshing liquid; they were using it for a funnel.

I fastened the camera to my belt and took another look at the workshop. There was nothing sinister about it; everything was typical, right down to the overflowing ash tray on top of the refrigerator and the cigarette burns on the table edge. Still, something struck me as odd; the two sides of the room were out of balance. I went to the table where the heater lay and ran a gloved finger over the top. Sawdust, grit and ash residue collected on the material. Then I looked at the workbench; it was just as cluttered, but in a suspiciously random way. I tested the surface; my glove came away clean.

The rubbish bins, despite smelling like rotten eggs, yielded nothing suspicious—no containers marked with a skull and cross bones or a hand-drawn map of the area with circles and arrows revealing the plan of attack. That proved nothing and only heightened my suspicions. If they'd thought to clean up the evidence then they were doing something they didn't want connected to them. That could mean a dead end, but these two didn't strike me as criminal masterminds; they wouldn't have been very thorough.

I crawled under the workbench, shining my torch into the crevasses between the floorboards. The floor was crisscrossed with tiny grit furrows that told of a recent sweeping, and the smell of rancid cooking oil and eggs grew stronger. Still, I found nothing of interest and was about to give up when I brushed a layer of dust away from a knothole and uncovered what looked like a cluster of frogspawn. Three pea-sized beads were wedged inside, each with a dark centre protected by a pliable, translucent shell. I removed my glove and teased them out with a fingernail.

A loud bang from behind caused me to yelp and smack my head on the underside of the workbench.

The fox that had been investigating the rubbish bin, drawn no doubt by the smell, darted back into the woods, leaving the bin on its side and its contents strewn across the floor. I rubbed my head. The wig had cushioned the blow, but that hadn't kept me from seeing stars. I gave myself a mental kick. Letting the fox sneak up on me was sloppy; a real crime fighter would not have

5

allowed that. But then a real crime fighter's heart wouldn't be pounding.

I scooted out from under the workbench and took a quick look outside. No one around. No suspicious noises. I took a few deep breaths to calm myself and went back inside. The beads had become soft and sticky in my hand; I nudged them from my palm onto the workbench and inspected them. They were little rocks wrapped in plastic. The plastic seemed to be made to dissolve in water and the rocks looked like something I remembered from chemistry class. The solution snapped into place and made me go cold. The two holes, the numerous jugs, the mixture of smells, the bucket; add to that the suspected gang of vandals and the horrid odours and it all became clear. They were constructing the world's largest stink bomb.

The blocked drainage pipe was the barrel; the second hole was for the payload. Whatever concoction they had brewed up would be forced into the flats. And that's what worried me. The beads were the propellant with a crude, time-delayed coating. They were clever, but did they know what they were dealing with?

I rubbed my palms on the fabric of my suit, then put my gloves on and selected the least damaged pellet. At the other end of the shack, I found a pint glass and poured the dregs from the bottles and cans into it until there was an inch of liquid in the base. I set it on the far side of the table, dropped the bead inside and retreated, counting out loud as I made for the other end of the room. "One, two, three." At the wall I turned and crouched behind the workbench to watch. "Four, five, six."

The bead fizzed and bobbed in the glass as the liquid cut through the protective layer. I hoped I was wrong; I hoped the beer simply foamed or popped.

"Seven, eight, nine."

The glass exploded.

A crack, like gunfire, careened off the walls and a ball of flame sent shards in every direction. I ducked, and when I looked again to where the glass once stood there remained only the shattered base, a wet spot and a plume of smoke.

I raced out of the shed. Caesium was the only substance on earth that could do that, and somehow these clowns had managed to get some. They might be clever in a sophomoric way, but pouring caesium into water could kill them both, never mind what might happen to the drainpipe. I belted through the woods and back into the estate, not slowing until I was midway through the overgrown garden. There had been no explosion, so

6

nothing had happened yet. If my mission was to succeed, I needed to catch them in the act.

I pulled out my camera and IRB device, activating both as I trotted to the edge of the building and slid into the shadows.

I could just make them out in the dim light; two grey figures squatting next to a hole, each with the glow of a cigarette floating in front of their face. They smoked in silence.

As I crept up behind the bush, the tall man tossed his dog-end into the hole. "That plug should be set by now. Let's finish this."

The smaller man knelt and picked up the traffic cone, easing the narrow end into the pipe. "That's it; put it in the hole, nice and tight."

"Said the actress to the bishop."

"Stop it, Derek," the small man said without looking up. "You're killing me. Now do something useful and hold this steady."

He left Derek holding the upended traffic cone and came back with the bucket. "Get ready. After these hit the water we'll only have a few seconds. You'll need to pull the funnel out and help me plug up the hole."

This was the money shot; even in infrared, it would be clear what was going on. I aimed the camera and IRB.

"Steady now. I don't want them all to go in, just a couple will do."

I pressed the shutter.

The night lit up in stark white and the men stared like squirrels caught in the high beams.

"Shit," I said.

"What the—" Derek said, clamping his hands over his eyes.

"Fucking hell," the short man said, dropping the bucket into the funnel. The next sound was the clatter of beads cascading down the cone and into the pipe. "Derek, run!"

They charged towards me, the short man in front while Derek staggered behind like a pole-axed bull. I jumped up, ready to make tracks myself, and smashed boob-to-face into Shorty. I flew backward and we tumbled to the ground, landing in a shockingly intimate position.

"What the fuck?"

"Uh-uh," I said, struggling to get my breath back.

"You dick-wit," he shouted at my breasts.

Derek shambled past us, unaware of our blossoming romance.

"Get down, Derek!"

7

In a final act of chivalry, Shorty rolled off of me and dived behind the forsythia bush.

The earth roared and heaved, erupting in a geyser of mud and raw sewage as the bathroom windows in the flats exploded. I rolled onto my stomach. Shards of glass and clumps of foul-smelling mud fell around me. It was over in a moment and a silence much deeper than the quiet of an early morning settled around us, bringing with it an amazing stench.

"Derek, are you all right?"

"I think so. You?"

They struggled upright. Lights snapped on in the windows above us.

"What the hell's going on out there?" a voice called.

"We'd better haul our arses out of here," Derek said.

I rose to my hands and knees, still struggling to find my breath. When I did find it, the nauseating stench made me want to give it back.

"No, stay put," Shorty said. "I have an idea."

Several torch beams wavered around us like amateur searchlights. "I've called the police," a voice from above said. Then another light snapped on. "Who's out there?"

I stood upright and opened my mouth to speak, but Shorty got there first.

"It's me, Carl. I'm with Derek. We captured the yob who's been vandalising the place."

"Well don't just stand there, cut his bullocks off."

"I can't, she's a bird."

"I don't care if it's Margaret Thatcher. Cut her bollocks off."

These old folks were a feisty lot.

The area lit up around us like a scene from a prison break movie, with most of the lights trained on me. I looked up, one hand shielding my eyes, the other pointing towards Carl and Derek.

"I didn't do it. It was them."

"Sure. And pigs will fly," said a voice.

"Tell it to the coppers," said another.

"You're nicked," said Carl.

"But you're the vandals," I said.

Carl looked at me with his mouth open for a few moments then brought his chin up to meet his upper jaw. In the distance, sirens sounded.

He smiled. "And who do you think they're going to believe? The loyal caretakers, or some freak in black pyjamas sneaking around in the middle of the night?"

"Why you . . . little weasel." It wasn't my best insult, but it was all I could do under the circumstance. "I have proof."

Derek edged towards me. I stepped back. Carl stepped forward. "What proof?"

"Pictures. I have them right . . . shit."

The camera! It had flown out of my hands when we collided. I had no idea where it was.

"You don't seem so confident now. Be interesting to see what the police make of your story."

Derek jumped forward and grabbed my arm. Carl lunged for the other but I swung away and kicked his knee, sending him howling to the ground. I slammed my foot down on Derek's instep, but my soft soled shoes had no effect through his heavy work boots. He tightened his grip on my arm and grinned. So I tripped him.

The three of us lay sprawled in the muck, Carl still thrashing and holding his knee like a kid trying to milk maximum sympathy out of a minor scrape. With my free hand I pulled a wrist-restraint from my belt and gave Derek a chop on his elbow. He grunted and lost his grip. I pushed away from them and snapped the restraint around their ankles, binding the two of them together. They both reached down and began clawing at the nylon strip. It was too good an opportunity to pass up; I lashed another restraint around their wrists.

Carl stopped his histrionics. "Who are you?"

I had never anticipated being asked that question; I was invisible, I came and left without a trace. No one was supposed to see me. "I am the night."

"That's Batman," Carl said. He looked at Derek. "She thinks she's Bat Girl."

"Whoever she thinks she is," Derek said, "once the coppers arrive, her name will be shit."

"Don't you mean your name?"

Carl looked at me. "You seem to forget it's your word against ours. And theirs."

He pointed to the building where several dozen angry faces peered down. I paid no attention. I planned on being gone when the police arrived; I just needed to find my camera and get away. Then I noticed that many of the lighted windows were empty and I began to wonder how many people were itching for the opportunity to thump the person responsible for their misery. In the distance, the sirens grew louder; the shouts of the residents were at ground level now, and getting closer.

"Do you think the police are going to believe you tried to stop a girl from vandalising this building and she overpowered the both of you?"

Carl stared at me in disbelief. "But you just did. Or do you think the cops will believe we did this to ourselves?"

The sirens drew closer. Angry voices echoed around the end of the building. They would be on me in moments. But truth was on my side, I just needed to stand my ground. That's what a real crime fighter would do.

Then the police cars turned into the court, silhouetting the figures of the enraged mob racing towards me.

The mob was too fast to be made up of pensioners; there were young fit men among them, mixing in with the long term residents. None of them sounded like they wanted to talk this through. The camera was in the weeds, I didn't have time to search for it without getting caught. And if I was captured, I would no longer be invisible. And neither would Rachel. What would Wonder Woman do? Wonder Woman would zip over at the speed of light and have the camera in a flash, then hold the mob back with her lasso of truth.

That's what Wonder Woman would do.

I ran.

Chapter 2

I RACED AROUND THE crater, away from the mob, towards the trees, stumbling through the bushes. My pursuers, with the advantage of torchlight, were gaining. I pulled out my own torch and switched it on. It made me visible, but I could move faster.

I squeezed through a gap in the thicket and came up against the brick wall.

"She's in there!"

The pounding feet grew louder. Torch beams wavered through the undergrowth. I jumped, grabbed the top edge of the wall and vaulted over as the mob broke through. I landed on the pavement, safe from my pursuers but standing on the street, mud-caked and wearing black pyjamas. All I lacked was an electric sign to hang around my neck flashing "arrest me" in red.

A patrol car—siren wailing, blue lights flashing—screamed down the main street. If they looked my way they couldn't miss seeing me. I froze, waiting for the inevitable, but they flew past and screeched into Keymer View Court, so intent on getting in on the action that they missed the main event. I stuck close to the wall and moved away from the junction. I was safe enough for the minute but sooner or later the mob behind the wall was going to discover what a beautiful thing co-operation was and begin boosting members over the top.

The opposite side of the street was lined with a row of identical bungalows from the post-war era. Some had lights on and, as I looked, more windows winked into life. Ahead of me, the road dead-ended; beyond, the land was covered in trees and low shrubs. I raced towards it, but I wasn't going to make it without being seen. Behind me, the commotion grew louder and I turned to see hands and a few heads bobbing above the parapet. Before the people in the houses had a chance to pull on their cardigans and join the chase, I jumped at the wall and pulled myself over. Inside I eased to the ground and crouched among the bushes as shouts and pounding feet echoed in the street.

"This way! She went this way."

"No, over here!"

The voices were a mixture of Indian and east European accents. There seemed to be only a handful of them. I peered

11

through the bushes at the growing collection of spectators and police. The residents who had chased me were making their way back towards the building now, chattering and gesticulating to the waiting cops.

The police began cordoning off the scene of the crime, lighting it up with criss-crossed beams from the headlights of their patrol cars. The police threw long shadows over what looked like a miniature mock-up of a World War I battle field as they urged the crowd back and unravelled rolls of crime scene tape. Before long, the place would be crawling with detectives, Scene of Crime Officers and, for all I knew, sniffer dogs.

I headed in the opposite direction, towards the back corner of the estate, keeping to the shadows. A sharp crack sounded as I stepped on a large twig. I froze, hoping the hubbub around the bomb crater would drown it out.

"Did you hear that?" It was one of the PCs. In a moment, I was caught in the beams of half a dozen torches. I jumped into the clear ground between the building and the undergrowth and ran. There was no way they could catch me. They would have to get around the hole and I had too much of a head start. I reached the rear wall in seconds, vaulted over in a single, fluid move and landed in front of three startled men.

The standoff lasted for several seconds. Only one of them had thought to bring a torch, but his foresight ended there; he was wearing nothing but a pair of pyjama bottoms. The other two were dressed in shorts, tee shirts and loafers with no socks. They all looked cold, tired and uncertain. I knew I could take them on and outrun them; I had the advantage of surprise and martial arts training. I had considered taking up judo or karate, but the method I had settled on was a little known discipline, adopted by the Israeli army, known as Krav Maga. I was drawn to it, not so much for its methods, but by its philosophy, which was neutralise and escape. It was the perfect match for an anonymous crime fighter who didn't want to dominate and only needed to get away.

That had been the idea, at any rate. The problem was, these people were the people I was here to help, so thumping them would not be in my best interest.

The one with the torch recovered first and lunged towards me. I ducked, tucked and rolled. When I sprang to my feet, I was behind them, and already running. I gained a fair lead but in the dark I couldn't run quietly enough to lose them or fast enough to stay ahead of them. The torchlight jumped around me as they tried to point it while running. I headed to where the ground sloped towards the railway tracks. At the crest, I ducked behind a tree, pulled my torch from my utility belt and threw it down the hillside. It made a satisfying racket as it bounced and rolled to the bottom. I held my breath.

They came within ten feet of me, then turned and followed the noise. As they skittered down the slope, I exhaled and headed the other way, coming out on the road well away from the rising excitement at Keymer View Court. Once on the street, I bolted back to my car.

The Batmobile it was not, nor was it an invisible jet, but the eight-year-old Ford Escort had some of the qualities of a perfect crime fighting car—it was dark and anonymous. No one was going to remember it parked among other cars on a quiet side street. As a bonus, it got great mileage and hadn't broken my budget.

I was covered in mud, twigs and leaves so before pulling out, I cleaned my face and fluffed out the curls of my black wig as best I could. At first glance I would look like any other person out for a drive at two o'clock in the morning. That was all I could hope for; a closer look, or sniff, would arouse suspicion. I was dripping with stench and, in the confined space of the car, the smell closed in on me. Turning on the fan made it worse. As I pulled away, I rolled the window down and sucked in the cold, fresh air.

On the way out of town I passed two more patrol cars coming in with lights flashing and sirens blaring. I made it to the outskirts of Cuckfield before I had to pull over from shaking so hard.

I rested my head against the steering wheel, gripping it tight while my shoulders shook and my arms quivered. A jumble of thoughts fogged my brain; I seized them and sorted through them, looking for the source. The mission had failed; that was the focal point. But failed how badly? The desired outcome had not been achieved, but I had escaped; they didn't know who I was.

Also, I had found the vandals, and had acquired irrefutable proof of what they were doing. If I hadn't lost my camera, I could have forwarded the photos to the police, as I had planned. And if the police had done nothing, I would have sent the photos to the newspapers, or the local television stations; to anyone who might shine a light on them and make them pay for what they had done. This was my prime objective; to show people that they cannot hide from their misdeeds.

Granted, going up against a gang of vandals wasn't the most glamorous mission I could think of, but I didn't have the advantages my fictional counterparts enjoyed. Clark Kent's job puts him in contact with more villains than his Superman alter ego can handle, and Diana Prince works in military intelligence where she can eavesdrop on top secret conversations and cherry-pick worthy assignments for Wonder Woman. As Rachel Davenport, International Travel Consultant for the Holiday Depot, I gather intelligence from people like Susan Delaney, who works at the sandwich shop next door to the office, and the only mission I had found for Nadia so far was one involving local youths, cheap cider and nervous pensioners.

That was why I had gone to Keymer View Court dressed in a black Microprene bodysuit that smelled like the inside of new car—to rumble a band of teenage hooligans who had been terrorising the tenants. Susan's aunt Gladys lived in a first floor flat in the south block. She and the other tenants had been hearing noises in the night and terrible smells began permeating the flats. She was sure a gang of youths, engaged in some unspecified but nasty behaviour, was responsible. The other tenants were fed up with it; the police couldn't do a thing for them and the landlord wouldn't install security lights. Many of them were moving out, but Aunt Gladys was too old, too frail and too strapped for cash to move. She was terrified, and Susan was worrying herself sick trying to think of a way to help her.

This would, I felt, be the perfect crime-fighting debut for Nadia, a chance to see if she could do some real good in the real world instead of just being someone I pretended to be when I didn't want anyone to recognise me.

Yes, I am *that* Rachel Davenport. You've probably been wondering what happened to me; I know the media have, and they haven't let their lack of facts temper their speculation. But all that talk about a nervous breakdown and locking myself in my room for two years was utter nonsense. They couldn't believe I was simply tired, and weary of life in the public eye, so they invented stories about me to keep the rumour mill churning. In a way, they are as much responsible for Nadia as anything else. Nadia first appeared as my cover, a means of escaping, of allowing me to move about undetected. Over the years, Nadia took on substance, and when I made my successful escape to Sussex, Nadia came with me.

After establishing a safely anonymous life, I had no further need for Nadia, but then the idea of becoming a clandestine crime fighter arrived and would not go away. So I found a job as a travel agent, refined my Nadia persona and waited for the right opportunity. Now it had come, and it had not turned out anything like I had anticipated.

I focused and took a few breaths. The mission was not over yet; I could assess the situation tomorrow and initiate damage control if necessary, but for now I needed to get back to being Rachel. Someone might be along any minute and, if it wasn't the police, it was sure to be some misguided good Samaritan (though try to find one when you need one) who would stop to help me and become an unwitting witness to the biggest crime in Sussex since the acid bath murders. I steadied myself and pulled back onto the road.

Ten minutes later I arrived at uStoreIt on the outskirts of Crawley. It was a large storage facility—an acre of tarmac butting up against an Audi dealership on what used to be farm land—containing a few dozen parallel rows of storage lockers. I drove through the orange glow of the entrance into the gloom beyond. My unit was at the back, in a dimly lit quadrant of garages. It was a double, or at least that's what the brochure said, and that would be true if you owned a Smart Car and a Mini. But that didn't matter to me. It was unobtrusive, unobserved and anonymous. The lease was in the name of Petra Parker, a slim redhead who had paid the first year's rent in advance. The manager had accepted cash and asked no questions.

I manoeuvred the car inside, closed the door and turned on the light. The single fluorescent bar flickered and caught, revealing the sparse furnishings: a dressing table—supporting a three panelled mirror, battery powered lamp, wig stand and a six-inch plastic figurine of Wonder Woman—a wardrobe and a chest of drawers.

This was my answer to The Fortress of Solitude, Paradise Island and The Bat Cave—a cube of concrete and corrugated steel, smelling of motor oil and cobwebs despite my efforts to scrub it clean. I called it The Citadel of Serenity, not because I thought of it as such, but because every crime fighter needs a headquarters with a flashy name. Even the Thunderbirds had Tracy Island.

I stood in the small space between my car and the dressing table, dripping, shivering and reeking. Changing back was not going to be as straightforward this time. I piled my shoes, gloves and utility belt on the floor. Then I peeled off my bodysuit and added it to the heap. It no longer smelled like the inside of a new car, more like a waste treatment plant.

Aching with cold, I sat at the dressing table in my shorts and tee shirt to remove my wig. It was secured with extra-long kirby grips, poking through the wig cap and into my real hair to lock it down tight. It had not budged during the night's debacle but, gratifying as that was, finding and extracting the kirby grips with numb fingers made me wish I had not been so thorough.

I arranged the wig on its stand for inspection. It was jet black, a high-end model that looked as real as you could get but now it smelled like a wet dog, its curls clumped together in damp loops. I would need to wash it, along with all of my other gear. I hadn't counted on that.

The rest of me didn't look so good, either. My gloves and bodysuit had kept me from getting any superficial wounds during my tactical retreat, but there was a smashing welt developing where I had landed on my torch after colliding with Carl. I was also mud-streaked, and my shorts and shirt clung to me with reeking dampness. I stripped them off and scrubbed my neck, arms and what I could reach of my back with half a pack of moist towelettes. I needn't have bothered; it was about as effective as tossing an air freshener into a skip and only drove the chill deeper into my flesh. With my teeth chattering, I opened the wardrobe and pulled out the cotton blouse and jeans I had worn earlier. My knickers and bra were also damp but I had nothing in the way of undergarments at The Citadel and I was not going to go commando.

I dressed in a fumbling palsy of cold and wrapped up in my fleece. When my hands stopped shaking, I pulled off my wig cap, removed the brown contacts and used the remaining towelettes to scrub off my make-up. A pair of glasses—tortoise-shell frames with plain glass lenses—completed the transformation. Rachel Davenport now stared back at me from the mirror; Nadia was gone.

I shook my head and brushed my hair with my fingers. It was light brown and cut short, stopping just above my collar. Keeping it short helped in fitting the wigs on so they looked more natural and kept any stray hairs from showing. When I was young I wore it long and curly; I started cutting it short when I took up gymnastics and then grew it long again when I entered the beauty pageants.

That was all far behind me now, but not far enough. I hadn't stepped on a stage in four years, but even in private life the residue of fame clung to me like an obsessed lover. When the public realised I no longer wanted to be their darling, their former adulation turned to suspicion, and finally to hostility.

They felt betrayed. So did my manager and mentor, Paul Evans. And so did I.

I was shocked to discover that doing nothing caused more of a sensation than all of my accomplishments put together. The tabloids couldn't understand why I wanted to be left alone and voiced their disapproval, as if they had made me a star and, in return, I now owed them an interesting life. When I refused to cooperate, they speculated: I'd had a mental breakdown, I had become a recluse, I had an incurable disease, I'd become a lesbian.

Paparazzi camped on my street, waiting for a glimpse of me, and shouted questions at my mother when she went to the shops. Was I preparing for a comeback? Had I found religion? Was I going bonkers? And later, when they followed me to university, I had to wear disguises to go out unmolested. This deception appealed to me; pretending to be someone else gave me freedom and kept me safe. I cultivated a character and named her Nadia Penric—an anagram of Diana Prince, Wonder Woman's secret identity. Nadia was my saviour; she protected me and shielded me from the glare of the celebrity searchlight.

That was how I got through university, by ignoring the media as Rachel and thumbing my nose at them as Nadia. By the time I received my degree—a Masters in Applied Mathematics—I felt as comfortable being Nadia as I did being myself.

I don't know when the idea of keeping Nadia alive occurred to me. I knew that getting my private life back would require deception and stealth but, once attained, there would be no need to live as two separate people. Nadia's primary mission would be over; I would no longer need her protection. But someone else might. There were other people in the world who were being hurt or terrorised but were powerless to do anything about it. Nadia could help them; she could go on being a protector.

By mutual agreement, I skipped my graduation ceremony. The university was afraid it would turn in to a media circus and I saw it as my chance to escape once and for all. While the local and national press flocked to Newcastle hoping to catch a glimpse of Rachel Davenport, Nadia Penric boarded a train heading south.

That had been just a few months ago. In that time I had taken on an anonymous job, built a quiet life and remained hidden. With my new haircut and no make-up I looked nothing like the old Rachel; I became invisible and, even though I was using my real name, the media's radar hadn't picked me up. It's not that they hadn't made an effort; my mother was grilled by a few journalists after I failed to show up at graduation. She told them the truth; she didn't know where I was. Soon, Rachel Davenport, the famous recluse was forgotten and Rachel Davenport, International Travel Consultant took up residence in Haywards Heath while Nadia Penric quietly acquired her crime fighting accoutrements and waited.

I rooted around in the bottom of the wardrobe and found a Marks and Spencer carrier bag. It was extra-large, but I still had a job stuffing the bodysuit, clothing and residual paraphernalia inside. After a final check that everything was turned off and in place as much as it could be, I slid the door halfway up, ducked under, then closed and locked it.

If someone had been watching, they would have seen a tall, dark and slender woman walk into the garage, and a somewhat shorter, paler, limp-haired Rachel Davenport emerge.

Chapter 3

I SET OFF FOR the car park outside a nearby Co-op—a seven and a half minute walk away. Tonight, weighed down by the carrier bag and the night's activities, it was closer to ten.

Unlikely as it was that I would be spotted walking out of uStoreIt, especially at this time of night, I didn't leave through the front gate. Instead, I went to the back where I slipped through a gap in the fence and walked along a footpath that wound through the narrow strip of woodland separating uStoreIt from the neighbouring housing estate. At the road, I took a cut through the brush and emerged onto the pavement far away from the pedestrian crossing and the CCTV. Once across the road, I resumed the path, which entered the Maidenbower estate as a paved pedestrian pathway shielded from the houses by a high wooden fence.

During the day, I would have walked down the pavement, but at three in the morning, it was best to avoid exposure. I headed towards the Co-op, where a parade of shops and offices surrounding a car park served as a sort of town centre for this neighbourhood of Crawley.

My red VW Golf was where I had left it, near the centre of the deserted car park, under a street lamp but away from the security cameras that guarded the entrances to the Co-op and Boots. I put the carrier bag on the back seat, then thought better of it and transferred it to the boot. Even so, the smell assaulted me as I pulled away. Fifteen minutes later, I reached my home in Haywards Heath, wondering if I shouldn't have just worn the clothes home for all the good stuffing them in the boot had done.

My home is a three-bedroom semi-detached, with a drive running down the side. It is in a quiet cul-de-sac on the edge of town; a house old enough to be of solid, spacious construction but new enough so that indoor plumbing had not been an afterthought. I chose it because anyone not belonging there would be easy to spot, not stopping to think that my comings and goings would be just as easy to track. I pulled in with my lights off and nudged the car forward so I could slip out and steal across the back garden to the door of my conservatory without—

"Rachel, there you are."

—Dee spotting me.

Dee Burket wasn't the only reason I went to such absurd lengths to keep my identities apart, but she was the most immediate one. She, her husband Nigel and their twin toddlers, Harry and Simon, lived in the other side of the semi. Our back gardens were separated by a low hedge—a very low hedge that had been trimmed just before I moved in. I suspected Dee of orchestrating this bit of gardening in anticipation of her new neighbour and felt it would seem churlish of me to erect an eight-foot wooden fence.

The light went on and Dee stepped onto her patio, a white terrycloth dressing gown cinched tight to her skinny frame and her feet shoved into furry pink slippers. "I was so worried."

"Worried? What for?"

"I was up with the twins when I heard the news; I knew you were out but I didn't know where you'd gone."

"I went out for milk."

"Milk? Such a big bag for just some milk. And you've been gone since midnight."

She was just a few years older than me; why did I feel like I was being cross-examined by my mother?

"I guess I lost track of time browsing in the dairy section," I said.

She looked puzzled for a moment, but soldiered on. "Sweetie, if you're out of milk, just knock on my door, no need to run into town."

"Oh, I couldn't, not this late at night. You need your sleep, and I'd wake the twins."

She waved a dismissive hand. "Oh, don't you worry. I'm up with them half the night anyway."

That settled it; next time I'd go out the side window.

"Well, thanks for the offer. Have a good night."

I put the key in the lock and pushed the door open a crack, hoping it would signal the end of the conversation.

"But I didn't tell you what happened."

This wasn't going to be good. Bad news and Dee were made for each other.

"There was a terrorist attack in Burgess Hill," she continued, when I showed no sign of trying to wheedle it out of her.

I stopped, glad that the darkness would keep her from seeing the colour drain from my face. "A what?" My voice came out in a raspy whisper.

"Oh, I know. It's awful, isn't it?" she said.

"A group of Islamic men, and even some women in those habeeb outfits—"

"Burqas."

"Whatever. They blew up Keymer View Court. Dozens were killed. The place is swarming with police, and I wouldn't be surprised if MI5 gets involved, as well."

In half an hour, that would be gospel, and MI6 would be leading the investigation. I was too depressed for words; all I could do was stand and stare at her. Under the circumstances, keeping my mouth from dropping open counted as a small victory. Then Dee's mouth turned down at the corners; she sniffed and wrinkled her nose. "What is that smell?"

I shrugged and pretended to examine the bottom of my trainer. "I must have stepped in something."

"No, the sewers must be backed up; to smell that bad you'd need to roll in it."

She chuckled at her own joke. I opened the door to my conservatory just wide enough to slip the bag in, then mumbled something about the late hour and tried to follow it.

Dee stepped forward, her patio light glowing behind her like a halo. "You don't suppose they're here, do you?" she asked.

"Who?"

She was only a few yards away now; I wondered how she could stand the smell. "The terrorists?"

"I can't imagine why they would be."

I inched further through the gap in the door, struggling to break eye contact.

"It might be an organised assault."

"On the Gander Close sewer system?"

"They attacked Keymer View, so anything is possible."

I gave her a slow and thoughtful nod as if taken in by her logic. "Shouldn't we go inside then, and lock the doors?"

She gasped and brought her hand to her mouth. "Oh my. I hadn't thought of that. And I left the boys on their own!"

She ran to her door, turning to me just before going in. "You weren't meeting a man tonight, were you?"

There was a strained playfulness in her voice but subtlety was not one of Dee's strong points.

"I was shopping, Dee."

"I'm not prying, it's just that, I worry about you, being alone with all these terrorists about."

"Thanks, but I'm doing fine." I slammed the door as I went inside and immediately regretted it. Dee wouldn't get the hint that I was irritated by her meddling, she would just think I was upset about her news. And about being single, making her that much more determined to rescue me. Dee was a natural mother and assumed it to be the desired status of all females. I'm sure she suspected I was a lesbian. I liked Dee, but at times I felt that hedge couldn't grow fast enough.

I picked up the bag and manoeuvred through the dark kitchen and into the living room before turning on a light. In the enclosed warmth of the house, the stench returned with a vengeance. It wafted through my jacket, which I could take, but it reared up from the Marks and Spencer bag like a malevolent snake, wrapping itself around my neck, choking the breath out of me. I climbed the stairs and entered the bathroom, flicking on lights as I went. Without pausing, I turned the shower on and climbed, fully clothed, into the bathtub, hauling the Marks and Spencer bag after me.

Thirty-seven minutes, one bottle of shampoo and half a tube of face scrub later, I descended the stairs, pink from the hot water and furious scouring, wearing my blue fleece housecoat and carrying everything I thought might fit in the washing machine—my jacket, my blouse, undergarments, even my trainers. Nadia's Microprene suit had been scrubbed, turned inside out, scrubbed, turned right side out and scrubbed again. It now hung in the shower, along with Nadia's shoes, gloves and utility belt. I had shampooed the wig twice, wearing it on my head, and then shampooed my own hair three times. The wig was now drying in the back bedroom, fitted over some balled up newspapers so it would hold its shape.

The nylon restraints had scrubbed up fine and were now on a towel next to the wig. The IRB device was gone, lost in the scuffle along with the camera, and of course I had thrown away the torch. These were replaceable; the IRB device was just a cheap torch fitted with coloured cellophane. I could buy another set of torches at Wilkinson's for less than a fiver, and I still had some cellophane left. Though without the infrared camera, it wouldn't be of much use.

I stuffed the sopping bundle of clothes into the washing machine and set it for a hot wash. That was the last of it, but I knew I wouldn't feel everything was done until all traces of Nadia were removed from my house. It felt strange having her there, as if a friend had showed up unexpectedly to stay the night. There was nothing to be done about that now, so I put all my concerns about her and the night's mission into a mental lock-box in the back of my mind; it was a trick Paul had taught me.

"Concentrate on what you can do, not on what you can't."

His voice, always there; calming, cajoling, cheering. Despite everything, it was impossible not to miss him. I shut him out and concentrated on his advice.

I needed sleep, and that I had control over. With luck, I could get three hours in. Part of the preparation for the mission had been a three and a half hour nap between eight and midnight, so I didn't expect any difficulty getting through the next workday. I had learned the benefits of catnapping while on the gymnastic circuit, and used it to my benefit in the beauty pageants. Another useful trick Paul had taught me.

I went into my bedroom, dressed for bed and slid beneath the covers. It was hard work keeping the night's events from sneaking back to the forefront of my mind, and even more difficult to stop mulling over the depressing spin Dee had put on them, but years of practice paid off. I set my mind to thinking of a way to get out of the mess and slipped into sleep.

Chapter 4

AMANDA LOOKED UP FROM her newspaper the moment I stepped through the door. "Did you hear what happened?"

She was sitting at her desk with the *West Sussex Weekly* spread out in front of her, bulging over her keyboard and crimped up against her computer screen like a rucked up carpet. I gave a mental sigh and walked past her so I wouldn't have to force myself to look interested.

"Yes, terrorists blew up Keymer View Court," I said.

At my workstation, I stowed my handbag and turned on my PC. When I looked at Amanda, she was scanning the interior pages of the paper, concentrating hard enough to crease her foundation make-up. "Really? When did that happen?"

"Last night," I said.

Amanda consulted the front page again to see if she had misread the headline, then held it up so I could see for myself. It read, "Ram-Robbers Strike Again."

"Well, there's nothing about terrorists in here," she said, "but the PC Supply Shop on Queens Street was robbed on Wednesday."

I felt relieved; not by the crime, but by the timing. The ram-raid had succeeded on its own merit, not because every policeman, policewoman and PCSO in Sussex had been chasing non-existent terrorists around Burgess Hill. That I could deal with.

"Oh, that's terrible," I said.

Amanda laid the newspaper on her desk. "I'll say. All those boarded up businesses are making the town look tatty."

She inclined her head, tucked a stray blonde lock behind her ear and began to read. "Raymond Morgan and his wife Julia received a shock when they arrived to open their Queen Street shop on Thursday morning."

I hate when people read to me; I always feel like I'm in a care home and my niece has come to visit and doesn't know what else to do to entertain me.

"Sussex PC Supplies, which has been operating since 1986, was the fifth victim of an organised ram-raid carried out by an unknown gang of thieves. The shop suffered extensive damage when a vehicle smashed through the plate glass window and security screen to gain entrance to the shop. Most of the Morgan's stock was lost in the raid.

"'We're not sure if we can go on,' said a distraught Julie Morgan . . . "

Oh God, now she was doing the voices.

" . . . 'our life savings was put into this business—'"

She was cut off when Martin Palmer returned from the store room carrying an armload of brochures. "Why are we engaging in amateur dramatics; what will our customers think?"

Amanda blushed and folded the paper. "But there aren't any customers. We're not even open yet."

"We will be soon, and when the customers come in I want my team ready and acting professionally."

Martin is the type of manager who reads all the latest management books and likes to call his employees a team, as if that alone will make the business turn a profit. In truth, the only management decision he's made that has had a positive effect is to not wear The Holiday Depot's trademark red blazer. Amanda likes the blazer because it makes her look like a Virgin Atlantic flight attendant, but Martin favours a blue sports coat, because wearing red makes him look like a sunset with legs.

He dropped the brochures on his desk. "We're pushing a special last-minute deal on holiday flights to New York. I want these placed in the rack near the door and a notice added to the window display."

Being the manager, Martin doesn't have to do any actual work. He sits at his desk in the rear corner playing patience all day. But for now he was deep into his morning routine: place briefcase along left side of desk, even with the rear leg, adjust computer screen and then adjust it back to where it had been, do the same with the keyboard and picture of his wife and daughter, sit, adjust chair and switch on the computer. It was the same every morning, six days a week. Next he would ask Amanda to get him a coffee and demand to know where James was while I set up the day's display.

"Amanda, would you . . . hey, what's wrong with the computer?"

Like a well-trained horse that keeps going without its rider, Amanda started towards the door. "No, I don't know why James is late," she said.

The door chimed as she opened it and joined the sparse flow of foot traffic on West Street.

"What's wrong with your computer?" I asked.

Martin jammed at random keys with a fat index finger. "I don't know; it just won't work."

Unlike Amanda, Martin was more like a mouse in a maze finding his memorised pathway blocked. I went over to his desk before panic set in. "It's telling you it can't find the network."

"Yes. But why?"

I looked at his round face and saw, not panic, but complete helplessness. He was a middle-aged middle-manager in charge of a branch office with sales figures that, to be kind, were unremarkable. His best strategy was to lay low and hope no one noticed him. But ringing up the corporate help desk to complain about a computer failure would draw unwanted attention to his store and his sales. He no longer brought to mind a confused mouse, but a rabbit caught in the headlights.

"Would you like me to have a look at it?"

His eyes glazed with gratitude. "Could you?"

I went to my desk and fumbled around in my handbag until he lost interest in me and went back to staring at his empty screen, then I went to Amanda's desk, picked up her newspaper and headed to the back room where the server was.

It wasn't much of a server room, just an area the size of a guest bedroom stacked with boxes containing brochures. On one side of the room was the door to the new employees' toilet, which was in the process of being finished off, though no discernible progress had been made during the weeks that I had been working here. On the other side of the room, sitting on a table, was the server, sprouting wires like some latter-day hydra. I ran a quick diagnostics check and found the router was malfunctioning.

It turned out to be a software fault, which was a good thing as I didn't think Mr and Mrs Morgan would be in the mood for much business today. I reset the router then began leafing through the paper. It was a weekly and had just come out that morning, so I didn't expect any mention of Nadia's misadventure in it. Besides, there wouldn't have been room to fit it in between pictures of the primary school kids dressed up in Halloween costumes, a report from the Warnham allotments concerning Mary Farnsworth's prize pumpkin and updates of the perpetual investigation into the financial shenanigans of local councillors.

A quick check confirmed this and I allowed my hopes to rise. Then I thought about the dailies, and the internet. I logged onto the server, opened a browser and checked a regional newspaper's website. They had published an article about the mishap; I read it with my mouth open.

Mystery Woman Vandalises Flats

At 2:17 Friday morning, police were called to the scene of a disturbance in the Sussex town of Burgess Hill. Caretakers of Keymer View Court surprised a lone woman in the act of sabotaging the drainage pipes but were unable to stop her from setting off an explosion.

"She was amazingly quick and strong," stated Carl Hanson, head groundskeeper for Sawyer Enterprises. "We tried to stop her, but she fought us off and restrained us before we knew what was happening. I think she was trained by terrorists."

Mr Hanson and his assistant, Derek Fletcher, were assaulted and bound together with nylon restraining cuffs and were unable to stop the mysterious woman from setting off an explosive device that damaged eleven flats and destroyed a large portion of the drainage system.

The police arrived within minutes of the explosion, but the woman had fled the scene.

Police are asking anyone with information to contact Sussex Police. The suspect is considered dangerous and police advise that, under no circumstances, should she be approached.

I did a quick search but found no mention in the national papers. That was good news, at least. I folded Amanda's paper and went back into the shop. Amanda had returned and was presenting Mr Palmer with his coffee. She looked at me through narrowed eyes. I wondered how she could see past the mascara. "So, fixed the server, did we?"

"As a matter of fact, I did."

"And you needed my paper to do it?"

I held the paper out to her. "Yes. I used it to beat the router into submission. Reboot your workstation, Mr Palmer; it should be all right now."

She leaned close to my ear. "You know, I could have fixed that server," she said in a low voice before snatching the paper from my hand. She started towards her desk, then stopped. "Are you sure you weren't back there fixing the plumbing? Your hair smells like a sewer."

I turned away to pick up the brochures, hoping I wasn't blushing. "I'll start arranging these now."

Martin laid a hand on the top of the pile. "Thank you, Rachel. Really."

I thought he might ask me to marry him, but James came through the front door and broke the mood. Amanda had not yet settled at her desk and took the opportunity to thrust her red blazer clad breasts in his direction. "Good morning James."

James, one side of his blazer collar turned up, nodded in her direction. He managed to grunt a greeting before slumping into his chair. I seized the opportunity to escape.

"Glad you could join us, James," Martin said.

James ran a hand through his thick hair, a habit he had when talking to Martin. I wasn't sure if it was a nervous tick or if he was attempting to draw attention to Martin's bald head. "Sorry, Mr Palmer, I had a late night last night."

Amanda snorted, but Martin kept a benign expression on his round face. Then he stood up. "Before we open our doors to the general public," he said, "I have an announcement to make. I've arranged a team building exercise for tomorrow; something fun and unusual, something that will be a benefit to the community and an opportunity for us to work together as a team."

"Hold on a minute," James said, slumping further into his seat. "You're telling us we have to give up our Saturday afternoon?"

"No, not at all. This will take place during our usual working hours; you won't have to give up any of your free time."

Amanda looked perplexed. "But the agency—"

"The agency will be closed tomorrow. I'll expect you all here at the usual time. Dress casually. Very casually."

"You mean wear clothes we won't mind getting grubby."

"Well put, James."

"So what will we be doing?" Amanda asked, looking worried.

"Be here tomorrow morning at nine thirty; you'll find out then."

Chapter 5

A T TWELVE THIRTY-FIVE I visited the loo and had a sniff of my hair. It did have a whiff about it. Chagrined, I left for lunch. It hadn't been the busiest of mornings and I had been able to do a bit of research into the real Keymer View saboteurs. Our work stations are locked into the corporate web sites but I found a way around their firewall and into the free-roaming wilderness that is the Internet. Still, it wasn't as straightforward as it should have been; Martin might play patience most of the day, but between games he takes an interest in what we're doing. Being seated at the desk closest to his, I needed to maintain the pretence of arranging a Christmas excursion to Disney World for the Bogbottom family or some such thing.

The desks are situated with Amanda at the front near the plate glass window so people can see a perky blonde with an up-turned nose whose store-bought tan accentuates her blue and white neck scarf and red blazer. James, who, despite a perpetual hangover, exudes an air of boyish charm and cockiness that can be mistaken for confidence, is in the next work station. Next to him is an empty workstation and the new girl, the plain-looking one with the mousey hair, sits in the back next to the boss where he can keep an eye on her. But by turning my screen away from him and remaining aware of the progress of his games, I was able to gather a little information.

First, and most disturbing, I was finding a growing number of references to last night's incident. Fortunately, most journalists still keep up a facade of responsibility, so Dee's account of a full-blown terrorist attack wasn't being repeated, at least not yet. By noon, there were a dozen or so articles rehashing the same facts and marginally enhancing the story each time, so if something interesting didn't happen soon, I might be seeing this on the national news by dinner time. I prayed for a train derailment or a coup in Belgium.

Carl and Derek, it turned out, did work for Keymer View Court, or more precisely, Sawyer Development Enterprises, a local company owned by Kevin Sawyer. The pair of them made up the entire maintenance and grounds keeping staff for the four properties Sawyer managed, so it was no wonder Keymer View

Court was in such ropy condition, especially if these clowns were intent on making it more unattractive rather than fixing it up.

This gave me something to think about when I left the office and stepped into the thin October sun. There wouldn't be too many more of these agreeable days, so I decided against a salad and fruit juice at Costa's and pushed my way through the crowd towards the Bishopric. Horsham is a nice town if you look up. The buildings range from bland sixties architecture to Georgian and Victorian, with moss-covered slate tiles and ornate spires on some of the more quaint structures. Looking up, you are transported back in time; but at pedestrian level, it's wall-to-wall plate-glass.

I walked down the pedestrianised street, past the derelict fountain and beyond the swirl of litter and leaves outside of McDonald's, to where a pair of adjacent restaurants—The Black Olive and The Merrythought—offered outdoor dining. I looked for an empty table in front of the Black Olive and struck lucky. I'd beat the rush, but now that I had claimed a table I had to go inside to place my order and that meant either abandoning my territory or leaving something behind to hold my claim, only to come back and find it stolen and my table taken anyway. Others around me weren't having the same difficulty; they were in couples.

I wished I had worn my Holiday Depot blazer; I wouldn't mind having that stolen, but I was fond of my fawn jacket. Maybe I could leave a shoe.

Then someone called my name. Being a relative newcomer, not many people aside from Dee know me, so I assumed they meant some other Rachel. But they called again, louder this time.

Two tables over, in the Merrythought Restaurant section, Alex Marsh was waving to me. I waved back and beckoned her over. She beckoned me to her table. I beckoned again. She stamped her foot, pointed at me and then at her table, so I defected to the Merrythought.

Alex is the only person I know outside of work in the whole of southern England. She lives in the flat above the Merrythought—hence her misplaced sense of loyalty. I met her during the first weeks I worked in Horsham. Every time I walked by the restaurants or stopped in for lunch, she was sitting at a table outside the Merrythought. After nodding to each other for a few weeks we started sharing a table. I remember my relief at the prospect of chatting to a fellow human being about something other than cheap flights to Barbados and was ready to change my mind about the reserved southerners when I discovered she was an American; the locals still remain aloof.

Alex is a few years older than me, but shorter, with black hair and an athletic build. She watched me with dark eyes and a benign smile as I took my seat.

"It's so good to see you," I said, and meant it. "It's been weeks; I was worried."

She looked perplexed for a moment. "Oh, that. No, I'm fine. Much better, in fact."

Alex had been in what she termed "recuperation mode" when I first met her. She'd suffered some sort of unspecified accident but was, unusual for an American, reluctant to talk about it.

The waitress, a willowy girl with long, limp hair, took our order. They might have waitress service at the Merrythought, but the Black Olive served a roast vegetable baguette that I didn't mind fetching myself. I considered sending the waitress over for one, but ordered a tuna salad instead.

"I've joined the Sussex Police," Alex said after the waitress retreated. "As a Special Constable."

I tried to think of something to say, but the best I could do was nod; at least I managed to keep myself from groaning out loud.

"I've been busy training, but that finished two weeks ago. I started work last week."

"What brought this on?"

She shrugged. "I needed something to keep me busy; I was going bonkers after all those weeks of not being able to do much."

"Couldn't you have volunteered at Oxfam? Why a cop?"

"Why not?"

She seemed put off by this so I switched my line of questioning. "How can you be a Constable? You're an American."

"I have permanent residency," she said, "and that's all they require."

"And you're already working?"

"Yes, right here in Horsham, which is convenient; but being new I get all the odd shifts."

"What days?" I blurted, hoping she hadn't been one of the cops chasing me around Keymer View Court.

"Oh, it varies. I was on this past Monday and Tuesday, but I was off after that so I missed the big excitement."

"What big excitement?"

"The break in at the computer shop."

"Thank God."

"What?"

I felt myself blush. "I mean, thank God no one was hurt. I hope they were insured."

Our meals arrived. I dug into my salad and hoped for a change of subject.

"They're getting more brazen, these ram-raid thieves."

"Well, now that you're a Policewoman, maybe you can catch them."

"They're a bad lot all right, but they're nowhere near as dangerous as the lunatic woman who blew up those flats in Burgess Hill."

I spit soda through my nose and launched into a coughing fit.

"Are you all right?" Alex asked as the fit subsided. I nodded, blowing my nose on my napkin.

"She seems a bit of a kook. She just walked into the courtyard, subdued the two caretakers and dumped explosive chemicals down the drainpipe. For no reason. Christ knows what she'll do next."

So this was going to be the topic of conversation. It was bad enough being referred to as a terrorist, now I was a kook, as well. "Are they sure she was the one who did it?"

Alex took a bite of her sandwich. "Well, she was the one running around dressed up like a ninja."

"But that doesn't mean she did it."

"What's up with you? Why are you so quick to come to the defence of a mad bomber?"

"I'm not. I'm just saying. Did anyone see her do it?"

"Yes. The caretakers caught her red-handed. That's why she assaulted and restrained them."

"Oh."

It wasn't looking good.

"And she's certain to strike again. I only hope no one gets assaulted next time."

Assaulted? Those lying bastards; Nadia hardly touched them, and I was getting a bruise where I fell on my torch after colliding with Carl.

"But don't worry; someone that unstable won't be hard to catch. I expect she'll go to an institution."

Unstable? I checked my watch.

"I have to be going back to work. It was good seeing you," I said, and got up.

32

To my surprise she stood up with me, put a hand on my arm and kissed the air next to my right ear. "I hope to see you again." She pulled back. "I hope this doesn't sound like I'm being a pushy American or anything, but you're good company. Maybe we could meet after work for a drink some time. When you're not busy."

Terrific. My first friend in my new location is someone who thinks I'm a lunatic and wants to see me locked away. I tapped into the years of experience that had taught me how to smile no matter what. I hoped it looked convincing. "That would be nice."

Alex wrinkled her nose. "The town must be working on the sewer again."

"Yes. I've noticed that, too. When would you like to get together?"

"Well, I'm busy tonight, and I'm working over the weekend, so it will have to be sometime next week. We can meet here on Monday to discuss it."

"That would be great; see you then."

Back at work I brooded at my desk, forcing smiles for the benefit of my customers until I thought I would go mad. At two o'clock I went into the toilet, waited fifteen minutes, then tiptoed to Martin's desk.

"Mr Palmer," I whispered, "I'm afraid I have to leave."

He looked up from his game of patience, his face a mixture of concern and suspicion. "We're pretty busy, Rachel. Are you sick?"

I hesitated for effect. "No. I'm just having some problems. Of the female variety."

His face went red. "Oh. I see. Are you, I mean, will you be all right? Do you think you can manage to stay for at least a few more hours?"

"I can explain exactly what's wrong if you like."

"No. No need for that."

"I'm really sorry about this, Mr Palmer."

I left the silence for him to fill.

"All right."

"Thank you."

"Rachel?"

I turned back towards him.

"You will be okay, won't you?"

"Don't worry, Mr Palmer. I'll be fine."

He went back to his game. "Good. Then I'll see you here at half nine tomorrow morning."

Chapter 6

MENTALLY KICKING MYSELF FOR not claiming to have terminal Chlamydia, I walked to the bus station to wait for the Park and Ride bus. The only way I was going to get out of this was to prove what really happened. And the only way that was going to happen was to get my camera back or convince Carl and Derek to tell the truth. Neither option filled me with optimism.

I took the Park and Ride bus to my car and drove out of Horsham attempting to fight the urge to drive to Burgess Hill to sneak a look around Keymer View Court. The police know criminals are compelled to return to the scene of the crime; they would have it staked out. It was the sort of thing an amateur would do. Or a lunatic. I made it as far as Ansty before turning south. It wouldn't hurt just to drive through Burgess Hill.

When I reached town I drove down the London Road, then turned off towards Keymer. Surely someone just passing by wouldn't draw any attention. I turned onto Oak Hill Park and headed for Keymer View Court, feeling the way I imagined an alcoholic who had just convinced himself it would be all right to go into a bar to admire the whisky bottles must feel. I needn't have worried about the place being staked out; the entrance was choked with cars and people. One more wasn't going to make a difference one way or the other.

I drove past and found a place to park around the corner on the street next to the brick wall I had jumped over the night before. I changed out of my blazer and into my jacket so I could blend into the crowd and walked back to the entrance.

Cars were parked all around the central garden and up on the scruffy patches of grass in front of the buildings. Two moving vans were squeezed among them. A growing throng of people had gathered in front of the south block where a man was gesticulating to their awed attention. As I neared them on my way to join the crowd in back of the building, I saw that it was Carl, giving a one-man theatrical version of the preceding night's events, playing all the characters.

Out back, among the onlookers and the locals ready to give their versions of events, a few Police Community Support Officers guarded the boundary of the crime scene. The police had cordoned off a generous area so once I was able to elbow my way to the front, I had a good view of the previous night's carnage.

The hole was still gaping and stinking, though the stench wasn't deterring the crowds. The broken windows had been boarded over and the muck was churned up with footprints but otherwise the scene was unchanged. The border of blue and white tape made it look like a tableau in an outdoor museum.

I noted the forsythia bush and found the place I had been standing when Carl ran into me. I calculated the impact and the angle the camera would have travelled and traced it to a weedy patch of ground right at the corner of the display area where a PCSO was standing guard.

The ebb of the crowd pulled me back as a new wave surged forward. It was like being in the Louvre with a bus load of sixth formers viewing the Mona Lisa, everyone eager to get a peek, then just as eager to get away. I separated myself from the herd and sidled up to the PCSO. He didn't notice me. He was watching the crowd, his gloved hands clasped behind his back in an "at ease" pose. His baby face was covered in fine stubble and lined with fatigue; his eyes were red-rimmed and drooping. I did a stealthy survey of the weeds.

"This is a crime scene. Move away."

I was no more than three feet from him, but if my proximity had caused him alarm he did a good job of hiding it; his demeanour radiated boredom rather than authority.

"Sorry—" I looked at the name tag pinned to his day-glo vest. "—Officer Harris, I was just—"

"I'm a PCSO."

"Okay, PCSO Harris, I'm interested in maybe becoming a PCSO myself. I was wondering if you could give me some insight."

He looked at me as if I had just unscrewed my head and was about to drop-kick it into the hole. Then his bored expression returned. "Try the Job Centre."

He turned away, having determined I was just an average nutcase and not dangerous. I took advantage of his lack of interest to do a thorough study of the weeds; they had been disturbed, but not trampled. Someone had walked through the patch, but had they been searching, or just passing by? Overall, I supposed it didn't matter; the camera was obviously not there.

"Are you still here?"

"I'm just wondering, you know, what the job is like?"

He rubbed a gloved hand over his stubble. "This is the biggest crime to hit Sussex in twenty years. The real police and the detectives have been questioning people; the SOCOs have been gathering evidence, and I've been standing here since four o'clock this morning, guarding a hole in the ground. If you want that kind of glamour, you're crazier than you look."

He turned away again, this time with more resolve. I looked at his shoes. They were grass stained and muddy and about the size of the footprints in the weeds. But that proved nothing. As if to accentuate that fact, as soon as I turned away I saw another set of muddy shoes that were also the same size as the footprints in the weeds. I looked up and saw Derek. I drew a sharp breath and looked beyond him, as if his presence hadn't registered. He looked through me, as well, gazing over the crime scene with keen disinterest before walking back towards the courtyard.

I milled around a few more minutes then headed out front without saying goodbye to my new best friend, PCSO Harris.

The key to proving my innocence was the camera. The most likely people to have found it were Carl and Derek, and a likely place for them to stash it would be their workshop. I followed the tarmac walkway to the rear of the estate and slipped through the opening. No one was around; nothing had happened here to gain anyone's attention. I moved along the short path and found the door to the shed open. The work table was still there, but all of the bottles and cans had been removed. Smart, getting rid of the evidence. I took a step closer and peered inside.

"Can I help you?"

I let out a yelp. Derek was on the far side of the shack, a can of Fosters in one hand, a cigarette in the other. He slipped off his stool and ambled across the room.

"Sorry," I said. "I was—" What? Looking for the camera I dropped last night? You haven't seen it around, have you? "—looking for a loo. I thought there might be one in here."

"You thought wrong." He gestured with the hand holding the Fosters. "Loo is around back. Some people call it a bush."

He laughed, revealing gaps in his yellow teeth. I smiled and apologised again. He was blocking the door, and my view into the workshop, but I had the element of surprise on my side and he had no one to help him. If Nadia were here, she could restrain him and search the shed, but I couldn't risk acting while I was Rachel Davenport; it would blow my secret identity. I turned to walk away.

"I've seen you before," he said.

My cheeks burned. I kept my back to him, struggling to remain calm.

"You were out back by the hole." He took a noisy slurp from the can. "Some shit, that, eh?"

I exhaled. "Yes. Incredible."

"We tried to stop her, the crazy woman who did it. Me and my mate, we went for her but she fought us off. She was trained by terrorists, you know. Coulda killed us."

I didn't know if he was trying to impress me or convince himself he didn't need to be ashamed about being beaten up by a girl. What I did know was, his story was word for word what I'd read in the paper; he and Carl must have rehearsed it together. I glanced over my shoulder at him. "That was brave of you," I said.

He shrugged in an attempt to appear modest.

"Shame about the outcome, though," I continued. "I hear she beat you both up and tied you together."

His smile went flat and his eyes narrowed. I looked forward and continued down the path.

"The bush is free if you need it," he called.

I went out through the main entrance and returned to my car.

My camera was a dead end. Somebody had found it. Did they know its significance? It didn't bear thinking about; all it meant was that I had to find another way to prove my innocence. I decided on the direct approach; it couldn't make things any worse.

The office for Sawyer Developmental Enterprises was in Crawley. I had memorised the address during my research that morning. If Nadia paid him a visit and told him the truth, he might become interested in what his caretakers were up to. If he looked into it, they might be found out.

I drove home for a quick but thorough shower, with scented soap this time. Then I looked through my wardrobe for an appropriate outfit. Nadia in a black Microprene suit wasn't going to make the proper impression. In fact, Nadia in any outfit was a bad idea, so I picked out a smart, professional trouser suit as a base to work from. I checked on Nadia's outfit. It was dry, so I put it, and the rest of her gear, into a holdall.

I did a quick appraisal of myself in the hall mirror and went back to my car, checking first to see if the coast was clear. It was broad daylight, and Dee was certain to be watching out for me. She did not disappoint; I practically fell over her as I stepped out of the conservatory.

38

"I saw someone in your house," she said. "I thought you were being burgled."

"No, just me. Listen, I have to—"

"You usually aren't home this time of day; are you all right?"

"Yes, I'm fine. I just took the afternoon off."

I headed to the car eager to get rid of the holdall before she wanted to know what was in it.

"Well, I'm glad I ran into you anyway. I've been wanting to ask you—"

"I'm sorry, Dee, but I'm in a bit of a hurry."

I deposited the holdall in the boot. She didn't seem to notice. Instead, she stood in my way as I tried to get to the driver's door. "Oh, are you off for a job interview? You look very smart."

"No. I mean, well, sort of."

"I understand. Hush hush and all that. Don't worry; you can count on me not to spill the beans."

"Okay, thanks, now—"

"Nigel and I would like you to come for dinner tomorrow night."

"Well, I—"

"That's if you're not busy. I know you're single and will probably have made plans already."

Which meant she would be checking to see if I was still home, choosing to remain on my own rather than take up her offer.

"Why, that's very sweet of you."

"Seven for seven thirty. See you then."

"Yes," I said as she walked away. "And thank you. Should I bring anything?"

From inside her house I could hear the twins squalling. "Just yourself. Looking as nice as you look now."

She disappeared inside.

Shit. A set-up.

I got in my car and drove to Maidenbower. At this time in the afternoon the car park was packed. I circled the perimeter three times, then made my own parking space at the end of a row, trusting that I wouldn't return to find my car clamped. The only visible souls were a scattering of shoppers and a cluster of youths in hooded sweatshirts and drooping trousers drinking cans of Stella and hovering around the bins next to the side of the Co-op. None of them were watching me, but I detoured to the Newsagents anyway. Someone might observe me driving in and walking straight off and find that suspicious, which might lead to unwanted attention.

"Never let your guard down, always give your best."

Paul's words.

I bought a pack of Polos and joined the queue at the till. While waiting, I scanned the rack of newspapers, flicking over the usual portents of doom from the national newspapers. Then I saw the regional tabloid and groaned out loud. The woman in the queue in front of me scowled.

The front page of *The Southeast Enquirer* afternoon edition featured a photo of the carnage at Keymer View Court and a headline—in extra-large type—screaming, "Terrorists Demolish Burgess Hill Estate".

I stepped closer to the counter so I could read the first paragraph. Someone had decided this couldn't be the work of a single woman and had managed to come up with witnesses claiming to have seen a second or third perpetrator. They had somehow kept themselves from declaring the gang to be Muslim extremists but did come to the conclusion that, as their intent seemed to be to terrorise, they were de facto terrorists.

"Can I help you?"

The shop assistant, a middle-aged woman wearing a nurse's tunic two sizes too small for her and a purple witch's hat, frowned at me.

"Oh, uh, sorry."

I laid the Polos on the counter and fished some change out of my handbag.

"That's awful, isn't it?" the faux-nurse said.

"Pardon?"

She nodded her head towards the rack of papers. "Those terrorists. We're not safe anywhere." She held out my change. My mouth opened but no sound came out. "I know," she said. "Terrible, isn't it?"

I walked across the car park in a daze. When I was clear of the parked cars the hoodies, who had organised an impromptu game of football using a pumpkin from the Halloween display in front of the Co-op, saw me and made kissing noises in my direction. I tuned them out and concentrated on one thought: damage control.

"It's never as bad as it seems," Paul told me. "You can always fix it, or at least mitigate it."

He was right, of course. Somehow, I had to contain and control. Visiting Sawyer may not help, but it couldn't hurt. I had only a few hours to set the record straight before the evening news.

I arrived at The Citadel by the footpath and the gap in the fence. The interior smelled of eau de landfill but otherwise everything seemed in order. I put Nadia's things away and then took the blonde wig out of the wardrobe and set about putting it on. I fastened it down with kirby grips and checked the results in the mirror. Not bad, but there was still too much Rachel and not enough Nadia.

I looked over my assortment of contacts and chose the blue ones, then I applied enough make-up to inspire confidence and put on a pair of discreet fake-pearl earrings with a matching necklace. Rooting through the bottom drawer, I found a respectable-looking pair of shoes with interior lifts. I put them on and stood in front of the dressing table.

"Good afternoon, Mr Sawyer," I said, in a posh London accent. "My name is Clar Knekt."

It was another one of my secret identities and, like the others, it was an anagram of a crime fighter's secret identity. The name fit my current persona; I was no longer Rachel, I was Nadia, disguised as Clar. I exchanged my big handbag for a smaller, professional woman's sized bag and slipped a few of Clar's business cards inside. The only information on them, beside the name, was an address and a mobile phone number; the address was fake and the number was for Nadia's phone.

Fifteen minutes later I parked on Stephenson Way in Three Bridges, outside an austere, breezeblock building with "Sawyer Development Enterprises" emblazoned over the door. I checked myself in the rear view mirror and drew a shaky breath. All this from trying to help out a defenceless old lady! This wasn't what being a crime fighter was supposed to be like.

A bitter wind hit me as I climbed the bare cement steps to the entrance. I put on my best pageant pose and pushed the door open, releasing a waft of warm air. The reception area was no less austere than the outside surroundings. Burnt orange carpet covered the floor, a water cooler stood in the corner and a single bulb hung from the centre of the ceiling throwing stark light into every corner of the room. An Ikea work station angled across one corner, occupied by a computer terminal, phone and a receptionist with pink hair who glanced up as I entered and then went back to reading her *Hell-o!* magazine. She looked to be in her late twenties, and dressed as if she was sixteen. Next to her, in her low-cut, sleeveless top and glitter make-up, I appeared absurdly over-dressed, but I hoped that might give me an edge.

I stood in front of the desk and cleared my throat. The receptionist looked at me over the top of magazine. "Can I help you?"

"Is Mr Sawyer in?"

She eyed me with open suspicion and laid the magazine aside. "Are you a reporter?"

"No."

"You're not the Old Bill, are you? Some sort of undercover copper or something? Because if you are, you need to show me your warrant card."

I took a business card out of my handbag and laid it on top of her magazine. "I'm not the police. I just want a moment of Mr Sawyer's time."

"Well, we're sorta busy. In case you haven't heard, we've been attacked by terrorists."

"That's what I'm here about."

She leaned back in her chair and folded her arms. "So if you're not a reporter, then you must be a solicitor."

"I'm neither. I have information."

"What kind?"

"The kind Mr Sawyer might want to hear."

She didn't move. Neither did I. We stared at each other for half a minute before she reached for the phone, never taking her eyes off of me. "Mr Sawyer. Sorry to bother you." She picked up the card and examined it. "There's a Clar Ka knee ket here to see you. Says she's got information and that she's not a cop or a reporter or anything."

She looked at the card one more time before tossing it in the waste bin and returning to her magazine. "What sort of name is Ka knee ket?"

"Ka NEEK," I corrected. "The T is silent. It's Norwegian; my father is from Oslo."

"Fascinating. Mr Sawyer will see you now. Through that door."

I thanked her with more cordiality than I felt and walked into the inner office, wishing I had thought to bring a briefcase instead of a handbag.

Sawyer was sitting at a large, wooden desk, typing into a small laptop. He was fit going on flabby, with just a hint of grey at his temples. His blue, oxford shirt was open at the collar and a thick wedding band circled the ring finger on his left hand. He looked up when I walked in and gave me a salesman smile. I hate salesmen.

"Good afternoon, Mr Sawyer," I said, striding forward with an outstretched hand. He stood and offered his. "I'm Clar Knekt."

I stated the name with a confidence I didn't feel. The notion of using anagrams no longer seemed like such a good idea; there are only so many convincing names you can assemble and, in retrospect, Clar Knekt was not the best one I could have chosen. "Thank you for seeing me on such short notice. I hope it's not an inconvenience."

He gave my hand a brief shake but spent a few additional moments admiring the front of my suit jacket. "Not to be blunt, but it is an inconvenience. As you have no doubt heard, we had a serious incident at one of my properties last night. I have been visited by reporters and the police and I am trying to rectify the damage without being allowed onto the crime scene. Now, I agreed to see you because you claimed to have information. Is that still the case, Ms *Kaneche*?"

"Yes."

He nodded at the chair in front of his desk. "Then please sit down."

I pulled the moulded plastic chair close and leaned in so I could keep my voice low. "I represent the woman who was involved in the incident at Keymer View Court last night."

Sawyer sat in his padded leather chair, leaned back and folded his arms over his chest. "This *is* a surprise. Are you here to tell me she's turning herself in?"

"No. I'm here to tell you she is innocent."

"Ms *Kennet*, are you going to try to convince me this woman, your client, was not at Keymer View Court last night? I'm afraid there are a number of witnesses."

"No, my client was there. But she did not conspire to damage your property. She was there attempting to stop your caretakers from damaging your property."

He leaned further back and clasped his hands behind his head. "This is a serious allegation. Why should I believe you, as opposed my caretakers, the witnesses and the police?"

"I realise how this looks, but none of those people, aside from your caretakers, saw what took place prior to the explosion. Your caretakers say they surprised my client in the act, my client says she surprised your caretakers in the act."

"And I have to ask you again; why should I believe you?"

"It's the only logical scenario. Emotions are running high at the moment, but once the excitement is over, the police are going to start asking themselves what is more likely, that two strong men with intimate knowledge of the grounds dug a hole and planted a bomb, or that a lone woman somehow transported all the equipment needed to do this to the site and then fought off two men who surprised her?"

Sawyer's brow creased. He leaned forward again. "You are forgetting that my employees, loyal employees who have been with me for several years, were found by the police bound together with nylon restraints. Now, they didn't do this to themselves. If your client is capable of that, then she is capable of the rest. I would suggest your time might be better spent talking her into turning herself in. Isn't that what a good solicitor would do for her client?"

"I never said I was her solicitor."

"Then what are you?"

"I'm representing her interests."

"And impersonating a lawyer."

This time I leaned back, but kept my hands folded in my lap. "I realise this all sounds a bit unusual, but I'm only asking you to have a closer look at your caretakers, their story and their workshop. My client is interested in clearing her name, but to do that someone needs to expose the truth. We were hoping you would help."

Sawyer didn't answer. He stared at me, glanced at the phone, and back to me.

"Your client does need help, Ms *Kaneut*, in the form of a real solicitor, as might you."

"Me? What for?"

"You're telling me you know who the perpetrator is. You are withholding evidence from the police."

"But she's not guilty."

"Then you should have no problem talking to the police. In fact, they asked me to call them if I came across any information they might be interested in." He reached for the phone and lifted the receiver. "I think this qualifies."

"I have proof," I blurted. He hesitated and put the phone down.

"I'm listening."

"Photos. My client took photos of your caretakers digging the holes and pouring in the chemicals."

"And you haven't taken these to the police, either?"

"My client would rather this be solved without police intervention."

He tented his fingers, rested his chin on them and stared at the desk top a long time before responding. "Who else knows of this proof?"

"Just my client and myself."

"Then if you can bring the proof to me, I will look into it."

"Well, it might take a while—"

"And I would like to meet your friend, I mean, your client, as well. Then perhaps we can solve this without, as you say, police intervention."

"Well, I'll ask her. But I make no promises."

"Then neither do I. Bring me the photos. Bring me your client. Then we'll sort this out. Between ourselves."

"Okay. If I promise that, will you take a closer look at your caretakers?"

He held my gaze, then nodded and leaned back. "All right. You have a deal. But it must be soon."

I could have kissed the smarmy bastard. "Thank you, Mr Sawyer. My client will be most pleased, and grateful." We stood and shook hands. "I'll call my client to make arrangements."

I tried to pull my hand away but he held fast. "And how can I get in touch with you?"

He released my hand and I fished a business card from my handbag. This felt like progress, but I wasn't sure if it was the right kind of progress. Still, I had no choice. "You can reach me on my mobile."

He took the card and studied it. "Thank you, Ms Ka Knee Ket."

"It's Ka NEEK, the T is silent. It's Norwegian; my father was born in Oslo."

Outside of Sawyer Enterprises I sat in my car, waiting for my insides to stop shaking and wondering if they had bought the story of Ms Clar Knekt and her father from Oslo.

In truth, my father was born in Barnsley. He lives in Spain now. I haven't seen him in eight years and I missed him now more than ever. I wished I could talk to him about what was happening because, in a way, he started it all.

Nadia was the natural result of what I was as a teenager, and what I was as a teenager was the natural result of what I was as a child. And what I was as a child all came down to my father discovering—during a bank holiday afternoon game of Trivial Pursuit—that I was a genius. Or so he thought. He based this conclusion on the fact that I knew the correct answer to every question he and my mum got wrong.

His conviction solidified when he quizzed me on every question in the box and I continued to get them all correct. My mum thought it was cute. My dad thought it was cute, too, but he saw an opportunity.

That was how I became that adorable little kid on the telly with the green eyes and curly hair who knew just about everything. Once it became clear I was on my way to becoming the nation's darling, my dad quit his job to manage my career. The next few years were a blur of news shows, interviews and guest appearances, which culminated in my MasterQuiz hat trick—winning the championships in the child, adult and celebrity divisions—when I was ten years old.

By then, I'd been a celebrity half my life, and I hadn't had a say in it. Not that I would have had much of an opinion at that time; for me, it was normal life. I found it odd, chatting with classmates at school, to discover none of them had ever been on the telly, or met the Prime Minister. As time went on, I found myself more and more left out when it became clear I had nothing in common with them. I'd experienced huge media success, but remained friendless. During those early, frantic years, my dad was my best friend.

When I turned eleven, I displayed an aptitude for gymnastics, and I took to it with a vengeance. Here was something I was good at, something I chose and wanted to do. I had talent, but without my previous media exposure, I would not have advanced very far. With my fame, came money for training, eager tutors and an adoring nation willing me on. That was when I met Paul.

Paul Evans was my coach and mentor, a young man who, like me, had shot into the spotlight at an early age. At twenty-seven he had already had some national successes, so my dad contacted him, hoping to lure him away from his latest protégée. Paul was thin and agile, with close-cropped hair, a serious countenance and more knowledge about gymnastics and coaching than anyone I had ever met. He was hungry for a champion; we were made for each other.

Paul took over my training. He worked me hard and I advanced at an increasing pace. It took a while for my dad to realise my "brainy kid" days were behind me; I was Rachel the gymnast now, and he saw his role diminish. Although he tried to stay involved, Paul became my de facto manager and my father started spending a lot of time at the pub. The toxic atmosphere in our house grew in direct proportion to the time he spent drinking. Then one day, he announced he had taken a job as a property manager. In Spain. He left the next morning.

We didn't hear from him for three months, until the divorce papers arrived. My mother didn't seem concerned; my sister blamed me for wrecking the family. I threw myself into my training and Paul became my surrogate father, as well as my friend.

Two years later, when I won the European Gymnastics Championship, my routines were polished and my impish smile a permanent feature on the competition floor, but inside I was empty. This worried Paul; I was his Olympic hopeful, he needed me happy, willing and compliant. In a bid to rekindle my enthusiasm, he enrolled me in the Miss Teen England competition. I did it because I craved a diversion, but I felt sorry for the other girls. I was the nation's favourite precocious child, their rising athletic star and, as I soon discovered, with enough judiciously applied make up, almost anyone can be beautiful. Losing was not an option.

It was, no pun intended, my crowning achievement. But it was also a huge mistake. My regal duties, which consisted of opening shopping centres and speaking at graduation ceremonies, cut too large a slice from my practice time for Paul's comfort. I held on, because that's what champions do, but it was the worst year of my young life. My relationship with Paul became strained as the Olympic dream drifted further from his grasp. When I retired the crown to the next Miss Teen England, I told Paul I was quitting gymnastics.

He did not take it well.

So I slunk off to university, followed by the tabloid hounds. And now I'm a fugitive terrorist.

I let out a sigh, put the car in gear and pulled away from Sawyer's office; everything leading up to this point came down to my knowing the answers to those bloody questions, and my father never thinking to ask me why. He assumed I was a genius. The truth was, a few months earlier, during a rainy and boring Sunday afternoon, I had opened the Trivial Pursuit game, read the box of questions and memorised the answers. I memorised them, along with the *Encyclopaedia Britannica*, *The Radio Times* and everything else that came in front of my eyes.

I'm not a genius; I'm a freak. But no one, not my dad, not even Paul, knows that everything I accomplished was founded on a lie.

Chapter 7

I ARRIVED AT THE Holiday Depot just before normal opening hours the next morning. Being a Saturday, the market was in town and vendor stalls crowded around the Shelly fountain in the Bishopric and spilled up West Street, bringing with them the scent of fresh cut flowers, vinegar and an occasional waft of grilled sausage. Nearby, a kiosk dispensed old-fashioned sweets from big glass jars. I considered nipping over for breakfast, because nothing says, "Good morning" like a cherry whip or bag of jelly beans, but decided against it. The toast and tea I'd had after my morning run would have to see me through.

I was dressed in jeans, a flannel shirt over a tee shirt and an old denim jacket. With no clue what we were supposed to be doing, I felt it best to come equipped with a versatile wardrobe.

I was not ready for a day of team building. The news last night had been shocking and robbed me of the sound sleep I had been looking forward to.

"A community cowers in fear as an organised group of terrorists targets their homes."

That was the lead on the regional news. The national news toned it down somewhat but it remained clear that the two to seven people (depending on whose report you believed) Nadia had turned into were still the prime suspects. The police had issued a bland statement about person or persons unknown being sought for questioning, which left the press with very little to do except chase their own tails. They were starting to report on their own reports, and each version strayed further from the truth; I needed to do something to deflate or divert the coverage soon, or tonight's evening news would have me in league with the Taliban.

"Any publicity is good publicity."

Those were Paul's words: easy to say when you're being coddled by the media, but I wasn't used to bad press. In each of my previous incarnations I'd been treated well by reporters and journalists, at least until I stopped giving them what they wanted. So perhaps what I needed to do to stop the speculation was provide a better story, one that would confirm Nadia to be one of the good guys.

Amanda arrived, breaking me out of my reverie. Her powder-blue running outfit had pink piping running down the sleeves and trouser legs and her blonde hair was pulled into a tight ponytail. A pink sweatband encircled her head like a low-flying halo and she carried one of those jogging water bottles shaped like an oblong doughnut.

"What do you think Mr Palmer's going to make us do?" I asked. "Try out for the London Marathon?"

"We're still representing the company, no matter what we're doing today. You look like you're dressed for mucking out stalls."

"Is that what he's got us doing?" said James, ambling up behind Amanda. She turned away and my retort, which would have been witty and scathing, withered on my tongue.

James wore tan denim trousers, oxblood loafers and a double-breasted reefer jacket, causing me to wonder if the whole team building thing was a practical joke set up to make me look like a homeless person hanging out with social workers.

Before I could speculate further, Martin approached from the direction of the Bishopric, dressed in jeans and an old sweat shirt. "Glad you could all make it."

He clapped his hands and rubbed them together, the way I imagined he did when presented with a roast dinner. I got a sinking feeling; if he was this happy about the project, it wasn't going to be good. "This way, ladies and gent."

We marched against the swelling tide of shoppers squeezing between the shop fronts and the vendor stalls and onto the open area of the Bishopric. When we passed the Merrythought I glanced at Alex's flat, wondering if she was watching our strange parade wandering out of town while everyone else was barging in, or if she was on duty and dedicating herself to catching the Keymer View terrorists. Or if, being a normal person, she was having a lie-in, which is what I wished I was doing.

We crossed Albion way, passed the kebab shop on the corner, the bookmakers, the mortgage lenders and The Pedaller's Bike Emporium, where the co-owners, dressed in lyrca cycling outfits, were setting sleek bicycles up in a neat row in front of their shop. I assumed them be the owners because there had to be a law forbidding employers to inflict such a fashion travesty upon their employees. I sidestepped around the taller of the two as he arranged another bike at the end of the row and continued onward towards my mysterious task, wondering if there might be any legislation protecting us from whatever Martin had in store.

I had never walked to this side of town before and was uncertain what to expect. We passed a few more fast food outlets, an undertakers, pub and Ford dealer in quick succession and then, about forty metres beyond the entrance of Bishops Court, I saw it: a pillbox.

It had been excavated from the decades-deep layer of weeds, brambles, ivy vines and fallen leaves that had encroached on it from the verges of Bishops Court. Someone had hacked a semi-circular, weed-free perimeter around the site, making it the most prominent feature, aside from the bus shelter, on that part of the road. I noticed it was a Type 20, more commonly known as a Vickers machine gun pillbox. The Fortifications and Works, or FW3, branch built them in pairs, so its twin was likely buried under the Collingwood Bachelor furniture showroom across the street. I could tell it had been modified from the official design, with the door opposite, instead of to the side, of the main embrasure. But this wasn't unusual. Nor was the fact that it appeared to be made of brick, as brick walls were sometimes used as moulds to pour concrete into, and then left in place to provide extra protection. What was unusual was that this brick appeared new and was covered in spray paint. A trio, consisting of a man, woman and either a very short person or a child of about twelve, scrubbed away at the graffiti with varying degrees of enthusiasm.

"You're not expecting us to help clean that up, are you?" Amanda asked.

Martin marched onward. "Team, I'd like you to meet the members of the Bishopric Historical Restoration Society."

They stopped their scrubbing and turned around. I recognised the woman and child from the photos on Martin's desk. The other man, with the two-day beard, pattern baldness and goofy grin, was unfamiliar.

Awkward introductions ensued. Martin's wife, an affable woman with a round face, wide hips and a loose jumper that didn't hide the fact that she was braless, was Lillian. The spindle on legs with the long brown hair and pinched face was their daughter, Judith. The other man, with the moist handshake and eager brown eyes, was Philip.

"You are going to perform a great public service this morning, team," Martin began. More than I wished to be anywhere else, I wished he'd stop calling us "Team".

"This FW3 Type 20 pillbox—"

"Excuse me, Martin," Philip piped in, "but outside of Norfolk they were referred to as Vickers MMG emplacements."

Oh great, a battle for the title of Über Anorak.

"Of course, but I didn't want to confuse my team with minutiae. The important thing is, this World War II pillbox was rediscovered, through the efforts of our friend Philip here, and renovated by the Bishopric Historical Restoration Society. As you know, next Sunday is Remembrance Sunday. The Lord Lieutenant has agreed to pay tribute to our war dead with a ceremony and the placing of a wreath at this site."

He waited while we grasped the enormity of the honour.

"As you can see, there are some who do not show proper respect for our armed services and their continuing sacrifices, so we must do it for them."

"And by that I assume you mean we have to clean it up," Amanda said.

"With many hands, it will be easy work. We spent weeks clearing this site and restoring the fortification to its former glory; this is just a bit of paint."

"But it will have sunk into the bricks. It's not going to come out." She squinted towards the writing. "And what does it say, anyway? Is it an anti-war slogan?"

Martin cleared his throat. "It says, 'Tag'."

"Tag?"

"Yes. On each wall and the roof. And there's more inside."

I imagined it was perpetrated by a budding wannabe who heard that, to be a real graffiti artist, your signature needed to be a tag. That measured up to what I imagined the creativity of the local troublemaker was. Someone with a bit more awareness would have at least painted swastikas.

We were divided into teams, with Amanda and James working together and Philip assigned to me. We had the pleasure of cleaning the empty Special Brew cans, kebab leftovers and used condoms out of the interior in preparation for covering over the impromptu artwork. I gave Martin grudging credit for realising small unventilated places and copious amounts of paint remover didn't mix. Instead of scrubbing down the inside walls with turpentine and a wire brush, he elected to paint it in institutional beige.

Amanda conspired to keep herself as close to James as possible, and Philip followed suit. Not with James, with me. He followed me down the concrete steps into the musty and dank interior and busied himself by clearing the bit of floor next to me, even though the inside of the pillbox was cosy enough without intimate company. To top it off, he began bombarding me with scintillating conversation.

"Most of the entrenchments still in existence have been on the maps since the end of the war. A new excavation like this is a rarity; we were very excited by the find."

I bet he was. I also bet he spent his Saturday nights surfing the Internet or meeting up with his anorak buddies. Not that I had anything to brag about.

"After the ceremony, we're going to have it registered as a national historic site."

I picked up a grease-stained wrapper, holding it between my thumb and index finger despite the rubber gloves Martin had provided. "I think the locals would like that," I said, dropping the wrapper into a black bag. "The opportunity to get drunk and shag in a historic monument doesn't come along every day."

He turned away, grabbed a double handful of debris and shoved it in to the bag in silence. Part of me was thinking, "Result!" but the part that knew what it was like to be made fun of sent a jolt of regret into the heart of my conscience and I found myself wishing I could make it up to him.

"Being buried for so long didn't do it any favours, did it?" I tried after a few minutes of tense silence.

"How do you mean?" he said, not looking my way.

"This model usually has three embrasures, but the two side rifle ports have been bricked over. You've done a lot of reconstruction work."

It was the wrong thing to say. He followed it up by pointing out an array of riveting details—such as the missing machine gun mount, the absence of a blast wall outside the entranceway and the extensive brick work that had replaced the disintegrating concrete in the walls and ceiling—all of which I knew. It was one of the downsides of my affliction. I know a great deal about a lot of things, but that doesn't mean I'm interested in them.

After that he appeared to think we were going steady and mooned around after me like a pole-axed heifer. At one point, when I emerged through the narrow door to gulp down some fresh air and a sudden row in one of the nearby flats caused me to hesitate, he bumped into me from behind.

The row grew louder. I looked towards Bishops Court where a string of harsh words spewed from a first floor flat, carrying a payload of pejoratives beginning with "f" and "c." A female voice was in the mix but the argument was dominated by a male.

"Ah, number 24, at it again," Philip said.

When I refused to take the bait, he pressed on as if he had my rapt attention. "I used to live there. You can see my old flat, there on the end."

He pointed to a bank of windows on the second floor. Through the jumble of branches I could see there were no curtains and no knick-knacks on the windowsills. The windows where the squall was building up were covered in white net curtains, through which I could see two figures gesticulating in animated debate.

"I could see this from my window," he continued. "That's how we found it. I didn't know it was a pillbox; it just looked like a big lump of earth covered in ivy and holly bushes. But then one day it occurred to me how it was just the size of an FW3 Type 20."

I could tell he wanted me to be impressed. I did my best.

"So one day I hacked a path through the brush and dug through the thicket until I found these walls. You can't imagine how excited I was."

I assured him I could.

"That's when I called Martin, and we put together a restoration team. It was hard going, and it took us weeks but we wanted to get it done by Remembrance Day."

"So you found this just a few weeks ago."

"Two months."

"And you've moved in the meantime?"

"Well, it wasn't the best of flats. The landlord was unresponsive. The rent kept going up. And those two were the last straw."

He looked up to where the fight was beginning to simmer down. "Chantelle was all right on her own. A little crass but generally quiet. Then a few months ago, Keith moved in and all hell, sorry, I mean, well, things got worse."

At last, I was becoming intrigued. Fighting for people who couldn't fight for themselves was Nadia's mission, and I thought making life hell—or, as Philip might say, heck—for the neighbour-from-heck would be a satisfying and safe way for Nadia to prove herself.

"What did he do to make you move out?"

"No one thing; it was more an accumulation of events. All the swearing, fighting, dope dealing—"

"You think he's a dealer?"

"I don't think he is; I know he is. Cars came and went at all hours, roaring in and parking on the grass where they're not supposed to. People running up to his flat and then back out ten minutes later. I told the police about him, but they never did anything."

"That's a shame you had to move just because of one jerk. What about your other neighbours? How do they—"

"It all worked out for the best. I have a second floor flat in the Forum, with a big balcony and a spectacular view. You should come and see it."

"Um, thanks. But not today."

I looked at my watch. It was eleven fifteen. "We'd better get back to painting. I think we have just enough time to finish before my shift ends."

He nodded. "What are you doing after? We could have lunch together."

Somehow spending more time with a pillbox enthusiast I had endured a fun-filled morning of picking up used condoms with failed to appeal.

"Sorry, but I have other plans."

And I did. Or at least Nadia did.

Chapter 8

AT THE STROKE OF noon I put down my paintbrush, turned in my gloves and bid a moon-faced Philip farewell. Martin thanked me and turned back to his work, measuring the pillbox entrance for the metal security door he was planning to install later that afternoon. As added protection, Judith and Lillian were slathering the outside walls with a clear, graffiti-proof paint. They had thought of everything, except how to keep the locals from using the gun port as a urinal.

Amanda and James, I assumed, had already sneaked away, but then I heard giggling from inside the pillbox. I wondered if they were getting high on the fumes from the latex paint or considering joining the pillbox club, or both. In the end, I decided I didn't care and left them behind, making me the lone skiver.

I walked back towards town, passing the entrance of Bishops Court just as a woman with brittle blonde hair, skin-tight jeans and a pair of stiletto heels clacked out of the drive. As she reached the pavement, a man leaned out of the neighbours-from-hell's flat and shouted down to her, "Cunt."

She raised two fingers towards the building and shouted, "Go fuck yourself."

Charming, the pair of them.

As I watched her stalking away a plan began to form, and by the time I reached town I knew what I was going to do. A simple plan, nice and neat, where nothing could go wrong.

Back at my house I cleaned up and changed my clothes. The morning had been cool but the day had warmed up so I put on a light jacket, found an old, dispensable handbag and my spare camera and left for The Citadel.

Being a Saturday afternoon, the Co-op car park was packed so I ended up parking illegally, with all the other illegally parked cars, in the school car park across the street.

Once inside The Citadel, I changed into a black skirt, sleeveless blouse and platform shoes. Then I added the brown contacts, make-up and the black wig. The result was Nadia without the skin-tight Microprene. Not bad, but for my current mission, I needed to go a little heavier on the make-up. After adding another layer and some fake glitter nails, I felt I looked sufficiently slatternly. All I needed was some surveillance equipment.

I laid the handbag on the dressing table and cut a hole the size of a ten-pence piece in one end with a pair of nail scissors and smoothed out the edges with the toenail clippers from my vanity set. After loading it up with essentials to lend it some verisimilitude—including £200 in twenty pound notes—I tucked the camera in and spent a few minutes practising with it.

The idea worked better in my mind than in practice. The camera, small though it was, made an obvious bulge in the end of the bag, and turning it on and pointing it at the hole was awkward at best. After a couple of tries I found I could manage a jumpy movie clip, with sound—the sound of my hand rustling around inside my handbag—and not look as if I was rooting for loose change.

I put on a faux leather jacket that was two sizes too small and perfect for the look I was going for, got the Escort out and headed towards Horsham.

I parked in the multi-storey on Black Horse Way and walked to the Bishopric, intent on getting to the flats before I changed my mind. As I walked by The Pedaller, head down, staring at the pavement and thinking about how I was going to get my life back, a man backed out of the doorway carrying a BMX bike and I ran head first into the rear wheel. Startled, I yelped and lashed out, pushing the offending spokes away, which caused the man to spin around and lose his balance. He fell towards the open doorway, but managed to career off the wall and tumble into the row of bicycles.

The display fell like dominos, but not as fast. It was more of a crash, tip, crash, tip that seemed to go on for ages. The man, in a lime-green and white Lycra cycle outfit, lay sprawled on top of the jumble of cycle casualties with the BMX on top of him.

I was too shocked to move and too mortified to utter a sound. I stood, staring down at him; the smartest woman in Britain looking like a complete idiot. He didn't look very clever either, though. His eyes were blue and bulged out in surprise, his arms and legs splayed out in a near-perfect "X". From his vantage point, he had a perfect view up my skirt, but his outfit and position made me think that we were about even on that score. "I am so sorry," I said.

He attempted to get up but the shifting pile of bikes beneath and on top of him made it awkward. I reached a hand out to him just as a skinnier, shorter version of the bike man, and wearing the same outfit, leapt through the door. "What in bloody hell do you think you're doing," he shrieked, batting my hand away.

The initial ruckus had gained the attention of the handful of people at the nearby bus stop and, now that it was heating up, the queue outside KFC was becoming interested.

"I'm trying to help this gentleman up."

He glared at me while the man lying on the pile of bikes grinned.

"I don't mean now, I meant before."

"She didn't do anything, Malcolm," the other man said. "I backed out of the door without looking and ran into her. Now help me up."

Malcolm removed the BMX and then we each grabbed a hand and pulled. He gained his feet and rose to his full height, which was a good two inches taller than me, even with the three-inch heels on. All the while he kept looking at me, a grin splitting his unshaven face. "Are you alright?" he asked.

"I'm supposed to be asking that of you."

"But I ran into you first."

"Well, I'm all right. I didn't hurt you, did I?"

"No," he said. "I'm fine."

"The day's not over," Malcolm said, moving between us to start picking up the fallen cycles.

The man smiled and watched him with amused affection.

"My brother, Malcolm," he said. "I'm Robin."

I shook his outstretched hand. "I'm Nadia."

I said it before recalling I was supposed to be under cover. Though I supposed it shouldn't matter; I wasn't hiding from him.

"Nadia," he said. "Nice name. If you ever find yourself in need of a bicycle, please think of me."

He released my hand and I backed away, then stopped when I thought of the trouble backing up had visited on him.

"Sorry," I said. "I will."

I could feel the eyes of the KFC crowd on me as I made my way towards the block of flats. In all, it hadn't been a bad encounter, if you ignore the unorthodox ice-breaker. He hadn't looked at me as if I were a freak, or an imposter. He didn't seem to notice my hair or my fake nails. In short, he took me as a real, authentic human being. He even liked my name.

I held my head a little higher as I neared Bishops Court; I could do this.

Ahead of me, the Bishopric Historical Restoration Society was still at it. A van had parked at the kerb and some workmen were fitting the metal door while the crew stood by and watched. I was surprised to see James and Amanda, standing side by side, among them. The pillbox looked like a proper historic artefact; the paint had been scrubbed away and the anti-graffiti coating dulled the modern brickwork, helping it blend in with the remaining bits of the original structure.

As I watched, Philip and Martin looked my way, but gave no sign of recognition.

I continued into Bishops Court, which consisted of a few grassy areas skirted by tarmac rings. The blocks were arranged in a geometric shape that, if viewed from above, would look like a series of Ys stuck together. The arrangement ensured that each flat had access to natural light in both the front and the back and looked, from my vantage point, like two thirds of the interior of a brick and glass hexagon. The flats had generous windows, petite balconies and flowerbeds at the front. In their day, they must have looked like a work of art.

Currently, the flowerbeds—despite heroic efforts by a scattering of tenants—were a tangle of thistles and bindweed. Ivy climbed the sides of the building and, as I scanned up to number 24, I noticed a fine crop of grass and saplings sprouting from the clogged rain gutters.

The flat was quiet, but I could see Keith through the net curtains prowling the front room, talking on his mobile. I pulled a piece of paper out of my handbag and pretended to consult it. I walked around the grassy circle outside his flat, scanning apartment numbers and doing my best to look confused. On my second turn around the circle, as I passed beneath his flat, he stepped out onto the balcony and looked down at me. "Can I help you?"

Loose jeans hung low on his hips and a white tee shirt stretched over his torso. There was little to impress there, but he seemed to want to show it off. He spread his hands wide on the balcony railing as he leaned over to peer down my cleavage.

"I'm looking for Philip."

His unshaven face scrunched with the effort of thinking. "Philip? The bloke who used to live in number 28?"

"Yes. I suppose that would be him."

"He moved."

I stuck out my bottom lip. "That's odd. I met him two months ago. He gave me his address and told me to look him up if I ever came to Horsham. When did he move?"

His shoulders hunched. "Dunno. He sometimes plays with his pillbox out back. I think he was there this morning. You could try there."

He slid his hands closer together and stood upright with an air of finality.

"Oh, that just sucks. I'm going out tonight and I wanted to party."

I put the paper back in my purse and turned away. I'd dangled the bait; the rest was up to him.

"Party?"

Hooked him. I looked up. His dull brown eyes had taken on a lustre of interest.

"Yeah, you know, I want to have some fun, and Philip said he could help me out."

He shook his head. "Philip?"

I didn't blame him for being incredulous, and didn't want to give him time to think about it.

"Well, thanks for your help."

"Wait a minute."

His eyes narrowed. He looked to his left and right and leaned far over the balcony. "You're looking for something, right?"

I nodded, and cast my own furtive glances.

"I might be able to help you. We can't talk here. Come up. My door is around that end." He pointed the way I had come in. "Number 24."

I found the double doors with the sign for flats 19 to 27 above them and stepped into the hallway. The tan tiles were warped and water stained, and the walls painted a dull and cheerless yellow. A wide, curved stairway—perfect for carrying mattresses, love seats and armoires up and down—led to the flats above. I checked the camera and headed up.

He opened the door as I approached, whisked me inside and shut it behind me.

The flat was bright and airy, a welcome change from the gloominess of the hallway. The interior doors were painted white and fitted with translucent glass panels to aid in light transfer. Despite the mushy-pea green carpet and the cracks running up the walls, it was more inviting than the newer builds that look as if they've been modelled after prison cells.

The rooms might have been large, but the hallway wasn't, and the confined space forced us to stand uncomfortably close. From this distance, his unshaven face and tousled hair looked less like a calculated come-on and more like someone who hadn't bothered to shower. He smelled that way, too.

He eyed me up and down. "You looking to buy?"

I nodded, trying to maintain my poise. This was easy to do if I was covering for a misstep after an awkward dismount, I had done that thousands of times, but here I had thrust myself into theoretical territory. I was face to face with a drug dealer and had no idea what move I was expected to make next. Fortunately, my lack of guile and his eagerness made it easy for me.

"What's your name?" he asked.

"Why?"

"I like to know who I'm doing business with. You can call me Keith."

"Then you can call me Kit. Kit Walker."

He did another slow appraisal of the front of my jacket. "Well, you don't look like a nark, Kit."

Then he turned away. I followed him past the open kitchen door into a large sitting room with curtained windows and French doors leading onto the balcony. The furniture was old but well-kept. And it matched. Newspapers, bills and other household flotsam covered much of the dining room table, but the clutter rested on plastic place mats. This flat was female and Keith appeared as out of place as I felt.

"What are you after?"

For my plan to work, I needed him to sell me something serious. A bag of pot was only going to cause him minor inconvenience. "Do you have any ecstasy, or cocaine?"

He smiled. "Coke, eh? My kind of girl. How much?"

"Can you handle an 8-ball?"

He stepped closer, his cockiness beginning to fade. "Are you sure you're not a nark? You don't look like the sort of bird who can support this kind of hobby."

"You'd be surprised what I support."

I pulled the notes out of my handbag and fanned them out for him to see. He looked at the money, then studied my face, his brow creasing under the unfamiliar strain of organised thought. This was not something I had counted on. My outfit was designed to keep him looking at my chest instead of my face. My crime fighting suit was a better disguise, along with darkness and distance. Here in the brightness of the sitting room, he was looking beyond the charade and taking in my real features. I knew where he was heading; I can put on the talk and wear tarty outfits and pancake make-up and hide beneath a curly wig, but my face didn't show the wear and hardness of a street-wise user. I needed to divert him before he could arrive at that conclusion.

"If we're not going to do business," I said, stuffing the bills back in my handbag, "then I'll be going."

I made to walk by him but he put an arm out to stop me. "Who said anything about that? Just wait here. I'll be right back."

He walked out of the room and pulled the door closed behind him. This gave me ample opportunity to turn on the camera and make sure it was pointing at the hole. I heard him open a door and rummage around in the hallway. I eased the sitting room door open just as he pulled a shoe box from the back of the airing cupboard. He set it on the floor and lifted the lid, revealing rolls of notes and a jumble of plastic bags filled with pills and powder. He caught me looking and popped the top back on the box. "Wait in there," he shouted.

"Sorry," I said, "I thought you were ready."

I retreated to the sitting room. I hadn't filmed much, but with luck it would be enough. And I wasn't done yet. In the hallway I heard the door slam, then there was some rummaging around in the kitchen. I hoped I hadn't angered him too much. I paced the room to ease my nerves. The dining table and chairs were from Habitat, the sofa and bookcase from IKEA. The books were a range of Mills and Boon novels and basic business books. I wondered if Keith had ambitions beyond dealing or if they were Chantelle's books.

The door opened and Keith returned carrying a wadded piece of cling film wrapped around a generous helping of white powder. He tossed it on the table where it landed on an overdue phone bill containing an array of 0900 numbers. I decided the books were Chantelle's and the phone bill was his and speculated that it might have been the cause of this morning's row. He grinned and looked at me with eyes that held no malice despite his recent outburst. "This what you came for?"

I nodded. We agreed a price and I counted out the notes, turning my body to keep my handbag pointed in what I hoped would be an incriminated direction. I held out my hand with the bills on my palm; he scoped them up and set the cocaine in their place. All in front of the camera lens.

"Thanks," I said, stepping towards the door. He moved in front of me.

"What's your hurry? I thought you wanted to party?"

The smile was still on his lips, but it had left his eyes.

"I do, but I'm meeting up with some friends."

I continued to walk forward, but he remained in front of me, backing up as he spoke. "What's a couple of minutes? I just gave you a sweet deal on an 8-ball, the least you can do is share a line." He spread his arms, planting one hand on each wall of the hallway. "And I insist."

If he meant to make me feel menaced, he failed; he was in the perfect position for a swift kick in the groin and I would be out the door before the first wave of nausea griped him. I turned to give myself better leverage and, through a gap in the bedroom curtains, caught a glimpse of bleached blonde hair and tight jeans on the pavement outside. I relaxed and smiled, for real this time. "Well, I don't suppose my friends will mind if I'm a few minutes late."

I went back into the sitting room. Keith pushed the papers aside and placed a glass coaster on the table. I put the 8-ball next to it. He slid it towards me. "You serve it up."

"I don't have any gear with me."

He undid the twist-tie holding the 8-ball together, fished a ring of keys from his pocket and, using the business end of a brass Yale key as a spoon, scooped out two piles of fine powder.

"Now line it up."

His eyes had regained their edginess. He ground a fist into the palm of his other hand, flexing his biceps as he did so. I ignored his antics, pulled my library card from my wallet and smoothed the powder into two neat lines. He looked on, smiling. I wiped the card between a thumb and forefinger and stuck it back in my wallet, catching a familiar scent as I did so.

"Something wrong?"

I put the wallet in my handbag hoping my cheeks weren't as flushed as they felt. "No, not at all."

He turned his attention to rolling up a ten-pound note and I took the opportunity to touch my index finger to the tip of my tongue. I did flush now. Even as the sweetness of the icing sugar spread across my tongue, rage and humiliation blossomed in my cheeks. I sucked it down and put on my beauty pageant smile. He might have won the first round, but I still had the advantage.

"After you."

He offered the rolled-up note. I hesitated just long enough to hear the footsteps in the hall, then plucked it from his fingers and bent over the lines of sugar. The door opened.

I bolted upright, glared at Keith and then at the puzzled Chantelle. "Who the hell is she?" I demanded. "You told me you didn't have a girlfriend."

Chantelle's eyes widened. Then she saw the coaster and the lines. "Bastard."

She strode forward; Keith shrank away from her, bumping into the table edge and knocking the lines of faux coke on the rug. "Babe, it's not what you think."

"Don't you 'Babe' me." She turned on me. "And you. What do you think you're doing here, as if I didn't know. Crack whore!"

I decided to let the slur stand; the look on Keith's face wouldn't have been more satisfying if I had kicked him in the bullocks. I raised my hands in a gesture of surrender. "Hey, I'm the victim here. He lied to me."

"Get out."

I stepped around Keith and the screaming woman and left through the open door.

"Here, you forgot this."

I turned around just as Chantelle hurled the remains of the 8-ball at me. It hit the side of my handbag and exploded in a sweet, confectionary cloud. I dusted myself off as I clomped down the stairs, my footfalls drowned out by Chantelle's screams.

"You promised."

"It's not what it seems."

"Get out."

I heard thumping and a loud crash followed by Keith swearing. I pushed through the double doors into the glare of the afternoon sun. At last, a satisfying conclusion.

Then the doors burst open behind me and Keith charged out, lunging in my direction.

Chapter 9

I SHOULD HAVE HAD no trouble avoiding such a clumsy attack, but my platform shoes and tight skirt hampered mobility to the point where he was able to cut off my escape to the road. I sprinted towards the inner circle and spun around, crouching and facing him as he approached.

My stance gave him something to think about; he stopped beyond my reach and we faced off, circling each other like anorexic sumo wrestlers. "You bitch," he hissed.

I smiled. "And you're a bastard."

I glanced up in time to see Chantelle fling open the French doors and throw an armload of clothing over the balcony. "A homeless bastard, at that."

He whipped around. "Babe, no."

"Don't you 'Babe' me. You take your shit, and your drug-dealing rat arse out of here and go move in with your latest slag."

I put my hands on my hips. "Hey, I'm not a slag."

She disappeared into the flat, her voice booming through the open doors as if through a megaphone, "Yes you are."

Keith had his back to me, his arms bowed away from his sides like a body builder who had completed too many reps, his hands balled into tight fists. I felt a similar feeling stirring but it wasn't full rage, just a curious annoyance. A slag? That's the thanks I get?

Chantelle returned with another armload of clothing and toiletries. It landed on the concrete, the razor shattered; the shampoo bottle oozed a blue puddle. Keith shouted some more and stamped his feet like a tantrum-prone two year old. Chantelle whipped around and stomped into the flat again. When she returned a few moments later, she had the shoe box.

"No you bitch. Don't you fucking dare."

But she did. The box had a soft landing on top of the heap of clothing, but the top flew off and it bounced and rolled onto the concrete, ejecting rolls of notes, some loose bills and bags of assorted drugs along the way.

"You bitch."

He scrambled towards his stash, grabbing at the baggies and stuffing them out of sight under the pile of clothes.

"Now fuck off," Chantelle screamed. "The both of you."

She looked at me as if I was somehow at fault then went inside, rattling the glass on the French doors as she slammed them. Keith stopped his scavenger hunt. "I'll fix you, you bitch. Just wait."

He stood over his pile of possessions, his body shaking, the back of his neck looking as if he had been in the sun too long. Then he kicked the pile, scattering shirts, pants, socks, bags of powder and money over the lane. When he saw what he had done, he kicked it again, and again, emitting a pejorative for emphasis each time his foot connected. I pulled out the camera and filmed him as he kicked and flailed and cursed, focusing in on the drugs when the opportunity arose. When I felt I had enough, I trotted to where the breeze was scattering loose notes and gathered up as many as I could. It wasn't as much as I had paid him for the sugar, but it was close.

He stopped his tantrum and turned towards me. "Give it back."

He stood in the middle of what looked like an explosion in a laundry, his face red and sweating, his fists ready.

"I don't think so," I told him. "I don't pay more than a pound for a box of icing sugar."

He grinned, but there was no humour in it. "You ignorant little whore. You thought you could put one over on me. Guess you thought wrong."

I held up the camera and the money. "I'd say we're about even." I stuffed them into my handbag. "For now."

He lunged towards me with admirable speed. I crouched, readying myself. When he was nearly on me I tucked and rolled into him. I was almost too late; his knee connected with my side sending a bolt of pain through me. An instant later he thudded to the ground. I stood up, rubbing my side.

I thought that would take the fight out of him but he swore and staggered to his feet. I almost felt sorry for him; his comfortable world was falling apart and all he had to do to make himself feel better was beat up a girl. I could at least let him score a few points. He shambled towards me and swung his fist wide. I ducked and kicked his legs out from under him, sending him—grunting and sputtering—back onto the grass. He still refused to stay down, but when he came up this time, he was holding a knife. It was a slender thing, with a black handle and a long, shiny blade. He pointed it towards me. I focused on it and readied myself. "Not so confident now," he said. "Nobody makes a fool out of me."

"You're right; you're doing a good job on your own."

I waited for his move, then I heard shouting and saw a man running towards us. Keith struck and I paid for my distraction. I grabbed his arm a fraction too late and the blade cut through my jacket and into my left forearm. Blood began to flow. I wrenched his arm back until he dropped the knife, then brought my platform shoe down hard against the inside of his ankle.

Keith howled and stumbled backward as the man reached us and pulled me away. My shoes tripped me up and I fell against him.

"Get out," the man screamed, "or I'll have the cops on you."

My arm ached, blood seeped through my jacket. I couldn't let him turn me in. I prepared to hit him with my bleeding arm, the only one I had free, when I saw his wispy, silver hair. He was about my height and had a strong grip for a man who appeared to be in his seventies. He steadied me and pulled me away from Keith, back in the direction he had come from. "Bad news, that one," he said. "You're hurt. We need to get that taken care of."

He brought me into another section of the building where the lobby was not quite as dilapidated as Chantelle's. He pulled a hankie from his pocket and wiped the blood dripping down my sleeve and pressed it over the cut. I put my hand over his. "It's okay, I can hold it."

He nodded but watched me and I got the feeling his chivalry wasn't so much about staunching the flow of blood as it was about me not bleeding all over his tidy lobby.

He lived on the top floor. We walked up together, his arm locked in mine and I allowed myself to be guided into this stranger's flat, still unsure of his intentions concerning the local constabulary and myself. But I fancied my chances with him better than with an angry and knife-wielding drug-dealer.

On the top landing, the door to number 36 was ajar. He pushed it open. "Maggie, you all right?"

"Yes, dear."

The frail voice was followed by a frail woman with a haze of white hair shrouding her head like a halo. As she shuffled through the open doorway of the sitting room, her eyes shifted between me and the man I assumed to be her husband. "Howard," she whispered, "there's a strange person in our flat."

Howard eased me forward closing the door behind me. A clanking, not unlike the slamming of a jail cell, tugged at my attention. The door frame was steel, with three bolts holding it closed, and a heavy-duty intruder chain for good measure.

"Rough neighbourhood?" I asked.

He looked at his handkerchief, blossoming into shades of maroon and burgundy where I held it against my arm. "You might say that."

The woman came towards us, smiling.

"This is my wife, Maggie."

She stared up at me, her pale eyes dull and moist at the corners. "You're a pretty young thing, aren't you?"

Hampered by holding the impromptu bandage, I stretched out my left arm and touch the paper thin skin of her hand. "I'm Nadia," I said.

"Pleased to meet you." She looked at Howard. "Shall I put the kettle on?"

"That would be nice."

She shuffled to the kitchen in frayed slippers and busied herself amid the tea cosies and trivets.

"You can wait in the sitting room," Howard said, "I'll get some bandages."

He left me to find my own way and I walked into a room that, even though it was chilly, felt warm. A rose-pattern sofa occupied the area that, in Chantelle's flat, was used as the dining room. It was surrounded by end tables sporting Tiffany-lookalike lamps on lace doilies. A dark wood entertainment centre had possession of the far corner and a pine table with two matching chairs stood against the wall between the sitting room door and the balcony. The balcony doors, like the windows, were hidden behind thick, vanilla drapes, giving the room a soft glow.

I took off my jacket and laid it, bloody side up, on one of the chairs and was inspecting my wound when Howard entered the room.

"I heard the kerfuffle and took a look outside," he said. "I generally don't get involved with the neighbours, but things looked like they were getting out of hand."

He edged me over to the dining table so he could put his medical paraphernalia down and dab at me with damp cotton wads. The cut wasn't deep enough to require stitches, which was good news.

When he finished dressing my wound, Howard returned his gear to the medicine cabinet, leaving me alone in the sitting room. I went to the window and parted the drapes an inch so I could peek outside. Keith was gathering the last of his stuff, using a large tee shirt as a makeshift sack. He had his drug-box tucked under his arm, but beyond that he seemed unconcerned about what he took. His toiletries were broken, squashed and scattered like toys around an angry baby's pram. I turned back to the room and found Howard standing behind me. "You're free to go," he said. "I won't call the cops on you."

This was getting ridiculous; the more good I tried to do, the more people treated me like a criminal. I had to turn this around. "And why would you?"

His ears turned a darker shade of pink.

"Let me guess. You saw me in Keith's flat, saw how I'm dressed and decided I was a crack whore."

He cleared his throat. "Most people who—"

"I'm not most people. While you were looking, taking in the drama, didn't you see me filming him?" I dropped my handbag on the table and pulled out the camera. "Would you like to taste the residue? It's icing sugar." I held up the camera. "I have evidence of his drug dealing here." I pulled the curtain open so he could see Keith stalking away. "I got him kicked out of his flat. Your neighbour from hell, gone and soon to be arrested, and you want to call the cops on me?"

"So, you're a detective? An undercover cop?"

The hand holding the camera in triumph dropped along with my righteous indignation. After castigating him for thinking I was a criminal, was I now going to admit to being one? I decided on the bold approach. "I'm a crime fighter. And, yes, I'm undercover. Sort of."

He rubbed a hand over his grey stubble and looked about to say something when Maggie came through the doorway carrying a tray and he turned to help her.

They put the tray on the table. On it were three matching teacups in a rose pattern similar to the sofa, all sitting on matching saucers pooled with spilled tea.

"I put milk in your tea," Maggie said. "I hope you don't mind. Do you take sugar?"

"No. Thank you."

"Howard, bring over the good chair."

Howard brought a cushioned chair to the table and held it for me. "Please sit, Nadia, and have some tea."

When the three of us were seated, I lifted my cup. Howard waited for it to touch my lips, then said, "Nadia is a crime fighter, Maggie."

I wasn't sure if he was mocking me or trying to amuse his wife. Either way it was a struggle to keep tea from shooting out of my nose.

"Really? Like that nice Mr Barnaby from the telly?" Maggie asked.

"I don't know. What would you say, Nadia?"

I set my cup down. "Look. I know it's unorthodox, but is trying to bring some justice to this world such a terrible idea?"

He stopped grinning and sipped his tea in silence. "Don't you think it's a dangerous thing to be doing?"

"I can take care of myself."

He looked at the bandage on my arm. The cheek. As if it wasn't his fault I got stabbed.

"Do you solve many crimes, dear?" Maggie asked.

"Well, no. I'm sort of new at this."

Howard looked at me over his teacup. "You're the woman who blew up Keymer View Court, aren't you?"

I set my cup down in lieu of dropping it. "Yes. I mean, no. I mean, it wasn't like that."

I sighed and looked through the opening in the curtains. It was sunny and clear, with the sky painted that deep blue hue reserved for fine autumn afternoons; it was much too cheerful a day to think about going to jail. "Honest, I didn't do anything wrong."

"Then you shouldn't worry about going to the police. You've got half the country convinced we've been targeted by terrorists. Don't you think you should explain yourself?"

I nodded and stared into my teacup. "I know, but it's complicated."

"It's your secret identity, isn't it?" Maggie said. "Crime fighters don't like people to find out their secret identity."

I gave her a wan smile. "Something like that."

I looked at Howard. "Are you not going to call the cops on me now?"

"No, you've already got yourself into enough trouble, and now you almost got yourself killed. Maybe you should think about taking up a different hobby. You don't seem to be very good at this."

I drew in a deep breath but he held up a hand before I could start my tirade. "I'm entitled to my opinion. You'll do as you will, and I won't try to stop you. But you can't keep me from thinking that it's reckless and dangerous." He paused, then added, "I admire what you are trying to achieve, but I worry about where this is taking you."

He lowered his hand; I let out my breath.

"Things are not going to plan, I admit that, but I will turn it around. Wait and see."

69

It felt surreal to sit, chatting about something I had kept secret for so long. I had always envisioned myself being invisible, just a random force that appeared from time to time and then disappeared. I didn't expect to tell anyone what I was doing because I knew no one would understand, or believe. Yet these people accepted me, they didn't agree with me, but they accepted me. How that might affect my mission and whether it was a good or bad thing was something I would have to consider later. For now, I was distracted by a wave of elation. My eyes grew hot. I gazed into my tea cup. "I should go."

"Finish your tea, dear," Maggie said.

I took a sip. And then another. Maggie filled the awkward silence.

"Our grandson, Geoffrey, knew all about crime fighters. He was mad about them, always with his nose in a comic book. He really liked Captain America. Is that what you do?"

I thought she was making a joke but when I looked at her, she appeared genuinely interested. "I think of myself more as Wonder Woman," I said.

"Oh, I remember her. She seemed nice, but Geoffrey wasn't keen on her. So is crime fighting what you do for a living?"

"No, I have a regular job."

Maggie nodded. "I see. Crime fighters don't make a lot of money, do they?"

"No." I looked at Howard. "But I'm trying to bring some good into the world. That's payment enough."

"Fighting bad guys; that sounds more fun than typing. That's what I used to do. Are you the one who tied up young Carl and Derek?"

"Um, yeah, I guess I did."

"I think that's marvellous. They're not very nice people, you know."

"You know them?"

"They're the caretakers here," Howard said. "Although I use the term loosely."

"You mean Kevin Sawyer owns these flats, too?"

"Yes. He took them over about a year ago. That's why the place looks so seedy; he doesn't seem to like his properties, or his tenants. My feeling is he's trying force everyone to move out so he can persuade the council to allow him to raze the place and throw up some breezeblock barracks."

"That's awful."

He smiled. "That's just my paranoia talking; he knows the council would never allow that, not while we're still here. We moved in when the flats were first built, back in '62. We're the last of the original tenants, and as such, we have a lifetime lease. He can't revoke it or allow the building to be condemned as long as we're still here."

"And you're not planning to leave voluntarily?"

"This is a perfect location, and the last place I want Maggie and I to spend our twilight years is in one of those old folks' prisons. No, the only way he could get me out of here is by planting a few sticks of dynamite under my bum."

"So why is he running the place down?"

"Bad economic climate, money's short. Who can say? It may be as simple as Carl and Derek being incompetent."

I drank down the rest of my tea, wondering if Sawyer deserved another visit.

"So what did happen at Keymer View Court?" Howard asked.

I thought about telling him the story, starting the ripple of truth to push back the wave of misinformation, but then decided it wouldn't be fair. "I'm sorry, Howard. You and Maggie have been very kind, but you're already in danger of being arrested for harbouring a fugitive."

"But we didn't know you were a crime fighter when we invited you here," Maggie said. "Isn't that right, Howard?"

Howard nodded.

"So, is what they're saying about you true?" he asked.

"No. But I can't tell you any more than that, for your own good. There are some things going on that I don't understand myself and I don't want to be guilty of spreading more misinformation."

I got up and put on my jacket. "Besides, I am Nadia, Defender of Truth, Champion of Justice," I winked at Howard. "The truth will prevail."

Howard showed me to the door and released the bolts. I felt a soft hand on my arm. Maggie looked up at me, her eyes shining. "Do you have an invisible plane? Wonder Woman always travelled in an invisible plane. Do you have one?"

I smiled. "No. I'm afraid all I have is a car."

"Oh, that's a shame," she said. "I would have liked to have seen it."

Chapter 10

WHEN I LEFT THE building, I took a cautious look around to make sure Keith wasn't hiding in the bushes. There didn't appear to be an ambush waiting either on the ground or from Chantelle's apartment, so I headed towards the street. As I rounded the corner I saw Carl and Derek loitering near the entrance. They saw me and came forward, each hefting a two-foot length of pipe.

"I had a hunch you'd be behind this," Derek said.

I looked behind me, as if they might be talking to someone else. "What do you mean? Who are you?"

Carl stepped forward. "Nice try," he said. "I'd recognise those bristols anywhere. I was real close to them the other night, if you recall."

He looked younger in the daylight, but his sly expression was more visible. And he looked fit, despite his padding of fat. Derek tapped the bar against the palm of his hand and kept his eyes on me as he moved away from Carl, blocking my way. I didn't think I could get past them without one of them landing a blow. And that would be enough. To my right were the rows of garages; a dead end where I would be trapped. My only option was to back up, keeping enough distance between them and myself so they couldn't attack, and hope Howard was curtain twitching again. I backed away a step at a time. They advanced twice as fast. If I turned, they would be on me and I couldn't outrun both of them. I was in sight of Howard's flat, but Carl and Derek weren't.

Then a black BMW with tinted windows roared into the entrance and chirped to a stop ten feet behind them. The door flew open and Kevin Sawyer jumped out. "What's going on?"

He walked between Carl and Derek. I stopped backing up and allowed him to approach. "Mrs Abruzzi in number 14 called to tell me there was a domestic dispute in progress. Are you responsible?"

I backed up a few more paces. "No, that wasn't me. And these men seem to think they know me. I think they mean to harm me."

Carl and Derek continued their approach, keeping themselves separated, covering either side of Sawyer. Behind the BMW I saw Keith sneaking back into the entrance.

Sawyer grabbed my wrist and twisted. "Is this her?" he asked, looking straight at me.

"That's her all right," Carl said. "Isn't she the one, Derek?"

Derek nodded and tapped his palm with the pipe.

"Klar, isn't it?" Sawyer said. "Klar *Kunt* or some such nonsense." His gaze drifted from the front of my jacket, to my skirt and back up again. "I must say, you look a lot more attractive now than you did in my office yesterday."

Keith closed in, ambling in our direction, in no hurry.

"Her name is Kit Walker," he called. "She wanted to buy drugs off of me but I told her I didn't do that sort of thing. And then she stole my money."

Sawyer glanced at Keith then smiled at me. "You have interesting leisure pursuits, blowing up buildings, stealing, taking drugs—"

"That wasn't me. I don't know what you're talking about."

Without looking he pointed at Carl who pulled a mobile phone from his pocket and dialled a number. From within my handbag came the muffled tones of the Hawaii Five-0 theme.

"Aren't you going to answer it, Ms *Kunt*, or is it Walker?" He pulled me closer. "You mentioned some proof you had concerning the unfortunate business at Keymer View the other night. Why don't we take a ride so we can discuss what we should do about it? We can invite your friend; it seems you and he have unfinished business."

I could escape Sawyer's grasp, but winning a game of tag against the four of them was not something I wanted to try, not with my platform shoe disadvantage. I was wondering how far I could hope to run in bare feet before I stepped on a broken Budweiser bottle or a puddle of last night's regurgitated kebab when Sawyer's grip loosened. Carl and Derek lowered their weapons, hiding them behind their backs, while Keith turned and scurried back to the street. Then I heard a familiar voice.

"Good afternoon, Mr Sawyer. I see you've met Nadia."

Sawyer looked smug. "Nadia, is it then?"

Good going Howard.

At least he had created a diversion. I pulled my wrist from Sawyer's grasp. Howard arrived and stood close. "Nadia wasn't the one causing the problem," he said. "She was helping."

"Is that right?"

"You should thank her. That tenant in 24, the one I've been calling about, has been moved on."

"And this was her doing?"

"Howard, I don't think we need to relive the whole sordid event for them, do you." I looked straight at him, furrowing my brow, hoping he would get the point.

"She's quite remarkable."

"Howard."

"And, well, he's gone now. If Carl and Derek can help me clean up the mess he left behind, we can start putting things right again. Don't you think so, Mr Sawyer? And about my gas heater, here it is nearly November and I haven't seen any sign..."

While Howard talked, I gave a small wave, mouthed "Goodbye" and walked away, stepping between Carl and Derek, neither of whom lifted a finger, or more to the point, a metal bar, to stop me.

I managed to hold myself together until I turned the corner out of the entrance, then my wobbling legs threatened to give way and I leaned up against a low brick wall, trembling, hugging myself and drawing deep breaths to keep from crying. Who was I kidding? A crime fighter, Wonder Woman? I pushed the emotions aside. It wasn't fear causing me to shake, or doubt, it was shame. This could be done, I was sure of it; the problem was, I was doing it badly, and there was no room for that. I needed to regroup and rethink my strategy. I could still claim a win.

I held my head up, forcing a confidence surge that lasted about half a second. Across the road, Keith paced the pavement, eyeing me like a snake evaluating a tasty mouse, then, to my left, Carl and Derek turned the corner out of Bishops Court. Broken bottles or no, I kicked off my shoes and ran.

I had the element of surprise on Carl and Derek; they were trailing me but they couldn't have imagined I was daft enough to wait for them outside the court. That fooled them good and proper. It took several seconds for them to understand what was happening and by then I was halfway to the intersection. Keith, on the other hand, wasn't as far behind, but he was on the opposite side of the road, loping past the Panda House Chinese takeaway, still looking for a break in traffic. So far, I had the advantage, but that could turn at any moment.

I couldn't weave through the traffic on Albion Way fast enough to lose them in the crowded town centre and if I tried to outrun them, I was sure to step on something that would give them the advantage. I had to lose them, and quick.

Ahead of me, Malcolm was bringing bikes into The Pedaller. He lifted one and turned in my direction, his eyes registering recognition and annoyance. Instead of running past him, I dodged into the shop.

The place was small, made smaller by the jumble of bikes, bike parts, racks of accessories, spare wheels, air pumps, streamlined helmets and Lycra fashion items displayed throughout the limited floor space. A bare wooden stairway led to an upper floor but I saw no sign inviting customers to the ladies lingerie department on the first floor, so this was the whole shop. Robin stood behind a cluttered counter leafing through a pile of papers. He looked up. "Can I help you? Oh, Nadia; here to knock over some more of our inventory? You'd better hurry, Malcolm is bringing it in now."

I heard Malcolm clanking behind me.

"Back door," I said.

"Pardon?"

"I ran to the counter. "I need to go out your back door. Now."

"We don't have one. But don't tell the fire brigade. It's too blocked up with—"

I didn't let him finish. I came around to his side of the counter and ducked down. "Some men are after me," I hissed. "Help me, please."

"This is bollocks," Malcolm said.

"Just keep bringing the bikes in," Robin said. "I'll handle this."

"She's trouble."

I heard Malcolm step outside, then shout, "Hey, watch it," as several pairs of feet thudded on the floorboards. I squeezed myself into a ball and tucked into the nook where the counter met the wall. It was a tight fit and smelled of grease and oil and the comforting aroma of old wood.

"Can I help you?" Robin asked.

"A girl came in here." Carl's voice. "Where is she?"

"You mean that crazy woman in the leather jacket?"

I kicked him in the shin.

"She ran out the back."

They must have attempted the same because Robin jumped to the end of the counter.

"Hold on. No one is allowed back there. Health and safety regulation. I couldn't stop her, but I'm not letting you go through. If you're looking for her, she's outside somewhere; I suggest you search there."

75

A mini-stand-off followed. From my hiding place, I saw Robin expand his chest and place his hands on his hips. I thought it might come to blows but then Keith's voice broke the tension. "She can't have gone far. I'm going out to look for her."

I guess being beaten up once a day was his limit.

"Alright." Carl again. "Go to the corner and see if you can spot her. Derek, you go around the back."

His voice faded as they left the shop and split up, fanning out in a cooperative effort to find me. At least I was now being chased by bad guys, people I could justify hiding from and take some pleasure in outwitting. So things were turning around after all.

Robin stepped back behind the counter but continued to look ahead, giving no sign that there was a woman sitting on the floor next to him. "You certainly have their attention. Mind if I ask what they're after you for. I think it's the least you can do; I fancy knowing if I'm hiding a criminal or a runaway bride."

I started to unfold myself.

"Don't get up," he said, shuffling through the pile of papers. "They keep passing by, looking in here. I think they're suspicious."

I leaned back against the wall. Sitting on the wooden floor with just my skirt for padding was making my bum numb. I raised myself up on my hands until the feeling came back, then settled down again. "I'm not a criminal, or a reluctant bride. One of those men is a drug dealer, the other two are caretakers for Sawyer Enterprises."

"And they're after you because you, what, trampled on their opium plants?"

"No, nothing like that. It's two separate incidents. They don't even know each other."

Robin stopped shuffling papers and looked down at me. "Let me guess. You're a councillor of sorts who brings people together by providing them with a common enemy."

"It's complicated. Can we just agree that I did some things that pissed them off?"

On the far side of the counter, another bicycle thumped to the floor. "I told you she was trouble," Malcolm said. Heavy footsteps trailed out the door.

"He's right, you know, you are trouble," Robin said. "But your friends look like more trouble, so I'm not going to let them get you; they didn't look like they wanted to invite you to tea."

76

"No, I can guarantee you that. Look, all I have to do is get to my car. It's not parked very far away; I just have to make sure they don't see me."

He gathered up the papers and stuffed them into blue plastic file folder. "That won't be easy, but I have a plan."

He disappeared into the front of the shop, then returned with a canary yellow jumpsuit, rubber shoes, helmet and a rucksack. "Here, put these on."

I looked at the rucksack. "What is this for?"

"Your civvies."

It took me a moment but I realised my skirt and jacket were never going to fit under the jumpsuit, and if I removed my blouse and bra, I wouldn't stand out as much, as if I wasn't going to be visible from outer space clad in yellow Lycra.

"I'll help Malcolm with the stock," he said. "You give a shout when you're ready."

"Do you have a changing room?"

"You're in it."

"But, couldn't I crawl into the back room?"

"No, no," he said, walking away, "they'd see you through the windows."

From the glib edge in his voice I knew there was no chance of that, he just liked the idea of me squirming around half naked behind his counter.

I wriggled out of my clothes and into the yellow cocoon. I've worn bodysuits for as long as I can remember, but somehow the garish colours preferred by the members of the biking fraternity make me feel self-conscious. I used to wear a white body stocking when I performed; my coach thought it made me look angelic. This outfit made me look like an ad for Colman's Mustard.

Without my bra on, the tight fabric made me look as if I had well developed pecs, and with the hood stretched over my wig and hiding the black hair and curls, I might pass for a man. At the very least, the disguise would fool Keith and Sawyer's men long enough to get out me of their reach.

I stuffed my spare clothing and my handbag into the rucksack, strapped on the helmet and stood up to signify I was ready. Robin was standing near the door, his bike suit augmented with a helmet and leather gloves, a bike on either side of him. "You can ride, can't you?"

I shrugged the rucksack onto my back and adjusted the straps. "Well enough."

Outside, I straddled the bike, a lightweight hybrid with thin, knobby tyres, low-slung handle bars and fifteen gears. Robin's bike was one of those odd-looking contraptions that folds into a clever package you can fit into a make-up case, but in his startling attire, he didn't look out of place on the bike, or vice versa. Derek was two doors down, standing at the corner. He even looked our way but didn't recognise us. I was standing in the only place where I could remain inconspicuous while dressed like Big Bird. A wise man hides a cyclist in a bike shop.

We pedalled away from Derek, towards Bishops Court and Martin's pillbox. It wasn't until Malcolm came back out on the pavement to fetch another bike that Derek saw something was wrong. "Hey. That's her."

We pedalled faster. I ratcheted up the gears from first to tenth in short order and then couldn't figure out how to get into eleventh. I gave up and concentrated on pedalling. I heard running footsteps but they were far behind and falling further away. When I got to the brick wall I skidded to a halt and dismounted. About ten feet ahead, Robin stopped, as well. "What the hell are you up to?"

"I left my shoes here."

I scooped them up and was about to take the rucksack off when Sawyer's car pulled out of Bishops Court. He spotted me, squealing his tyres to swing the nose of the BMW my way. Gripping a shoe in each hand I grabbed the bike and ran forward with it just as Sawyer's car jumped the curb and grazed up against the wall where I had been. By the time I jumped on the bike and started pedalling, he was already backing up. Cars screeched and horns blared as he cornered backward into traffic and shot forward after us. Robin was twenty feet ahead of me, hunched over the handlebars, pedalling furiously. So much for chivalry.

I leaned forward and pumped as the car gained on us.

"Follow me," Robin shouted.

He swerved into the entrance of Tanbridge Court and I followed. Sawyer, who had been close on my tail, skidded to a stop, backed up and turned in after us. We cut through a gap in the trees and across a small car park onto Blackbridge Lane. Behind us, Sawyer reversed back onto the road. I followed Robin as he jumped the pavement and biked up a driveway, across a back garden and onto a footpath leading between a row of large and affluent properties. From there we crossed another road and pedalled into a copse of trees, exiting onto school playing fields.

The black BMW raced up the road in front of the school as Robin led us through a gap in the hedge where a bike path ran behind a row of houses. We were out of sight of the road here, safe for the moment. Robin coasted to a stop. I pulled up next to him.

"We need to get away from these roads where he can't follow us," he said.

I nodded, stuffed my shoes in the rucksack and got ready to ride.

The path led to a narrow lane. Robin ventured out first, checking for Sawyer's car, then signalled me to follow. We sped down the empty road but soon the growl of an engine came up fast behind us. Robin went up onto the pavement and I followed. The car slowed to match our pace, though Sawyer could do nothing but glare at us. Then we veered off onto a path that ran along the river Arun. We were still in sight of the road but were twenty feet away and protected by trees. Sawyer revved his engine in frustration, then darted ahead and disappeared around a bend.

"Do you think he went to get reinforcements?" Robin called.

"I doubt it. It would take too long; we could be anywhere by the time they arrived."

"Then he may be planning to cut us off at the end of the path."

I expect him to turn around and double back, but he continued forward. As the path looped around the curve, he detoured back onto the road and switched into high gear. I struggled to keep up, still unable to get the bike into the top gears. Ahead, Sawyer's car angled across the path where it ended at the Tanbridge schoolyard. Sawyer climbed out and stood beside it, waiting for us.

We zipped by in silence. Sawyer was so intent on watching the path he almost missed us and, by then, we had entered the school grounds. Robin led us through an open gate, onto a paved footpath that ran along the edge of a meadow. I looked up the gentle slope and saw that Robin was heading for a narrow pedestrian bridge spanning the dual carriageway. Once we crossed it, we would be home free. I downshifted and began to relax.

Then from behind came a deep thud and the screech of tortured metal. I glanced over my shoulder. Sawyer was bulling his way through the gate, leaving one gatepost leaning drunkenly and the other gouging the side of the BMW as the engine revved and the tyres squealed. I pedalled faster, building speed and momentum.

The screeching stopped and I chanced another look back. Sawyer was free of the gate. He swung the bulky car wide and began to sink in the soft soil, but then he manoeuvred one side of the BMW onto the paved path and began closing the gap between us. I focused on the bridge and pedalled double-time.

Ahead of me, Robin cycled onto the bridge. He rode a short distance, then stopped and looked back, an expression of alarm on his face. "Hurry," he shouted.

I had no energy to spare for a reply; all my strength and concentration focused on my legs, my arms, my breathing. I pumped with everything I had as the BMW growled behind me.

The bridge was a few metres away when I felt a thump and shot forward. The bike shuddered and I struggled to maintain control, to keep on the path and not go over the embankment. I slipped between the steel walls of the bridge as a deafening clang exploded behind me and the roadbed gave a slight lurch. Wobbling to a stop, I took a quick look behind me.

Sawyer had driven into the end of the bridge. If he had been expecting his car to squeeze onto the narrow walkway as if in a cartoon then he was disappointed. The grille was smashed, the headlights shattered and Sawyer himself was hidden behind the deployed airbag. His arms flailed, punching at the bag, encouraging it to deflate.

"Come on," Robin said.

The bridge led to a Tesco's car park and from there we rode along narrow lanes and a series of bike paths, coming to stop on a rise overlooking a landscape of undulating, hedge-rimmed fields.

"Pretty, don't you think?"

I took a breath to calm myself. "Yes, it is."

"Do you think we've lost him?"

"I think so," I said. "Even if he's not still stuck in the meadow, I can't imagine him finding us out here."

Robin grinned. "Then let's take a ride."

With that, he pedalled away.

"Hey, wait up."

He led us through a maze of paths and lanes, riding at a moderate pace. After a while, my heart rate dropped to pre-panic levels and I allowed myself to enjoy the cool wind on my face and the waning warmth of the late afternoon sun. At length, we came to the edge of an impressive complex of medieval buildings.

"That's Christ's Hospital," Robin said.

"He has his own hospital? I wasn't aware he was sick."

"It's a boarding school, established by Edward the sixth in 1552. The students still wear medieval-style uniforms. A lot of people think it's funny, but I like it. There's comfort in tradition; do you agree?"

I looked at him, wondering if he was serious. We had just escaped from a gang of thugs, and now he was giving me a history tour.

"Are you a local?" I asked.

"Born and raised. I grew up in Pound Hill, and I live in Southwater, just down the way. I ride here all the time. It's soothing."

"Yes," I said. "It is."

We rode past the buildings onto a road that took us under the A24 and back towards town. At the top of Tower Hill road, he stopped at a large white building with blue trim and a sign reading, "The Boar's Head."

"What are you doing?" I asked.

He rested his bike against the brick wall outside the entrance. "Stopping for a pint. What's it look like? I don't know about you, but I like a drink after a nice ride, and a narrow escape."

I dismounted and leaned my bike next to his. "Okay. But I'm not going in there dressed like this."

He waved towards a collection of picnic tables. "Have a seat, then. I'll buy."

I was seated, with my helmet and hood removed, gazing over a fetching countryside speckled with orange, red and gold when he returned carrying two glasses. "A pint of Tanglefoot, that will put you right."

He sat next to me and I took a long drink. I hadn't realised how thirsty I was. He sipped his pint and said nothing. I continued looking at the sunset, letting its serenity seep into me, realising that I felt relaxed and relieved and almost happy for the first time in a long time.

"Thank you," I said.

He nodded. "Are you ready to tell me who you are and what that was all about?"

I watched the sun, it was red now and just above the horizon, half obscured by pink clouds. "You already know who I am. And that was a case of mistaken identity. Those men thought I was someone else."

"You'll have to do better than that. I think you owe me."

81

"I do. So I'll do you a favour. I'm a woman you helped because you are a decent, kind and brave man. Believe me, that's all you want to know."

We drank in silence, but not the strained and awkward variety. He seemed at ease, satisfied with my answer.

"And you are," I said.

"I am what?"

"Decent and brave. I owe you."

"I know."

He looked at me, grinning. "You're a challenge; I love a challenge."

The sun disappeared behind the green landscape; the air turned cooler.

"You should listen to your brother; I'm trouble. We ought to head back to town now."

When we arrived at the multi-storey car park on Black Horse Way, dusk was settling in. I pulled to a stop outside the pedestrian entrance, got off the bike and removed my helmet and hood.

"This your stop?" he asked.

"Yes. Thank you."

"No, thank you," he said, "for a memorable afternoon. I'm looking forward to hearing the rest of your story."

I shrugged the rucksack off my shoulders so I could get at my car keys. "What makes you so sure you're going to see me again?"

"You're wearing over a hundred quid's worth of my equipment."

I looked down at my florescent bodysuit. "Oh, yeah."

"Unless you'd like to give it to me now."

I hugged the rucksack to my chest. "I think not."

He smiled and dismounted, folding his bike and attaching it to a harness that he strapped onto his back. Then he mounted the bike I had been riding.

"In that case, I'll see you again," he said. "Or I'll hunt you down like a dog. But only because I want my equipment back, you understand."

Chapter 11

IT WAS FULLY DARK by the time I pulled into The Citadel. I peeled off the Lycra suit, pulling it inside out in the process. The inner lining was a dull grey that I think would have suited me better. I changed into Rachel's clothes, put Nadia's clothes back in the wardrobe and dumped everything else—day-glo bodysuit, biking shoes and gloves—into the rucksack.

As I walked down the dark lane towards the Co-op, the thought that had been nagging at me since Howard's comment forced its way forward. I was rubbish at being a crime fighter.

After all the months of crafting Nadia and the whole secret identity thing, I'd been on active duty two days and already I had the police, a drug dealer, two thugs and a building developer after me. I was in debt to a shopkeeper and the person who I hoped to become best friends with had sworn to track me down and arrest me. And the papers thought I was loony.

It was a depressing thought. How could I be this bad at something? I'm Rachel Davenport, I can do anything.

"You're invincible," Paul told me, and I believed him.

But it was time to face up to it; what I was doing was crazy. It was dangerous, ill-advised and, okay, a little bit illegal. If I quit now, just abandoned The Citadel, sold the car and cancelled the re-mailing account, Nadia would disappear. I would be out of danger and I could count my time as a crime fighter a success because I had completed two missions without getting caught. And I had been responsible for getting Keith kicked out of his flat; that should make up for the faux pas at Keymer View Court.

I cut across the darkened car park to my car, warming to the idea; I felt almost cheered by it. Besides, hadn't I done enough already? If I was retiring from being famous, I shouldn't be fooling around meddling in other people's business and risking my hard-won anonymity. I felt lighter for having made the decision—it felt right.

Just then, an Indian boy came out of the Co-op carrying a bag of groceries and walked across the car park. The group of youths, who seemed to have no other occupation aside from loitering outside and drinking, began to taunt him.

"Hey, what's that costume you're wearing?"

"He's trick or treating, dressed as a Paki."

"Let's give him a treat. Hey Paki, over here."

He continued walking, ignoring them as they and their taunts followed. There were five of them and one of him. I didn't fancy his chances and neither did he; he kept his head down and sauntered on. I did the same. It was none of my business. My decision was made, and it felt right.

Whooping and shouts split the quiet night.

The gang had surrounded the boy and knocked the bag from his hand. They were already playing football with it, scattering cans and broken glass across the tarmac. Then they turned on him and in a moment he was on the ground, surrounded by yelping youths. And the kicking started.

My decision was made; and it felt like a mass of rationalisation. This was what Nadia was born for.

I unzipped the rucksack and yanked out the bike suit; it would do. I threw my glasses into the rucksack and struggled into the suit, tugging it on, grey side out, over my jeans and shirt. Fabric strained and ripped; Robin was not going to like this. I mangled my arms into the sleeves and was already running towards them as I pulled up the zip and stretched the hood over my hair.

I didn't have the utility belt so I had no restraints and I wasn't wearing the Kevlar gloves. There were five of them and one of me; I didn't fancy their chances, they were about to meet Nadia, and she was angry.

They didn't hear me coming. They were clustered around the boy, kicking and shouting, feeding off each others' energy like sharks around a wounded seal. They were going to carry on until they were exhausted, or he was dead, or both. I launched myself at the nearest one, landing square on his back, driving him forward, over the victim and bowling down two of his companions. The four of us landed hard on the pavement. The two on the bottom cracked their heads against the concrete; the one I landed on met it with his face. He howled in pain and I sprang to my feet just as the remaining two stopped kicking the helpless boy and turned on me.

The nearest one, wearing a floppy, hooded sweatshirt, wispy beard and a snarl, charged at me. I caught him by the hood and threw him on top of his two inert companions. The one with the bloody face struggled to his feet and lurched towards me. I moved backward, drawing the last one away from the victim and his support network. His eyes blazed with mindless rage but they

84

cooled when he realised he was facing me alone. He stopped advancing, took a tentative step backward, decided he liked going in that direction and ran away.

Two others were on their feet, advancing. "Chris, you fucking coward. She's a girl."

The two boys I bowled over remained motionless on the ground, as did the victim. I began to worry that they might need medical attention but the two coming towards me didn't look like they wanted their play time interrupted by calling 999. They moved slow, feigning menace. Then the one with the bleeding face pulled an ebony wand from his pocket and flipped out a six-inch blade. I wasn't getting cut again. I dived for him, blocked his knife hand and cracked the side of his head with my elbow. He grunted and dropped like a sack of potatoes. I stomped a foot down on his wrist, kicked the knife out of his reach and snatched it up.

His cohort—hood up, jeans sagging—advanced from the side. When he saw me pick up the knife, he stopped. I bent down, placed the point against the tarmac and stomped on it, snapping the blade off at the hilt. I dropped the pieces and stood facing him. "Want to play now?"

He snarled an obscenity and came at me. I sidestepped, grabbed the leg of his trousers and tugged. He managed a few tangled steps in his red and white stripped boxer shorts before stumbling over his dazed companion, writhing and swearing and trying to pull his twisted trousers up. I kicked the pieces of the broken knife far enough away so they couldn't find them and sprinted to check on the victim.

He was bleeding from his mouth and nose, his eyes bruised and swelling. He winced as I tried to help him up. "Are you all right? Can you stand?"

"My arm."

It was hard to understand him through the blood and accent. I felt along his sleeve. He winced again.

"Where do you live."

"Cawdry."

He said it clearly, as if well-practised. The two I had used as bowling pins began to moan. One of them sat up, holding the back of his head.

"I'd get myself to an A&E if I were you," I told them.

He stared up at me but didn't appear threatening. Behind us, the ringleader was back on his feet and coming our way. "Let's get you home," I told the boy.

I headed straight for my car, even though the path took me in the direction of the other two trouble makers. I stood tall, mustering as much dignity as an ill-fitting, inside-out biking bodysuit would allow. They were both standing up now. The one adjusting his trousers looked harmless, but the other, the one whose face I had introduced to the tarmac, glared at me. "Paki," he spat, "Go back to where you came from or you'll get more of the same."

I stopped. His eyes widened and he took an involuntary step back.

"It took five of you to beat up someone smaller and younger than you; and you were all beaten up by one woman. I'd suggest you go, or you'll get more of the same."

He snarled a few more interesting racial observations, then he and his companion disappeared into the darkness at the edge of the car park. I half-escorted, half-dragged the boy to my car and helped him into the back seat. I hoped the gang had dispersed; I didn't want them to see my car, or mount a counter attack while we were vulnerable. I jumped into the driver's seat and screeched onto the street.

The boy guided me with a few garbled directions and after navigating a confusing maze of short, curved roads, we pulled into a housing estate that looked remarkably like all the other housing estates in the area. I wondered how a newcomer would be able to find their home returning from the pub on a dark night.

I parked illegally and pulled the boy out of the car. His house was a mid-terrace in a block of four that took up less room than my semi-detached. I pressed the door bell, found it didn't work, and knocked. A babble of voices erupted and a stout, brown woman in a loose fitting shift answered the door. She looked at me, then at the boy and screamed.

"Sanjay!"

That was the only word I understood. The rest was a babble of broken English and her native language. Two smaller children, a boy and a girl, rushed up behind her and added to the cacophony.

The woman grabbed the boy, and he screamed. The children clustered around our legs, wailing. The screaming woman released Sanjay's arm and hugged us both while the blubbering children tugged at Sanjay's jacket. I manoeuvred the howling cluster through the door.

"What happened?"

An older child, a girl, came from the direction of the kitchen, dressed in jeans and a loose tee shirt and holding a mobile phone.

"Sanjay was attacked," I told her. "He needs a doctor."

She spoke to the woman. I helped Sanjay to a sofa that was draped in an old, tattered blanket in an attempt to hide an even older and tattier covering. The girl stood still as if in shock. The mother continued to scream. The children cried.

"Get some cloths and cold water," I shouted. "And dial 999."

"Who are you?"

She didn't ask it in a belligerent way, but as someone who was simply puzzled. I became aware of what I must have looked like to her, and the others, and, for that matter, Sanjay. I'm surprised they didn't call the cops straight away. Sanjay spoke to her. Blood sprayed from his mouth onto the floor. Her eyes grew wide, then she turned and ran into the kitchen.

The mother stopped screaming and put a hand on my shoulder, mumbling the same word over and over.

I pulled away. The daughter returned with wet tea towels and she and her mother began dabbing at Sanjay's swollen face.

"Did you call the ambulance?" I asked.

The girl nodded.

"I need to go. Will you be all right?"

She nodded again, tears streaming from her eyes as she mopped blood from Sanjay's lips.

I extricated myself and headed for the door. The mother followed and hugged me until I thought my ribs would crack, repeating the same word again and again.

"She's saying thank you," the girl told me.

"Help Sanjay," I said, and slipped away.

I ran to my car, aware of other family groups gathering on their doorsteps, some watching me, some watching the still open door of Sanjay's house. Perhaps they would assume a silver-clad spaceman had landed to torture the family next door. At least they were all still screaming and crying in there; the witnesses would know they were alive when I left them.

It was cold and dark and felt quite late but it had just gone half six. I could be home by seven and in a bath by seven oh five. I would have to find a secluded place to stop so I could take off my outfit, otherwise Dee would be certain to see me and wonder what I'd been up to.

Dee. Oh dear God.

I was supposed to be at her house for dinner.

Chapter 12

EVEN WITH STOPPING OFF at a lay-by to remove my crime fighter bike suit, I still made it home by six fifty-five. I tore up the stairs, flinging clothing as I went and jumped into the shower. Five minutes later, my make-up scrubbed off, my hair dripping wet, I stuffed myself into fresh clothes. I wasn't sure if it was a causal dinner or not so I put on grey trousers and a cream blouse. No need for a coat, I was only running next door. I squeezed a bit more moisture out of my hair with a towel, checked my bandage—it could do with a change but I had no time—and ran downstairs. It was seven fifteen. I was surprised Dee hadn't called, or at least pounded on the wall. As I ran out the front door, my mobile began to ring.

I jumped over the low wall separating our front porches and knocked on Dee's door. Through the decorative bottle glass I saw her put the phone down and my mobile went silent. She smoothed her skirt and trotted across the room. "I was getting worried," she said, opening the door.

"Sorry. I got stuck in traffic."

"Thank goodness you're safe."

"It was just a traffic jam."

"No, the Keymer Court Bomber, they say she was in Horsham this afternoon."

I tried to speak but when I opened my mouth, nothing came out.

"She was fighting with a man from Bishops Court over a drug deal. I hear she nearly killed him, then she took an old man and his wife hostage."

"Aaaaahhhhh," was all I could manage.

Dee smiled.

"Well, you're here now, so let's not worry about any of that."

Easy for her to say.

She wore a lavender jacket and matching skirt topped off with a string of pearls, making me feel underdressed in my plain blouse with damp patches from my dripping hair. No matter; it was only Dee and her family. And the strange man in the twill trousers and sport coat holding a drink and chatting with Nigel by the gas fireplace.

"Come over here," Dee said. "I'd like you to meet Stephen Green."

The floor was clear of toddler debris and an unnatural, adult silence pervaded the room.

"Where are the twins?"

Dee smiled. "My mother-in-law has them. I thought it would be nice to have a grown-up evening for a change."

She directed me towards her husband and his companion, who turned and extended his hand. "Stephen Green," he said.

I returned his firm, businesslike grip. "Rachel Davenport."

Nothing special, indeed. What is it about married people that they can't just leave their single friends alone? Is it misery loves company?

"Stephen works with Nigel at Sun Alliance in Horsham," Dee said.

"I'm a claims adjuster."

I nodded as if I understood and was impressed.

"Rachel works in Horsham, too. On the high street."

This perked up his interest, thinking perhaps I was a fellow claims adjuster. "What do you do?"

"I work for a travel agency. The Holiday Depot."

"I think I know the place. Is it the one near the Edinburgh Woollen Mill?"

"No, that's Thomas Cook. We're down near Poundland."

I didn't try to curb his disappointment by pretending my job was more exciting than it was. I wasn't here to impress him; I was here for dinner.

Dee got me a drink of non-alcoholic grape juice and we stood around the dancing flames of the fake fireplace engaging in the sort of small talk that makes me wish I'd taken a vow of silence. It might have been livelier if we'd had high-octane drinks but Nigel had to retrieve the twins from his mum after dinner, Stephen had to drive home and Dee was afraid of getting tipsy for fear of accidentally drowning the boys while giving them a bath. That left me as the sole candidate for alcohol, but it's no fun being the only intoxicated person in the room, so I opted to go along with the no-alcohol crowd.

Too bad; it might have made the evening more interesting. As it was, the men talked to each other in adjuster jargon, leaving Dee to give me her latest observations on how cute the twins were and fill me in on all the amazing things they were doing, such as producing babbling sounds that might be words and taking three steps in a row before landing on their well-padded bottoms. I struggled to be impressed, but anybody can walk; when they could do a back flip dismount, then I'd take notice.

Don't get me wrong, I understand children are the biggest thing to happen in a person's life, but they're not the biggest thing to happen in my life, so when a friend ditches her kids to have a grown up evening, it might be nice to talk about something other than nappy changing, feedings and bowel movements. I managed to get in a few pithy observations about the weather and then my repertoire was exhausted. What was I supposed to do, tell them I had just beaten up a gang of five yobs and done battle with a drug dealer? That might have put some sparkle in the conversation, but it would have looked like I was just showing off.

I felt alone and wished I was back with Howard and Maggie, or Robin. They were people I could talk to, people who knew me. Perhaps they didn't know a lot about me, but at least they knew a different, more exciting part of me. I supposed if I was going to keep Nadia around after all, this was something I would need to get used to.

Just before I considered poking myself in the eye to relieve the boredom, Dee suggested we sit, arranging us family-of-four style around a rectangular table with her and Nigel at the heads and Stephen and myself staring at each other over the baby's breath in the centrepiece.

"This is so nice," Dee observed.

What was nice? Forcing Stephen and me into awkward proximity or not having to spoon-feeding either of us?

"Yes," Nigel agreed. "It was a great idea to get my mum to watch the children for the evening so we could entertain guests."

The edge in his voice suggested he had entertained other plans and tweaked the awkward meter up a notch.

"Thank you for having us," Stephen said, beating me to it. I seconded it, but it sounded lame and insincere. "You are to be commended," he continued, aiming his comments at Dee. "You must be so busy with the twins, yet you found the time to make this wonderful dinner."

Now I didn't feel so bad about sounding insincere.

"Nigel talks about the twins all the time," Stephen continued. "They sound like quite a handful."

Dee gave a brave smile. "Yes, they really fill my days, especially now that they're beginning to walk."

Nigel grunted into his Yorkshire pudding. "And her nights, and pretty much every moment in between."

"No one said being parents was going to be easy," Dee said in a sing-song voice.

"So how are things at the office, Nigel?" I asked, hoping to derail the conversation before it had a chance to gain steam.

"Busy," Dee said. "He spends quite a bit of time there. Some days I fear I'll forget how to speak in multiple syllabic words."

"Is that so, Stephen?" I asked.

He looked at Dee and hesitated.

"I mean about you being so busy?"

"Oh, yes. We have a lot of business at the minute. I'm putting in a bit of overtime myself. It can be a little stressful, but I don't mind. It beats the alternative."

"And the overtime comes in handy," Nigel said. "Nappies don't grow on trees, you know."

"But some things are worth more than money," Dee said, "like seeing your son taking his first steps. Don't you think so, Rachel?"

I almost choked on my broccoli. "I wouldn't know. I'm single."

"That's right," Dee said, as if this was news to her. "And you're single, as well, aren't you, Stephen."

"Um, yes, I am," said Stephen.

"If he's smart, he'll stay that way," added Nigel.

"Rachel is new to the area," Dee continued. "She moved here few months ago; I don't think she's met many people yet."

I was beginning to think I had become invisible when Stephen addressed me directly. "So where are you from?"

"Manchester."

"You'd never know; you don't have an accent."

"I'm trying to fit in."

Stephen paused for a moment, then smiled as a new thought occurred to him. "Say, do you know you have the same name as that kid, the one who was on MasterQuiz?"

"You don't say. No one has ever mentioned that before."

"She went on to do something else, didn't she?"

"I think she became a gymnast," Nigel offered.

"Yes, but didn't she—"

"She was voted Miss Teen England a few years ago," Dee said.

"Yes, that's it," Stephen said. "She became a lesbian; the stress became too much for her."

"So they've determined that stress is the cause of homosexuality?" I asked him. "Tell me, how stressful is your job? Are you thinking of batting for the other team?"

Conversation ceased. The quiet clank of silverware on china filled the room. I was shocked myself; it wasn't something I would normally say. In fact, it had felt like someone else was saying it. After an excruciating ten seconds, Stephen broke the silence.

"I'm just saying, you know. I mean, that's what I heard. Sorry I brought it up; I guess you get that a lot."

The banter lightened up as dessert approached. With Dee recalling the main purpose of the evening, talk began to centre around Stephen and me, what we did, what we hoped to do. There was no probing of our pasts, which was a relief to me, but it left me wondering what Stephen was hiding.

After homemade pear tart with cream and lingering over a postprandial cup of tea, I felt I could make my excuses without appearing as if I would sooner have the earth open up and swallow me than spend another moment treading around the brittle facade of marital bliss. When I did, Stephen jumped out of his chair and offered to walk me home.

"I live on the other side of that wall," I told him.

"Even so, I insist." He looked at Dee and Nigel. "If you will excuse me for a few minutes."

"Or a few seconds."

I thanked them both for a lovely evening and showed myself out with Stephen close behind. In order to be merciful, I didn't take the shortcut over the separating wall but, instead, walked down the path to the road, went five steps along the pavement and turned up my own path.

"If you're in a hurry to get back, you can just jump over to their porch," I told him when we reached my door.

"I think maybe I'll give them a few minutes to talk things through."

I wasn't sure what he was implying by that; they were going to need all night, and I wasn't going to stand out here with him that long, and he was not coming inside with me. Not on a first "here's a single man, why don't you date him" encounter.

"I think maybe they should have taken advantage of an evening alone."

"Ah, but then they couldn't have brought us together," he said. "After all, it is the duty of married couples to introduce their single friends to each other so they can share their bliss."

I laughed, hoping Nigel and Dee wouldn't hear. "Not quite 'bliss' though, is it?"

I wondered what I was supposed to do next. I had exhausted all small talk and gone above and beyond to remain chipper and witty and now the words had dried up leaving an uncomfortable silence. He wasn't expecting me to invite him in, was he? Or was I somehow supposed to signal to him that it was okay to kiss me, which it was not.

It occurred to me I was on virgin ground, so to speak; nothing this normal had ever happened to me before. Normal, pleasant-looking boys—the type who grow up to become normal, insurance adjuster type people—never approached me when I was Miss Teen England or a world-class gymnast or the smartest kid in the country, unless it was for a photo-op or an autograph. I'd spent my life surrounded by a support network, and other gymnasts, beauty queens and super-intellects and their support networks, none of whom gave a toss about me as a person; to them, I was a threat or a commodity. My time was structured to the second, with practice sessions, competitions, regulated meals and mandatory sleep intervals interspersed with the occasional interview. There was no time to fritter away having dinner with the neighbours or allowing their single friend to walk you home and make small talk with you on your front porch.

Stephen was staring at me. The silence was becoming unbearable. Whatever it was I was supposed to be doing I was not doing it. Should I be giving him some sign that I wanted to see him again? Did I, in fact, want to see him again? And if I did, what did that imply? Perhaps I should look at it from the negative side. Did I *not* want to see him again? He was attractive, witty and intelligent. Was that enough to warrant spending unsupervised time together? Was there room in my life, or Nadia's life, for that?

"You seem far away."

I pulled my gaze from the middle distance and looked at his eyes. They were dark blue flecked with grey. He looked puzzled. "Sorry. I was drifting."

He wants you to give him a sign. Do something, Rachel, anything. He's going to think you're retarded.

I stuck out my hand. "It was a pleasure meeting you."

He shook my hand, but without conviction. "Did you have a good time tonight?"

"Yes."

"Do you think you might like to do it again?"

Was he asking me out? Was this how it was done?

"Yes," I said. "Yes, I would."

"I'll call you then."

I gave him my number and thought that would seal the transaction but there was another awkward pause and then he leaned in to kiss me. I turned my head and offered him my cheek then went inside so he wouldn't see me blushing. I was sure I could have handled that better. Maybe if I'd had more practice. But that isn't the sort of thing you can rehearse with a teammate. I decided not to think about it. He would call, or he would not.

In the quiet hours of the morning I woke with a suddenness that told me something was wrong. I lay in the dark, holding my breath. Then I heard the trippy tune of my mobile coming from my handbag.

The only person with my phone number was my sister and she would never call me at three o'clock in the morning. With the exception of the occasional, drunken ex, no one calls anyone at three o'clock in the morning, unless it's a family member with news of a birth or death. But I didn't have an ex and no one I knew was pregnant, and I didn't want to think of the final possibility. I threw the duvet aside and hit the floor running, fending off fantasies of my father in a mangled car or my mother surrounded by people in white coats and attached to a machine that let out a low wail as its light drew a flat line across the screen.

My handbag was on the chair in the corner. I dug through it until I found my phone. It wasn't ringing.

The sound came again, from deeper inside the bag and, as clarity of thought seeped further into my sleep addled brain, I realised it was the Hawaii Five-0 theme. I dug out Nadia's phone. "Number Withheld" flashed on the display.

"Hello?"

Silence. Then the sound of low breathing.

"Bitch. Don't think I won't find you."

The caller hung up.

I stared at the silent phone for a moment, feeling stung and violated. This was my house; Nadia's life was not supposed to intrude here. Bad guys didn't annoy Bruce Wayne at his home (Alfred would turn them away if they did) and Lex Luthor never showed up at Clark Kent's flat. But life was simpler back then; stalkers needed ambition, drive and tenacity; now they just need a phone number.

I had given Nadia's number out to only one person, but it had not been Mr Sawyer on the phone. Perhaps, in addition to giving it to his henchmen, Sawyer had also shared it with Keith; that was who my money was on.

I turned the phone off and put it back in my bag, then took out my own phone and laid it on the bedside table; now that I was primed for a family tragedy, I wanted to be ready when— no, if—the phone call came.

Chapter 13

A CRIME FIGHTER'S SUNDAY morning isn't much different from anyone else's, especially when you're being Clark Kent and not Superman. I took advantage of the end of British Summer Time by sleeping in, getting up at half six instead of half five. Then I warmed up with twenty minutes of aerobics and went out into the grey dawn for a six-mile run to clear my head.

Being a crime fighter wasn't turning out like I expected, and now that I thought about it, I couldn't say what I had expected. Although Nadia had come to life of her own free will, I had shaped her and help bring her into the world in a controlled and deliberate way. The crime fighting idea had not been as well directed, which was why running off and performing random good deeds had produced unanticipated results. It all had to do with goal management.

"If you have no goal," Paul said, "you don't know where you're going, and you can't tell when you arrive."

And that was the problem; Nadia had no real goal, just an ongoing mission. If I was going to make any sort of progress, I needed to define a goal and work towards it.

The sun was up when I returned. I put on my dressing gown and ate a simple breakfast of muesli and wholemeal toast while sitting on the sofa watching the morning news.

There were wars in the Middle East, the world was in economic meltdown and in Yorkshire someone was sure to be growing the world's largest aubergine, but the lead story was about the terrorist they were now calling the "Keymer Court Bomber."

I watched with a critical eye, putting as much emotional distance as I could between myself and the events; it allowed me to better analyse the damage and helped my muesli go down easier. They started off with Nadia's vitals: five foot eight, about nine stone five, dark eyes, black curly hair, armed, dangerous, the usual. That part wasn't bad; they hadn't discovered anything critical that might lead them to me, though I could have done without the armed and dangerous part. Then they cut to a special report on her activities.

It wasn't all bad news. The co-presenters, a distinguished older man and a solemn younger woman with conservative brown hair and a poppy pinned above her left breast, reported the facts about an altercation outside of the Co-op the previous evening. There was no CCTV footage but the facts seemed to be that a woman dressed in a silver bodysuit intervened when a gang of youths attacked an Asian boy. The boy was in hospital and the mother credited the mystery woman with saving his life.

The quote they got from her was encouraging. "She's a good woman; she saved my son." At least that's what the subtitles said. It went downhill from there:

"Three of the five youths required treatment at a local hospital and police are seeking the woman in connection with several incidents of grievous bodily harm. It has also been reported that she brandished a knife at one of the youths. It is believed the woman is the same person responsible for the explosion at Keymer View Court on Thursday night. The public are reminded that the woman is considered dangerous and should not be approached. If anyone has information, they should contact the police.

"Police also confirm that a domestic dispute at Bishops Court is also linked to the mystery woman. 'A drug deal gone bad,' is how police describe the incident that culminated in a knife fight in the courtyard."

It seemed to me they had little evidence for this assertion, but they persevered, citing the general description and bizarre activity as circumstantial proof. The background footage consisted of a slow pan of Keith's post-tantrum debris, which Carl and Derek had opted to not clean up. It had a crepuscular look to it, so I assumed it was the report Dee had alluded to the night before. A voiceover reported the sparse facts, and I began to wonder how they were linking this to Nadia when the scene shifted and Howard and Maggie appeared in the frame with a perky blonde newscaster wearing a cream-coloured, double-breasted coat adorned with the obligatory poppy.

"Howard Oaks, of Bishops Court, and his wife Margaret witnessed the altercation," the newscaster said to the camera. Then she turned to Howard and Maggie. "What did this look like to you, Mr Oaks? Was this woman here to buy drugs?"

"The man who attacked her was a known drug dealer," Howard said. "But the woman was not here to buy drugs."

Well done, Howard. He was wearing a brown jacket, Maggie a fleece and scarf; they were at the entrance of Bishops Court and looked as if they had been ambushed by a BBC news crew while on their way to buy a litre of milk, had poppies pinned on them and dragged in front of a camera.

"Then what do you think the altercation was about? What was this woman doing here?"

The microphone moved back to Howard, but Maggie leaned forward. "Her name's Nadia and she's a superhero, like Wonder Woman. She was here to fight crime."

The newscaster looked as shaken as I felt. She recovered her poise and moved on while I sat, open mouthed. "The police report that you spoke with the woman. How did that come about?"

Howard leaned into the microphone. "I went down to break up the fight and brought her back to our flat."

"We had tea," Maggie said. "She was ever so nice."

"And how did you come to suspect she was the Keymer Court Bomber?"

"She told us she was," Howard said. "She wanted to tell us her side of the story."

The newscaster hesitated. "And what did you do then?"

"I notified the police."

It was a good tactical move. Sooner or later someone would have tipped the police off about the woman involved in the dispute having gone up to his flat. Howard might be willing to bend the truth for a good cause, but he wasn't going to lie outright, and Maggie would have told them anything they wanted to know. Going to the police before they came to him would keep them from being charged with obstruction; I just hoped they gave the police a favourable view of Nadia. I know Maggie would have, but I expected the police might be sceptical of her answers. The newscaster, however, exploited the opportunity with a total lack of shame. "You are the only people who have, so far, had a conversation with this woman. What is your impression?"

This time, she positioned the microphone in front of Maggie. "She's innocent, you know. But she can't go to the police herself or they'll discover her secret identity."

"So you're saying this woman believes herself to be a comic book superhero, like Wonder Woman?"

"Oh yes, except she doesn't have an invisible plane. She has a car."

"Does that strike you as a bit strange? Do you think this woman may be mentally ill?"

To her credit, the newscaster directed the question at Howard.

"She struck me as a sane, intelligent young woman with a unique idea of how to make the world a better place."

"And how do you respond to the charges brought against her by the police?"

"That's not for me to respond to. I don't think she's dangerous, if that's what you're asking, she's just different."

"Different how?"

Howard turned away from the newscaster and looked straight into the camera, straight at me. He gave a smile and a wink. "She's a superhero, of course."

The camera switched back to the studio, where both the presenters were barely suppressing grins. "We thank our news team for that report from yesterday evening, and the revelation that Sussex has its very own superhero," the woman said. "But is she a menace, a maniac or a misguided do-gooder? Call or text us your opinions."

"The question everyone wants answered, of course," her partner said, "is who is she?"

The woman nodded. "Yes, that is the question of the day: Who is Nadia?"

From there they segued into a story about the investigation of local councillors. I switched off the telly, put on some laundry and took a long bath, mulling over what I had seen.

From the little I knew about Howard, he struck me as a sincere man, someone who liked order. If you were looking for faults, you might say he lacked spontaneity, but to me that meant he liked to think things through before acting. A careful man.

He had called the police, but he had taken his time. Was it to think, or to allow Nadia to get away, or both? And the interview might have had a spur-of-the-moment look to it, but to me it felt orchestrated. I had no way of knowing what he had told the police, but I suspected it more or less mirrored what he told the newscaster. My feeling was he had taken the opportunity to do what Nadia wanted to do but couldn't, which was to ease the collective mind of the population. "Don't worry, you're not being attacked by terrorists, it's just your run-of-the-mill crime fighter doing what crime fighters do."

Now the focus was on Nadia's mental health, but that didn't matter; the media was changing tack, perhaps I could help steer them.

I dressed and had another look at the bodysuit Robin had lent me. One leg was torn where my trainer had pushed through and the other was split up to the knee. There was no way to repair it so I cut it into small pieces and put it in a bin bag for anonymous disposal somewhere between here and The Pedaller. It wouldn't do to have Nadia's Silver Surfer outfit found in my dustbin. I'd just return the remaining gear to Robin and pay for the outfit.

While waiting for the laundry to finish, I turned on my laptop to surf some online newspapers and check my finances. I closed it after a short time, uncertain which one worried me more. I was going to have to be careful if I expected to make it to the end of the month without cutting further into my dwindling savings. It was a harsh reality to face, especially after having had so much in reserve for so long. I'd amassed a respectable bank balance from prize money, endorsements and television appearances over the years, and had—during the months I had spent in my room, supposedly having a nervous breakdown—started doing some online purchasing and trading of stocks and bonds. It was the perfect hobby; I never had to see anybody, I could buy or sell or not depending on how I felt, I could stay in my pyjamas or in bed, for that matter. It wasn't a pastime I took up with my usual fervour, but I still managed to increase my portfolio a fair amount before I decided to try going to university.

It's ironic; back then I had a lot of money and nothing to buy; now I had to choose between making my car payment and buying new shoes. Fortunately, I'm not that concerned about shoes.

So how does the smartest person in Britain end up broke? That was easy; I paid my own way through university, and maintaining a secret identity turned out to be more expensive than I thought it would be. Plus there's the main reason—I'm not that smart. I bought my house, laid a huge down payment on it so my mortgage would be low and six months later, the markets crashed. True, my monthly outlay is pretty low, but I'm living in a place that is now worth about two thirds of what I paid for it. Like I said, I'm not that smart; I just know a lot of facts.

I ate lunch while running the dryer, then packed everything I needed into my handbag and the rucksack, picked up the bin bag and started towards the conservatory just as Dee knocked on the front door. I sighed, walked back through the house and let her in.

"So?" Dee said as soon as I opened the door. She looked tired, as usual, but her voice was chipper.

"So, as in . . . ?"

She stepped into the living room and laid a hand on my forearm. "How did it go with Steve?"

Another test. No doubt they grilled him when he returned to their house; now she wanted to know if my side of the story matched his.

"Nothing *went*. He walked me home, all of fifteen feet. We chatted. I went inside."

She furrowed her brow. Then I added, "And he said he'd call," which perked her back up.

In truth, I had forgotten about his promise to ring me; if I had been listening for the phone during the morning, it had more to do with the midnight caller than Stephen's promise.

"But do you like him?"

"I don't know him." I could see by Dee's semi-frown that I wasn't giving the correct answers, so I added, "He seemed a nice enough guy; if he does call, I'll go out with him."

Dee squealed her delight; I set my teeth to keep from cringing.

"He will. I just know it."

And I was sure she did.

"I hope you forgive us for setting you up like that, but I know how lonely the single life can be and I wanted to help." She leaned closer, as if there was someone around to overhear us. "If you ever want to talk, I'm just on the other side of that wall."

Great. Just what I needed, someone living next door I could spill my love life to. Or, in this case, someone else spilling it to her husband on my behalf. Dee squeezed my arm and released me. "I have to get back; the twins are corralled in the sitting room but you can never tell what they might get into."

"Can't Nigel watch them?"

Her gaze flitted to the door. "He's out."

The silence stretched. Was I supposed to ask where, why? At length she noticed the bin bag. "Are you taking the rubbish out? They don't come until Tuesday; if you put it out too early it might attract foxes. Or worse."

"It's not rubbish; I'm just taking a few things to the charity shop."

She sucked a breath and put a hand to her mouth as if she just remembered she had left the twins playing with a box of matches and a straight razor. "Oh, I have a sack of old baby clothes that has been waiting to go for weeks but I haven't had the time. Would you be a love and drop them off for me?"

I drove to the Co-op with the rucksack on the back seat and a bag filled with recycled baby outfits up front in the passenger's seat. The bin bag containing Nadia's Silver Surfer suit was at the bottom of a skip at a building site outside of Cowfold. I found a spot and left the baby clothes in the car; no crime fighter would be caught dead with a pile of baby outfits in their secret hideout. Besides, if I left them in my car, maybe one of the local yobs would steal them for his pregnant girlfriend and save me the trouble.

There was no sign of the previous night's altercation, but the headline on a news poster outside the Co-op read, "Wonder Woman Saves Youth from Gang Attack." Intrigued, I went inside to scan the article. It was in the local daily, and it took up most of page one, putting "District Councillor Denies Bribery Charges" into the B slot. I was impressed, and hopeful. Eyewitness accounts, which could only have come from the gang members, made references to Spiderman and the Silver Surfer, but the media seemed content with Wonder Woman, which pleased me on many levels.

Wonder Woman was the template for Nadia; I had read all the comics and found her to be an inspiration and a good role model. Maggie passing the idea on to the media, and the media picking it up had been an unexpected coup, and a step in the right direction; Wonder Woman was a much better moniker than The Keymer Court Bomber.

So far, so good. But the final paragraphs brought a return to reality—grievous bodily harm, knife wielding, armed and dangerous, do not approach—no matter how you cut it, Nadia was a fugitive.

"You planning on buying that paper before you start on the crossword?"

"Oh. Sorry."

I paid for the paper and dropped it in a dustbin on my way to the garage.

Ten minutes later Nadia drove out, wearing a red tee shirt and thigh-hugging jeans with calf-high suede boots. I topped it off with a knee length felt coat, even though it was still sunny and mild. I wasn't concerned with being spotted by the cops; if the police were stopping every curly haired brunette they came across, they'd be pretty busy by the time I arrived. Still, it made no sense to take chances, so I parked on the outskirts of town on Blackbridge Lane, where Robin and I had had our near escape from Sawyer, and walked to The Pedaller from there.

My route took me past Martin's pill box, which I was surprised to find in pristine condition. I took a peek through the gun port, into the dim interior, and smelled the fresh paint. I wished him well; it wasn't every day the Lord Lieutenant came to commemorate something you and your fellow anoraks dug up.

Bishops Court didn't look as pristine, but it did seem a little quieter with Keith out of the way. Then I had a sudden thought that Chantelle might have taken him back, or that he might be hanging about waiting to harass her, or find me. I quickened my step and took a deeper interest in the few pedestrians and the cluster of punters outside the King's Head pub.

When Hawaii Five-o rang out from my handbag, I let out a yelp. When I fished the phone out, "number withheld" appeared on the display.

"Good day, Ms Kunt, or shall I call you Nadia?"

It wasn't Keith, which was good news; it was Sawyer, which wasn't. I looked around as I talked to make sure I wasn't being observed. "What do you want, Mr Sawyer? Are you ready to admit it was your men who sabotaged Keymer View Court?"

"There's no need for that; the police seem satisfied about what happened. And I see you have branched out; assault and grievous bodily harm. That's a charming addition to your CV."

I relaxed a bit; if he were watching me that would have been his first ploy. "Is there a point, Mr Sawyer?"

"Just to say I'm disappointed that we were unable to continue our conversation yesterday, and I look forward to seeing you again."

"There's a flaw in that plan."

"And that is?"

"You don't know how to find me, but I know how to find you."

I cut him off then, but just before my finger hit the button I heard him say, "For now."

I put the phone back in my handbag and walked into The Pedaller. Robin was at his post behind the counter talking to a lean, silver haired man about a gel bike seat. I browsed the racks of bike tyres, air pumps, helmets, gloves and other biking paraphernalia while waiting for them to complete the deal. When the man left with his high-tech, bum-moulding support device, Robin followed him to the door and stopped at my side. "I told you I'd see you again."

He looked more normal today, in faded jeans and pullover with his bike shop logo emblazoned across his pecs. His blonde hair was pulled into a ponytail, but a telltale ridge circled his crown where the bike helmet fit over his head. I wondered if it was a permanent feature. I smiled and held up the rucksack.

103

"You're seeing me, but not the fetching outfit you loaned me. I'm afraid this is all I can return."

"The suit?"

"Ruined."

He took the rucksack and laid it on the counter. "I didn't expect it to come back in pristine condition. I'm sure it will be fine, whatever you did to it."

"No. Believe me, it's beyond use."

"My god, what did you do after I left you off? Your friends didn't find you, did they?"

"It's a long story, but you don't need to worry about it."

He paused a few beats to wrestle his curiosity back into the closet. "You look different. Better."

I did a slow twirl for him and walked to the counter. "I only dress like a tart when I'm on duty."

He raised his eyebrows. "Are you trying to tell me something?"

"No, I'm not for sale. And I'm not a cop."

"You are a mystery, though."

"And determined to stay that way. It's safer for you."

He leaned forward. "Now you really have my attention. There's no way we could explore this further, is there?"

I was tempted; another bike ride through the countryside might be just what I needed. Before I could speak, my phone rang. I snatched it out of my handbag; it was Rachel's phone with an unknown number, but at least it was a number. "Sorry, I need to take this. And I don't think it would be a good idea to get you involved any more than you are."

He laid a hand on my arm. "Ah, but we are destined to become more involved."

"What makes you so certain of that?"

He released my arm. "You still owe me for the bike suit."

I pressed the button but didn't speak until I was at the door. Behind me, I heard Robin talking, as if to himself. "Papers say a woman wearing a silver bodysuit fought off a gang attacking a boy last night. As I recall the suit I loaned out had a silver lining. Strange, that."

I smiled at him, waved and stepped out the door.

"Hello, Rachel"

It was Stephen. We exchanged pleasantries as I wandered past the dry cleaners and the funeral parlour. As I approached Bishops Court he came to the point, which was pizza, with Rachel, at seven o'clock Monday evening. It seemed a bit sudden; weren't men supposed to leave a woman hanging for a week or so before calling? But in truth I didn't have any other plans. "Yes, that would be fine," I told him.

"Anywhere special you'd like to go?"

"They tell me the Oak Barn on the Cuckfield Road is pretty good; I've always wanted to try it."

"Great. I'll pick you up at six thirty."

A familiar tune erupted from my handbag.

"What's that sound?"

"My other phone. Look, I've got to go."

"You have two phones?"

"It's my work phone."

"But I thought you were a clerk for a travel agent."

"And that means I can't have work emergencies?"

The tune grew louder, more insistent. "I'm sorry, I've got to take this call. I'll see you tomorrow. And by the way, I'm a travel consultant."

I hung up and snatched up the other phone.

Silence. Then the sound of someone breathing.

"I knew you'd come back," Keith said. "I like the boots. Did you buy them with the money you stole from me?"

If I hadn't been wearing a wig the hairs on the back of my neck would have stood up. The windows of Chantelle's flat had the curtains drawn, but that meant nothing. I did a slow scan of the street.

"Don't bother looking around, you won't see me. But I can see you. You went to visit your boyfriend at the bike shop. Where are you going now, to see my ex-girlfriend? Were the two of you in it together?"

He wasn't in the flat, or Bishops Court. The silence meant he wasn't outside, but he might be in a car, tailing me, in which case he could follow me back to my car, and The Citadel. That must not be allowed to happen. I didn't want him to think I was afraid but a tactical retreat was what this situation called for. I turned off the phone and ran.

I needed to get off the street, so I darted behind the pillbox and followed a short path through the undergrowth to the rear of Bishops Court. Hugging the perimeter, I ran until I found another path leading to the nearby Tanfield flats and onto Blackbridge Lane. I looked up and down, saw no one lurking about, ran to my car and sped away.

I drove out of town and spent some time touring the A24 and various roundabouts in Crawley to make sure I wasn't being tailed. When I got to The Citadel I turned my phone back on. There were three messages, all from Keith, each one calling me a name worse than the one before, and speculating on how I spent my free time.

I changed into Rachel and drove home with the realisation that, for better or worse, Nadia now had a goal: eliminate the threat.

I turned on my laptop and logged into the server at the Holiday Depot, and from there logged onto another, anonymous server. When I was sure I couldn't be traced, I set up an e-mail address for Nadia and used it to open a Twitter account. Once logged in, I followed a number of reporters and news presenters who had made favourable comments about Nadia's exploits and the one who had posed the question, "Who is Nadia."

And then I tweeted, "I am Nadia."

A sense of serenity returned as I turned off the laptop. The pebble was in the pond, I just had to wait.

And start the ironing.

Chapter 14

THE NEXT MORNING, WHILE getting ready for work, I checked Nadia's Twitter account. She had 17,324 followers, and there were 287 e-mails in her IN box. I didn't have time to read them, but I scanned down the subject list and mentally reviewed them as I drove to work. Most were from journalists requesting interviews in the hope that I was for real; the rest included a mixture of supporters, detractors, vile suggestions and ads for enhancing various body parts, some of which I did not possess.

I had a few minutes to spare so I nipped into the news agent to see what the printed world was making of Nadia's coming out.

"Wonder Woman Saves Youth From Yobs"

It was an improvement, and it wasn't in the local papers, this was in *The Gazette,* on page two, just across from Erica and her fulsome breasts, who worried about climate change and how to develop renewable energy. Erica worried, that is, not her breasts.

The article concentrated on gang violence and took the police to task for making me the criminal. It also left out the fact that the youths were all native Brits and the victim an immigrant and managed to avoid mentioning the unfortunate incident at Keymer View Court. *The National Observer* took a different view, arguing the dangers of vigilantism and stressing that Nadia was most likely mentally ill. *The Echo*, in addition to a semi-factual, front page article under the banner, "Sussex Superhero Saves the Day," echoed *The National Observer's* concern, and blamed it on the coalition government. *The Daily News* blamed the immigrants.

All in all a mixed review, and one I wasn't too displeased with. I put the papers back in their respective piles as other customer's edged past me. Raj's news agent was crowded as commuters jostled to buy their morning papers, but it was small enough that I would be noticed reading and not buying if I wasn't careful. I decided to buy just one so I wouldn't look like I had too much of an unhealthy interest in the news. I scanned the headlines looking for something of interest. When I saw the front page of *The Southern Counties Courier*, I felt my optimism fade, and as I joined the queue to pay for it, the nagging worry in the pit of my stomach began chewing its way into my bowels. I paid for the paper, sat on a bench outside the Black Olive and looked at the front page. "Police Assemble Task Force to Hunt Down Bomber."

It was the headline, in bold, oversized type; not even local government corruption and the looming shortage of road salt could push it to a less conspicuous position.

"Sussex Police have confirmed that they are committing 'all necessary resources' to tracking down and apprehending the woman known as The Keymer Court Bomber. A variety of key personnel from across the district have been assigned to an internal task force, lending their unique abilities towards this goal. 'It's a small force,' said Chief Superintendent Hollander, 'but we've put our best people on it, people whose special talents make them well suited to this sort of investigation. We expect to have this woman in custody by the end of the week'."

I dropped the paper onto the bench next to me and rested my head in my hands, fighting back the cold squeeze of terror that had begun to grip my gut. This was disturbing on several levels, but it wasn't an insurmountable problem. At least that's what I kept telling myself.

"Don't give in to the fear," Paul whispered. "You give it power when you surrender to it; face it down and put it back in its little box where it belongs."

I ran the article over in my mind. The first concern, of course, was Nadia. How safe was she? And how solid was the wall separating her from me? The other concern was the stubborn determination of the local press to keep pushing the bomber angle. I could understand the motive—Nadia was not a hero to the residents of Keymer View Court—but they refused to even give her name. They seemed to want to keep the anger alive. That had to be turned around.

The outcome rested on the team. Who were they? Were they good enough to hunt down Nadia? Put in that perspective, the problem was simple, either they would succeed, or Nadia would, and as Nadia carried all the advantages, this revelation wasn't a setback at all. Unless, of course, you compared the current reality to the original plan—wherein Nadia was unseen, unnamed and secretly responsible for random acts of good— then it became an unmitigated failure; just four days into Nadia's crime fighting career and the whole county knew who she was. That counted as a clear failure, and that made me angry.

Focus. I forced myself to remember the European finals, where an awkward dismount had cost me points. I was furious, but Paul forced me to focus. "Anger is energy that needs to be channelled," he'd told me. "Contain it, make it work for you."

I struggled to do that now, but this wasn't anger, it was panic. They were closing in on Nadia.

"You look like you could do with a pick-me-up."

I looked up. Alex was standing in front of me. She picked up the paper and sat down. "Are you all right? You look like you're going to be ill."

"I'll be fine. Just a rough weekend is all."

Alex smiled and scanned the paper. "Been a while since I've had one of those. I guess I'm just an old fuddy-duddy these days. Hey, I see the councillors are back in the news. We've been investigating a few of them for suspected bribery."

"Should you be telling me this?"

"It's public knowledge; I'm not giving away state secrets. And look here. Wacko Woman is at it again. We've been investigating her as well. In fact, she's my first major assignment; I've been put on the team they're talking about here, the one tasked with hunting her down and bringing her in."

Then I did throw up.

Half an hour later, cleaned up and fortified with a cup of tea, I sat at Alex's kitchen table, apologising for the umpteenth time.

"Look, it's fine," she said, making her own tea. Being an American, I thought she'd be having coffee but she must have gone native. "We've all been there."

I hadn't, but I didn't press the issue. I just nodded and sipped the soothing liquid.

Alex's flat was tiny, consisting of a single bedroom, a sitting room and the kitchen, which was just large enough to fit a small wooden table and two chairs.

"And it could have been much worse; at least no one was out there eating breakfast while you blew chunks."

"Oh, please, don't make me laugh. It hurts."

She sat across from me and lowered her head so she could see my downcast face. "Feeling better?"

I looked up. "Yes. I'm just over tired. It's not like I was even drinking over the weekend; just a glass or two of non-alcoholic wine on Saturday night."

"That's a shame."

She said it to be ironic, but in truth it was a shame. At twenty-two I had never been binge drinking, had never had a best friend I could hang out with and tell all my secrets to. All I'd had were competitors, the media and Paul. I suddenly felt very lonely. "You know what you said last time we met, about going out for a drink sometime."

"Yes."

"Could we meet on Saturday to have a few drinks and a chat? I promise not to throw up."

I thought that would make her laugh but she looked solemn. "I'm sorry, but I'm on duty this weekend."

I nodded, hoping I didn't look as disappointed as I felt.

"But I really would like to. Look, why don't we meet for lunch and we'll make a definite date. Okay? Twelve thirty, in the Merrythought. Or outside if it's still nice enough."

I looked at my watch. Work had started ten minutes ago. "Sure. That would be great. See you then."

I picked up my handbag and she walked me to the door. Halfway down the stairs I recalled Dee's baby clothes still sitting in the front seat of my car. "Alex," I called. "Can we make it the coffee shop in The Forum, instead? I have to take some stuff to the Salvation Army at lunch so I'll be over in that area."

"Not a problem. See you then."

I arrived at work fifteen minutes late.

"Good afternoon," Amanda said.

She was sitting at her desk reading the paper and talking with James, who had his chair turned in her direction. As a team-building exercise, the pillbox make-over seemed an unqualified success, at least for Amanda and James. Martin already had his coffee. He looked up as I sat at my work station. "Are you all right?"

I thought about hanging a sign around my neck reading, "I'm all right. Really." It would save time and my sanity. Instead I smiled at him. "Yes. I'm fine. Sorry I'm late; I got stuck behind a tractor on the A272."

He nodded. "I want to thank you for your help on Saturday. Your efforts were most appreciated, by myself, the Bishopric Restoration Society, and the nation."

I shrugged in a self-depreciating way. I doubted an OBE would be coming my way any time soon. "I was glad to help."

"But you left too soon," Amanda said. "You missed the show."

"There was a mighty kerfuffle at the flats," she continued without waiting for encouragement. "Just as we were leaving, some lout and his girlfriend had a stand up row out in the courtyard."

110

"Charming," I said. "So sorry I missed it."

"But you don't know the best part—it was her."

She held up her copy of *The Daily News*. "She was the one. It was Nadia, Wonder Woman, and I actually spoke to her."

I perked up. "When?"

"You keep saying that," James said, "but I never saw you."

Amanda glared at him. "And I keep saying that you boys were too busy admiring the door to notice."

She turned to me. "I was standing on the pavement and saw her come out of Bishops Court. She waited there a while so I went over to ask if she was lost or something. I didn't know, of course, that she was *the* Nadia."

I couldn't believe I was hearing this, and I realised I must look as if she had my rapt attention. I tried to adopt an insouciant attitude but failed.

"She told me about being a crime fighter and all, and that she was doing it to show the world what women are capable of."

James grinned and shook his head. "She did not. You're making that up."

"Am not. It's true."

Martin cleared his throat. "Then shouldn't you go to the police, Amanda?"

"Yeah," James said, his grin widening. "The cops would like to hear your story, I bet."

"Well, they've already interviewed that old couple," Amanda said, "and I don't have anything to add to that."

Then someone asked, "What happened after you talked to her?" I realised it was my own voice. Amanda brightened.

"Not much. I thought she was a nutter and I went back to get James. When I looked again, she was gone."

Terrific. Amanda had noticed just enough to feed her fantasy but had missed seeing anything of real value.

"I think what she's doing is great. She's striking a real blow for women—"

"Then you should go to the papers," James suggested. "They would like your story."

"I could but, well, I don't want a lot of publicity."

I watched her upturned nose but it didn't grow so much as a millimetre.

"Besides, I don't need to. I already friended her. A crime fighter with a Facebook account, is that the coolest thing? I suppose I should go write on her wall, too, see if she remembers talking to me."

"Her what?"

111

"She's on Facebook. Didn't you know?"

In the distance, Martin's voice came to me, as if I were underwater. "Rachel, are you all right?"

I dropped my head onto the desk. "No. Not at all."

James speculated about the tractor that had made me late, intimating that it might have been a bottle. Amanda snorted. "Lightweight."

That morning, of all mornings, contained three times the normal number of hours. Customers began to trickle in soon after, but three hours later I looked at the clock and it was still nine twenty-five. Two hours after that, it was ten fifteen.

I handled a few accounts, sending them to Timbuktu for all I knew, all the while expecting the police, with Alex in the lead, to come busting through the door to arrest me. Each time that thought occurred I had to resist the urge to crawl under the desk and curl up into a ball.

Six hours into the day, at eleven o'clock, Martin came to my desk with a cup of tea and a worried look. "Rachel, I'm sorry."

I looked up. "For what?"

"Last Friday, when I let you leave early, I thought you were having me on." He put the tea on my desk. "Have you seen a doctor?"

"No. Really, I'm sure I'll be fine."

He grunted a neutral reply and went back to his desk, leaving me feeling guilty. "Thanks for the tea," I said. "And thanks for Friday."

"What about Friday?"

"For letting me go home when you thought I was lying."

I sipped the tea. It was time to take charge again. Even when I slipped off the bar and landed flat on my face and was sure I was out of the competition, Paul made me get back on. "Things are never as bad as they seem," he said. And he was right, although in that competition I had come in third; this time I had to come out on top.

Nadia was known; there was nothing I could do about that. But now she was being hijacked and I could, and would, do something about that. I needed to control my publicity, and not allow any more lies. The battle to salvage Nadia's reputation had begun, and it would be fought in the media, where she could move about freely. I was optimistic about my chances, even as I reminded myself that it was not the main event. Manipulating the media was a side-issue, a tool to help attain the actual goal.

112

Public opinion was one thing, thugs—and the police—quite another.

As the clock neared half-twelve, I locked down my work station and went to lunch. Both Martin and Amanda noticed my early departure, though Martin maintained the least critical expression.

I retrieved Dee's bag of baby clothes and walked across the open expanse of the Forum with its bronze sundial and minimalist fountain, made up of rows of erupting geysers. It was off now, identifiable only by a large damp area scattered with leaves.

As I passed the Esquire coffee shop—a cylinder of glass topped with a peaked roof that looked like a squat, round aquarium wearing a coolie hat—I noted that Alex wasn't there yet. I hoped she arrived before the place filled up; a handful of people had already resigned themselves to the outdoor seating area and, mild as it was, I would rather be snug inside.

I descended the wide steps into Sainsbury's car park, dodging traffic and car washers, who scuttled around like worker bees with wet rags, until I found the drop off bins. With Dee's package delivered, I made my way back towards the forum, concentrating so hard on what my next move should be that I bumped into a man wiping down the windshield of a maroon Audi Quattro.

"Sorry."

He turned towards me and grunted. It was Keith. I nodded, as I would to a complete stranger, and kept walking, hoping I hadn't gone white.

Then I heard the sound of a wet rag hitting the bonnet.

"Hey, you."

I kept walking, straining to not quicken my step; it had nothing to do with me. Footsteps, loud and fast, then a hand on my shoulder spinning me around. I prepared to defend myself the way I thought a normal person would. Running and screaming seemed a good option. "What do you think you're doing?" He looked at my eyes, my face, I tried to turn away. "Let go of me or I'll call the police."

"It's you," he said. "You're the one who stole my money."

"What are you talking about?"

I struggled out of his grip and he grabbed my arm just above where he'd cut me.

"Now we'll see."

He pulled at my jacket, trying to wrench my arm out of the sleeve. Now seemed to be a good time to start the screaming and running away. "What are you doing?" I screamed. "Help."

I twisted my arm against his grip and broke free, then tore away, dodging between the cars, heading towards the Forum where I hoped the presence of people would work in my favour. My flat shoes made running easier than it had been the first time I ran from him, but he was in trainers, and wasn't wearing a skirt. I zigzagged through the car park, trying to pick cars parked close together so I could run through while he had to squeeze between or go around. But he moved like a weasel, and by the time I reached the base of the steps he was barely ten feet behind me.

I flew up the stairs and headed towards the coffee kiosk, screaming. A hand punched me between the shoulders and I went down, sprawling onto all fours, grating off several layers of skin against the rough paving stones. He was on me in an instant, his knee in my back. I let out a whoosh of air and lay motionless as he jerked my arms behind my back and pulled my blazer off. When he saw the wound it would be all over; he would know. Nadia would be unveiled; he could find her, Sawyer could find her, the police could find her, and the press—smelling blood—would start to circle.

He worked my blouse sleeve up. I struggled and squirmed but couldn't stop him. I couldn't even slow him down. I felt as if I were dying; there was no rage, just a sadness that it had to end this way. I was already missing Nadia and dreading the media feast. Not to mention the inside of a jail cell.

Then my arm wretched back. Pain shot up my shoulder but Keith's hands stopped clawing at my sleeve and his knee left my back. I rolled to my side, gasping for air. Alex was on top of Keith, pinning him face down, his arms behind his back, her knees on his shoulders. "Don't move, scumbag."

"It's her. She stole my money. Check her arm."

"Shut up, or I'll gag you."

"You can't gag me; I know my rights."

"Well I don't; and I will."

She looked confident and in control, but she had the advantage of jeans; it's hard to be dignified in a street fight wearing a skirt. I straightened mine, covering my thighs.

Alex looked at me. I didn't think I could stand one more "Are you all right?" but instead she shook her head with a wry smile.

"This just isn't your day, is it?"

114

Half an hour later I was back in Alex's apartment, sitting at her table, drinking another cup of tea. Turns out Alex was a Girl Scout when she was young and still always came prepared. She had a can of police issue Captor spray—the latest in incapacitation technology—and, after showing it to Keith, he considered his options and decided to settle into sullen silence. The police arrived shortly after, taking statements, cuffing Keith, offering first aid and, of course, asking if I was all right. The local newspaper also made an appearance but I avoided their questions so I would be listed only as an unidentified female.

"So what was that all about?"

I looked at the scrapes on my hands. Scrubbed down and disinfected they didn't look so bad, but they were already forming some fetching scabs, along with the burning patches on my knees.

"I have no idea. He must have mistaken me for someone else."

"I think that's apparent. I just wonder why?"

"What do you mean?"

"Well, you don't look anything like her."

I sensed this was heading to a Bad Place. "Who?"

"The Mad Bomber."

"I thought the papers were calling her Wonder Woman now."

"They are, but to us she's still the Mad Bomber. And there's bad blood between your attacker and this woman. Witnesses saw them fighting outside of Bishops Court. We suspect it was a drug deal gone bad."

Leave it to the police to look for the negative.

"Maybe this woman is trying to help."

"If she is she's doing a rubbish job of it. All she's done so far is stir up a known drug dealer so he's begun to attack random citizens. We can only hold him for so long; he'll be back on the street tomorrow unless you press charges."

The police at the scene had already asked me this, and I had told them I would think about it. I had. "He didn't do much of anything. He just chased me and pushed me."

"It's still assault. And if he did it to you, he'll do it to someone else. If you don't press charges, someone else is going to be hurt."

My face grew hot as tears of frustration pooled in my eyes. Keith wasn't going to attack anyone else, but Alex couldn't know that. He was after me, and I needed to deal with it in my own way. I had to protect Nadia, I had to protect myself. What hurt was having Alex think I was a coward.

A tear slid down my cheek. "I'm sorry. I can't."

Alex reached across the table and laid a hand on my arm. "I know it's hard, and frightening, but we'll protect you. If you stand up to him, he won't be able to hurt you, or anyone else."

I covered my face with my hands. "Oh god, I'm sorry. I'm so sorry. But I can't."

She let me sniffle a while, then she got up to fetch a tissue for me. "It's all right. I understand."

I felt her comforting hand on my shoulder, but heard the disappointment in her voice.

"I wish you did," I said to no one. "I really wish you did."

Alex rummaged in her handbag and produced a Sussex Police business card. "If you change your mind, or if Keith bothers you again, give us a call."

I took the card and limped towards the door. "I will. But right now I need to get back to work."

"Rachel."

I turned towards her. She was leaning against the table, her arms folded over her chest, looking as miserable as I felt; like she had just lost a friend. "Take care of yourself, okay?"

I nodded and opened the door.

"See you around," she said, as I closed it behind me. I didn't bother to acknowledge the lie.

Chapter 15

STEPHEN KNOCKED ON MY door thirty-one minutes after six. I put his lack of punctuality down to not wanting to appear too eager. I managed not to limp, and kept my hands in my pockets to hide my wounds as he walked me to his cherry red BMW Z4. He held the door for me and we drove off. As we passed by the house, a curtain twitched on Dee's side and I knew I'd be in for a grilling the next day, if not when I got back.

"I'm afraid I didn't make reservations," he said.

"I'm sure they'll have a table. It's Monday night."

"But you never know. There's an Ask on Station Road, why don't we stop by there? If they have a table, we can go there, if not, we'll go on to the Oak Barn. And if they're full, it's a take away."

He grinned and I wondered if that's what he was secretly hoping for.

Downtown Burgess Hill was crowded for a Monday evening. He parked at the pay and display at Martlets shopping centre and we walked to Ask. The Oak Barn had its own car park and, I'm sure, a number of free tables.

Ask turned out to be crowded but not full. We were assigned a table near the kitchen and an over-eager waiter named Scott. Stephen accepted the suggested starter of olives, ordered the wine and we settled down to the business of stilted and awkward conversation. We'd already exhausted our jobs, so tonight was devoted to out-of-work hours. Stephen, it turned out, liked football and was quite keen on computer games. I know nothing about football and only used a computer to manage my portfolio. Since I couldn't tell him what I really did in my time off, we seemed doomed to banalities about the weather until he mentioned he was a runner and after that the conversation became easier.

We chatted about shoes and heart monitors and the competitions he'd won and I even managed to use it to explain away my bruises. "Slipped running this morning," I said, exposing the heels of my hands. "That's where these came from. And my knees are chewed up, as well. One of the hazards."

"It's your shoes."

"My shoes?"

"You're wearing the wrong shoes for your class. They must be too heavy for your feet. I wear Saucony and I have never fallen while running."

I lowered my hands. "Good for you."

The entrée of Risotto Fruitti di Mare was good, but when you have your heart set on your favourite pizza, anything else is bound to be a disappointment. Stephen was driving, so he'd ordered just a half bottle of wine, and insisted we have a dessert and coffee afterwards, just to be sure.

"Thank you for a lovely evening," he said, as the coffees arrived. "You're good company, easy to talk to, and very attractive."

"You're too kind," I said, mocking coyness.

"Have you ever thought of wearing make-up?"

I fought the urge to be offended. "I thought you said I was attractive."

"You are. That's just it. You'd be so much more attractive if you, you know, brought out your better features."

"I used to wear make-up when I was younger. It made me look like a tart."

He smiled and lifted his hands as if surrendering. "I can see this is a bad subject. Can we forget I brought it up?"

We headed for the safe ground of work and I learned more about insurance underwriting than I ever wanted to know. I also learned that most of his colleagues weren't as up to the task as he himself was, though Nigel was a good egg. We drove back to my house in companionable silence and he walked me to my door again. This time I let him kiss me.

It was an odd sensation, feeling the lips of a near stranger pressed up against mine. I was wondered how I was expected to respond when I felt his tongue probing against my teeth. I opened slightly and he slipped in. It all seemed a bit clinical, as if we were dating by the numbers: dinner, lips, tongue. I expected the numbers would ratchet up from there.

"Are you going to invite me in?" he asked, when he came up for air.

I'd let him into my mouth; he wasn't coming into my house. "Sorry, it's getting late and half five comes early."

He nodded. "Morning run?"

"Yes, and an exercise routine.

He leaned forward for another kiss. I kept my teeth clenched this time.

118

"Can I see you again? Maybe we can have a race; I'd give you a head start."

"I won't need it."

"It's a date, then."

Chapter 16

THE NEXT MORNING, WHEN I got off the park and ride bus and headed for the Holiday Depot, I turned on Nadia's phone. There were seven messages. Four were unimaginative and anonymous harassment calls that I assumed originated from Sawyer and none were from Keith, who at least had the courage to announce who he was. I didn't entertain the idea that he had given up on me; he was probably just busy.

The remaining three calls were a concern. They were all from the same number, and that number had the same pattern as the numbers on the card Alex had given me. The police had Nadia's name, and now they had her phone number. The phone was a disposable mobile so it was untraceable, but the idea that they were closing in made me numb. I pushed aside the panic—I would have no repeat of yesterday's disaster—and dropped the phone into my handbag.

"When it looks like they're gaining on you," Paul had told me once, "keep moving and don't look back."

I didn't look behind me, but I did look left as I rounded the corner of West Street. I told myself I was being prudent and looking out for Keith, but I knew I was hoping to see Alex, sitting outside of the Merrythought, having an early breakfast. Maybe she would call me over, we could talk and she would forgive me for being the coward she thought I was. But that was a fantasy; I turned my back on the Bishopric and kept walking.

Martin was opening up as I arrived. He started to open his mouth as soon as he saw me.

"I'm fine," I said.

He turned the key and held the door for me. "You gave us quite a fright yesterday. We were all very concerned."

I took that to mean he was worried about having to pay me while I was out on extended sick leave.

"It frightened me, as well, but after a night's sleep, it doesn't look so big and bad. Some crazy guy pushed me in the car park. Unfortunate, but hardly the end of the world."

I dropped my bag on my desk and showed him my hands. Abrasions and scabs ran along the base of my palms and up the side of my thumbs, but otherwise I showed no evidence of the encounter since I was wearing trousers instead of a skirt. "See, good as new."

"Just be careful when you go out. And if you see this nutter hanging about, let me know."

I nodded, switched on my workstation and checked my accounts while Martin settled into his routine. A few minutes later, I noticed him shifting in his seat as if something was wrong and I realised we were still the only two in the office.

"Would you like me to get you a coffee, Mr Palmer?"

He looked towards the door, at the empty work stations, then at his desk and sighed. "Yes, that would be very kind of you."

I went to the sandwich shop next door and stood in the queue, ordering a coffee for Palmer and splashed out on a tea for myself. The smell of baking wafted over me like a reassuring blanket—the scent of fresh croissants, pain au chocolat and comfort. If they released a perfume called eau de bakery there wouldn't be a lonely woman left in the world.

"Hi, Rachel."

I looked at the woman taking my money. "Hi Susan."

On most mornings, that was the extent of our banter, unless she had some gossip to spread, like today. "You heard about the explosion, right? Well, that was the last straw for my aunt. She's moving out. So are most of the others."

"I'm sorry to hear that."

She shrugged. "To tell the truth, I'm relieved; the property was run down and there was no security. I mean, imagine, a woman, blowing up buildings. I tell you, you're not safe from terrorists anywhere these days."

"That's the woman who saved the boy on Saturday," someone from behind me said. "She's not a terrorist, she's a hero."

"Then what's she doing blowing up buildings?"

"They're two different people," said another person.

"Police don't think so."

"She's a nutter, that's what I think."

"Well I know a mother who doesn't feel that way. Wouldn't you want her around if your boy was getting trampled on by a pack of yobs?"

"Not if she comes over to blow up my house afterwards."

"I think she's what the lady on the news said she is: a superhero."

"You mean a vigilante."

"The police are painting a bad portrait of her because she's doing a better job than they are. That's what she said on her Facebook page."

"The Sussex Superhero has a Facebook page? Batman will want one next."

A hot cup in each hand, I ducked out the door, leaving the banter behind. I felt it was a small victory; not everyone was against Nadia, and the Facebook page I had set up the night before was already getting noticed. I had first done a search of any others and found four purporting to be Nadia. The price of fame. Then I had set up an authentic page for Nadia and posted the link on each of the other's walls. She already had over 7,000 followers, and they would read what I wanted them to read. So far that had not been much; my profile caption was, "The Sussex Superhero," my avatar was an image of Wonder Woman and my status update said only, "I am Nadia."

Still, it was a start, something to build on if it suited me. Working the media and turning public opinion was important, but it was a side show. Sawyer was the main event. It was in his interests to keep Nadia a fugitive; otherwise he would be helping the police catch her. He believed Nadia did have the photos and he was keen to get his hands on them; all I had to do was find out why. It would also help if I could find out who really did have my camera, and I thought I might have a clue who that was.

I walked back towards the Holiday Depot and stopped in my tracks. A young woman in a sleeveless blouse and jeans was wearing a large black button with white lettering reading, "I am Nadia." I stood, staring as she walked by. Then I saw another, and another. I noticed some people, men and woman, wearing black tee shirts with an expanded message containing the news presenter's question, "Who is Nadia?" at the top in small print, and "I am Nadia" covering much of the front. It brought a smile to my lips and an uneasy flutter to my stomach at the same time; the tide was turning, but where was it taking me?

Back at my desk, with Palmer caffeinated but still jumpy with worry about Amanda—who wouldn't surprise me by arranging a mugging for herself so she could top my attention-grabbing antics of the previous day—I set my screen at privacy angle and logged on to the Internet.

I had done a bit of research on Sawyer before I saw him the first time, but now I sought out every piece of information I could find. At nine o'clock exactly, Amanda arrived with James in tow. Since they weren't technically late, all Palmer did was look at them over his computer screen and wish them good morning. Amanda looked at his cup of coffee, my tea and glared at James. I imagined an earlier row with her ingratiating punctuality pitted against his insouciance and the winner being a compromise that suited neither of them.

"Did anyone watch the local news this morning," she said, "the ram-raider thieves struck again last night."

Good ploy to keep conversation from centring on me.

"Some hairdresser in Stan's Way; I think it was called Hair Today, Gone Tomorrow." She giggled at her own wit. "You should see the pictures. All the glass smashed and the shelves ransacked. Terrible, wasn't it, James?"

"Sure. Awful."

Satisfied that she had pulled the spotlight her way by announcing that they had slept together—or, at the very least, had watched the morning news together—she settled down at her work station and began leafing through the paper she had brought, exchanging occasional, secretive glances with James. As giddy and infatuated as they were, it just seemed a bad idea to get naked at night with someone you are obliged to sit next to all day. What was it Paul used to say, "Never shit where you eat."? Good advice, rarely taken.

I downloaded my research and saved it to my flash drive, then readied myself for work. It was a slow morning, giving me a lot of time to obsess over the law closing in on me, and Keith tracking me down. On the plus side, with few people coming through the door, I didn't have to look up from my computer screen and get ready to run very often. I did my best to compartmentalise it, and set a time to ponder over it for later in the evening, but something kept gnawing at the back of my mind.

As noon approached, I realised what was troubling me. I asked Martin if I could take an early lunch and, after enduring admonitions about talking to strangers and my promises not to wander into dark alleys, he let me go.

I walked up West Street, keeping an eye out for Keith. I couldn't be obvious about it and, if I did run into him, I would have to keep up the pretence that I regarded him as nothing more than a random stranger who had gone berserk on me. Enough reason to be afraid, but having to be wary while I was Rachel was a new wrinkle. This hadn't been part of the plan—even needing to be wary while I was Nadia hadn't been part of the plan—and the sooner I got the plan back on track, the better.

My current mission wasn't part of the plan, either, but my mind wouldn't let it go. I made my way to East Street and turned down the twee little lane that was Stan's Way. The practised calm and opulence of Perdie's Linens and Tristan's Restaurant jarred against the tragedy just beyond. The hairdresser's was a stand-alone building, a newer build, small and with floor to ceiling windows in two walls. Or, should I say, used to have; now it had two gaping holes covered by strips of crime scene tape.

The business, despite Amanda's joke, was called The Cutting Edge and there wasn't much left of it. The black leather seats inside the shop were criss-crossed with angry slashes, and bottles of creams, washes, dyes and other beautifying goos lay smashed and oozing beneath the shelving units scattered around the floor. From the state of the mirrors, it was evident that someone was going to have about 875 years of bad luck.

I was pleased to find that the police had already vacated the scene; this would not be an opportune time to run into Alex. The residual police presence consisted of a female PCSO, standing at ease in front of the untouched door. The only other people on the scene were two men in matching charcoal suits, holding clipboards. I took them to be insurance adjusters, and noted with relief that neither of them was Stephen.

I didn't need to pretend to be shocked, but I stood there gawping at the scene for a few more seconds, my hand over my mouth. Then I approached the PCSO. She was about my height, but more solidly built. Her manner appeared calm and competent, suggesting she might be easy to talk to, but she adopted a defensive stance as I came within range. Smart woman; never let your guard down. She wore a yellow high visibility vest and a name tag that read 'Doyle'. I felt an immediate and absurd kinship with her, even though she would have gleefully arrested me if she suspected who I was.

"Can I help?" she asked, in a voice that did not invite me to approach any further.

"I had an appointment here this morning."

Doyle relaxed. "You don't anymore." Then added, just in case I was blind or had the IQ of a gnat. "This is a crime scene."

"This is so awful. Poor Chantelle. I wish there was something I could do. You don't know where she is now, do you?"

"Pardon?"

"Chantelle. This is her place."

"I wouldn't know that. And if I did, I would not be at liberty to divulge that information."

I turned to the charcoal suits, who had been close enough to overhear. "Can you tell me where Chantelle is?"

They exchanged a look. "No, but Ms Blake's whereabouts isn't something we would discuss, either."

I smiled and backed away.

"Sorry, it's just such a shock, I'm sure she must be terribly upset. I know I would be. I'll come back in a few days."

Doyle nodded and resumed her stance, feet spread, hands clasped behind her back, brown hair tucked up under her cap. "I think that would be best, Miss."

I returned to East Street, the niggling in my mind satisfied. I didn't know what the police were making of this, but it wasn't the work of the ram-raiders; it wasn't their style. Tucked as it was into the mini-pedestrian zone of Stan's Way, The Cutting Edge was inaccessible to vehicle traffic, particularly a vehicle capable of smashing through a window and carrying away the goods. And any foot traffic in or out would be captured on CCTV cameras. No, this had Keith's fingerprints all over it, literally; this was his revenge on Chantelle and it made me wonder what he had in store for me when he found me. If he found me.

I hoped the police would have better luck catching up with Keith than they were having with the ram-raider gang. An arrest for this break-in, coupled with his history, might be enough to take him out of the picture, at least for five to seven years. The prospects were good: as an amateur, he was more likely to leave the police something to work with than the gang, who moved with professional precision. They tended to favour targets on the periphery of the town, outside the reach of the CCTV cameras, and with access to main roads where they could smash, grab and run within minutes.

I walked down East Street, wandered through the Carfax and stopped at Panino's Café for lunch. As I munched my tuna and cucumber sandwich, my mind played over the recent robberies and I subconsciously pulled a map of Horsham into my head and constructed a four-dimensional diagram involving area and time, turning and twisting it this way and that as you might to an imaginary Rubik's Cube. As I sipped the last of my ginger beer, a sudden snap in my mind made me sit bolt upright and spill the rest of the drink on my blouse. I dabbed the damp spots with a napkin as the mental picture faded but left the unwanted knowledge behind. There was a pattern to the robberies. I had seen it.

I knew where they were going to hit next, and when.

Although I was certain I was right, I doubted I could convince the police. If I went to them as Rachel, they would just think I was a publicity seeker. And after the raid happened as I predicted, they would think I was in league with the robbers. So I wrote that option off, telling myself I now had no choice but to go with option number two. If Nadia could capture the gang in the act, the police would have to admit she was working for the cause of justice, or at least stop calling her a wacko bomber. And even if the police refused to see the truth, a win here would help tilt popular opinion further in her favour. It was perfect. The only downside was she couldn't afford another cock-up, so this one had to be handled with caution.

I fanned my blouse as dry as I could and buttoned up my jacket to cover the damp patches. Then I went across the Carfax to the Non-Stop Party Shop. If I hurried, I could reconnoitre the area around the business before my lunch hour was up. It would be dark when I got out of work and I wanted to get the lie of the land while it was still light. This would give Nadia a better advantage.

Three minutes later I left the Non-Stop Party Shop with a large pack of fireworks. The star-spangled carrier bag bumped against my thigh as I quick-walked down West Street towards The Pedaller.

Chapter 17

I ARRIVED AT MY spot just before 1 a.m. I knew they wouldn't strike before then, as the street had a kebab shop on the corner and three pubs within shouting distance. It would take at least an hour for the post-pub crew to get their kebabs and the street to return to some level of quiet. I slipped into the shadows of the shrubbery outside the Albany House Office across the street from The Pedaller, dressed in my Microprene suit, gloves and black wig. I was also wearing a heavy overcoat against the cold and had a bobble hat pulled over my hair. The look was not that of a glamorous crime fighter but it had the dual advantage of keeping me from freezing to death and, if some random drunk stumbled upon me looking for a place to take a pee or heave up his nights allotment of lager and kebab, he might mistake me for a homeless person instead of a ninja.

The ground was damp and cold, so I squatted down as opposed to sitting. I had a clear view of The Pedaller; its glass frontage covered by a heavy mesh security curtain. I reached into the warmth inside my coat and unclipped the camera from my utility belt to take a few practice shots. The light from the street lamps provided enough illumination for a decent night shot, but it required a slower shutter speed so unless the thieves agreed to line-up for a commemorative photo, I wasn't going to get anything the police would be interested in. That's where the item stuffed into my coat pocket came in.

To the uninitiated it might look like a tomato soup can, but it was, in reality, a flashbang. More flash than bang, I hoped, because noise was not what I was after. I had constructed it after dinner, while watching a CSI rerun. The can wasn't part of the device; it was just a means of protecting it. The mixture of gunpowder I had extracted from the fireworks was bundled in a paper towel, wrapped with aluminium foil and looked a bit like a leftover sausage with a fuse sticking out of one end. The idea was, once the gang smashed through the shop front and began ferrying bicycles to their truck I would light the fuse and roll the can into the road. I had compartmentalised the powder so it would go off in a sequence of two or three flashes, each one lasting about half a second. I judged that would give me enough time for at least two clear shots of the thieves, who, with luck, should be looking directly at me with startled expressions on their faces.

That was the plan, at least. I'd run it over and over in my mind through dinner, telly, bomb preparations and fending off calls from Keith and Sawyer and accepting one from Stephen. He had called while I was scooping explosive powder onto the paper towel, making me spill some on the coffee table. We chatted a while about nothing in particular and then he began angling to come over with a bottle of wine and a movie. Although the idea did have some appeal, I'd looked around at the pile of gunpowder, soup can, foil wrap and fuse and decided to tell him I was tired. I did ask for a rain check, which seemed to mollify him, but he was less than overjoyed when he hung up.

A car approached and I tensed, but it roared by without slowing, or observing the speed limit. I flexed my leg muscles to try to coax some warmth and blood back into them and ran the plan through my head again, mimicking the motions, making the actions into a routine. Light the fuse, roll the can, ready the camera, shoot, shoot, shoot. Then skedaddle. Slip through the alley, into the shadows and back to the car. Nothing could go wrong.

Turned out I had a lot of time to think about that. By two o'clock my legs were deep in REM sleep and I would have been myself if my shivering hadn't kept me awake. I didn't entertain the idea that I might be wrong about the date and place, but that didn't take into account outside factors, like the gang getting a flat tyre on the way to the heist, or this robbery interfering with one of the key gang member's darts night. By half two, I was wondering how I was going to get through the next day with only two hours sleep and regretting that I hadn't had the luxury of giving the can a few practice rolls or seeing what the flashbang would actually do when it went off.

These thoughts worried me less than my lack of sleep; if it went wrong, if the flashbang didn't go off or if it made an ineffectual fizzle, I would disappear. No one would know Nadia had been there. I would be no better off, but no worse off, either.

At two forty five I decided I would wait until three o'clock and pack it in.

At two forty eight, the ramming van arrived. I heard it before I saw it, a low, menacing growl that echoed off the silent buildings and rolled down the street like distant thunder. Then it came into view, a rust-flecked, hybrid vehicle that looked like the mutant offspring of a moving van and a humvee. A steel grille covered its snub nose and the bumper appeared to be an iron girder. Eccentric though it was, on a motorway, it would blend into the mass of traffic, but here on this deserted street, there could be no question as to its intention. It prowled past my hiding place like a jungle beast in search of prey. I kept still and watched it roll by. Through the tinted windows of the cab I made out the shapes of at least two people; the storage compartment on the back could hold any number of others but I placed the gang numbers at four based on the amount of goods they had been able to pack away in previous robberies.

As the lorry turned onto Albion Way, I memorised the registration number even though I expected it would be stolen. Once the vehicle drove out of sight I realised I was holding my breath and let it out with a whoosh. The engine rumble grew faint, then revved loud as the robbers circled the roundabout and returned at increasing velocity. I rose into a low stoop, keeping to the shadows, flexing feeling back into my limps, readying the camera, checking the flashbang. This was all going to happen quickly and everything had to be done right; there would be no prize for coming in second.

The drone of the engine grew into a frantic roar as the mutant machine screeched through the red lights and turned a sharp right onto the Bishopric. It jumped the curb without slowing and rammed straight into the front of The Pedaller. The glass panel exploded in a shower of glittering shards. The steel curtain crimped in the centre but didn't leave a hole large enough for a man to squeeze through. They wouldn't have time to attempt a second run; the crash would have already alerted everyone in a half-mile radius and time was a key ingredient in their plan. I thought they might decide to drive away, leaving Robin with a ruined shop and me with nothing to show the police. Then the rear doors of the storage compartment flew open and two men jumped out carrying a thick chain.

With practised precision, they looped the chain through the mesh barrier and around the lorry's bumper. Another roar of the engine and screech of tyres and the lorry sped backward, snapping the chain tight and wrenching the barrier away. It tore loose, ripping wood and glass with it, and clattered to the pavement. The two men, dressed in dark clothing and black balaclavas, scrambled through the breech as the lorry roared forward, pulling up near the shattered shop front.

Another man, also clad in black, jumped from the cab and began removing the chain from the bumper while the first two ferried bikes from the shop into the back of the lorry. At least this is what I assumed was happening. The lorry, being parked in front of The Pedaller, obscured much of my view, making it difficult to know what was happening inside. It also meant I was not in a position where I could get a decent photo of the thieves in the act. I was wavering between improvising and retreating when the shouting started.

Inside the shop the subdued clanking and grunts of the robbers was joined by a cacophony of unintelligible shouts. The man working the chain looked up, startled. He left the chain and peered into the dark shop.

"Get him."

Then a cry of pain. The voice was Robin's. I dropped the camera into my pocket and raced into the street, yanking off my hat and unbuttoning my coat as I ran. I dodged around the front of the lorry, my coat flapping behind me like a black cape. The driver was staring out of the cab window, the chain man standing nearby, both looking into The Pedaller. As I jumped onto the wreckage of the security curtain the noise alerted them. The chain man spun around in time to see a lithe figure clad in black with a cape fluttering behind her leap into the air and land a kick square in his chest.

He flew back, landing on top of the jumble of bikes lying on the pavement. Behind me the door of the cab opened and the driver jumped out. I saw him from the corner of my eye: a large African man in camouflage trousers and a black jacket. I whirled around, throwing my weight against the door, slamming it shut on him. It caught him across the thighs and banged the top of his head. His balaclava softened the blow but it still emitted a satisfying clunk. When I yanked the door open he made a drunken lunge for me. I dodged aside and tripped him as he staggered past, sending him face first onto the crumpled security curtain.

I shucked my coat, pulled two nylon ties from my utility belt and strapped his hands to the metal rods of the curtain. Chain man was just getting his breath back so I flipped him onto his face on the pavement and secured his hands behind him, then I jumped through the broken window into the shop.

It was small enough in the day time, but at night, with all the bikes stored inside, there was little room to move. The clutter, the darkness and the confusion of thumps, bangs and shouting made it difficult to discern what was happening. Two figures crouched near the counter, edging towards the wall where another figure stood, backed into the corner, swinging a bicycle pump and shouting. The rubber hose of the pump whistled through the air like a whip, dinging off the counter and nearby racks as Robin swung it wide, keeping the robbers at bay.

"Get the fuck out of my shop."

The tight quarters put me at a disadvantage. They were bigger and stronger and there were two of them. I relied on speed and outmanoeuvring my opponent; the only advantage the shop offered was surprise.

I jumped on the back of the nearest robber, digging my knees into his side to keep myself in place, and yanked at the back of his balaclava, stopping his breathing and putting him off balance. We tumbled backward. I threw my body weight sideways as we fell, spinning us around so that I landed on top of him with my knee in the small of his back. I pulled his arm up and slipped a restraint on it. He bucked beneath me like a bull but I hung onto the back of his jacket, riding him as he kicked and shouted and dragged us towards the lorry with his free arm. When we came into range of a fallen display stand, I released the lock hold on his arm and latched the other end of the restraint to it.

He bellowed and thrashed and clawed at his stationary arm like a bear caught in a trap. I jumped away, avoiding his flailing feet and turned in time to see the two dark figures near the counter lunge at each other. Robin swung the pump and landed a blow on the side of the man's neck. The robber bulled forward, body-slamming Robin into the corner, crushing his shoulder against the wall. Robin grunted and dropped the pump. I dived towards them, rolling into the man's knees, sending him backward onto the floor. I rolled onto all fours and came face to face with Robin. He was slumped in a heap, his teeth gritted, his eyes squeezed to slits. His lips turned up for the briefest of moments when he saw me. "So you are Wonder Woman."

He said it with smug satisfaction; only a man would pause at a moment like this to point out he had been right. I laid a hand on his shoulder. He winched.

"Your shoulder is dislocated."

"I know."

"I'll fix it. Don't go anywhere."

A surge of pain cut short his bark of ironic laughter. I turned my attention to the man behind us, surprised to find he had not moved. I crawled towards him, ready to jump if he made a grab, but he remained still, emitting a curious wheezing that grew higher in pitch with each laboured breath. The wheezes stopped, and he began to convulse.

I scrambled to him, pulled off his balaclava and brushed his sweaty hair away from where it had gathered around his neck. He was an Asian man, young, dark skinned. At the side of his neck, just under his jaw, a darker bruise swelled to the size of an orange. His body jerked as he tried to get air through his blocked breathing passage. I pulled off my gloves and felt the base of his throat. There wasn't much swelling there. I looked into his dark eyes; they were bright with panic.

"I'm going to perform a tracheotomy," I told him. "You've got to remain still. Do you understand?"

His eyes grew round, but his head moved.

I had, sometime in my early teens, read a medical encyclopaedia. There were descriptions of several operations in it, all of them more complex than the instructions for how to perform a tracheotomy. It wasn't such a difficult operation, at least that's what the book led me to believe, but it required a scalpel and some tubing.

"Robin, I need a knife."

All I heard in response was a moan.

I recalled the locked glass cabinet next to the wall. There had been Swiss Army knives displayed in it. I snatched up the bicycle pump and ran to the display, swinging wide, aiming for the centre where the thick, tempered glass would be weakest. The pump clanged and jumped in my hands. Nothing happened. I swung again. And again. I thought of the man behind me, dying because I couldn't break into a display cabinet. I swung again. The glass shattered. Jagged hunks thumped to the floor and fell into the case. I grabbed one of the knives and went back to the injured thief.

I opened the blade. It was small, but sharp. I placed the point at the base of his throat, feeling for a ridge in his trachea. His hands came up, clawing at the knife, his throat, my arms. He needed restraining and Robin was not in a position to help.

"Look, you're going to die if you don't cooperate. Give me your hands."

He did, and I pulled them above his head, securing them to the base of a shelving unit. It took only a few seconds, but to him it must have felt like most of what was left of his life. I straddled him, placed the knife on this throat and pushed down. It slid in with surprising ease and I stopped for a moment, doing my best to hide my amazement. I moved the knife forward in a sawing motion until the slit was about an inch long, then I turned the blade to open the cut.

He sucked in a huge lungful of air and blood and hacked so hard the knife popped out and clattered to the floor. I got off him, watching helplessly as his body wracked and convulsed and his arms strained, pulling the rack until I feared it would fall on us.

I turned to Robin. He was struggling to remain conscious. I needed a tube, something he could breathe through. I grabbed the air pump and examined the hose. It was narrow, and had a narrower bore, but it was all I had. I hacked off a two inch length, pinned the man's shoulders to the floor and looked him in the face. "Suck it up. I need you to be still, just for a few moments. Can you do that for me?"

I felt his body tense and strain against the urge to cough. I slid the knife back into the cut. "Hold still."

His body went ridged. I turned the knife and slipped the tube in. Blood seeped around the edges. I didn't want any more blood going into his lungs and I couldn't let the tube slip in there, either. I squeezed the cut closed as tight as I could and gripped the tube with blood-slicked fingers. "Okay."

He sucked in so hard I thought I was going to lose the tube, then his spasms took over and the tube popped out like a champagne cork. The wound on his neck sprayed a mist of blood droplets into my face. I turned away and saw Robin, still slumped in the corner, his face a mixture of misery and shock. "Tape," I yelled.

"Uhhh?"

"Tape. I need to tape to hold the tube."

He pointed with his chin. "There's some gaffer tape behind the counter."

I glanced into the thief's eyes. "Don't breathe."

There was a long, recessed shelf behind the counter. I groped in the darkness, throwing the accumulated clutter onto the floor feeling for a roll of tape and hoping I might stumble upon some tissues or cotton wadding or, if I was going to fantasise, some surgical gauze. All I found was tape. I reeled off a strip as I ran back to the man, then I realised I had no tube. I scrambled for the air pump and cut off another length. Then I reached under the man's jacket, yanked his tee shirt out as far as I could and slashed off a hunk.

The man was doing his best to hold still, but he was losing the battle. I mopped at the blood around the wound, wrapped the cleanest end of the cloth around the tube and shoved it though the hole. He sucked in air.

"Wait."

I strapped tape onto his neck as if it was a package I was readying for shipment, then wound a narrow strip around the tube to anchor it. He pulled another breath and I held mine. The tube stayed in place, his hacking began to subside. And in the distance, I heard the sirens. I scrambled to Robin.

His left arm was clutching his right, which hung limp from his shoulder, the odd configuration visible through his shirt. For the first time I noticed he was barefoot and wearing nothing but baggy boxer shorts and a thin tee shirt. I put my hand on his shoulder, feeling the position of his socket.

"What are you doing here?" he rasped.

I prised his left hand away and held his forearm. "Saving your ass. What the hell are you doing here?"

"Malcolm and I have been taking turns sleeping upstairs. Worried about the robberies. Why—"

His words turned into a brief yowl as I pushed his shoulder against the wall and levered his arm upward. Unlike the tracheotomy, which I had only read about, I had seen this done, and done it myself, a number of times. I felt the joint pop into place. He leaned back, flushed and sweating. "Where did you learn to do that?"

"I took a correspondence course."

The sirens grew louder.

"I have to go."

"Will I see you again? I could show you some other bike trails. Prettier than the last."

"In the middle of all this you're asking me for a date. You're a lunatic."

"I'm not the one dressed in black pyjamas pretending to be Wonder Woman."

"Pretending?"

I ran my hand over his shoulder. "You need to put some ice on that, pronto."

His left hand gripped my wrist. "Tell me how I can find you."

"I owed you a favour. Let's call it even." I pulled away. "The less you know about me the better off you'll be."

"You can't make that decision for me."

"I just have."

"Wait."

But I was already moving. I stopped to check my patient. He seemed okay for now. The tube moved a fraction as his breath sucked and wheezed through the small hole. I cut away his restraint and crab walked over his body. When I felt a hand grab

134

my arm I had a moment of disbelief so strong it made me dizzy. Was I going to have to neutralise a man who was all but dead? But the grip had no urgency in it; I looked down. His eyes were no longer wild and desperate; they were half closed, calm and conveyed a sense of peace. He mouthed the words, "Thank you."

I nodded and jumped over the other man before he had the chance to strike out at me and bounded onto the pavement. The driver was thrashing and cursing, still fastened to the security gate, but the chain man was gone. I looked around and saw him staggering across the road. The police were close, but he stood a good chance of ducking into the alley between the chippie and the KFC before they arrived. I picked my coat up from the pavement and fumbled for the flashbang and lighter.

Chain man shuffled across the road like an extra in *Return of the Living Dead* so it wouldn't take much to hold him for a few seconds. I lit the fuse and bowled the flashbang towards him like a skittles ball, aiming so it would roll wide. I wanted it to go off near the far kerb to disorient him and draw the attention of the police. It all went to plan until the soup can hit a bump in the road and changed direction. It curved towards the man, rolled between his legs and, to my relief, another ten feet before exploding in a loud pop just as the police careened around the corner.

I averted my eyes as the street became a collage of glaring light laced with sharp-edged shadows. I heard the squeal of tyres as the police car braked and fishtailed. It skidded past the lorry, bounced onto the pavement, sent a rubbish bin spinning into the air and crashed into the pay and display meter in front of Same Day Dry Cleaning.

I saw the two officers struggling against the air bags as steam hissed from beneath the crumpled bonnet. Kebab wrappers, KFC buckets, chicken bones, bits of broken glass and other unidentified debris settled onto the windscreen, roof and boot of the mangled car. A mixture of emotions shot through me, but over all I felt a strange sadness tampered with disbelief; less than five minutes ago it had all been under control.

I let out a sigh, grabbed my coat and ran.

Chapter 18

IF THE SCUFFLE AT The Pedaller had been a football match, I would say it ended in a draw, even after my spectacular own goal. The newscaster struggled to keep the smile from her face as she recited the story tagline on the morning news:

"Mysterious Sussex superhero thwarts ram-raider gang; police thwart pay-and-display meter."

It was the lead story on the regional news and came in third, after a refinery explosion in Kuwait and the latest Parliamentary scandal, on the national news. The report started off favourability, noting how Nadia had subdued the gang and performed an emergency tracheotomy before—as one of the robbers had observed—disappearing into the night like Batman.

Then the newscaster paused and looked into the camera for a beat, letting us know the punch line was about to be delivered.

"Police have a different view, stating that the woman threw a homemade bomb at their car as they arrived at the scene, causing them to crash. They have now added possession of an explosive device and attempted murder of a police officer to the growing list of charges against her."

I nearly choked on my muesli; it stuck in my throat as my stomach turned to a block of ice. Murder? This was getting way out of hand. Then I noticed the newscaster and her partner were still smiling.

"Do you think this will result in another war of words?" the co-presenter asked.

"There's no reason to think otherwise. Most people wanted by the police don't have their own Twitter account and Facebook page, but it's a wonder that they don't; with each accusation, Nadia has countered with her own version of events, so the public will be looking forward to another update."

I turned off the telly and opened my laptop. As I finished getting ready for work, I logged on to Nadia's Twitter and Facebook accounts. The connection was sluggish, due no doubt to half of southern England trying to log on simultaneously. When I got in, I found hundreds of messages, about half of them encouraging, some threatening and some, which I assumed to be from the police, advising Nadia to give herself up. I wondered how long the police had tried to trace the accounts before they gave up. They had, according to *The Daily News*, attempted to force the providers to shut the accounts down and this was giving the Internet crowd a great Freedom of Speech soapbox to preach from.

I also noted that the 'I am Nadia' merchandise was trending on Twitter and appeared to be selling faster than local entrepreneurs could crank it out. Some people were bidding up to one hundred pounds for a tee shirt.

I typed in a few succinct messages to set the record straight and then, unable to resist, I wrote, "It's not my fault that they can't drive."

I hadn't meant to make an enemy of the police, but there was nothing I could do or say now to convince them I was on their side. They had accused me of buying drugs, so I posted the video of Keith having his tantrum and scooping up his drugs on YouTube. They accused me of brandishing a knife, so I told what had really happened. The single incident I had not countered was the explosion at Keymer View Court, an omission not overlooked by them or some of the newspapers.

Still, I felt encouraged, even if I felt less than heroic.

While the notion of "disappearing into the night like Batman" was a pleasing image, the truth was less elegant. In reality, Nadia tore around the corner in a blind panic and had sneaked to her car while sirens and blue flashing lights invaded the neighbourhood. It had been nearly dawn by the time I arrived home and now, after two and a half hours of fitful sleep, I was preparing for my day and looking like someone who had been out running wild into the early hours.

At least my Rachel persona had the advantage of not needing to do her hair or worry about her wardrobe, but a touch of make-up would go a long way towards making me look more awake and less like a gadabout. I managed the drive to Horsham well enough, but fell asleep during the 5 minute journey from the park-and-ride to the bus station.

The morning turned out to be a busy one, with people booking holiday excursions to Disney World with the family, or dirty weekends in Corfu with the mistress. At midday I turned off my workstation and turned on my phones. Both of them beeped. I listened to Nadia's messages first.

"Quite the busy little woman these days." Sawyer. "And you're building a following. That won't protect you, you know, it will merely make it easier to find you."

Then there was Keith's somewhat shorter but more cogent communication: "I'm coming for you, bitch."

On my phone, it was Stephen, calling to make a date for our foot race. He genuinely wanted to race me. What sort of date is that? I dropped the phones into my bag and went out, intending to visit the newsagent on the corner of the Bishopric and Albion Way. It would be a good idea to check out the local papers to see what sort of press Nadia was getting, and what sort of trouble she was in. I headed that way and got nearly ten feet before Paul's voice invaded my thoughts. "Are you acting rationally or on impulse? There is a wide gap between doing what we want to do and doing what we should do. Don't walk into it."

I admired a display of glasses in the Optician's window while I thought it over. The newsagent was a small one, cramped, narrow, not good for browsing. But going there would take me past The Merrythought, and near to The Pedaller. Was this what I was really after? If so, I was making a mistake. I went to WH Smith's instead.

As I walked up West Street, my phone began to ring. But which one? I had changed both phones back to the standard ringtone so Nadia's wouldn't stand out as much, but now it left me wondering what to do. If Nadia's phone was ringing, it might be a trap; Keith could be watching, waiting to see if I answered. And what if he was close enough to hear it ring? I went into Next, browsed my way to the back and checked for messages. It had been Nadia's phone, but it hadn't been Keith gloating that he was watching me. This caller's number was not hidden, and the sound of the voice made the hair on my arms rise up. "Nadia, this is Specials Police Constable Alexis Marsh. I want to help you. You are not in any trouble, but you need to talk to me about what you are doing before you or someone else gets hurt. I understand what you are doing and I admire you for it, but you need my help. Please call me."

My chest tightened. I drew a shallow breath to ease the dizziness. First Nadia's name, then her number and now the only friend I had was trying to trick Nadia into turning herself in. Admiration, indeed; all Alex had for Nadia was a desire to see her face down on the pavement with her hands cuffed behind her back.

I left the shop but no longer felt a desire to check the news. The phone call hadn't been from Sawyer or Keith but that didn't mean the next one wouldn't be. And even if my own phone rang, I couldn't answer it; how would I know if it was my phone or

Nadia's. I headed back to The Holiday Depot, feeling as much a prisoner as if Alex had already captured me.

Amanda looked up when I arrived. "My, that was a quick one? Where'd you do it, in the car park?"

"What are you on about?"

"You went to meet your boyfriend."

I shook my head in disbelief. "That's preposterous."

"Oh come off it. You're showing up with bags under your eyes, sneaking off at lunch and coming back all flushed. Spill it; who are you seeing."

"No one. And even if I was, it's none of your fu . . . darn business."

I went to my desk.

"Hmm, maybe I am wrong," Amanda said. "You're much too grouchy for someone who just had a shag."

I sat at my desk and ignored her. Martin looked up from his computer with the worried expression of someone afraid they might have to do something managerial. When I made no sign of replying to Amanda, he relaxed and returned to his game.

The front of our office was plate glass and, while much of it was covered with posters promising holidays in warm places at amazingly low prices, it was still possible to see me if you looked beyond the showpiece that was Amanda. That meant I could even be trapped here. Keith would have had little difficulty tracking me to the Holiday Depot, and although he would be hesitant to confront me here, I still felt like a cornered rabbit. I went to the employees' toilet to turn off my phones, then felt like a paranoid idiot for having done so.

An hour later, when Kevin Sawyer walked in, I stopped feeling paranoid and made the switch to panic. Then Paul's voice forced its way through the fog. "Focus. You're in control. You know you can do this. Head up, eyes front, exude confidence and they will see a winner."

I had to assume Sawyer and Keith had formed some sort of loose alliance, and that Keith had told him he suspected I was Nadia. This was the test. Keith's suspicion was deep, but Sawyer's was second-hand; this was my chance to put him off the scent.

I glanced up at him with the same interest I would show any other customer. He made an awkward pretence of browsing the racks of brochures, moving towards my workstation. I smiled up at him. "Can I help you?"

He studied me, searching out similarities between me and the woman he'd met in his office. To help confound him, I left my seat and stood next to him so he could see my conservative dress and short stature. The mistake I'd made with Keith was to let him linger on my face too long. That couldn't happen again. I let him take in my unadorned features, limp hair, glasses and green eyes with the bags under them, then looked away.

"Crete is very popular right now," I said. I pulled a brochure from the rack and handed it to him. "What is it you have in mind, some winter sun, or are you looking for a family holiday?"

My flagging countenance may have done more to hide my identity than all the other machinations. He moved his gaze up and down my frame once more for good measure, then placed the brochure into my un-manicured hands. "I'm here to book a business trip," he said and went to Amanda's desk.

After she got him seated, she looked at me and winked. I returned to my desk, doing my best to appear unconcerned. Amanda chatted and giggled and strode back and forth between the printer and her workstation. Ten minutes later, tickets in hand, he left without a backward glance.

I drew in a long, easy breath. Unless he was a consummate actor, he had no inkling of who I was. He and Keith might both be after Nadia, but they had different motives. Keith was simply a Neanderthal who had been beaten up by a woman in front of witnesses. The money was a good excuse, but that's all it was; he needed to hurt Nadia and, as far as he was concerned, hurting me would be just as satisfying. But Sawyer had a bigger motive, and I needed to find out what it was. Knowing where he was going would be a good start.

After I gave Sawyer enough time to get away, I went to Amanda's desk. "That man who was just in here; did you book some flights for him?"

Amanda looked up. "Oh, you mean that man you let slip away, and who preferred to have me book his trip for him? That man?"

There was no kindness in her eyes; she had the advantage, she knew it and was enjoying it.

"I'm just wondering where he was going, that's all," I said. "He seemed to be wavering between Crete and Paxos; I'm curious about which one he chose."

"Hm, why the sudden interest in clients' holidays, I wonder. Could he be the man you have been slipping out to meet? Is that why you came back from lunch with the hump? Has he stood you up and now he's in here booking a holiday trip with his family?" She smiled and looked at James. "What do you think, James?"

"Huh?" James said.

"Stop playing games and just tell me where he went."

"Can't. Client privilege."

"Amanda, you're not a barrister."

She looked at her screen, moved her mouse around and clicked. I knew she was closing the documents she had been working on with Sawyer. "For all I know, you could be stalking him," she said, still looking at her workstation screen. "Maybe he dumped you and you turned into a bunny-boiler. He must have had a reason to not make the booking with you."

"That is just preposterous. If you're not going to tell me, just say so."

"Ladies," Martin said. "Please conduct your personal conversations during personal time."

I returned to my desk, my cheeks burning. "Sorry, Mr Palmer."

Amanda said nothing, but her smirk told me that Sawyer's destination would remain hidden from me.

But perhaps Nadia could find out.

Chapter 19

IT WAS DARK WHEN I left work and walked to the bus station. When I got off the bus at the park and ride and started across the car park, a car zoomed towards me, pinning me in its headlight beams. I jumped out of its path as it streaked by, my heart pounding. The car didn't beep or swerve or stop; it raced across the tarmac and screeched into an empty slot. No one got out. I thought about confronting the driver, but as I was alone in a dark car park, I decided that might not be the best strategy. Instead, I found my car and drove away, my mind going over the events of the past twenty four hours.

Despite my optimism of the morning, I had to admit that last night's caper had not achieved its primary objective of proving to the cops that Nadia was one of the good guys. But that was becoming a given, so perhaps it was time to accept that she was destined to remain outside the law, a vigilante crime fighter like the original Batman, instead of best buddies with Inspector Gordon like the TV Batman. Peter Parker managed to operate outside the law, as well, but the plan all along had been to model Nadia after Wonder Woman, who was respected and admired by the guys in the white hats, and Diana Prince didn't have to scuttle around dodging small time pushers and sleazy property developers.

Nadia saved a life last night, and stopped a robbery; if that wasn't good enough for the cops, then walking on water and raising the dead wouldn't change their minds, either. I sighed and turned onto the A272.

It was the usual stop and go traffic up to the junction with the A23 but after that the cars thinned out. Still, I didn't notice I was being followed until I turned onto Perrymount Road into Haywards Heath.

It wasn't a clear conviction, just a feeling. The headlights behind me were the same pair that had come up behind me when I left Horsham. That in itself was not unusual, I was not the only person who commuted from Haywards Heath to Horsham, but I couldn't shake the feeling that they matched the headlights on the car that nearly ran me down at the park and ride.

I thought of all the tricks I could employ to see if I was being tailed, and to lose them if I were, but that would give me away. I wanted to pound my forehead on the steering wheel in frustration; Nadia was supposed to make me free and keep me out of danger but I felt as if a noose was tightening around my neck.

I could do nothing but drive forward, leading whoever it was closer to my home. Cold panic rippled through my stomach. If this were a competition, what would I do? How would I pull a win out of this? I concentrated but came up with nothing. Giving away the fact that I knew I was being followed didn't seem like a good idea; they would just try again in a less obvious manner, and I would be forever looking over my shoulder.

Then an idea did come to me, a way I could keep secret the fact I knew I was being followed, yet still not lead them to my house. It was a simple idea, and one I had used in competitions. As a plan started to solidify, Paul's voice broke into my mind. "If you feel you're going to lose, you don't have to compete."

He would tell me that to cajole me into competing when I felt I hadn't a chance in hell of winning. It was a challenge meant to push me, to make me do what he felt I should do, rather than what I believed I could do. It always worked, and it would work now, but in a different way. I may be on my way home, but that didn't mean I had to go home.

I drove to the shopping plaza in the centre of town and parked in the middle row. The car followed me in. It parked two rows behind me but no one got out. I got a shopping trolley and went inside, cruising the aisles at a leisurely pace, picking out items at random, wondering how long I could stay in the shop without raising suspicions and what I was going to do when I left.

After half an hour of arbitrary shopping, I went to the till with the longest line. Eventually, a lanky teenager with black hair and blacker make-up greeted me and asked if I wanted help packing my groceries in a tone suggesting it was the last thing she wanted to do. I resisted the urge to tell her "Yes," and then she charged me five pence apiece for two carrier bags and gave me a withering look because I was killing her planet.

Back in the car park, the more immediate concern of being followed by person or persons unknown took precedence. I put the carrier bags on the back seat and resumed driving towards town. The mystery car followed. Where could I go now? The police station seemed like a good idea; maybe a normal person might have noticed the tail by now and become suspicious. I couldn't know, and I couldn't chance it. A normal person might be going to visit friends, however. Okay, so I had no friends to visit, but the person following me didn't know that.

I was nearing my neighbourhood now. If I pulled into my cul-de-sac they would find my house for sure. I continued up Gander Hill instead and parked in a drive between tightly packed houses. I pulled my car up as far as I could, took the groceries out and carried them around to the back door. The car slowed to a crawl; I could sense the driver watching me as I walked up to a door near the back of the property. There were lights on in the house and, through the window, I saw two men sitting at a small table having dinner. It looked like pasta in white sauce and chilled chardonnay were on the menu. I didn't want to disturb them but I couldn't just stand there holding two bags of groceries so I stepped up to the door, put a cheery smile on my face and knocked.

A man wearing a maroon jumper and white, linen trousers with knife-edge creases answered the door.

"Is Jenny in?"

"There's no Jenny here, luv. You've got the wrong house."

"Oh, I'm so sorry. I must have written the address down wrong."

"What address are you looking for?"

What address, indeed?

"Don't worry; I'll just call her."

"What's your friend's surname? We know most of the people on this street."

Again, the hard questions. He turned towards his companion. "David, do you know any Jenny that lives on this road?"

"Jill and Frank at number 57 have a Jenny, but she's eleven. What Jenny is she looking for?"

"No, really," I said, backing away. "I've taken up too much of your time already. Thank you for your efforts."

The mystery car had driven away as soon as the man had opened the door. I returned to my car, checking as much of the street as was visible from my vantage point. Whoever was tailing me had moved on. But had they parked down the street waiting to spot me leaving, or had they gone away, fooled into thinking I meant to stay there? I backed onto the road and drove into town, keeping an eye on my rear view mirror. There didn't seem to be anyone tailing me, so I drove home, pulling my car into the back yard so it couldn't be spotted from the road.

"Are you sure you want to park your car there?" Dee called from her back door. "If it rains, it will sink into the ground and you'll leave ruts. Those ruts will be a devil to get out, believe me; Nigel used to park his car in our garden at our first house, and it ruined the ground."

I stood next to my car holding my groceries feeling like an errant school child caught tracking mud into the classroom. "Sorry. It's just for tonight."

"Oh, is Stephen coming over? If there's not enough room in your drive for both of your cars he can park in ours."

Stephen? I had never called him back. It wasn't too late; I could tell him I didn't pick up my messages until after work. I could call him after dinner, after I calmed down.

"Um, thanks, but he's not coming over. At least not tonight. I have to go in now, the ice cream will melt."

Dee smiled in a self-congratulatory way. "Of course."

I packed my purchases away, changed into jeans and a jumper and pulled on a pair of pink fuzzy socks. I put on the telly for company and sat on the sofa wondering what to make for dinner. The jittering in my stomach was just about gone when my doorbell rang and my insides turned back into cold jelly.

I peered through the peephole. It was Stephen, wearing a leather coat and holding a takeout pizza and a bottle of white wine. It was hard to decide whether to admire his thoughtfulness or berate him for showing up uninvited when, for all he knew, I was in the shower getting ready for a night on the town. Then I thought it was time to get over myself and just take it at face value, along with the extra bonus of some company when I really needed it. I opened the door. "My, this is a welcome surprise."

I grabbed the pizza and closed the door. Then I counted to three and opened it again, figuring that was enough punishment for showing up unannounced. "Oh, and do come in."

He let out a nervous laugh and stepped into my home. "I hope you don't mind me dropping in like this, but I happened to be in the neighbourhood and thought you might enjoy some company."

It was a lie; a nice one, but a dangerous one. In truth I didn't live the sort of life that could accommodate people dropping in unannounced. For most people it would be merely rude, for me it was perilous. Still, I couldn't stop being grateful for the company. He and his bottle of wine followed me and the pizza into the kitchen. I put the pizza on plates while he hunted down some wine glasses and poured us each a generous portion.

"Cheers."

We clinked glasses and tucked in. Now that I felt safe I was ravenous; all the nervous energy I had built up found release in a three-cheese pizza.

"Is this your preferred topping," I asked, "or were you betting the odds."

He smiled. "I prefer ham and mushrooms, but I don't know what you like so I thought cheese would be safe."

"Good thought; for all you know I could be a vegetarian."

"But I saw you eat meat at Nigel and Dee's."

"I had the fish; that's a vegetable."

"But there was meat in the hors d'oeuvres.

"A polite vegetarian then, who doesn't like to pass judgment at other people's dinner parties."

"Never met one of those."

"I could be lactose intolerant, in which case this would have been a huge faux pas."

"True."

"I might even be a vegan."

"A non-judgmental vegan? I doubt it. Besides, if you were a vegan you'd be wearing sandals and lecturing me about my coat."

"Or I could be the type of person who doesn't like people coming over unannounced."

The mindless droning of the telly in the sitting room became the dominant sound. He looked shocked, but no more than I. The words had come out as if someone else had said them.

"Would you like me to leave," he asked.

"No. I'm sorry."

"If I'm intruding—"

"Stephen, I'm glad you're here, okay. But I have a busy life and you may have found yourself standing in my front garden holding a cold pizza and finding no one at home."

"You have other boyfriends?"

"I don't have *any* boyfriends, okay. I just had a frantic day and I want a nice, calm and peaceful evening. That's all."

"Are you saying you want me to stay, or go?"

"Please stay; but next time, please call."

We squared off, staring at each other, waiting to see who would blink first.

"I did call you," he said.

I blinked.

"I know. I'm sorry. I didn't return your call. I didn't get it until this evening. I was going to call after dinner."

"Then it's just as well I showed up when I did. Otherwise I'd have had to eat this pizza all by myself. And drink all this wine."

He tried a smile. I returned one. "Let's just say you had a good instinct and were brave enough to act on it. Can we leave it at that?"

We hadn't finished our pizza but the argument put us off the meal so we took our wine glasses and sat on the couch. He sat near me but not right next to me, keeping a respectful distance. I surfed through the channels, hoping for something riveting to watch.

"I brought a DVD," he said. "Would you like to watch it?"

I scrolled through some more channels. "Well, there doesn't seem to be anything on the telly."

He put his wine glass down and stood up. "It's in the car. I'll be right back."

He let himself out, leaving me alone on the sofa, surfing the wasteland that is freeview television. It felt comfortable, almost domestic. I surfed through more channels of mind numbing drivel and then saw Robin's face staring back at me. I sat forward and turned up the sound.

Robin stood next to a stern brunette newscaster on location at the scene of the crime. Behind them, The Pedaller's frontage had been boarded over with sheets of plywood with the painted message "business as usual" scrawled across them. In her trim blazer, the newscaster looked like a holiday-camp greeter transported to downtown Beirut. She talked straight into the camera, with Robin standing next to her, his arm in a sling, his eyes darting around in uncertainty.

"You can see behind me the destruction caused during the robbery. To my left is the damage caused by the police car."

The camera panned up the street, zooming in on the crumpled pay and display meter.

"And in front of me, those scars on the road provide evidence of the explosion that precipitated that crash."

More panning and zooming, this time to a faint burn mark on the tarmac.

Explosion? It was just a pop and a flash; that hardly constitutes an explosion.

"With me now is Robin Sanger, owner of The Pedaller, who was saved by Nadia, the mysterious crusader people are comparing to Wonder Woman and who police have dubbed the Keymer Court Bomber. Mr Sanger, can you tell us what happened?"

147

The camera centred on Robin who, I was pleased to see, wore a sport jacket and open collar shirt instead of his trademark Lycra bodysuit. If you get the opportunity to pimp your business on television, it's best to look like a businessman. He seemed fit enough after last night's adventure, despite the sling.

"I heard a crash about three in the morning and I went downstairs to confront the burglars."

"You were staying in your shop," the announcer prompted. "Because you were afraid of being robbed, isn't that right?"

"Yes. My brother and I have been taking turns sleeping in the storeroom over the shop. In case the robbers targeted us."

"And this was because you lacked confidence in the ability of the police to protect your business?"

"Yeah, I guess so. It just seemed a good thing to do."

"But the gang overwhelmed you, correct?"

"I was outnumbered."

"But this woman, Nadia, subdued all four of the robbers by herself? And I understand she administered first aid to you and one of the injured robbers, as well."

Robin shrugged, suppressing a wince of pain. This left hand moved towards his right shoulder, then dropped back to his side. "She had the advantage of surprise."

The newscaster stepped into the picture. "Nadia came from out of nowhere and thwarted the robbery. Do you have any idea how she knew you were being robbed?"

Robin put his free hand in his pocket and looked at his shoes. "No. I've never seen her before. She just . . . appeared."

His awkward lie caused a surge of affection in me, and I experienced a growing ache along with the realisation that visiting him again as Nadia would be too much of a risk to take.

"Who's that?"

I started, feeling a misplaced sense of guilt, as if Stephen had caught me in a compromising position. I pushed it aside. Neither was my boyfriend, and besides, Robin was interested in Nadia, not me. I looked up at Stephen. "No one. It's just a report on the robbery last night."

Stephen sat down, just a bit closer to me than before, his eyes on the television. "That's the guy the mad bomber saved? No wonder he needed a woman to fight his battles; he couldn't punch his way out of a paper sack."

"He looks pretty capable to me. And he held his own against the robbers before she showed up. He's got nothing to be ashamed of."

"Who said he did? And why are you defending him? Do you fancy him?"

"No, of course not. It's just that, the news said he was doing well enough on his own before she showed up."

"That's not what I heard. She swooped in and saved his bacon, that's what I heard."

I didn't press the issue. The newscaster came back into the frame and we both turned our attention to the telly.

"We're going live now to Trisha who is outside the hospital where Jazziah Halder, the robber who Nadia saved, is recuperating."

The scene shifted to another newscaster standing in a car park with what appeared to be the front entrance of a hospital some distance behind her. The bright lights washed out her complexion and drew the attention of people entering and leaving the hospital. She flashed white teeth at the camera. "Thanks Chris. Behind me you can see the hospital where Mr Halder is being held in a secure unit while he recuperates from his injuries. Doctors report he is in stable condition thanks to the quick thinking of the Sussex Superhero, who found time during her busy schedule of stopping robberies to perform an emergency tracheotomy after a blow to the throat closed off Mr Halder's air passage."

The newscaster paused to consult a piece of paper in her hand, then looked back at the camera. "Mr Halder has asked reporters to convey his sincere thanks to the mysterious woman and credits her with saving his life. He has further pledged to devote his life to keeping young people from choosing a life of crime."

"Would you like to see the movie, or are we going to watch the news all night?"

"Sorry, I got caught up in the story. I think that's sweet."

"What's sweet?"

"That he thanked the woman. It seems a nice gesture."

I sorted through the forest of remote controls looking for the one that turned on the DVD player.

"Yeah, but how sincere is that? He's a thug, for God's sake."

I found a remote that looked promising and pressed the big red button. The DVD player came to life. "Yes, but you didn't see his eyes."

I was halfway to the entertainment centre, glad he couldn't see my face.

"How could you see his eyes? He's in hospital. No one has seen him."

"There was a photo in one of the papers today. I saw it at work. I don't know which one it was."

The movie previews began to play and Stephen picked up the remote, claiming his rightful role as the man in the relationship. That seemed to distract him. When I returned to the sofa his attention was on the screen, his fingers punching buttons. I sat down, shaving another slice from the gap between us.

The movie was a light comedy, something with Hugh Grant, a good choice for a budding relationship with no scenes in it that would leave us cringing with embarrassment. Half an hour into the movie—without making any overt movements—our sides, thighs and knees were touching. He put his arm around me and I leaned against him, feeling his warmth. After a while I felt his lips brushing my neck. It was an unusual, but nice, sensation; gentle, soothing. When he began to kiss my ear a shiver ran down my back and nestled in my crotch. I turned my face towards him and let him kiss me, not minding when his tongue invaded my mouth. He put his other arm around me and drew me closer and I felt the warmth in my crotch begin to spread.

When the doorbell rang, we both groaned our disappointment.

"I'll just go see who it is," I said.

His hand held on to my arm, sliding down to my hand and slipping off the tips of my fingers as I got up and walked towards the door.

It was Dee, holding a cricket bat. "Rachel, I'm so glad you're all right."

"Why shouldn't I be?"

"There's a madman loose in the neighbourhood. He broke into David and Jeremy's house on Gander Hill. They had to fight him off with a putter."

I looked at her, trying to comprehend what she was talking about. "A putter?"

"Yes, you know, a golf club. The man was raving and began assaulting Jeremy. Fortunately, David is a keen golfer and had a putter handy."

"Have they called the police?"

"Yes, but the man is still at large. He's prowling around here somewhere; you need to protect yourself."

She held out the cricket bat. "I brought you this. You can use it if he breaks in."

"That's very nice, but I'm fine."

"Thank God."

She tried to peer around me. "I thought I heard someone go into your house."

"Yes, Stephen's here. We're watching a movie."

She beamed. "Why, that's wonderful. I'm so glad. And now you have someone to protect you."

"Pardon?"

"With a man in your life, you've got someone to watch out for you."

"He's not in my life; he's in my sitting room. And he's leaving after the movie is finished."

"Oh."

In truth, the idea of getting back to where we had left off and seeing where it led was what I'd had in mind, but I didn't like the implication that I couldn't take care of myself. "Are you suggesting that I should let him sleep with me in exchange for keeping me safe? "

Dee sighed. "You're making it sound like prostitution. It's just what a relationship is, a give and take for mutual benefit."

"Hell-o? Is that Dee?"

Stephen came up behind me and wrapped his arms around my waist. "I was wondering who was keeping you so long."

"I was just leaving," said Dee.

"And so is Stephen," I said.

Stephen pulled away as if he'd been stung. "What? Why?"

"I'm sorry, but you need to go."

"But the movie."

"I'll return it when I see you. Our race date is still on for tomorrow, right?"

"Yes, but I still don't understand—"

"You don't need to understand, you just need to leave."

Sulking, he went to retrieve his jacket. I turned to Dee, who was, for once, rendered speechless.

"No one's getting any benefits tonight. And thanks for this."

I took the bat.

"I'm sorry. I don't understand, but I'm sorry."

She went back to her house as Stephen came out, his brow furrowed, his hands shoved deep into his pockets. He pulled back when I tried to kiss him. "I'm really sorry about this. I'll see you tomorrow."

He left without a word, wheels spinning as he pulled onto the road and sped away leaving me alone in the night with an angry drug dealer after me. As the solitude encircled me like a cold fist, I began to wonder if I had made a mistake. Would it have been so bad letting him stay? With a clearer head and a cooler crotch I admitted I had made the right choice; I wasn't ready to open that particular door, not tonight, not with Stephen, and certainly not in trade for security services.

Wonder Woman might have the lasso of truth, the sandals of Hermes and the gauntlets of Atlas, but I had the cricket bat of justice. I went inside to protect my fortress.

Chapter 20

I WOKE TO MY alarm feeling haggard after a night of jumping at every bump and creak. The weather had turned colder overnight which made my morning run more invigorating; a welcome change, as I needed to clear my head. I resisted the urge to alter my route to take me past David and Jeremy's. Nothing would be gained by it and Keith might still be lurking in that area. It was his last link to me, where the trail went cold, and he might lack the imagination to do anything else but sit there and wait and hope I turned up. I decided I wouldn't oblige him.

After my run, conscious that my night time activates had been interfering with my exercise regimen and that I had a race with Stephen scheduled for the afternoon, I pushed the coffee table aside so I could exercise in the sitting room in front of the telly. I never exercise with the telly on—the mindless babble of talking heads tends to throw off my timing—but I wanted to see if the assault got a mention. Confirmation that the cops had made an arrest and that Keith was behind bars was too much to hope for, but sooner or later a break was bound to come my way.

When I clicked the remote, instead of the news, the movie appeared, picking up where it had left off the previous evening. I wasn't sure if I felt a pang of guilt or just a simple longing for normalcy as I pushed the eject button. I set the channel to the national news, expecting they would filter down to local happenings at some point, and started my routine.

When nothing of interest appeared, I tuned it out, concentrating on my squat thrusts. Then a police sketch of Nadia appeared on the screen, stopping me in mid-thrust.

It wasn't a perfect likeness, but it was close enough. Too close; the curly black hair, the shape of the face, the eyes, the make-up, all Nadia. The voice-over confirmed it was a sketch of Nadia compiled by police artists from descriptions provided by a number of witnesses. I hoped this was a segment from the local news, but when the camera cut away from the picture and returned to the show's hosts, a brunette with a pixie haircut and a white-haired man in a grey suit reviewed the full list of Nadia sightings for the benefit of the national audience. Then they replayed the clips from the previous night, giving Robin a

153

chance to fidget in front of the entire country. I hoped the interview threw some business his way; at least then he might believe some good came out of meeting Nadia.

The hospital interview had been updated, giving the latest condition of Halder and a reiteration of his pledge to reform. Then the hosts engaged in some light-hearted banter, speculating on where Nadia might strike next and asking the viewers if they thought she was a menace or a miracle, which I considered an upgrade from "menace or maniac." They had even set up a discussion forum; just log on and join the debate. And a lot of people were; Pixie gleefully read out a sample:

"Julie from Leeds wrote, 'Nadia is an inspiration. We should all learn from her example. Way to go, girl.'"

"Here's one from William in East Sussex," the suit said. "'Has everyone forgotten that this lady's first appearance involved a terrorist attack on a block of flats? That she has not killed anyone yet is the miracle. The cops need to lock her up so she, and the rest of us, will be safe.'"

"A rather harsh assessment of someone credited with saving two lives so far," Pixie said. "And one last one from Richard and Patty in Devon, who have started a Nadia fan club. 'We need to get behind Nadia. She's a one of a kind, and the cops only want to arrest her because they're jealous. Join our Nadia Now fan club to show your support.'"

"Well, good luck with that, you two," the suit said. "And now over to Mandy in Kent, where a local businessman has come up with some unique ways of dealing with the financial crisis."

I slumped onto the sofa, my routine forgotten, feeling like I was going to wet myself. There was no denying it; Nadia was famous. And with that sort of spotlight on her, it was only a matter of time before someone got to her, and to me. The question was, who? The cops, Keith, Sawyer or even an over-enthusiastic fan? After that, nothing mattered. The media would take over, I would be paraded in front of the nation again; a freak, and this time, a criminal, as well.

I turned off the telly and took a long bath, the cricket bat on the floor within easy reach even though I doubted anyone was going to break in. And if they did, the sight of a naked woman coming at them with a cricket bat should be enough to put them off.

By the time I returned to the kitchen in my robe and slippers, I had a plan: call in sick.

I had some tea and yogurt for breakfast and waited until I knew Martin would be in before calling. Somehow, calling in sick while you're in your robe makes it easier than if you're all dressed and made up and ready to go out. I did the requisite croaky voice and Martin responded with appropriate sympathy and well wishes. I hung up, too depressed to feel guilty. I thought of turning Nadia's phone on but decided that wasn't something I could face until I was dressed.

Ten minutes later, fortified by a pair of jeans and a jumper, I turned on the phone and found no messages. That, at least, was a good sign, but perhaps Keith was too busy dodging the cops last night to check in. I half expected my fan club to have the number by now, and I began to wonder if Nadia's escapades had become embarrassing enough for the police department to authorise the MI5 to triangulate her mobile signal as a way to track her down. I expected that might be a bit overboard, even for them, but I was debating switching it off just to be safe when it rang, startling me so that I nearly dropped it.

I looked around the kitchen as if someone might be watching me, then I pressed the answer button.

"Nadia?"

It was Alex.

"Nadia, I know you're there, please don't hang up. I want to help you. You need to talk to me."

I held the phone away from my ear, looking at it while listening to the squawk coming from the speaker, wishing I could say something, ask her to meet me for tea and croissants, or pizza and bottle of Pinot Grigio. Or even get angry with her, tell her how I felt about her lying to me, trying to get me to give Nadia up. Instead I cut her off, feeling lonely and disloyal. I turned off the phone and thought about making a plan. But Paul took over. "If you don't have a plan," his voice said, "how will you know if you're making progress?"

I'd made good progress without one, so far. Just not the sort of progress I was looking for. In truth, I couldn't think of any way out. The police were out for Nadia's blood, as were Sawyer and Keith. It mattered little who got to her first, the result would be the same: exposure, incarceration and a public pillory.

If I turned myself in it might go easier on me, especially now that I had a fan base, but the media wouldn't allow anything so subdued. They wouldn't have to dig hard to come up with the rest of the story, my life would be laid out for everyone to see again, the geek turned beauty queen, the ugly duckling, the freak. My family would see, Paul would see, the nation would gawp and laugh and, once exposed, I would have no place to hide.

I needed to stop thinking about it or I would drive myself crazy. There had to be something constructive I could do. Quit my job, maybe. Sell the house and move to East Anglia before they caught up with me. It had appeal, but it would take time and I had no idea how close were they getting or how much time I had left.

After lunch I turned on the phone. Another message from Alex and ominous silence from the boys. At one o'clock I returned the cricket bat to Dee and spent an hour exchanging apologies for the night before and explaining why I wasn't at work.

At three o'clock, my phone rang. I looked at the number. It was Stephen. "We're still on for after work, right?"

He sounded like he had recovered from last night's disappointment and, in truth, it was good to hear a friendly voice. Getting out of the house wouldn't do me any harm, either. "Sure."

"Can I meet you at the Holiday Depot after work? I could drive you home so you could change and we could go to the race course together."

That was going to be a bit awkward, and I didn't want him asking too many questions. I thought for a moment. "And where are you going to change?"

"I have all my gear with me and there's a shower here at work. I often take a run during lunch. That's the course we're going to race tonight. Or, I could change at your place."

Um. Yes, I'm sure he would like that.

"Why don't I meet you there; I have some errands to run after work."

He hesitated. I could practically hear his plans derailing. "Okay, I guess. Meet me in the main car park at Horsham Park. I'll be there about half five."

The rest of the day I spent hoovering, dusting and doing laundry. If the news crews did end up in my house, I wanted it to be clean.

At half four I put on my running outfit—a loose but opaque tee shirt over a jogging bra and a pair of silk running shorts. I put a track suit over this, wore an old pair of trainers and tucked my running shoes, towel and both phones into my gym bag.

I arrived in Horsham at quarter past five and parked in a dark corner of the car park, wondering how much of an advantage Stephen was enjoying by running on his home turf. At the far end of the car park, the gaudy lights of the bowling alley and Horsham's after hours club were glowing as they began gearing up for business. I took advantage of the time and turned on Nadia's phone. Nothing. No messages from Alex and continued silence from Sawyer and company, which was somehow more ominous than the threats.

A tap on my window made me yelp. I dropped the phone into the bag as if I'd been caught behind the playground fence sneaking a fag, and turned to see Stephen in a blue jersey with a wide stripe running across the front like a sash. His shorts matched his top. I lowered the window.

"Caught you."

His breath clouded, gooseflesh covered his arms. I wondered how long he had been watching. "You startled me."

I got out and kissed him. "Let's move. It's cold."

We walked to the top of a grassy rise at the edge of the car park. To our right, a paved footpath disappeared into the dimness of the park. Across the vast expanse sat the leisure centre, and midway a street lamp lit an area where several paved paths converged.

"We'll run to that light," he said. "There's a pond in the centre of the park. Run around that, past the tree at the end and then back towards the car park."

He started doing some warm up exercises. I took off the track suit, laying my glasses on top, and joined him, bending and stretching and warming my muscles. After a while we stood side by side, ready to go.

"Once around. First one back to the top of this rise wins."

"Fine by me,"

I began to settle into position.

"Ready, steady, GO."

He was off before I realised the race had started. I abandoned my preparations and raced after him, pumping my legs as fast as I could. I needed to catch up to him and match his pace but he was too far ahead. I wasn't keeping to my usual rhythm and my lungs began to burn before I reached the street lamp. I could see him in front of me, then he disappeared behind the bushes that surrounded the pond. I followed, determined to pass him, but the far side of the pond was in darkness, and he had the advantage of knowing the terrain. I gave up trying to close the gap and concentrated on keeping up with him and not falling over something in the dark. As we approached the lone tree that marked the end of the pond, he turned the corner too sharp and

157

slipped. He was up in a second. The gap closed by a few feet and he widened it by cutting in front of the tree.

Ignoring the burning in my lungs and the ache in my legs I pushed myself forward. I made the tree and did not cut in front of it. Now he was fifteen feet ahead, but it was a straight run to the finish line and it was well lit. I allowed myself to feel anger at his cheating; my legs pumped harder, determined.

The gap closed slowly but consistently. He was either allowing me to catch up, or was reaching the end of his endurance. He didn't strike me as the type to do anything but thrash an opponent as hard as he could, so I assumed the latter. He heard me gaining and gave himself a boost. I matched it, straining and pumping, reaching beyond the pain. The gap between us narrowed. With the finish in sight I was a foot behind him. I reached deep, pulling up the dregs of my energy. In a final burst, I drove myself forward, up the grassy incline, diving onto the summit a split second ahead of him.

We collapsed into a heap in the grass, laughing and panting on the cold ground.

"I won," he said.

"Did not; I came in an inch ahead of you."

"No. I had my hand out. I broke the line before you."

"What line? I don't see any line here."

He sat up and wrapped his arms on his knees, panting but no longer laughing. "The finish line was the top of this rise; I got here first. Are you saying I didn't?"

"Okay," I said, sitting up next to him. "We'll call it a draw."

His smile returned. "Call it what you want, but I still won."

I put on my glasses, picked up my track suit and we walked back to the car park. The cold air felt good on my skin and in my lungs, but by the time we reached my car, we were both shivering. I started the car, turned up the heater and moved the bag into the back, allowing Stephen to sit in the passenger seat to warm up.

For a while we just sat there, our breath clouding the interior, fogging the windows. When our breathing eased and the heat in the car rose, Stephen put a hand on my shoulder, drew me over and kissed me. I scooted as close as I could with the gearstick in the way and returned the favour. We kissed deep and long and when we parted I could see the fabric of his shorts rising into a blue tent.

"We should go," he said. "The car park will be filling up soon, and by the look of the steam on these windows they will assume we're up to something."

I sat up behind the steering wheel, unsure of what to do next.

"Would you like to come over to my place?" he asked. "I could make us dinner."

The blower from the heater wafted the aroma of my sweat-soaked outfit into my nostrils. "I'm not exactly dressed for dinner."

"We'll drop by your place. You can shower and change and leave your car there."

It seemed a sensible, safe and normal thing to do. And having Stephen following me would give me an excuse to pull my car into the back garden again without Dee tsking at me. "Sure."

He opened the door and a beeping sound made him pause. "What's that? Did I set off an alarm?"

"No, it's my phone. Sounds like I have a text message."

My phone was off, so the message was for Nadia. I waited but he made no move. "Aren't you going to check it?"

I reached into my bag and found Nadia's phone. As usual, there was no sender listed, just a brief message saying, "How do you like this?" and an attached photo. I pressed the button to download it.

"Trouble?"

I looked up and smiled. If he would just leave this would be a lot easier. "No, just a message from—"

I stopped as the photo came into view. It was a street scene, a darkened place I didn't recognise, but the man lying in a crumpled heap on the pavement I did. Even with his clothing ripped and bloodied and his face bruised I knew it was Robin. I felt my jaw wanting to drop. I held firm and looked at Stephen. "I'm sorry. I need to go."

He shook his head and folded his arms. "You know, you're making a habit of this."

"I'm sorry, it's a family emergency."

He looked unconvinced. "Or maybe you're running off to see someone else."

I suppressed a blush. I was, but that wasn't the point. "I'll make it up to you, I promise. But I can't . . . I have to be somewhere else tonight."

He got out and slammed the door. Politeness dictated that I wait until he got into his car and started it before I left, but this was no time for politeness, and I didn't feel he deserved much anyway. I put the car in gear and roared out of the car park.

Chapter 21

A S I DROVE OUT of Horsham I checked to see that I wasn't being followed, by Sawyer, Keith or Stephen. When I was certain I was in the clear, I pulled onto a side street and went through my handbag looking for Robin's card. No one would be answering the shop's phone at this time of day, but there was a mobile number as well. I dialled it and prayed someone would pick up.

"Hell-o"

It wasn't Robin. Had Sawyer taken his phone? If so, I wouldn't be giving anything away by talking to him. "This is Nadia," I said.

There was a brief silence.

"Don't you think you've done enough? Ever since you came into our shop we've had nothing but bad luck. And it's always attached to you."

"Malcolm?"

"Can't you just go away and leave us alone?"

"Malcolm, please, I've got to see him."

Until I uttered the words, I didn't know how true they were. My gut ached with guilt and the need to, if not put it right, at least ask forgiveness.

"That's not going to happen."

"Why not?"

A sigh from the other end of the phone. "He sent a message to me. He told me to keep you away."

It felt like someone had kicked me in the stomach. Everything had gone too far. Even Robin wanted me to stay away. Then I had a thought. "Was that the entire message?"

"That was the gist of it."

"Tell me the exact message."

Silence again as he debated with himself. "He said to keep you away, it would be too dangerous for you to see him."

The bands around my chest loosened; it wasn't a rejection, it was a warning. "Malcolm, I won't lie to you, it will be dangerous, but mostly for me. I need to see him. Please."

"I suppose I can't stop you. He's in East Surrey hospital. I'll warn him."

"Are you going to see him?"

"Of course, I'm leaving as soon as my sister gets here."

My mind whirled, grabbing at the first idea that came into reach. "What about your sister's boyfriend?"

"She doesn't have a boyfriend."

"She does now."

"What are you on about?"

"Wait for me. Please?"

A pause and a sigh. "All right."

I hung up and headed for The Citadel.

The booming of artillery fire and showers of coloured sparks greeted me as I parked the Escort and began to search for Malcolm's flat. The first explosion startled me, then I realised it was the fifth of November, Guy Fawkes Day; people would be out celebrating, setting off fireworks, lighting bonfires and engaging in controlled mayhem. That might work to my advantage; if I blew anything up, it would just blend in.

I had dressed in jeans and was wearing a tee shirt under my jacket. No Microprene suit tonight. My black curls were hidden under a knitted cap and I had traded in my heels for a pair of anonymous trainers with lifts in them. I wouldn't draw attention dressed like this, but I still kept my head down as I hurried across the tarmac, checking the numbers on the buildings. Malcolm lived on an estate in the west of Crawley so it hadn't taken long to get there from The Citadel. Still, every second was accompanied by the conviction that he had reconsidered his promise and had left without me. But there was nothing I could do about that; he would wait, or he would not. When I found Malcolm's block, I was relieved to find the lights on and two figures looking out the front window of the first floor flat I assumed to be his. I waved and jogged up the walk.

"We have to get going," Malcolm said, as he opened the door. "Visiting hours have already started."

I pushed past him into the small sitting room. "Sorry, but I'm not ready yet."

The flat looked like a college dorm cleaned by well-trained baboons. The furniture was spartan, the curtains were mismatched and the entertainment centre was new. Bike parts were strewn about on every available flat surface. I didn't know if he had a flatmate, but there was no girlfriend in the mix; no woman would live in this sort of clutter.

There was a woman standing in front of me who I assumed to be the sister. She was my height but made taller by the knee-high leather boots and tricorne hat. In between she was decked out as a military officer of dubious origin, complete with tunic and a sabre. I noted with some relief that the sword was plastic. She had made no effort to hide her mouse brown hair and it hung to her shoulders, covering her epaulettes. She placed her hands on her hips, assessing me. I assessed her back; she struck me as the type of woman who would insist on matching curtains. I held out my hand. "I'm Nadia"

"Christine," she said, shaking my hand. "And I'm pleased to meet you."

She opened her tunic, revealing an "I'm Nadia" button pinned to her blouse. "I bought this on Monday, before Robin even told me about you."

So Robin had shared our secret; was that because of my growing celebrity or because he felt I was worth knowing? And if he told her, who else knew? I felt the old insecurities flooding back, second guessing the motives of the people around me.

"Don't worry," Christine said, filling the silence. "You're safe with us. I admire what you're doing, Robin is smitten, and little brother won't dare spill the beans if he knows what's good for him."

Smitten?

I felt Malcolm's presence behind me. "You don't look like Nadia," he said.

I turned to him. He was dressed in loose white jeans and a baggy white jumper with horizontal black stripes. A red bandana circled his neck.

"You don't look like the bloke from the bike shop, either,"

I cast my gaze at his crotch then back to his eyes and smiled as he blushed. Christine stifled a laugh, Malcolm cleared his throat. "We're members of the Eastern Brigade Bonfire Society, and we have a bonfire ceremony to get to after we visit Robin, so can we go now?"

"Not yet." I stood next to him. He was just a little taller than me. "Can I borrow one of your outfits? A normal one; I don't want to look like a smuggler."

Malcolm just stood there, dumbfounded; Christine took my arm. "Come with me. You're my boyfriend; I'll fix you up."

She brought me to a cramped bedroom; at least I assumed there was a bed under the heap of discarded clothes. There was no wardrobe, just a rack in the corner with a hotchpotch of biking outfits, button down shirts, jeans and a single charcoal suit hanging from it. We found a pair of chinos, oxford cloth shirt and a corduroy sport jacket in the pile. The result said, "smart casual," but a smart casual that had slept in a doorway. I

162

hid the rest of my hair under my knitted hat and wiped off my make-up. Then we studied the result in the full-length mirror hanging on the back of the door, locking arms as if we were a typical couple out for a Sunday stroll.

"Do you think I'll pass?"

"I don't know. You look sort of delicate. We need to rough you up a bit."

She got her handbag and produced a bottle of foundation. "This will darken you up. From a distance no one will know its make-up. And if I play my part right, they'll be looking at me, not you."

She undid a few buttons on her blouse and pushed her breasts up, then used a cotton ball to dab the make-up over my face and neck. We resumed our positions. I looked like I had fallen asleep in a tanning booth.

"What do you think?" I asked.

Christine remained silent.

"Well?"

"I think this must be how a man feels when his wife asks, 'Do I look fat in this?'"

"That bad, huh?"

"The hat looks ridiculous, and I can still see your boobs."

She rummaged through the piles of clothes and came up with another black and white striped jumper. I pulled it on over the shirt and jacket and we resumed our positions.

"I think that will work," she said. "For tonight, at least, that outfit will blend in a lot better than the smart look. And it doesn't matter because we don't have time to fix it."

She gazed again at the unlikely couple in the mirror and undid another button on her blouse.

Back in the sitting room, Malcolm was standing at the door, waiting. "You don't look much like a man," he said as I walked by. He wrinkled his nose. "But at least you smell like one."

We crammed into Malcolm's Citroën C3 with me in the back. I used the time to smooth out the darker blotches of make-up using my finger as an applicator and the darkened window as a mirror. In the hospital car park, Malcolm pulled into a shadowy area between the lights.

"It's show time," Christine said.

We formed up with Christine and me in front and Malcolm following close behind. With explosions and flashes going off in the distance, we walked arm in arm, Christine with her shoulders back, leading with her breasts and me beside her, doing my best to become invisible. It wasn't difficult; I just pretended I was back at university. By the time we reached the crossing, I was in my role. I kept my head down but scanned the area for potential danger. Derek was loitering outside the entrance, mingling with the pack of smokers who were supposed to be enjoying their habit out in the car park. He didn't glance our way as we walked by, not even to check out Christine's hooters.

The glass doors slid open, emitting a warm gush of air carrying with it the unmistakable scent of hospital, a mixture of medicine, cleaning fluid and despair. The three of us entered the lobby.

"Wait here," Christine said.

Malcolm and I lagged behind while she went to the desk. I scanned the room. Carl was sitting in a cluster of chairs near the potted ferns at the far corner of the lobby. It may have been wishful thinking, but it he looked like he had a black eye. I hoped that meant Robin got in a few good shots. Lounging against the wall near the entrance to the wards, reading *The Daily News*, was Sawyer. Carl had a newspaper, as well, but he was playing Sudoku while Sawyer watched the room. His eyes didn't linger on us; he gazed around, checking the entrance, the waiting area, the reception desk, and finally held his paper aside to check his watch. They'd pulled out all the stops; all we needed were the cops and Keith and we'd have quorum for the inaugural meeting of the Nadia Penric Appreciation Society.

As if on cue, two Surrey PCs walked out of the corridor, right past Sawyer. Maybe they were there on general business, or to get a statement from Robin, or perhaps they had noticed the connection between Robin and Nadia and were hoping to strike lucky. If so, they had failed to notice the connection between the assaulted man in the ward and the people gathered in the lobby who had assaulted him. No, that would be too clever. They took up a position in the middle of the lobby, standing at ease, the younger one trying to emulate the stern countenance of his partner.

"I'm here to see Robin Sanger," Christine said to the receptionist.

This drew the attention of Carl and Sawyer.

"He's on Brockham ward," the woman said, "but you can't go in there wearing that sword."

This drew the attention of the police.

Christine stood back and put her hands on her hips. "It's plastic. It can't hurt anyone."

The receptionist bristled. "A hospital is no place for a weapon. I don't care if it's made of Swiss cheese."

The cops moved forward and Carl and Sawyer came closer, studying Christine.

"Those are the men who are after me," I whispered to Malcolm.

"Are they the ones who attacked Robin?"

I took his arm. "Yes."

He stiffened and tried to pull away. I held tight. "Now is not the time."

Derek walked by and glanced our way before joining Sawyer and Carl. I suppressed a shiver.

"Then what am I supposed to do?" Christine asked, her voice rising. "I came all the way up here to see him and now, because I'm carrying a bit of plastic, you're telling me I can't?"

I manoeuvred Malcolm away from the desk. All of them—the police, Sawyer, Carl, Derek—had their backs to us. "Come on."

I pulled Malcolm with me across the lobby towards the corridor.

"What about Chris?"

"She knows what she's doing. Now move."

We walked into the hallway, Malcolm looking at signs and leading the way as if he knew where he was going. We only had to backtrack once before we came to the ward.

There were eight beds, some of them surrounded by privacy curtains, none of them empty. The nurse at the desk directed us to the third bed on the left, one with the curtains drawn.

Malcolm moved ahead, reaching the bed first. I could hear him making sympathetic noises as I approached. Then I heard Robin's voice. "What, no flowers? You come all the way up here and you can't even bother to stop in a petrol station to get me some flowers."

His good humour was intact, but his voice was raspy. I waited, wondering how long I should give Malcolm when Christine came up behind me. "The cops made me leave my sword at the desk," she said.

"Thanks. That was brave."

She smiled. "No, it was fun. I even have problems walking into pubs with it sometimes, so I expected they'd give me attitude about it. Come on."

She pulled the curtain aside. Robin was lying down, his head propped up by three pillows. The bandage around his head and the large plaster on his right cheek hid most of his face. The parts that showed were bruised and puffy, the bruises turning a shade of purple tinged with yellow. His arm was strapped to his chest in a tight sling, his knuckles scraped and discoloured by disinfectant. When he saw us, he smiled. "Chris. And . . . " He narrowed his eyes and gazed at me. "Oh my God."

He looked at Malcolm. "I told you not—"

I held a finger to my lips. "It's not his fault. I insisted."

"Oh, you insisted, and Malcolm couldn't just stop—"

I leaned over him. "They're everywhere," I said, keeping my voice low. "The men who assaulted you, the police, the people looking for me, all of them. Do you want to turn me in now or are you going to deal with the fact that I came because I had to, and none of them, or Malcolm or you were going to stop me."

I backed away, my arms folded over my chest.

"Mum said she would come down tomorrow to see you," Malcolm said, filling the awkward silence.

"Tell her not to bother. I'm only here for observation. They're releasing me in the morning."

Christine held his left hand and stroked his shoulder. "Are you sure you're going to be all right?"

"It's just some bruises; I've had worse falling off my bike."

"But what about next time? Or the time after that?"

He shook his head. "There won't be a next time. The robbery was a fluke, and the men who assaulted me, well, they—"

"They're after me," I said. "And once they know they can't get me this way, they'll leave him alone."

Christine turned towards me. "You mean they'll go after someone else."

"I don't know. I never meant it to come to this. I don't know why they're after me, why they would do this. I'm so sorry I got you involved, I'm sorry you got hurt."

I stopped and put my hands over my face; I couldn't afford to cry, it would streak my make-up.

I felt Christine's hand on my arm. "Maybe the police are right about you; maybe you are a menace, even without meaning to be. I can't say for sure; you seem like a nice person, but you're a rubbish superhero."

That stopped the threat of tears, but I kept my hands in place to hide the hurt and anger I knew was showing on my face. I took a few deep breaths. "I'll make it right," I said, looking from Christine to Malcolm. "I don't know how, but I swear to you, I will make it right."

Christine smirked. "Now you're talking like a superhero. But if would sound more authentic if you said something like, 'By Thor's Hammer, I will make them rue the day they raised their hand against the mighty Nadia.'"

Robin gasped and wrapped his free arm around his abdomen. "Please, Chris, don't make me laugh."

"Come on, little brother," Christine said, taking Malcolm by the arm. "Let's give these two a moment."

She guided Malcolm away from the bedside, drawing the curtain as they left.

"They did this to you," I said when we were alone. "Those men who chased me into your shop."

He raised himself into a sitting position, grimacing as he pulled against the headboard. I bent over to help but wasn't sure where I could touch him that wouldn't cause more pain.

"I can't say for sure. They were wearing balaclavas. Jumped me as I was locking up and pulled me around the back. There were two of them. But I got in a few punches before they had me on the ground."

He stopped for a rest. I adjusted his pillows and pulled the thin hospital blanket up so it wouldn't leave him exposed in his equally thin hospital gown.

"One of them held me, the short fat one, and the tall one did all the work." He pointed to his face. "Mean bastard, that one. I got the feeling he was enjoying himself. He wanted to keep going but Shorty called him off. Said something like, 'That's enough. We want her to visit him in the hospital, not the morgue.'"

"I'm sorry. No, I'm beyond sorry. This is not how it was supposed to be."

"It's not all bad; if I had known this was all it took to make you come see me again, I would have done it earlier."

I smiled, leaning towards him. "Why would you want to see me again? I bring nothing but trouble."

He leaned closer. "Let's just say I'm intrigued by the mystery."

His lips were swollen. I wondered if kissing them would cause him much pain.

"How did you find out?" he asked.

"They took a photo of you, after they beat you up; they sent it to me in a text."

"On your phone?"

"Yes."

He pulled back, sitting straight, his puffy eyes narrowing. "The bad guys have your number, but I don't?"

I stood up and sighed. "I can't just hand it out willy-nilly. I'm incognito."

"So now I'm just some willy-nilly?"

167

"No, but I'm not supposed to be contactable. It's bad enough the cops have it without—"

"The cops. What did you do, post it on the community centre bulletin board?"

He lifted his left hand, then let it fall on the bed. If he could have crossed his arms, he would have. Instead, he stared ahead in silence.

"I thought you liked the mystery."

He turned in my direction, silently appraising me. "That's a different look for you. I like it."

"Are you trying to tell me something?"

He grinned. "No. But without all that hair and eye shadow, you're really pretty."

"If that's your idea of an apology, I accept."

He looked at me in mock surprise. "Apology? What do I have to apologise for?"

"For being so shirty when you don't get your way."

I leaned down and put my lips close to his ear. "How good is your memory?" I whispered.

"Pretty good. Especially when someone tells me something important."

I whispered my mobile number to him, then turned his head and touched my lips to his swollen mouth.

"If that's your idea of an apology, I accept."

"Apology? What do I have to apologise for?"

He pressed his lips against mine. "You'd better go," he said. "I don't want to give people the wrong impression about my brother's mate."

"Actually, I'm supposed to be Christine's date."

"Then you'd really better go; I don't want to be found snogging my sister's boyfriend."

I ran my fingers over his bandaged arm. "Take care."

"What are you going to do," he asked as I pushed the curtains aside.

"I don't know. But I will make it right, I swear."

"Let me help you. We could make a great team."

"I don't know. How would it look if The Sussex Superhero had a side-kick named Robin?"

I waited in the corridor while Christine and Malcolm finished their visit, then we walked to the car together. In the lobby, Carl and Derek were still in position, as were the two PCs, but Sawyer was gone. I guessed that the time he'd been checking his watch for had arrived, necessitating his presence somewhere else. I thought a good plan would be to follow him to wherever that was.

We made it to the car without anyone coming out after us and we all felt a palpable sense of relief as we pulled onto the main road.

With the visit out of the way, Christine and Malcolm were all business, discussing how they were to get to where they needed to be to catch up with their bonfire buddies. I worked on the foundation make-up and had most of it off by the time Malcolm pulled into the car park and stopped by my car. "We'll drop you here, there's no time to go inside."

"What about your clothes?"

"Bring them around to the shop next time you decide to visit some mayhem on us."

"Be careful," said Christine.

I got out and they were away before I even got into my car, leaving me standing in the car park wearing men's clothes and a striped jumper. Inside my car I pulled off the jumper and made do with the rumpled preppie look. My jeans and blouse were still in Malcolm's flat but that wasn't a concern; getting out of this mess, and getting Robin out of danger, was my only concern. My handbag was where I had left it, hidden under the passenger's seat. I wouldn't need everything that was in it, just my credit cards; I slipped my card holder into the inside pocket of the blazer and stuffed my handbag back under the seat.

Sawyer was the key. It was almost a certainty that he was leaving on his business trip tonight, and I needed to go with him. The trick was finding out where he was going, but I knew just how to do that.

I drove back to Horsham, parked in a residential area and walked to Black Horse Way, the narrow street that ran behind the Holiday Depot. There was a delivery bay in the back for when the shop used be a clothing outlet. The bay doors were gone, replaced with a standard metal door. Next to the door was the window leading into the server room.

It wasn't late and the celebrations were still gearing up, with flashes and popping going off one after the other, and there were more than the usual number of people on the streets. That was good; it provided cover, but Black Horse Way, not being in the pedestrian area, remained quiet and deserted. Even so, I kept to the shadows, wishing I was wearing something darker than the tan corduroy jacket.

I checked the window. It was held closed with two simple latches at the bottom. I used my Nectar card to test the gap and forced it through the crack, slipping one of the latches. The card snapped, but the latch came free. I dredged through the wallet, searching for another expendable card. My Pasties Plus loyalty card seemed a good choice; it was more flexible than the Nectar card, better for slipping a lock and I wondered if they might make that a selling point. I managed to bend it into the crack and slip the next latch, ruining the card in the process. The window swung out. I tested it by raising it a few inches. No alarm. I buttoned Malcolm's jacket so nothing would catch on the window frame, took a quick look around and slipped inside.

The window swung shut behind me and I crouched in the dark waiting for my eyes to adjust. I moved across the small room and opened the door to the main office; it was silent, lit by slices of ambient light from the street lamps leaking in between the posters covering the plate glass shop front. Satisfied that I was alone, I eased the door closed and went to the server. The server itself was never turned off so all I had to do was flick on the monitor. The screen glowed like a spotlight; no one was going to see it but I worked quickly just in case.

I bypassed the login and searched through the database for the previous day's transactions. There was nothing for Sawyer. I searched again and still found nothing. I was beginning to wonder if he had booked under a pseudonym when I noticed there were other transactions missing, and they were all Amanda's. She hadn't saved her work to the server, as company protocol dictated. Martin was going to read her the riot act when he found out, but that wasn't going to do me any good at the moment.

I turned off the monitor and crept into the office area. There were motion detectors, but I knew they were aimed at the front door and the central area of the room. I squeezed myself against the wall and brochure racks, moving slow, wondering how long it would be before someone noticed me.

When I reached Amanda's desk I switched on her work station and turned the brightness down as low as it would go. It still lit the room like a beacon. I tapped a key and when the password screen appeared I let out an audible groan.

This was so unfair. Why couldn't she have just done her job properly? And how was I supposed to guess what a person like her would use for a password when all she could think about was—

I typed J A M E S on the keyboard and the Holiday Depot logo appeared. Amanda's files had four Sawyers listed, but only one had recent activity. I pulled up that account and checked the last transaction. A return ticket to Fuerteventura, leaving tonight at 10 p.m. and returning on Sunday afternoon, a three night booking at the Dunas Club hotel and a rental car.

It was too late to catch his flight, but with luck I could arrange tickets from my home computer for tomorrow morning and book a room at the same hotel. I logged out, powered down the work station and saw PCSO Doyle looking through the front window at me. Her torch beam swung through the room and centred on my face. I dived to the floor and scrambled towards the rear. Above the noise of the security alarm I heard her shout from the street, "Alex! Intruder."

I charged into the server room and ran to the window. I was halfway out when I heard footsteps running down the alley between the office and the Vision Express building next door. I slipped back inside, groped my way to the employees' toilet and pulled the door closed.

It was pitch black and quiet. I put my hand on my chest to steady my breathing and muffle the sound of my pounding heart, which I was sure they could hear in the street. Now that getting caught had become an option, I assessed my situation. I had no make-up on and was still wearing Malcolm's clothes. Without my black bodysuit and utility belt, I couldn't even claim to be acting in the capacity of a misunderstood crime fighter, I would simply be cross-dressing Rachel Davenport, the breaking and entering employee. And to be caught by Alex, of all people. I had come to believe she couldn't think any lower of me, but if she found me here . . . it didn't bear thinking about.

I held my breath and listened. They were at the window, talking loud enough to be heard over the alarm.

"This was open when I got here." Doyle's voice. "I expect whoever it was is long gone by now."

Light leaked through the gap beneath the door, growing and shrinking as they shone their torches around the server room.

"We'll need to contact the security company."

The light beneath the door flickered like a strobe, I heard a clatter, then Alex's voice. "I'm going to check the premises; the intruder might still be in there. Give me a boost."

More clattering as Alex, her Kevlar vest, hi-vis jacket, torch and utility belt attempted to climb through the window.

"Shouldn't we wait for backup?"

"This will only take a minute. Help me, my belt's caught."

I sighed. She was going to come in, open the toilet door and be very, very surprised. Unless I could conjure up some real super powers, like making myself invisible, I was going to spend

171

the night in jail. The first of many, I supposed. Then I realised I did have super powers—I could see in the dark.

I felt around and found the toilet. Sitting on the closed seat, I called on my memory to reconstruct the room just as it was the last time I saw it from this perspective. I concentrated and it swam into focus, the sink, the pipes, the PVC casings over the electric wires, the horizontal supports between the wall studs, the jutting frame of the door. When it all locked into place, I moved.

Two small steps through the blackness. I was at the sink. I reached for the tap and bumped my hand. It wasn't right; things were out of place.

I returned to the toilet, lifted the lid and sat. The perspective would be subtly different from this angle, but it would be enough. When I had the room memorised, I moved again. This time my hand landed on the tap and I felt a surge of elation; it was going to work. I reached up, grabbed a support, climbed onto the sink and then up the door frame where I sat hunched under the low ceiling.

Outside the door, Alex's struggling and the strident whooping of the alarm covered my movements. I braced myself, my arms and legs locked, holding me in place like a resting spider. Peter Parker, eat your heart out.

I waited. Alex fumbled and swore and landed on the floor inside the building. The light moved again, growing and shrinking as she checked the back room. My arms began to ache, the muscles in my thighs trembled. I had to hold on, even a slight slip would give me away. Complete darkness and receding footsteps as Alex checked the main office, then the light reappeared and the door flew open, bathing the toilet in sudden, harsh light.

The beam travelled around the tiny room, making me visible in the ambient light, but Alex was looking down, checking under the sink, in the corner and behind the toilet, just in case the intruder was midget.

I held my breath and strained to steady my arms. The door closed. I waited, willing Alex and her partner to go away.

"Ellen, hold the window open for me," Alex said.

I heard more clattering as Alex left the office. The window closed. I heard their voices fade as they walked away. They would remain, guarding the unlocked window, until the security company showed up or Martin arrived.

That thought moved me to action. I dropped to the floor in a perfect dismount and ran to the main office. Alex and Doyle

172

might split up, with one in the back and one guarding the front, so I had to be quick if I was going to get out unseen. I turned the lock on the front door and ran outside.

The street was filled with groups of young revellers in varying degrees of sobriety, enticed by the mild weather and the carnival atmosphere. Away from the wail of the siren, the more dominant sound of exploding fireworks took over. I spotted a smattering of smugglers and now wished I had kept Malcolm's jumper.

I walked up the street, straggling behind a group of young girls in the hopes it looked like I belonged with them. The girls were waifish, wearing spike heels, spaghetti strap tops and skirts that almost came down to their thighs; if I could fool anyone into believing I was one of that group, it would be by claiming I was their chaperone.

"Working late, doll?"

I looked over my shoulder, ready to run. A group of boys, no older than the girls in front of me, came up from behind. Their eclectic attire contrasted with the uniform outfits of the girls; too bad they all looked as if they shopped at the local recycling bin. Each one held a can of beer. My interrogator took a sip and smiled. "You robbing that travel place? I seen you coming out of there."

"No," I said, turning away. "I work for the security company."

The last thing I needed was a conversation with someone who, drunk as he was, might remember the face of the woman he saw running away from a break in. I had hopes they were losing interest in me when one of them spoke up. "Hey, you know who she looks like?"

"Yeah. She's not quite as pretty but she looks like that superhero bird."

I put up my collar and broke away from them, heading into the Carfax where I could get lost in the crowd.

"Yes. You're Nadia, aren't you?" one of them shouted.

The girls looked at me as I passed them. Their leader turned to the boys. "No she's not."

With that, she pulled up her dress, revealing black lace knickers with white lettering reading, "I am Nadia."

173

Chapter 22

I PULLED INTO MY driveway just before eleven. Nadia's car—along with the wig—was parked on a side street in Maidenbower. I was still wearing Malcolm's clothes but I was now Rachel; a butch Rachel, perhaps, but no one was going to see me. I jumped out of the car and jogged to the conservatory door.

"Rachel. There you are."

I turned the key and opened the door as Dee came out of her house and started my way. "How was your date with Stephen? Nigel tells me you had a race date; how romantic."

I stepped inside. "Not now, Dee. I'm in a hurry."

"But—"

"And whatever Nigel heard about the race, I won, not Stephen," I said, and closed the door.

It was time to call on another super power. I could fly. Okay, so I don't have my own invisible jet, but I could always use someone else's. I opened my laptop and booked a 7 a.m. flight out of Gatwick on lastminute.com and got a deal on the hotel at the same time. It was after midnight when I finished, leaving me just a few hours to prepare and get to the airport.

I had to make the bookings in my own name because Nadia didn't have a passport. I would have to leave and return as Rachel Davenport; Nadia would have to travel in my suitcase. I threw Malcolm's coat, shirt and trousers on my bed and dressed in comfortable jeans and a loose tee shirt for travelling. Then I hunted down my suitcase, packed the basic necessities and quietly carried it to my car.

I returned to Maidenbower and parked the Golf on a tranquil side street among other cars where it wouldn't attract attention. In this neighbourhood, at this time of night, no one was setting off fireworks, or even out walking their dog, and the windows remained dark as I carried the suitcase to Nadia's car. At The Citadel I packed the wigs, make-up and a variety of outfits for Nadia, including her Ninja suit and utility belt. When I finished, the suitcase was jammed full.

It was nearly two o'clock when I slipped out of The Citadel. By then, I judged it was late enough to call the Holiday Depot without Martin or the police picking up, so I pulled into a lay-by and took out my mobile. It went to the answer phone and I left a message saying I had a family emergency and wouldn't be able to make it to work in the morning, and not Saturday, either. Then I drove to the airport.

Gatwick was almost deserted, so I had no problem getting into the car park and checking in. I was through security by four o'clock and managed to catch a fitful hour of sleep before boarding commenced. The flight took off on time and by eight in the morning I was over the Channel, enjoying a breakfast of lukewarm tea and a small muffin filled with enough preservatives to keep it, and me, fresh well into the next century. After that, I still had three hours of flight time to look forward to so I dozed off, waking at half ten to the warmth and blinding sunshine of the Canary Islands.

I cleared immigration, retrieved my suitcase and thought about how I was going to get into my hotel. If I arrived as Rachel and then turned into Nadia, it was going to draw suspicion. I thought it would be best to look like neither, so I bought a pair of large sunglasses a scarf and a floppy straw hat and went to the ladies to cover my appearance as best I could.

It was a forty five minute ride to Corralejo and the Dunas Club hotel through scenery with all the appeal of a slag heap. Despite the inhospitable landscape, several resort hotels were spaced out along the route, most of them brimming, some abandoned and a few under construction. It was hard to believe the sun had that much appeal, for that seemed the island's main selling point. There was no other reason to be here.

I checked into the hotel, keeping a watch for Sawyer. Even though I had convinced him I wasn't Nadia, he still might recognise me as the girl from the travel agency, so I kept my hat low, my sunglasses on and signed the guest register as Becci Wayne. The desk clerk looked at the signature and gave me sly smile has he handed back my passport. I smiled in return and thanked him without embarrassment or apology; I couldn't be the only guest who signed in under a fake name. I expected Sawyer had done the same, as a quick scan of the register revealed that no one with that name had checked in over the past day and a half. I declined the offer of a bellboy and took the lift to the second floor to find my room.

I passed a few middle aged couples in the corridor, marvelling at their fashion sense, and let myself into my room. It was bliss; quiet and empty with a double bed beckoning like a beguiling lover. I went to it and flopped onto my back, letting it tease me into giving myself over to it fully. This was the first time I felt safe in a week, and the sense of relief left me giddy, as if I had just been pardoned from a death sentence. I pulled off my scarf and sunglasses and gazed at the cracks in the fresh paint on the ceiling.

The thought of going back on Sunday loomed like a spectre. I pushed it aside and luxuriated in the unexpected relief of freedom and sank into playful fantasies of not going back. Fuerteventura was in the EU, I had every right to stay, or go to Spain, or France. I could get a new job, hire people to pack up my house and ship my belongings to my new location. I could even sell it, and have someone drive my car to me, or sell that, as well. Rachel, I kept reminding myself, wasn't wanted, yet. She could just say she was after a change of scenery. And Nadia would just disappear. No one would miss us much. Stephen would be upset for a while, and Robin would wonder why Nadia stopped coming around. He might even try to call. He was welcome to; I had her mobile phone with me, maybe I would throw it in the sea later today.

It all sounded so inviting, and plausible, so why was it a fantasy, why couldn't we stay, why shouldn't we disappear and become someone else, someone with the best qualities of Rachel and Nadia in one person? What was holding me back?

I opened my eyes. The bedside clock read 3 p.m.. I bolted upright, dizzy and disoriented and feeling the cold edge of panic. Paul's voice cut through me. "Eye on the prize. Eye on the prize."

I took several deep breaths and focused on the wall in front of me. In the mirror on the imitation oak dressing table, I saw myself, hair dishevelled, no make-up, and looking a bit frightened. Paul's voice came again, softer this time. "You're a champion; act like one."

I got off the bed and walked to the bathroom, shedding my clothes en route. I shut myself in the shower and turned it on full, letting the stinging jets of hot water drive away the fatigue and indecision. When I stepped out of the bathroom I was still without make-up, still five feet six inches tall, but I was Nadia, and I knew why I had to go back on Sunday: because superheroes don't run away.

I opened the suitcase and began the task of going after Sawyer.

The time I'd lost couldn't be recovered so I put it out of my mind. It may even have been put to good use as I now felt refreshed and better prepared for my mission, despite the fact that I was starving. The afternoon sun was still high and hot and a peek over the balcony confirmed the patio around the pool was still well populated by tourists lounging on deck chairs like lizards on a hot rock. Most of them were wearing skimpy two piece swimsuits or, God help us, just the bottoms of skimpy two piece swimsuits, turning themselves pink in places that should never see the sun.

I dressed in my own more modest but still eye-catching tangerine two-piece and wrapped a beach towel around my waist. I put on just a bit of make-up and donned the red wig. It was shoulder length and parted in the middle; simple, unobtrusive but attractive. The sunglasses hid my eyes from above my eyebrows to the top of my cheek bones, and with my suit on, I wasn't worried about Sawyer, or any other passing person of the male persuasion, looking too long at my face.

At the pool, I claimed a deck chair, positioned it so I could see the hotel entrance and settled in to wait. It wasn't a foolproof plan, but it was the only one I had, short of asking the desk clerk for Sawyer's room number. I supposed a woman asking for a man's room number wouldn't raise an eyebrow in this place, but I couldn't afford to attract attention. Instead, I read my book, keeping one eye on the entrance.

Two chapters later I moved my chair into the shade. Another chapter after that and I was too hungry to read. There was a restaurant and snack bar attached to the hotel. I wouldn't be able to see the entrance from there, so I went to the vending machine in the lobby and bought a Kit Kat and a packet of sour cream and chive crisps.

Back at the pool someone had taken my seat; the curse of the single traveller. I found another one and squeezed into a shady spot by the far wall. I was further away but still had a view of anyone going into or out of the hotel. After my sour cream crisps dinner and chocolate biscuit dessert I went back to my book. Six chapters later, I turned on my mobile phones because I was so bored even threats and intimidation would make a welcome diversion. Instead, all it did was remind me of what awaited me on my return.

Alex called again, dropping ominous hints that time was running out and things would go better if I came in of my own free will. There were no messages from Sawyer or Keith, though I found Keith's silence more unsettling. He didn't strike me as the type to let an injury to his ego pass; I figured he was either still in police custody or still obsessed with finding me via Rachel.

Rachel's messages were equally disquieting.

177

"Miss Davenport, this is Mr Palmer. What do you mean calling in like that and telling me you can't be at work? And for two days? I'm not running a charity here. You want time off, fine, take all the time you want. Don't bother coming back. I'll post your final pay slip on the last day of this month. If your company blazer has not been returned by that time, the cost will be deducted."

Before the implications even registered, the next message, from Stephen, came up.

"Where are you? I called your house. Nigel tells me you left yesterday and haven't been back. What do you think you're doing, disappearing like that?"

"And how is that any of your fucking business," I said aloud.

The hits just kept on coming. Now I was an unemployed fugitive with a pissed off wannabe boyfriend. What annoyed me most was how it intruded on my serenity, keeping me from enjoying my furtive fantasy. I turned off both phones and settled back into my book. Three chapters later the pool area began to clear out and two chapters after that I started to feel obtrusive. Blending into the crowd in an orange bikini was easy as long as there was a crowd of bikini-clad tourists to blend into.

I abandoned the pool, walked back through the lobby for a last look around and returned to my room where I dressed in a low-cut top, shorts and sandals. Then I went to the hotel bar, taking a seat near the end where I could keep an eye on the lobby.

"What is your pleasure?"

The bartender was slim, tall and tan. He wore a Hawaiian shirt and a name tag that read, 'Louie'.

"Lime and soda water, please."

"Five euros. Shall I put that on your room?"

I showed him my room key and he fetched the drink. I sipped it slowly, savouring the most expensive lime and soda I have ever tasted outside central London.

"You are having dinner in the hotel tonight?" Louie asked. "Would you like me to reserve a table? I cannot believe a pretty lady like you would be here alone, so I should reserve a table for two, si?"

He might not believe it, but his eyes were full of hope.

"I'm waiting for my boyfriend," I told him. "And we will be going out for dinner."

"Of course."

He walked away then, but there were only two or three other patrons at the bar, giving him plenty of free time to stop by to

178

ask if I needed anything else. I nursed my drink for as long as I could and was considering ordering another when Sawyer walked in.

He must have spent the day in his room because he came from the direction of the stairs instead of the street. He took a seat near me, leaving two empty stools between us—close enough to strike up a conversation should the opportunity arise, but far enough away to not appear creepy. He was dressed in a white linen shirt tucked into tan cotton trousers and looked every bit the uptight businessman, surrounded as he was by laid-back locals and Brits on holiday. He glanced my way as he sat down but there was no malice; he was just a man doing what men do when they encounter pretty women. I flashed an "I'm on holiday" smile at him and pulled out my book, hoping he would take the hint.

Louie appeared, distracting him.

"Pint of Stella," Sawyer said. "Room one two seven."

I sipped the melting ice in my glass and read while he gulped his beer and checked his watch. At seven o'clock he drained his glass and entered the hotel restaurant. A grinning hostess greeted him and steered him into the forest of linen topped tables, no doubt to a tiny one in the back reserved for people like us who travel on their own. I sucked down the last bit of ice in my glass and went upstairs.

Sawyer's door was locked and, assuming the latch was the same as the one on my door, I knew there was no way I was going to slip it with a credit card. His room was one floor down and four rooms across from mine, so it might be possible to climb onto his balcony, but not without attracting attention. The only thing I could do was stick with him and see where he went. Then a door down the hallway opened and a stout maid pushing a cart laden with linens, towels and packets of coffee and tea appeared. She locked the door with her passkey and trundled onward. I jogged after her. "Excuse me. I need your help."

She looked at me, giving no sign that she wanted me to continue or had even heard me. I motioned for her to follow me. "Over here. Can you help me, please? Con permiso?"

The woman looked at her cart as if reluctant to abandon it, but she came towards me. I pointed to Sawyer's room. "I locked my key inside," I told her. "Can you let me in?"

She held up her hands and shook her head. "No. No. Recepción."

"I'm in a hurry. No time." I pointed at my watch, just in case she understood sign language. "I need to get in now."

"Recepción," the woman repeated.

I looked up and down the hallway. We were alone. It was time to use another super power. I opened my purse and took out a ten euro note. "I locked my key in my room," I said slowly. "Can you help me?"

The woman looked at the money and back at me. She shook her head again, but made a come on gesture with her hand. I took out another ten euros. "Can you help me now?"

"Si."

I handed her the notes. She looked up and down the hallway, opened the door and hurried away, stuffing the folded notes into her ample bosom.

I ducked inside and locked the door behind me. Superman might have been able to bust the door down, but money has a power all its own.

I stood for a while, collecting my thoughts, wondering where to start.

He hadn't brought a lot with him, no scuba gear, surf board, beach wear or even a pair of shorts. There were two pairs of trousers and two white shirts hanging in the wardrobe, along with the coat he would need on his return to Britain. A small suitcase lay in the bottom of the closet next to a pair of oxblood loafers. The rest of the room was just as sterile. There were the usual bits and bobs in the bathroom, but no sign that he had taken a shower, though since he had arrived the previous night, he'd had a normal morning with the maids cleaning up after him.

The bed was also pristine. The only sign that someone had spent the bulk of the afternoon in the room was a saucer heaped with fag ends sitting on a table on the balcony. I went out to inspect it. There were enough butts to fill an average afternoon and several empty cans of Stella. I looked over the balcony wall at the pool area where I had spent the afternoon. Had I thought to look up, I would have seen him. We'd spent the whole afternoon in sight of one another; me waiting for Sawyer, and Sawyer waiting for, what, exactly?

There was only one reason I could imagine would keep him sitting here that long; he was waiting for someone, as well. All the cigarettes and beer cans were arranged around the single wicker chair, so if he did have a visitor, they had not sat on the balcony to talk, and the interior of the room showed no signs that anyone had sat on the sofa. He was either conducting his own surveillance or waiting for a phone call. I couldn't know if he had been looking out for someone, but I might be able to find out if he'd received a call.

I went back inside. There was a phone on the bedside table, along with a pad of hotel stationery and one of those little pencils you find in Argos. The top sheet of the pad was indented with the loops and squiggles of a hastily written note. I tore it off and held it up to the light at an angle. There were several words and something that looked like a time, or at least a colon followed by two noughts.

I went back to the balcony and picked a butt out of the ashtray. Kneeling on the terracotta tiles, I rolled the crumpled end between my fingers, sprinkling ash over the paper. Then I rubbed over the message with my fingertips, brushing the ash into the grooves, bringing the writing to life.

"Casa Hermosa, Avenida Magnifica. 10:00"

I shook off the paper and returned the butt to the ashtray, placing it as if I were creating a flower arrangement. Nothing looked out of place. Not wanting to chance sprinkling charcoal over his clean rug, I shook the note over the side of the balcony, folded it and put it in my pocket. If this were an adventure movie, the door handle would turn now and the bad guy would enter, leaving me, the heroine, to do something clever.

I did a quick check of the room to make sure there was no sign I had been there and started towards the door. Then I heard the sound of a key being inserted into the lock.

There was no time to think of a plan and I didn't feel clever or heroic, just scared out of my mind. I ran to the balcony and scooted into the corner where I was hidden from view by the curtains. It wasn't an ideal plan. He seemed to live on the balcony, so when he came out here, I would be caught.

I waited, holding my breath, but he didn't come out. I heard a key jangle as he tossed it on the bureau. Then I heard him in the bathroom. I breathed out. A reprieve. Could I get past him? He was sure to see me sneaking by if he hadn't closed the door. And besides, I couldn't count on him being in there that long. The best I could do with the time I had was to somehow get off his balcony. I climbed onto the wall and jumped.

There was a three foot gap between rooms, but it was a dizzying drop to the tiled patio surrounding the pool. I made it easily, landing in a silent crouch in front of Sawyer's neighbour's balcony. The curtains were open, but the door was closed and the room was empty. I tried the door. Locked. I climbed onto the far wall and jumped again.

In the next balcony, the door was open, and a couple was engaged in an imaginative and energetic sex act on the bed. The woman screamed, the man made an admirable dismount and rushed towards me, heedless of his nakedness, while the woman pulled a sheet over herself.

"What the—," he bellowed.

I waved my hands and shushed him. He stopped short, his face changing from rage to confusion, his resolution flagging. Two rooms away, Sawyer stepped onto his balcony. I stepped into the threshold; if Sawyer looked my way, he would see nothing but my back. "Sorry," I said in a stage whisper. "I was with my boyfriend next door and his wife came home unexpectedly."

The man smiled and looked back at the woman, who was now calm. "Always glad to help out a lady in distress," he said.

He stepped aside and made a sweeping gesture with his arm, inviting me into the room.

"Thanks," I said, keeping my voice low.

I started across the room, keeping my eyes averted.

"You are welcome to join us," the man said.

I looked at him. His resolution had returned and the woman removed the sheet, revealing an inviting pose.

"Um, thanks, but I think I've had enough excitement for one afternoon."

"Such a pity. Some other time?"

"Yes. Some other time."

I hustled to the door and pulled it open. The hallway was clear, save for a few unconcerned guests. I waved a "thank you" to the couple and left, walking past the other guests without making eye contact.

Back in my room, I drank a glass of water and paced the balcony to calm my jittery insides while puzzling over the meaning of the note. Ten o'clock wasn't hard to figure out, but what was Casa Hermosa, or Avenida Magnifica? I looked in the phone directory and on the tourist map of the island I had picked up in the lobby. There was no mention of either place, yet the name sounded familiar.

I sat in the chair, thinking back to all that had happened since arriving on the island. The landing, customs, the airport, the cab, the hotel ran through my head like a movie. I slowed the action down, checking details. There was something there, something between the airport and the hotel, during the taxi ride.

An idea came to me. It was a long shot, but if it didn't pan out, I could still get back to the hotel in time to tail Sawyer. If I hurried.

I went down to the lobby and asked where I could rent a motor bike. They directed me to a stall on Calle Taoro but warned me they would be closing soon. I ran down the pavement, dodging tourists and arrived just as a man in a straw hat and a flowered shirt that strained against his protruding belly began pulling down the security gate. "A bike," I said, as if I had just run a marathon across the desert. "I need to rent a bike."

"Closed, doll," he said. His accent was Australian, his demeanour insouciant; he hadn't even bothered to look at me.

"Please," I said. "I need a motorbike. My plane got in late, I'm supposed to meet some friends in Puerto del Rosario. I need transport."

"Take a cab."

He fished a heavy lock from the back pocket of his shorts.

"How much?"

He stopped and looked at me for the first time. "Come again?"

"I need a bike, you have bikes. What is it going to take for you to rent me one?"

He looked me up and down. "You're offering a bribe?"

"Yes. But money only."

"Shame," he said, but he lifted the barrier.

I looked inside the packed and tiny shop; it reminded me of Robin and I wondered how he was.

"One hundred euros."

"What? But your sign says fifteen euros a day."

"And unless you'll be bringing the bike back in five minutes, you're renting it for two days, plus insurance." He paused, smiling. "Plus the desperation fee."

"I'm not that desperate."

He reached up for the security barrier.

"Okay. A hundred it is."

I sighed. I supposed I should have been grateful he didn't charge double that. "Do you take Visa?"

"Sure do. Most bribes are paid for with Visa."

I selected a bike. We rushed through the paperwork. I signed away my life savings as collateral in case I returned it with a scratch on it, which I found a bit rich because he could buy a new one with the money he charged me. We shook hands and I wheeled the most expensive moped in Fuerteventura towards the main road. There was no way I was going to practise riding in front of that man.

I pedalled the bike through town, kicking on the engine when the road entered open desert and traffic dropped off to the occasional taxi or tour bus. The sun was going down, bathing the slag heaps in a red glow that made them marginally pretty. By then I was sweating from the heat, so the breeze, as the bike sped along to the sewing machine hum of its motor, was heaven.

About five miles outside of town I saw it, a faded, hand painted sign reading "Casa Hermosa" and an arrow pointing down an unpaved, rutted track. The track, which I assumed to be the Avenida Magnifica, curved over the expanse of rocky soil and ended about a mile away at what looked like a half-finished hotel.

I pedalled the moped through the ruts, eventually reaching a broad, flat area covered in cracked concrete. Dirt and rocks were strewn over much of the paving and weeds grew through the cracks, disguising what was meant to be a car park and causing it blend into the surrounding landscape.

The hotel, from this distance, looked more like an enormous set of concrete blocks that a giant baby had played with and then forgotten. The main entrance seemed complete, in an unadorned concrete way, but the wings that fed off of it ended in bristles of reinforcement bar, rusted with age.

A dusty white van was parked near the gaping hole of the entrance, its back doors open. As I watched, a man climbed out, picked up a box and carried it towards the hotel. At the same time, another man came out of the entrance heading for the van, and saw me.

He began shouting and waving. I couldn't understand what he was saying but it was clear he wanted me to leave and I obliged him as quickly as I could. I kicked the engine to life, jarring my teeth as I jolted over ruts and rocks on my way back to the main road.

Chapter 23

MY HOTEL PROVIDED A bike rack at one end of its tiny car park, but the rack was crammed beyond capacity so I chained the bike to a lamp post and headed to my room, detouring past the bar and restaurant to see if Sawyer was still about. He must have remained on his balcony because there was no sign of him. Of course, he could have slipped out and gone to his rendezvous early, or wasn't planning to go at all.

It might also be that the directions I had found were a complete fabrication, but I didn't think so; the men in the van were up to something, sort of a Spanish version of Carl and Derek. The choice I had to make was whether to stick with Sawyer and follow him to wherever he was going, or trust my hunch and get to the hotel first so I could be in a better position once he arrived. The latter seemed an all or nothing bet and smacked of desperation so, naturally, I chose that one.

I made a more rational decision about my surveillance method. I might not be an actual genius, but I do learn from my mistakes, and I have to admit my evidence-gathering techniques needed a re-think. On this outing, there would be no hidden camera, no microphone, no recorder; I was just going to listen and learn and hope whatever I found out answered the question of why he was after me.

I had a quick dinner at the snack bar and decided to treat myself to the full Nadia experience. I hadn't had the time or inclination to put on the complete crime-fighting outfit since my debut at Keymer Court. Every appearance after that had seen something missing so this time I would do it right, even though no one was going to see me.

Back in my room I put on the black bodysuit, pinned up my hair, secured the black wig, applied make up, put in the brown contacts and wished again I could be like Clark Kent and just jump into the nearest phone booth. Granted, the advent of mobile phones might force Superman into changing in hotel rooms but, even if that were to happen, Superman wouldn't have the problem of walking through the lobby wearing blue tights and a red cape. He could just fly off the balcony.

To compensate for living in the real world, I put on a white skirt and a jacket. I looked like a tourist in tights; a geeky tourist who thought sandals and a thick black leotard made an avant-garde fashion statement.

I walked through the lobby, smiling and nodding to my fellow tourists as we headed for our respective nights out. The pool area was crowded with people in cruise wear carrying drinks of various primary colours. I waded through them to the relative coolness and openness of the street, unlocked my bike and motored out of town.

When I was half a mile away from the Avenida Magnifica, I switched off the engine and coasted off the highway. Relying on the light of the waning gibbous moon to guide me, I pedalled the bike over the hard-packed moonscape until the road was well behind me. After hiding the bike behind a cluster of Verode, I took off the skirt and jacket, put on my shoes and gloves and continued on foot. I reached the car park in a few minutes and skirted around the edge, keeping to the shadows. The white van was gone, but someone was in the building. Flashes of light illuminated the empty gaps where the windows should be, as if someone was carrying a torch down the hallway.

The light bobbled along the far wing and entered the area that should have been the lobby. I crept closer, keeping low. A man with black hair and dark clothing was bent over something in the middle of the floor. I froze and waited. Soon, he and the light moved away, down another wing. I looked around for signs of anyone else and sprinted across the concrete, careful to step around the loose rocks and discarded bits of reinforcing bar. Inside, the lobby was dark and I slowed to a cautious walk.

At the far end I glimpsed a stack of breezeblocks forming a makeshift stairway to the first floor. I felt my way in that general direction, stepping over the occasional broken block or strand of wire. When I reached the base of the steps, the lobby lit up. A Land Rover pulled into the car park and up to the lobby entrance. I took the stairs two at a time, hiding behind a half wall bordering what was meant to be a balcony area overlooking the expansive lobby. Below, the man carrying the torch returned, shielding his eyes from the headlamps of the Land Rover.

The engine died but the lights stayed on. A car door slammed and a man carrying an attaché case walked in, casting a long shadow from the headlights. He was stocky, with beefy arms, straw hat and a manner that brought to mind Tony Soprano. He walked to the centre of the room, where a neat pile of blocks formed a pedestal, and laid the case on it.

Tony spoke to the man with the torch in rapid Spanish. The other man nodded and spoke back. I didn't understand a word. So much for intelligence gathering. I looked at my watch. It was five minutes to ten.

The two men strolled around the lobby. The man with the torch did the talking, shining his light into various corners and down the empty corridors. Tony nodded. "Bueno."

Then another vehicle arrived, adding light to the already glaring lobby. The lights died, the engine stopped, a car door slammed. Then Sawyer entered. Tony turned to him. "Ah, here we are, Señor Sawyer."

Sawyer looked uncomfortable, realising he was outnumbered and in a remote area with a man who, although he was smiling, exuded anything but comfort. He gazed up at the unfinished building, the gaping doorways, crumbling concrete and rusting reinforcement bars that bristled from the unfinished edges of the walls and ceilings.

"It's impressive," he said.

Tony laughed. "It would have been impressive had I been allowed to finish it."

"What went wrong?"

The man shrugged his bear-like shoulders. "Permits, fees, interference from my competitors. The usual."

Sawyer looked at the two men. "You weren't able to do anything about it?"

"No, my friend." The man made a sweeping gesture with his hand. "All of this, a waste. Usually some money in the right hands can move things along, but not this time." He put a hairy arm around Sawyer's shoulder and drew him close as if to whisper sweet nothings in his ear. "This is a special case; it calls for special measures, and you need to see these special measures. I invited you here just for this purpose."

He released Sawyer, who looked relieved. "I'm still not sure what this is all about."

"We have an arrangement," the man said. "You are not honouring this arrangement."

Sawyer went from relived to alarmed. "I am progressing, but there are problems. The councillors are under investigation, they are getting skittish. And there's this woman—"

"I'm not interested in your problems," the nice guy voice disappeared, replaced by the business side of Tony Soprano. "I am interested in your results. And I see none." He turned away, resting his arms on the table, looking at the attaché case. "But I do understand problems. It is how you make them go away that counts."

He opened the briefcase. It was filled with money. Sawyer looked at it with an expression of dread.

"One million euros, my friend. You will take this back with you, and use it to progress your problems. Si?"

He snapped the case shut.

"You want me to carry that back? Won't a money transfer be safer?" Sawyer's voice rasped as if his throat had gone dry.

The big man smiled. He cupped the side of Sawyer's face in one paw and patted his cheek with the other in a gesture that managed to be friendly and sinister at the same time. "You young men, you trust in technology too much. I transfer this, it is traced, you pack it in your suitcase—a respected business man—and no one suspects. Untraceable. This amount of money will help your councillor friends overcome their shyness. They see numbers in a spreadsheet, they do nothing, they see money in their hand, they feel courage."

Sawyer nodded; the man stepped away from him. "Now tell me about this woman."

I shifted my position to hear better, grinding grit under my shoe. I froze. They didn't seem to notice. Now I was in an awkward position but didn't dare move.

"She's some sort of amateur detective, but she knows something," Sawyer said. His observation was both an insult and an exaggeration. "If we continue with the plan, she will know what we did. She will go to the authorities."

The big man waved his hand in a dismissive gesture. "Then you find her."

Sawyer stared at his feet. "That's proving harder than I imagined. I've tried several times but she keeps slipping away. Even the police can't catch her. And if they get to her first, she'll tell them what she knows."

"Then you must try harder, my friend." He rubbed a hand over the black leather of the briefcase. "But that is your problem, not mine. Mine is getting the land and the permission to build on it. You are *progressing* that, si?"

"Everything is in place. But the woman—"

"A woman!" Sawyer jumped at the sudden shout. "I have spent millions and waited months and you tell me of a woman. No more. You will *progress* in your way or I will progress in mine. Usted entiende?"

Sawyer backed away, looking at his loafers. The big man drew a breath, calming himself; Good Tony returned. "Señor

188

Sawyer, I am trying to help you, because helping you helps me." He stepped away from the table and looked around the cavernous room like a king surveying his domain. "This was to be a great achievement, but petty minds blocked the way. They dishonoured me; they allow a rival is to finish this, my great work. But if I am not allowed to finish it, no one will." He smiled and looked at Sawyer. "Unlike you, I do not trust in technology. My methods are simple, direct and effective, as yours must be. I wanted you to see this, to see how I *progress* my problems, to give you courage to do the same."

Sawyer cleared his throat. "There are subtle differences between Fuerteventura and Britain."

"And you have told me you are able to overcome those differences, no?"

"Yes. Si. The technical problems have been overcome. It's just, well, there is that other issue."

He was afraid of me, afraid of even mentioning me.

I sensed something wrong. I looked from Sawyer to the big man, to the table. A panic rose in me; the other man wasn't there. Was he off finishing whatever job he was doing, or was he—

The wire whipped over my head and dug into the fabric of my suit. I propelled myself backward, knocking over my assailant. An elbow to his ribs and the wire loosened. An arm around my neck, squeezing. We rolled in the grit and dust.

"Let go you bastard."

The arm loosened. A knee dug into the centre of my back; my hands wrenched behind me and wrapped with wire as the man panted and chuckled. "A woman." It was a shout of triumph, as if he had just landed a forty kilo sturgeon.

He gripped my arm and dragged me to my feet, pushing me towards the stairway. We picked our way down through the shadows to where Sawyer and his companion waited, Sawyer with his eyes wide and the big man smiling in a way I found very unpleasant.

"That's her," Sawyer said. "That's the woman, Nadia."

"You see," he said, turning to Sawyer. "Good fortune smiles on industrious men." He grabbed my free arm in a grip that felt like a bear trap. "Miguel, gracias."

He and Miguel hugged with their free arms, the big man patting Miguel on the back. I would have joined the love-fest but my hands were busy being starved of oxygen.

"This is fortuitous. We can progress many problems tonight."

"If she followed me down here, she'll have left a paper trial," Sawyer said. We can get her passport, find out who she is."

The man sighed and pulled me in front of him, holding me by both arms as if presenting me to Sawyer. "I begin to think your problems are of your own making. What is the difference who she is? She is the woman standing in your way. No?"

Sawyer nodded. "No, I mean, yes. Si"

"Then tonight she no longer stands in your way. Problem progressed."

He shoved me back to Miguel as if I were a rag doll. Miguel's hands were smaller than Tony's but they dug into my arms with equal force. These guys weren't taking any chances, or giving me any opportunities.

"What are you going to do?" Sawyer asked.

"I am going to give you courage, my friend. I am going to show you how I solve my problems, the old fashioned way, and I will solve your problem, as well. When you see what I am willing to do for business, you will not be so timid in your actions."

Sawyer went white and looked as if he was about to throw up. "But there will be enquiries."

Another dismissive gesture from Tony. "A lone woman goes on holiday and disappears. It happens. There will be an investigation, but it will have nothing to do with us."

My hands stopped tingling and went cold. I focused my mind on one thought; getting away. I twisted my hands, straining against the wire until the blood began to flow back into my fingers.

"Miguel. All is ready?"

"Si."

"And Señor Sawyer. All is ready with you?"

"As I said, the, um, technical issues have all been solved, we were waiting—"

"Then you call your men. Now. It happens now."

Sawyer pulled his mobile from his jacket pocket, and with the slow, deliberate movements of a man walking to the gallows, punched in a number. "Derek? Yes. Everything is taken care of. You can go ahead. Tomorrow. As we planned." He ended the call and looked at Tony. "It will be done. Tomorrow night."

The big man nodded. "You see, Señor Sawyer. I am a man of action, not words. Now you will benefit from my actions, and I will benefit from yours."

He turned to Miguel. "You have the detonator."

Miguel nodded.

"We will drive up the avenue, to the big rocks near the road. We will watch from there. Make everything ready and meet us." He reached out a paw and cupped my chin. "Such a pretty señora joven. Too bad for you."

He released my chin and turned away. Putting his hand on Sawyer's shoulder, he picked up the briefcase, and the two of them walked back towards the vehicles.

"Tie her tight, Miguel," he called, without turning. "I don't want her getting away. And don't keep us waiting."

They climbed into their vehicles, the big man into the Land Rover, Sawyer into the sedan. Shadows swung across the open lobby as they backed away, turned and headed towards the road, leaving me alone with Miguel. We were in darkness now, him standing behind me, a firm grip on each arm. Even with my hands tied it should be a simple matter to disable him and hide in the desert. I steadied myself and kicked backward to connect with his kneecap. My foot swung into empty air.

The force of my kick unsteadied me. Miguel let go, pushing me as he did. I stumbled forward, struggling to keep my balance without the use of my arms. I was doing all right until I tripped over a broken slab of concrete and tumbling into the grit. I turned in time to keep from breaking my nose, but gravel and metal cut into my side.

Miguel laughed. "You are a feisty one."

He was near my feet. I tried to lash out again but I was too late. A loop of wire snaked around my ankles and pulled tight. I clenched my teeth to keep from screaming. He wrapped the wire until it was secure then dropped my legs and walked away as if he had just bulldogged a calf. I squirmed forward, grinding rubble into my side. Miguel ignored me. I made three feet before I found out why he appeared so unconcerned—in addition to binding my feet, he had also looped a cable around my ankles and had tethered me to a column.

I heard him walking around behind me, then he drew near. A light shone on my face, stinging my eyes with its intensity. I blinked and looked away.

"Señor Flores is right, you are a pretty one. Too bad you meddle where you do not belong. And too bad they are in a hurry. I would like to spend more time with you."

A hand reached out and slid down my shoulder, over my breasts and to my crotch. I didn't have to squeeze my legs together to keep him from feeling much, he had taken care of that by trussing me up like a Christmas goose. He should have planned ahead.

191

The light moved. Miguel withdrew his hand, went to the makeshift table and laid the torch on it, filling the lobby with an eerie glow. I heard noises, the slapping of cable against concrete, muttered curses, then a subdued shout of triumph.

My legs straightened and pulled tight, then I began to inch backward, losing the ground I had gained. I tried to see what Miguel was doing but it was all I could to do not scrape my face along the concrete. I put most of my weight on my shoulder, if I turned on my back, my hands would get chewed up and it wasn't worth thinking about being dragged across the floor on my stomach.

Then my legs began to rise and the pressure on my shoulder grew as I tilted further upward. My head cocked to a painful angle, rough concrete grated my cheek and scraped up the side of my face, threatening to pull my wig off. Then the top of my head left the floor and I was slowly spinning, suspended from a reinforcement bar jutting from the unfinished balcony. Nearby, Miguel grunted as he inched my body upward.

He had looped the cable around a column, using it as a makeshift winch. It worked until my full weight was in the air but now he appeared to be having problems. He was sweating and cursing and I was relieved when he gave in and tied the cable off; I wasn't thrilled about the prospect of being dropped on my head onto concrete. As it was, I was barely a foot in the air. But it might as well have been a mile.

The wires around my legs dug into my ankles as I eased forward and back like a human pendulum. I looked up at my feet and the cable holding them, suspending me like a side of beef in a butcher's window. Miguel finished securing the wire, fetched the torch and squatted down on the floor next to me.

He reached a hand towards my face and drew it back as I tried to bite him. He smiled. "Such a waste. I would love to make you feel better, but all I can promise is a quick end. The explosion will bring this whole building down on top of you."

He placed a hand on my chest and gave a soft push. "But you won't feel a thing; the blast will kill you."

I swung back and forth. He pushed harder, and harder again.

"Until then," he said, walking away. "Enjoy yourself."

He chuckled and left, taking the torch with him, leaving me swinging in the darkness.

So that was the game. In my research on Sawyer I had seen a downturn in his profits that brought him close to insolvency, followed by a sharp increase. I had put that down to a drop in the housing market; a combination of foreclosures and people not being able to afford to buy would create a need for rented flats. But Sawyer must have bypassed all that in favour of a quicker, surer return. His criminal partner was fronting the money for Sawyer to buy properties cheap and run them down so they could demolish them and build thousands of shoddy, overpriced flats and rake in some real money.

And now I knew why he was after me; I had proof of what he was doing, which threatened to expose the entire scheme. Until he got that proof back, he was hamstrung. Problem was, I didn't have the proof, and now that I had satisfied my curiosity, I was swinging in the dark, waiting for the big light.

The cable around my ankles felt like tendrils of fire cutting through my skin, but the wire Miguel had wrapped around my wrists was now loosening. I pictured the rocks on the side of the rutted path from the hotel to the road and calculated the distance. Whether they were going to set the explosion off remotely or by a timer, Miguel would need at least ten minutes to get to the rocks and settle in to enjoy the show.

I twisted my hands again. I could move them, but they were still tied tight. Too tight? I bent at the waist and brought my arms down, I mean up, to my hips. I can do this with my hands clasped, but tied at the wrists means an added level of difficulty. I curled as tight as I could, stretching and straining, inching my arms up until my bum popped through and I had my arms around my thighs.

I took a breath and scrunched further, working my arms along my thighs, to my knees, my calves and under the heels of my shoes. My shoulders ached, my abdomen burned, my feet were numb. I ignored the pain and pushed again. My feet slid through. My hands were now tied together with the cable running between them. I slid them upward, grasped with my wrists, pulled, grasped, pulled, and inched my way up the cable.

Sweat pooled inside my suit, my muscles thrummed. I pulled with the last of my strength. I was halfway to the top. I dug for strength and pushed again. I was suspended like a cradle now, with my hand and the cable forming the apex of a rough triangle, and my body acting as the base. Grasping the cable tight, I curled my legs under me and pushed for the bar. My gloved fingers brushed the metal. I pushed again and gripped the bar. I hung for a second, then pulled myself up and lifting my legs. The cable slackened but, instead of slipping off the end of the bar, it looped closer to the concrete. I lifted again. Again the cable coiled in the wrong direction.

Tucked into a ball, I chinned myself on the bar and knocked the cable with the side of my face, easing the loop away from the wall. I swung myself and used the bit of slack I had to walk myself closer to the bar's end. I whipped my head, hitting at the cable, crying in frustration. I swung my head harder, batting the cable with my chin. Then I slipped.

I dropped three feet. The cable snapped taut nearly ripping my arms out of their sockets. I hung with my hands at my feet, tucked into a ball, swinging from side to side. The cable clung to the end of the bar but my fall had bent it downward. I rocked my body, increasing my arc. On the third swing, the cable snapped free.

I arched my body, attempting to land in a dismount position, but tumbled to the floor instead, panting and cursing. I rolled onto my back and sat up. I was free, sort of. My hands were now in front of me and I wasn't suspended in air but I was still shackled to the column. I reached between my feet and felt for the cable. It was looped between my ankles and twisted on itself. I pulled at the loose end, bending it around and around, counting the seconds as I neared the end. At last it came free, I yanked it through and tossed it away. My ankles were still bound with wire but I had no time to free them. I got to my knees and lurched into a standing position.

I needed to get out, but they might see me if I went through the front. I remembered the hallways and hopped towards the nearest one. I started cautiously, not wanting to take the chance of losing precious seconds by sprawling across the floor. When I made the corridor, I hopped faster, springing forward, looking for a doorway. To my left, I saw a square of grey looming in the blackness. I turned and hopped towards it, expecting the blast to take me at any second. I pumped my legs, propelling myself across the concrete, nearing the window, timing my approach.

At the right moment, I pushed hard and leapt towards the square, diving through into the warm night.

I tucked and rolled, the gravel digging into my shoulders and back. I flipped onto my stomach, pushed myself into a standing position and hopped for all I was worth.

Twenty feet later, the world shook as a deep roar cut through the night. Hot wind slapped my back, throwing me forward. I fell to the ground and scrambled into a low depression as dust and grit settled around me.

The charges weren't set to explode outward. If they had been, I would have been vaporized. It was more of a controlled demolition, with the hotel collapsing in on itself in a cloud of

194

rubble, dust and smoke. I remained tucked in a ball, taking shallow breaths, until the ground stopped shaking and the dust began to clear. The once massive hotel was now a pile of broken concrete and metal. Miguel had not exaggerated; if I had been inside when it happened, no one would ever find me.

Tony and his gang would not be back, but the blast had to have attracted someone's attention. I wasn't in the clear yet. I rolled onto my back and worked the wire off of my ankles. When my feet were free, I set to work on my hands. I had to use my teeth and the going was slower. Then I heard sirens.

With my hands still tied, I picked my way over the rocky ground towards where the bike was hidden. The sirens grew louder. Lights flashed and tyres squealed as vehicles turned off the highway and onto the lane that led to where the hotel used to be. I was out of the range of their headlights but kept low as I moved across the landscape.

I found the bike and spent a few minutes working my hands free while more vehicles gathered in the ruined hotel's car park. In the distance I could see men wandering around, silhouetted in the headlights.

My body ached, my hands burned and tingled as blood began to flow and I could feel welts forming around my ankles and on my neck from Miguel's garrotte. My suit was ripped and caked with grit. It wouldn't do to return to town looking like the loser in a cage fight.

I removed the suit and stood in the warm night air in my knickers and bra, letting the soft breeze dry my sweat. I put on the skirt and jacket, zipped it up to my neck and turned up the collar to hide the welt. With luck, I should pass for a tourist coming home after an energetic night out, even though it was a bit early for that. Fearing I might run into Sawyer or one of his buddies, I removed the wig, unpinned my hair and combed it out with my fingers.

Then I wheeled the bike back to the road and pedalled towards town, not daring to switch on the engine until the flashing lights faded into the distance.

Chapter 24

I LEFT THE BIKE locked up outside the shop I had rented it from and walked back to the hotel. In my room, I took a shower, then spent an hour on the phone rearranging my flight. The earliest I could get was ten o'clock the following morning. It was the best I could do, so I saw no sense worrying about it. I climbed into bed and fell asleep.

The next morning, wearing the red wig, halter top and a scarf around my neck, I went to breakfast. Sawyer was sitting two tables away looking glum. He didn't look my way. After breakfast, I went back to my room as Nadia, changed into a long sleeve cotton blouse and a knee length skirt and left as Rachel, trusting in my sunglasses and floppy hat to get me past any unfortunate encounters with Sawyer.

I checked out, had the receptionist call a cab for me and went to the airport.

On this trip, the Casa Hermosa blended into the landscape, being little more than a pile of rocks. A few of the external walls remained, like an old ruin, but the bulk of the building was a mound of grey rubble. No emergency vehicles were there; they must have lost interest.

The cab dropped me outside the terminal, a building so uninspiring it made me think that the airport hadn't thought to build a departure lounge so they had commandeered one of the surplus hangers and given it a not very thorough make-over to correct the oversight. I had an hour before my flight departed, so I checked in, bought a bottle of apple juice and a Mars Bar from a vending machine, squeezed myself into a seat between a family of Americans and a group of hung over lads returning from a stag night, and settled down to brood.

Whatever Sawyer was planning was to take place that evening. My flight was due into Gatwick at three o'clock so I wouldn't have long to find out what it was. I had little idea of how to go about that, but I did have a place to start and from there all I could do was hope that, for once, luck would be on my side.

When my flight touched down at Gatwick, the first jolt of the wheels on the runway was mirrored by the full weight of my fugitive status landing squarely on my shoulders. I wondered what sort of reception I could expect from Stephen, and if Alex had tried to contact me, either as Nadia or Rachel.

I cleared customs and retrieved my suitcase in record time, then hustled to the car park and joined the M23. Barring traffic catastrophes, I would be at The Citadel within the hour. It was already dark so I decided I could save some time by driving Nadia's car into uStoreIt as Rachel.

A soft rain began to fall as I turned on to the Balcombe Road and drove through the uStoreIt entrance. I followed the lane past the rows of lockups and turned into mine. At the far end, in front of The Citadel, a Sussex police car idled in the darkness.

I braked hard and sat facing them. For a few moments we squared off, like gunfighters at high noon. Choking back disappointment and panic, I weighed my options. I couldn't hope to outrun them, not with them sitting in an idling car and facing my way. I would have to back up and they would be behind me, blocking my escape, before I could turn around. My only option was to fool them.

Doing my best to feign ignorance of their presence, I grabbed the floppy tourist hat from the back seat and pulled it low over my brow. Then I put on the hand brake and got out of the car, checking my handbag as I walked to the nearest storage unit. When I got to the door, I threw my hands up in disgust, turned around and went back to the Escort. It worked. The passenger door of the police car opened and one of the officers got out. "Excuse me, Miss."

A woman police officer walked towards me; I glanced her way and waved. "I forgot my key," I said.

The other officer, a man, joined his partner. Both broke into a trot, heading my way. "Miss, we need to talk to you."

"Forgot my key," I said again, then opened my car door and jumped in.

"Stop."

By now they realised their mistake. My tyres squealed as I tore out, backing up and pulling onto the lane with my car pointing towards the exit. The woman still thought she could catch me and charged at my car. The male officer raced back to the patrol car and roared away. I peeled out, zooming past the next row of lock-ups. I prayed I had enough time, and that the male officer would be a gentleman and stop to pick up his partner before undertaking a wild, high-speed chase. Feeling I'd made enough noise and burned enough rubber, I turned into the next corridor. It was empty and the far end was in shadow. I raced into the darkness, stopped and shut off the engine.

Two seconds later the patrol car sped past, its blue lights flashing, siren wailing. They didn't look my way, and if they had, they wouldn't have seen much, just a darker shadow in a patch of shadow.

I rolled my window down to listen. They appeared to be hesitating at the entrance, unable to decide which way I might have gone. They choose the fast route, and turned left towards the M23. I started the car and drove to the end of the units. The need to escape was suffocating, but I turned back towards The Citadel and parked outside. I jumped out of the car, rammed the key in the lock and wrenched the door open. I yanked clothing and accoutrements off of hangers and out of drawers and flung them into the back seat of the Escort, rushing to and fro as if the building were on fire. With the bulk of Nadia's wardrobe already packed in the suitcase, I was able to clear The Citadel in a few trips. After everything was out, I pulled the scarf from my neck and wiped down the all the surfaces.

I wiped down the door handles and pulled the door closed with my hand wrapped in the scarf. Then I scrambled into the driver's seat and, with my heart pounding and my breath coming in short, panicked gasps, drove sedately out of uStoreIt. No sense drawing unwanted attention.

Back on the road, I turned into Maidenbower just as two screaming police cars screeched through the entrance of uStoreIt. I located my car, parked a few slots behind it and transferred Nadia's gear, loose clothing and the suitcase into the Golf. Then I wiped down Nadia's car and wrapped the scarf around my neck. With The Citadel empty and rented in the name of Petra Parker, there was no way anyone could link it to me.

The Escort was another matter. The police had seen the car, but they hadn't come close enough to get a good look so it was very likely that, in the confusion, they had been unable to get the registration number. That didn't mean I had got away; they would be broadcasting the description to every patrol car in Sussex. If they found the Escort, they couldn't link it to The Citadel, but they could link it to me. If they had failed to get the registration number, however, there was no way to prove it was the same car they had chased out of uStoreIt.

I sat in the Golf, put on the wipers and took one last look around. No one was peeking out of any windows, so I was getting away unseen, but that was the only good thought I could salvage at the moment. Nadia's cover was blown. The police knew where she lived, knew what car she drove. With no place to change into Nadia, she was a good as dead. But right now I was safe. I was Rachel Davenport, driving Rachel Davenport's car going to Rachel Davenport's house. The police weren't looking for Rachel Davenport. Not yet, anyway. I allowed this thought to calm me and set off towards my home. And Nadia came with me.

Chapter 25

IT WAS BEGINNING TO sleet when I pulled into my driveway. My house was dark, no police cars were there waiting for me, but as I pulled my suitcase out of the back seat, Dee rushed out to greet me. "Where have you been?"

"Didn't you get my memo?"

She looked perplexed. I slammed the car door and walked past her towards my front porch to distract her from helping me unload and discovering the jumble of clothes hidden in the boot.

"We were worried. You just disappeared. Anything might have happened. Stephen has been beside himself. Why didn't you let someone know?"

I felt like exploding and screaming at her, taking all the frustrations of the past days out on her, but that wouldn't be fair and that's not what a superhero would do. She was merely being a concerned friend. And they were starting to be in short supply.

"I'm sorry. I just needed to get away for a bit. To think." I decided to try the sympathy ploy. "I lost my job and there's just an awful lot going on in my life right now."

Dee gave me an awkward hug. "You poor lamb. When you get settled, come over and I'll make you a cup of tea and we can talk. Starting a new relationship can be a challenge."

"I'd love to, Dee, but maybe tomorrow. I have a lot on my plate this evening."

"Oh, are you going to see Stephen?"

I felt a misplaced pang of guilt. Shouldn't he have been the first person I thought to call when I landed? To be fair, I'd been busy; being chased by the cops takes precedence over returning phone calls. "Not tonight. I've made other arrangements. I know he's worried. I'll call him tomorrow."

I unlocked my door and went inside, leaving Dee on my front porch. I had no idea how I was going to get past her dressed as Nadia but whatever I came up with it would have to be good. Dee would be on double alert this evening. It wouldn't surprise me if she called Stephen. I would have to change and get out fast. I pulled the door to close it but Dee held it open. "Actually, Stephen is here."

"What?"

"He came over earlier, to see Nigel."

More likely to check up on me.

"Tell him I'm sorry, I just need some space. Okay?"

I left Dee at the door and hauled my case upstairs. I dragged it into my spare bedroom and pulled out Nadia's wig and bodysuit. The suit was beyond redemption, but it was all I had, and I couldn't go chasing bad guys around in a skirt and blouse. The wig was a little flat but I could spruce that up in no time. I laid it on the desk, then dug out Nadia's make up case and went into the bathroom.

What I saw in the mirror did not inspire confidence. My eyes were bloodshot, the skin beneath them slack and darkened. I didn't look much like a superhero, and truth be told, I didn't feel much like one, either.

"Act like a champion; feel like a champion."

Paul again. I hated him in my head, hated that he was right. I was still only Rachel; when I changed into Nadia, I would be strong enough for what lay ahead. I picked up the eye liner and set to work. I did my right eye in blue liner and mascara and darkened in the brow. It was a strange thing to be doing in my own house, in my own bathroom. I put the eye liner down and picked up the lip gloss. Staring into my face, I coloured the right side of my lips. I put foundation on my right cheek, and a bit of rouge to give it some colour, then I put in one brown contact lens. The halves of two familiar faces stared back at me.

On impulse, I got the black wig from the spare room, folded it flat and held it to the side of my head. Turned to the right, I was Nadia, turned to the left, I was Rachel. It was hard to see if I was trying to hide one of them, or set one of them free. I felt giddy, as if reality had revealed itself to be a dream. Then I heard footsteps pounding up the stairs.

Panicked, I looked for a place to hide the wig. All I could think to do was throw it in the sink.

"What's going on here?"

I turned around, hiding the wig with my body. Stephen stood in the doorway.

"What's going on here is none of your business," I said. "I told Dee to tell you I would call you tomorrow."

"Sure, after you spend tonight with your other boyfriend. Look at you, all made up. And what's that you're hiding? A wig? You're playing the tart with someone else and being a tease with me. What is it with you?"

I felt an absurd sense of gratitude that it was Stephen who had found me; someone less self-centred would have figured it out.

201

"Stephen, I think you'd better leave."

"Not until I get some answers."

Unobservant as he was, I didn't want to give him a chance to see Nadia's stuff. So far, he hadn't noticed her suit or the utility belt, which were visible through the open doorway behind him. I stepped forward and pushed him into the hallway. "Answers tomorrow," I shouted. "Right now, leave."

It looked as if I had shocked him into complying. He took a few steps towards the stairs but turned his head and looked into my bedroom on the way. He went ridged with anger and stomped through the doorway with me following. "And what's this?"

He held up Malcolm's jacket, shirt and trousers. "You're fucking some other guy in here and turning me away with just a peck on the cheek?"

We'd done more than peck. I'd willingly done more with him than with anyone else, but I didn't think he would be convinced if I told him. "Stephen, can you just trust me that it's not what it seems. Just go and we'll deal with this tomorrow."

He threw down the clothes and grabbed my arm. "We'll deal with this now." He flung me down on the bed and landed on top of me.

"Stephen, no."

He pulled back and looked at me, then brought his hand down, smacking me hard across the cheek. My head jerked to the side and I tasted blood.

"This is what you've wanted all along."

I wasn't sure if it was Stephen's voice, or Paul's ringing in my ears. I was too stunned to move. He worked my skirt up and ripped my knickers off. It was happening again. How could it? I had Nadia to protect me, but Nadia wasn't here, Nadia was a fugitive, Nadia couldn't come to my aid. He yanked at his belt and pulled his trousers down. I felt him hard against me. No, not again.

A mouth pressed wet against mine. A tongue probed and retreated. I looked at him leering above me as he jammed a knee between my thighs, forcing my legs apart. "You want this."

Paul's face superimposed over Stephen's.

"No," I said, but it didn't stop him, as it hadn't stopped him before.

I had thought this couldn't happen. What was wrong? Where was Nadia? I was just a seventeen year old kid, I trusted him; I couldn't fight back. Nadia was supposed to fight for me now, but where was she?

I looked above me. Stephen's face was back, red with excitement and exertion, working my thighs apart, working his way between them. He grinned at me, a grin of triumph, the same grin Paul had shown. But I wasn't a seventeen year old kid anymore, and I wasn't Nadia Penric, and no one was going to come to my rescue.

"I trusted you."

I swung my fist up and caught the side of his jaw. His head snapped back and his grin turned to a snarl. He raised himself up on his left hand, raised his right to strike me, and I raised my knee, hard into his groin. His hand stopped in mid-arc and his knee slid from between my thighs. I gripped his left arm and twisted it throwing him off of me.

I leapt off the bed, intent on getting away but I felt a hand fist in my hair, dragging me backward, slamming me onto the mattress. He jumped in front of me, half hopping, half staggering towards the bedroom door, his ankles hobbled by his trousers. He fell against the door, slamming it shut, then turned to face me, panting, his erection throbbing. "So, you like it rough."

He kicked off his loafers and stepped out of his jeans, standing in his socks, feet spread, hands on hips, a wolfish gleam in his eyes.

Paul's voice, like a painful buzzing in my head. "I made you, I can take you."

Then it was drowned out by Nadia's voice, confident and calm. "You don't deserve this; you know what to do."

I smoothed out my skirt and stood facing Stephen. The buzzing in my head stopped, replaced by clear, crystal silence. "Out of my way, Stephen. I have work to do."

He came towards me. "Not until our work is concluded."

I punched him hard in the chest driving him against the door. As he sank to the floor, gasping for breath, I grabbed him by the shirt collar and dragged him to his feet.

"I trusted you," I screamed, slamming him into the wall hard enough to make the pictures jump.

"How could you do this?"

Again the pictures jumped.

"You had no right."

And again.

Now I saw fear in his eyes. Blood leaked from his mouth where he had bitten his tongue. His erection no longer throbbed but hung limp between his legs.

"What the fuck are you on about?"

203

I yanked him forward. I wanted to slam him again and again and again for all the pain and hurt and betrayal I carried.

"That's enough. You can't put it all on him."

This time it wasn't Paul's voice, or Nadia's; it was my own. And I was right; it wasn't his fault, not all of it, hardly any of it, to be truthful. I wrenched the door open and pushed him through, half dragging, half walking him down the stairs to the front door. I threw him face first against the wall, pushed the door open and slid him along the wall through the opening, leaving a smear of blood across the door frame.

Dee was on her porch, staring wide-eyed. "Rachel, what happened?"

I let Stephen go. He staggered a bit but kept his feet.

"What happened? I'll tell you what's happened. He . . . " I point at Stephen in case she thought there was some other man lurking in the shadows. " . . . tried to rape me, that's what happened."

Dee went white. Her mouth dropped open. I didn't wait to hear if any sound came out. I slammed the door.

"What about my trousers?" Stephen shouted.

Chapter 26

I STOMPED UPSTAIRS. YES, what about his trousers. I thought about cutting them to ribbons and throwing them out the window but by the time I got to my bedroom I had a better idea.

I stood in the hallway, took a few deep breaths to calm myself, then set to work. Nadia's outfit was dirty, scraped and torn in a dozen places. I used a wet cloth to clean it as best I could, then pulled it inside out and gaffer-taped over the worst of the tears. When I turned it right side out and put it on, no gaping holes were visible. It wouldn't hold for long, but I didn't think I'd have much time anyway. I went back to the bathroom, finished applying make-up, put on the wig and saw Nadia looking back at me from the mirror. She didn't look sparkly and new as she had on my first outing less than two weeks ago. She looked tired, but also rugged, like someone who has seen action and was ready for more. She looked like a superhero closing in on the end of a mission.

I put on the shoes and utility belt and was done; now I just needed to get out of the house. It had taken, I hoped, just long enough for everyone to gather inside Dee's living room. What they were doing or saying I had no idea and even less concern. I put a scarf over my head, donned my fawn jacket and picked Stephen's trousers up off the floor. In the kitchen, I used a steak knife to gouge a large hole in the crotch and threw them onto Dee's porch, slamming my door so they couldn't avoid hearing me.

When I heard them come out, I ran to the kitchen, slipped through the conservatory door and jumped in my car. Before they guessed what was happening, I was already tearing out of the driveway. All they could see was me in my coat wearing a scarf, no one would have reason to think it was Nadia. They would assume I was going somewhere to think, or to the police station. Only Stephen would be self-obsessed enough to believe I was on my way to see another man.

In a sense, I was; two to be exact. I headed for Burgess Hill and Keymer View Court, certain I knew where Carl and Derek would be, and why. Whatever they were doing tonight they would have to begin at their lair, and then go back to clean up.

They might even hang about to have a few celebratory drinks together, though anyone with any intelligence would go to a pub to supply an alibi for themselves.

The sleet was getting heavy by the time I parked and made my way around the side of Keymer View Court. I jumped the wall into the back of the south block and made my way towards the garages. From around the corner, I heard footstep and talking. I ducked into the shadows as three men, one carrying a cricket bat, walked by. They talked low and emitted the occasional chuckle but kept up their pace as if they were on a route march. They walked past me and disappeared around the far end of the block. They were, I realised, on patrol. The residents had probably never said a word to each other before, but I had brought them together by providing a common enemy. How touching.

I sprinted across the common area and out to the path leading to the workshop. Yellow light spilled out of the dusty windows, illuminating the wet leaves on the ground. I worked my way around, keeping silent, even though the noise coming from the interior of the workshop would cover any noise I made. They were sitting on the stools, each with a bottle of Bulmer's cider in their hand. Several empties were scattered on the table in front of them. As I watched, they each drank, slammed the bottles down with identical grins and took up the conversation, which seemed to begin and end with Brighton and Hove's football club. I went to the front of the shack, opened the door and walked inside.

The air was close, smelling of sweat and cigarette smoke. The conversation stopped. Carl looked at me with his mouth open as he set his bottle on the table. Derek took a swig from his and a final drag from his cigarette. "Well, well, look who's here."

He grinned and stood up while Carl continued to have problems keeping his mouth closed. Derek was going to be the difficult one, but I was going to enjoy it. Sound finally came out of Carl's mouth. "But, Kevin told us he had taken care of you."

Derek ignored him and moved around the table. I stayed where I was, guarding the door. No one was getting out of here until I was ready.

"What did you think," I asked. "That Mr Sawyer had eliminated me? Is this what you were celebrating, the demise of the woman who beat you up and spoiled your fun? Or are you providing an alibi for each other?"

Carl began to lose colour. "Why should we need an alibi?"

"Shut up, Carl," Derek said.

He moved closer, his hand resting on a length of copper tubing. I knew without looking that just within reach on the workbench behind me was a claw hammer, flathead screwdriver and short coil of rope. I kept my eyes on him.

"You've been naughty boys," I said. "Your master told you to do something today, and I'm here to stop it."

"But there's nothing to stop."

"Shut up, Carl," Derek said. He gripped the copper pipe and stepped closer.

"I think there is. I think you have something planned for this evening. Something big."

"And I think you've been poking around where you don't belong for long enough now."

"Derek, she doesn't know nothing. She's bluffing. Kevin said she can't hurt us anymore."

"Shut up, Carl."

"Mr Sawyer thinks I can't hurt you because he thinks I'm dead." I looked from Carl to Derek, who had moved beyond the table, the pipe clutched in his gnarled fist. "Isn't that right, Derek?"

"Dead? Listen, he told me no one was going to get hurt."

"Shut up, Carl."

Derek lunged forward, swinging the pipe down like a truncheon. I sidestepped, reached behind me for the rope and swung it towards him like a whip. It snapped around his neck and I yanked, pulling him off his feet. I jumped aside as his lack of balance and excess of cider caused him to crash hard into a rack of tools. He and an assortment of pliers, hack saws and hammers tumbled to the floor. I lunged towards him, zip-tie at the ready. He kicked and lashed out with the pipe. "Carl, get the door. Don't let her get away."

This brought Carl to action. He bounded towards the door but I didn't think subduing me was on his mind; he looked like a rabbit fleeing a hungry dog. I body slammed him into the doorpost and kicked the door closed. He raised his hands to ward me off, which gave me the opportunity to grab his wrist, twist him around and wrench his arm up to the middle of his back. He yowled in pain. I slipped the restraint on him, grabbed his flailing, free arm and pulled the nylon loops tight around his wrists. Out of the corner of my eye I saw Derek on his feet coming towards me. I pushed Carl to the floor and jumped up on the workbench, pointing at Derek with a gloved hand.

"Drop that weapon and submit," I shouted. It sounded corny, even to myself, but it had the desired result. Derek stopped and looked up at me; a confused expression on his weathered face. "Who the hell do you think you are, lady?"

I stood with my fist on my hips, legs spread.

"I'm Nadia Penric," I said. "Defender of truth, guardian of justice."

"You're a loony."

He swung the pipe at my knees. I leapt into the air, ducking my head to keep from hitting the ceiling. As I came down I kicked out, landing my foot in the centre of his forehead. His head snapped back, followed by the rest of him. He fell against the table, scattering bottles and cider and stools. I jumped down, straddling him, rolled him onto his stomach and landed on his back with both knees. I heard the air whoosh out of him and he went limp, enabling me to restrain his hands and feet.

Carl's eyes opened wide, shining with fear in his ashen face. "Jesus, lady. Are you really a superhero, like the papers said?"

"Yes," I said. "I am. And now you're going to tell me what you did this evening."

Behind me, Derek stirred. "Don't say nothing."

I turned away from Carl and rummaged through the workshop until I found a roll of gaffer tape. I peeled off a length and taped it over Derek's mouth.

"Now," I said to Carl. "What did you do?"

Carl wormed into a sitting position and scooted away from me towards the far wall. I walked with him until he backed into the corner.

"Well?" I said.

"Nothing. Honest."

I stepped closer. He cringed.

"There was a gas fireplace here, on that table. You made it into an explosive device, didn't you? Where is it?"

Behind me Derek thrashed and squirmed like a landed carp and made muffled sounds through the tape.

"There's nothing bad going to happen. Honest."

"Something bad has already happened. You blew up Keymer View Court. People could have been hurt or killed. You're driving people from their homes. Your boss tried to kill me. Don't tell me nothing bad is going to happen."

A sound, like the whimper of a Labrador puppy separated from its mother climbed up his throat. "Okay, it may not be totally on the up and up, but Kevin has it under control. It's all for show. No one will get hurt."

208

I squatted down so I could look him in the eyes. "You're the one who solved all the technical problems, right."

He nodded.

"And you mixed the chemicals that caused the explosion last week?" I thought about the assorted chemicals and electronics that had been scattered about on my first visit. "You're very intelligent, aren't you?"

A smile flickered on his quivering lips, but there was no humour in it. "A genius, that's what they told me."

"But it didn't do you much good, did it? All the kids picked on you, called you names, treated you like a freak."

He said nothing, but the fear left his eyes, replaced by surprise and curiosity.

He nodded his head. "Yes."

"Why didn't you go on to university? Make something of yourself?"

"What do you care?"

"You could have used your powers for good; instead you're a glorified gardener for a sleazebag slumlord, doing his bidding because you think it will please him, or because you can. I don't think you're a bad person, you can still make something of your life, but not if you let the events of this evening unfold without giving me the chance to stop them."

He took a breath to steady himself, then cast a glance at Derek, who was making quite a disturbance thrashing about. I thought about trussing him up tighter but didn't want to interrupt our discussion.

"Ignore him," I said. "Who do you take your orders from? Mr Sawyer, your friend over there? Neither of them have the intelligence you do, but you're letting them ruin your life."

His composure returned and a real smile crept onto his face. "You just don't get it. It's all set up; it will all go like clockwork."

"Why, because you set it up. Do you have that high an opinion of yourself?"

His smile turned to smugness. "The device is a masterpiece. It's so good, even you knowing about it won't make any difference; the police won't believe you if you try to explain it to them, they'll just arrest you."

"That clever, are you?"

Derek ratcheted his thrashing up a notch, suspecting, as I was, that Carl's ego was about to burst.

"Yes, I am. The device will activate in stages, allowing time for evacuation but not enough time for the fire services to get there. At the end of its cycle, it will leave no trace. It's perfect."

"It's bullshit. No one is that clever. You're putting people's lives at risk based on your ill-placed confidence in yourself."

"It's not ill-placed. The device cannot activate—"

"Let's call it what is it, shall we?" I shouted at him. "It's a bomb. You put a bomb in someone's home. And you call that clever?"

His smug smile remained. "You don't know what you're talking about, lady. The bomb is a work of art. When it activates, it releases gas into the room to make the occupants woozy. Once they are evacuated, gas will continue to fill up the room, creating the illusion of a gas leak. When the device goes off, the resulting explosion and fire will destroy all traces of it. Kevin will be on hand to get everyone out. He'll be a hero; the explosion will be an unfortunate accident. We all get what we want."

I gaped at him and felt true sorrow. "You really believe that, don't you?"

"I've checked everything, built and tested prototypes, it's all going to run smooth as silk. What makes you think it won't?"

"Because Mr Sawyer is in Fuerteventura."

Carl's smile dropped and his complexion turned a pasty white. "What are you talking about?"

"He went there on Thursday, right after you failed to catch me at the hospital. I followed him. That's where he called you from, after he thought he'd eliminated me. He's not coming back until Sunday."

"You're lying."

"Carl, you're the clever one, so listen up. Who made the bomb? You did. Who installed it?" I pointed at Derek who had passed out, grown weary or accepted his fate. Either way, he was lying quiet now. "I'm guessing your mate there didn't help you."

"Well, no, he had another job—"

"You're being set up, Carl. Your bomb is going to go off, people are going to die and all fingers are going to point to you."

For a moment I thought he was going to be sick.

"Tell me where it is, Carl."

He looked at the floor, shaking his head. "It's too late. Too late."

Now I felt tendrils of panic rising in me. "What do you mean? Has it gone off already?"

"The device, the bomb, will begin its sequence at eight o'clock. It will go off twenty minutes later."

I looked at my watch. It had just gone seven. "There's still time. Tell me which flat it's in, I'll go get it."

He looked at me, real pain in his eyes. "You don't understand. It's not here. It's in Bishops Court. Kevin needed to get that old couple out because of their special lease."

I grabbed him by the collar and shook him. "You bastard. You're going to blow up Howard and Maggie?"

He started crying then, real blubbering baby tears. "I didn't know, honest. I didn't know."

I let him go and stood over him. "How do I defuse the bomb?"

"You can't. If the fireplace is turned on, it will activate at eight o'clock and you can't stop it. The whole device is sealed, you can't get in it. Even turning the fireplace off won't stop it. The only thing you can do is get the people out."

I checked my watch again. Another minute gone, but I could still make it if luck remained on my side and I didn't end up behind a tractor.

"But the bomb, I must be able to do something to stop it?"

He shook his head, looking at the floor again. "I'm telling you, you can't. Even I can't. It's impossible to defuse and you won't be able to carry it out of the flat. It's too heavy; I had to use a hand truck to get it up there. You've just got to get away."

I left him and headed for the door. "You'd better hope I get there in time."

"Nadia," he called, startling me by using my name. I turned towards him.

"You've got to get far away. The bomb, it's real powerful. There's twenty pounds of C4 in it. It's behind the fireplace in the retaining wall between the flats. It should destroy both of them, and most of the two below. We chose the spot for maximum damage."

"Well done you," I said, not trying to hide my disgust. "You and your mate should be comfortable enough here until the police find you."

As I stepped outside, he called to me once more. "If Kevin thinks he eliminated you in Fuerteventura, how did you get here?"

I smiled at him. "I'm a superhero, remember?"

Chapter 27

I USED THE LAST of my restraints to secure the door from the outside. Derek wasn't going anywhere, but Carl might find his feet and figure a way to open the door using his teeth. Not that it mattered a great deal; what mattered was getting to Bishops Court in less than fifty minutes. On a good day, that run might take twenty minutes, but this wasn't a good day; it was night and it was Saturday. And the sleet was beginning to mix with snow.

I ran into the courtyard and cut a path straight across it towards where my car was parked. It didn't matter if anyone saw me; speed was paramount now, not stealth. I vaulted the wall, nearly slipping on a skim of ice, and sprinted to my car.

I wanted to avoid going through town so I turned south on the London Road and took the bypass to the A23. Despite the weather, traffic was moving freely. When I got to the A272, it slowed, but even then it moved without incident into Cowfold, where it became bumper-to-bumper and slowed to a crawl. I sat in traffic, willing the cars forward, resisting the urge to pound on the dashboard, blare my horn or otherwise draw needless attention to myself. All I could do was check my watch and pray no one in front of me had an accident.

At the roundabout, most of the traffic turned left for the A24 and speed picked up a bit as I headed up the A281. My watch said twenty minutes past seven. It was going to be close unless I could make better time. I put the wipers on high as the sleet and snow mixture changed to snow. At the sight of white precipitation, the rest of the drivers panicked and forgot everything they had learned from the Highway Code. Some hit their brakes and went into small but heart-stopping skids while other drivers, the wankers in the big people carriers who think they are invincible, zoomed around them on their way to an appointment with an accident.

I checked my watch and joined the wanker squad, my tyres skidding and slipping as I wove around the more cautious motorists. I made it through Mannings Heath and entered the outskirts of Horsham at twenty eight after seven. The traffic was thicker there, forcing me to weave onto the snow-covered pavements. On the hill climbing into the town proper, I pulled around a Frontera Sport and earned several angry horn blasts accompanied by creative hand gestures. I couldn't blame them; I was driving like a lunatic. I just hoped no one recognised my car.

As I came up by the Queen's Head the road was clear. I could see the railway bridge and beyond it the glow from the town centre reflecting off the falling snow. If Albion Way wasn't blocked with traffic I would make it.

Behind me, high beams glared, reflecting off my rear-view mirror and into my eyes. The vehicle came up fast, blinding me, then zoomed past. It was the Frontera I had cut off, exacting revenge. He blared his horn and swerved in front of me, forcing me to slam on my brakes. I managed to avoid hitting him, but my tyres locked and I went into a skid. My car slid over the thickening snow, jumped the kerb and crashed into a bollard in front of the PC Supply Shop. My air bag exploded, pinning me to the seat. The Frontera never slowed.

The airbag deflated. I sat, stunned, looking at my crumpled bonnet and the plume of steam rising from beneath it. I turned the key. The engine caught and, after grinding and hissing, settled into a stuttering rhythm. I threw it in reverse and tried to back away but my tyres spun on the ice. I knew I could get the car out eventually, but I didn't have the luxury of time. I jumped out of the car and ran.

On foot, I could go straight through town to Bishops Court. I raced down East Street and entered the pedestrian area that encompassed Middle and West Streets. The pavement was slick underfoot but I was making better time than I would have in the car. I could see the golden glow of McDonald's arches at the end of the street. I was almost there.

The weather hadn't discouraged the Saturday night revellers. West Street was dotted with groups of people on their way out for the evening or, by the looks of some of them, moving from one pub to the next. Clusters of boys in tee shirts and young girls dressed for a tropical climate wove their way along the street, unmindful of the falling snow and ice underfoot. I dodged between them, slipping in my rubber-soled trainers, marvelling at the girls who remained upright in high heels. People looked as I ran by but remained disinterested, apparently assuming I was a dedicated jogger. Then someone pointed me out to their companions and gave a thumbs-up sign. It started as a whisper, rippling along with me as I passed my place of erstwhile employment and approached the scattered groupings of couples by the Shelly fountain.

"Nadia!"

"Are you sure?"

"Yes, that's her. Look, it's Nadia."

"It is. Hey, Nadia!"

Then the chanting began. "Nadia, Nadia, Nadia."

I felt I should do something, so I waved as if I was the Queen passing by in her motorcade. The crowd cheered.

"Off to save the world again, Nadia?"

Some of the boys called to me, to show off their "I am Nadia" tee shirts; the girls pointed to their buttons and a random few exposed their undergarments. I kept running and gave another wave to more hoots and cheers. Their enthusiasm gave me a boost and I kicked my pace up a notch, as much to leave them behind as to make sure I arrived at Bishops Court on time. Encouraging as their support was, the last thing I needed was a crowd trailing after me chanting my name for every PC in town to hear. To my relief, the thought of following a superhero wasn't enough to divert them from the pleasures of the pubs. No one joined me on my run, and just a few of them continued chanting as I entered the dim area of the Bishopric. I passed the Merrythought. An involuntary glance at Alex's flat confirmed she wasn't home. I looked at my watch. I still had twenty minutes. The crossing for Albion Way was right in front of me. Beyond was The Pedaller, and Bishops Court. I was going to make it.

Then someone tackled me from behind.

Caught by surprise, I fell forward, breaking my fall with my hands and skidding on the slick pavement. Whoever had tackled me had their arms around my legs, pinning my feet down with their body. The next sound I expected to hear was a PC reading me my rights and I debated the wisdom of kicking a police officer, even if I had a good reason. From behind me, I heard a triumphant snarl. "Got you, bitch."

I kicked out and squirmed away, turning over as Keith jumped at me. I caught his nose with the heel of my hand and scooted backward, jumping to my feet and turning around to run. Behind me, Keith lashed out and pain shot through the back of my thigh. I fell to the pavement, holding my leg, looking up at Keith standing over me, his smile outlined by the blood running from his nose, a knife in his hand.

I kicked out with my good leg. He jumped back, his smile widening. "I'm going to enjoy this."

I felt blood seeping out of my leg, oozing into my bodysuit. I thought I could walk, but I wasn't going to have the chance with

Keith standing over me. I crawled backward as fast as I could, while Keith matched my progress with a slow amble. He avoided my efforts to kick him and he had the advantage. He remained out of range, biding his time, herding me deeper into the shadows. I was hoping I could make it into the thicket of bushes that lined the road; perhaps I could lose him in the undergrowth. Then my back came up against a tree. I couldn't move around it, or go forward. It was a standoff. I didn't have time for a standoff, and Keith didn't look in the mood for negotiating.

He held the knife towards me, just out of range. I braced against the tree, waiting for him to strike. He lunged forward, the knife going straight for my throat. I knocked his hand away and grabbed for his wrist. He was quick, but not quick enough to avoid my other hand. I punched him in the side of the neck with a gloved fist, sending him sprawling to the pavement.

"You bitch!"

I clawed my way up the trunk of the tree, gaining my feet. Keith recovered and came at me. Then someone from the group of smokers outside the Green Dragon pointed our way. "Hey, that's Nadia. And someone's after her."

I tried to move around the tree, into the thicket, but Keith lunged and blocked my way. There was no where I could go. Keith grinned, oblivious to the pounding feet behind him. I kicked again, trying to keep him distracted and away from me.

The crowd hit him like a freight train. Four beefy boys and Keith toppled to the snowy pavement beside me followed by their game, but lesser adventurous, companions.

"He's got a knife," someone shouted.

Keith never had a chance; he was pinned and pummelled and stripped of his weapon in moments. I slipped further into the shadows, testing my leg, fighting the pain. I could stand, but I wasn't sure if I could run.

Six boys were holding Keith now, gripping his arms, legs and neck, holding him spread eagle as he struggled and swore and spit.

"Nadia, who is this bloke?" one of them asked.

The growing knot of people crowded me in; the only way out was through the thicket and onto the road. I stood straight, looking at the growing throng, doing my best not to favour my leg. Bad form for a superhero.

"He's one of my arch enemies," I said, smiling at the group and surreptitiously checking my watch. Ten minutes to eight.

"Hey, that's the guy from YouTube, the drug dealer having the tantrum."

A murmur of assent from the crowd. One of the men holding Keith looked at him. "It is. You're a right wanker, mate."

"What do you want us to do with him?" another one asked.

"Deliver him to the authorities," I said, because I thought it sounded like something a superhero might say. And it would give the police something to do besides follow me.

The biggest, beefiest one smiled. "Don't worry, Nadia, we know how to take care of people like him."

Keith kicked out, screaming and twisting. "You bitch! You fucking bitch!"

The men held tight. The crowd turned to watch. I took advantage of the distraction and ducked into the shadows. I was at the guard rail in three steps, climbed over with difficulty and hobbled along the road looking for a break in traffic. Behind me, my absence was noted.

"Where's Nadia?"

"She just disappeared."

"She must have flown away. She really is a superhero."

When you're drunk, I suppose anything is possible. I performed an awkward sprint across Albion Way and limped towards the Bishopric, gritting my teeth, my thigh throbbing.

I passed by The Pedaller, still boarded over and still with the cheery "business as usual" sign across the front. Light glowed through the door—the only panel of glass still intact. I paused and glanced inside. Robin was at the counter, one arm in a sling, his face a study of blue and purple. He was hunched over a ledger, writing with his left hand. He looked up as I limped away. Slow as I was going, he didn't catch up with me until I was near the Ford dealer. "What are you doing running around out here? The police are looking for you."

"Really?" I said. "How could something like that have slipped my mind?"

He was having a hard time keeping up with me, even though I was moving at a leisurely jogging pace, but I didn't slow down.

He shook his head. "Come on, what's going on? Can't you stop for a second?"

"No. There's a bomb in Bishops Court that will activate in . . . " I checked my watch, " . . . eight minutes. If I don't stop it, it will blow up Howard and Maggie and who knows how many other people."

I pushed myself harder. He grimaced, trying to keep up with me. We moved in silence; he didn't speak until we had passed the Ford showroom and approached the entrance to Bishops Court. "You know, there is no such thing as superheroes."

"Look, I know it sounds crazy, but it's not a fantasy. You've been assaulted, that's real. We were chased by Sawyer, and he tried to kill me—"

"Kill you?"

"Yes, in Fuerteventura, when he blew up the hotel. That was real."

"Fuerteventura. Are you sure?"

I sighed. We were almost at Bishops Court. It was seven minutes to eight. "Yes I'm sure. I was there."

"Who are Howard and Maggie?"

"They're nice people, friends. Does it matter? He's trying to kill them. I have to stop it."

"Stop it? How are you going to stop a bomb?"

"It just has to be turned off. It's hidden behind their gas fireplace. I need to have the fireplace turned off before eight o'clock."

"You know, you are the most interesting person I have ever met, but I have to tell you, this sounds crazy. Even for you."

I looked at him. We had just turned into the court; in a moment I would see the lights in Howard and Maggie's flat. "No one's asking you to stay," I said.

"That's not what I meant—"

"You can just go now if you think I'm a loony."

"Nadia, can't we just talk about this for—"

"No. There's no time. I could already be too late."

We made it into the courtyard. Maggie and Howard's lights were on.

"Listen," I said, "this is my fight. You of all people should want to avoid me, but you're telling me you want to stay and that I can trust you. Is that right?"

"I do, and you can."

"But you don't trust me. And I can't trust someone who doesn't trust me. You either believe what I'm telling you or go back to your bike shop. Your choice."

He stopped then. I moved ahead, limping up the steps. With four minutes to spare, I pushed the doors open and entered the lobby, leaving him behind. Then a thought occurred to me. Suppose my watch, or Carl's timing, was off? I turned around. He was walking away. "Robin, come back."

He looked over his shoulder. "Don't you think we've—"

"I need your help."

He stopped, but kept his back to me.

"In the hospital, you said you wanted us to be a team."

"But you said—"

"I'm giving you a second chance. And after I prove myself to you, you'd better not doubt me again."

He turned around then.

I went down the steps, looking up at the balcony above me and the balcony above that, which led to Howard's sitting room. "If the bomb has activated, they may already have been overcome by gas. We won't be able to get in through their door. Howard's got it bolted up like a fortress."

Robin looked puzzled but at least he didn't walk away. "So what am I supposed to do?"

"You go up the stairs and try their door. They'll answer if they're still conscious."

"And what will you do?"

"I'll fly up to the balcony and get in through the French doors."

He kept silent for a moment. "This is a test, isn't it? You're trying to make me think you're crazy."

I didn't answer. I sidestepped into the tangle of weeds that served as a flowerbed and pulled myself onto the sill of the lower window. Pushing off with my good leg, I jumped to the lower balcony, grabbed the bars with my gloved hands and pulled myself over the railing. I looked below. He was still standing, gaping at me.

"I told you I could fly, now get moving."

He climbed the two steps and disappeared into the lobby. I regarded the second balcony. The first one had been easy, the next one might prove difficult.

I climbed onto the railing, slick with sleet, fighting for balance. The top of the nearest window was edged with a lip of concrete, and it was just within reach. I pushed off of that, my wound and the slickness making momentum difficult. I gripped the bottom railing of Howard's balcony, and hung there.

I chinned myself, and grabbed for the top rail. My hand hit and slid off the icy surface. I pulled and grabbed again, gaining purchase this time. I held on and moved my other hand to the top rail. Now it was a matter of vaulting over it and onto the balcony. I swung my leg up but couldn't get it to the lip of the railing. My hands were numb with cold; they began to slip. I struggled to hang on, my arms burning with the strain. I looked beneath me to the pavement. It was a long way down. My fingers began to slide.

Then strong hands gripped my wrists. I pulled and swung my leg up. My foot made it to the edge of the balcony and stayed. I clambered over the railing and came face to face with Howard.

"Nadia, what are you doing hanging off my balcony?"

"No time. We've got to shut your fireplace off."

"But—"

I pushed past him, he followed, his hand still on my wrist, trying to hold me back.

"It's a bomb, Howard. Mr Sawyer wants you out and he's willing to kill you to do it. We have to shut it off."

"But—"

I pulled against Howard's grip. He was remarkably fit for an old guy. I could have sucker punched him but that would have been rude. "I know it sounds crazy, but it's true," I shouted, above the telly. "You've got to let me turn it off before it's too late."

Maggie rose from the settee. "Oh, has Nadia come to visit? How nice."

"Howard, please."

"But—"

"But what?"

"It's not cold enough to turn on the fire."

I stopped struggling and looked at their new gas fire place. It was dark and empty. I let out a breath. Now that I wasn't acting like a lunatic, Howard released me and pulled the balcony doors closed. "You gave me a fright," he said.

"It sounds crazy, I know, but it's true. We need to call the police, and the fire brigade."

"What on earth for?"

The doorbell rang.

"Oh, more visitors?" Maggie said, shuffling towards the hallway. "And at this hour?"

"Your fireplace is lethal, Howard. We have to get out of here and evacuate the building."

"Are you sure? That seems a bit extreme."

"Trust me. If I'm right, we can save the building. If I'm wrong, everyone gets a nice walk in the snow."

Maggie came back with Robin on her arm. "Look who has come to visit. A nice young man."

Robin looked as dazed as Howard.

"Maggie, Howard," I said, "this is my friend, Robin."

"Oh," said Maggie, "like the bird?"

"You're Robin?" Howard asked. Then he looked at me.

"So, that makes you—"

"Don't say it."

Robin looked at me. "I see you made it. I didn't know you could fly."

"Really?" Maggie said. "Is that how you got up here?"

"No. Your husband pulled me up. Without him, I'd be a splat on the pavement."

Maggie nodded, her eyes bright with interest. "You should take the stairs next time. Shall I make some tea? It's cold in here."

Without waiting for an answer she shuffled away.

Howard turned his attention to Robin. "Nadia tells me my gas fire is a bomb. What do you make of that?"

Robin looked at his shoes for a few moments. "Well, given all that's happened, there's no reason not to believe it. And will it hurt to take precautions?"

I could have kissed him. "As I said, Howard, what's the worst that can happen if I'm wrong?"

Howard rubbed his chin. "I don't know, dragging a whole lot of people out into this weather. Some of them have babies."

"It beats the alternative. If you—"

I was cut short by the thump of a body hitting the carpet. We all looked towards the far wall, where flames flickered in the new fireplace and Maggie lay crumpled on the floor in front of it.

"Robin, get her!"

I opened the balcony doors. Robin and Howard rushed to Maggie's aid as I opened the rest of the windows wide, whipping the curtains out of the way for maximum air flow.

I helped them get Maggie to her feet. She was groggy, but semi-conscious. "Get her outside. Call the police. Get everyone out of the flats."

This time Howard didn't argue.

The three of us walked Maggie down the hallway, out into the lobby. Then I went back inside.

"Nadia, what are you doing?"

"I'm going to get rid of the bomb."

Robin dropped his half of Maggie, forcing Howard to scramble to keep her on her feet. He came towards me. I slammed the door and threw the bolts. "Get her out," I shouted through the door, hoping I was loud enough to be heard above his pounding.

I limped into the sitting room and shut off the fire. If Carl had told me the truth, the bomb would continue spewing gas until it went off. I judged I had just about fifteen minutes. I could smell the gas. I held my breath and felt around the edges of the faux front. As I suspected, they hadn't done a very thorough job of installing it. It might have been because they knew it wouldn't need to be there long but I suspected it was just their usual way of working. I slipped my fingers under a corner edge and pulled. The entire fireplace came away, revealing a grey metal box about two and a half feet square that had been set into the wall behind it. From the lower corner a small hole hissed as gas flowed from it.

I wrenched the box out of the hole, bringing dust and brick grit with it. It fell forward and I jumped out of the way as it crashed to the carpet. I tried to pull it free from the wall but it wouldn't budge. I looked for the problem. The gas pipe, a flexible copper tube, held the base in place. I needed to remove the nut attaching it to the bomb.

I tried to turn it with my hand but it was too tight. I went to the kitchen, flinging open drawers, looking for a tool; any tool, a hammer, a saw, a pair of pliers. All I found was a cork screw and a nut cracker. I took the nut cracker.

Back in the sitting room I gripped the bolt with the nut cracker and turned. It moved a fraction of an inch and then the nutcracker slipped. I crawled to the window to take a breath. Maggie, Howard and Robin were below, Robin on his mobile, Howard standing with Maggie. I sucked in cold air and returned to the bomb. I squeezed and turned and slipped again. Millimetre by millimetre the bolt turned until it was loose enough to unscrew by hand. I spun it off and wrenched the box free. It was a foot thick and heavy as a bag of bowling balls. Gas roared into the room from the open pipe.

I limped to the window again, coughing and sputtering. I heard shouting below but didn't stop to take it in. I went back to the pipe.

I needed to shut it off. I sat on the floor next to the wall and pushed the pipe with my foot, bending it over. I applied more pressure, praying it wouldn't break. It didn't, the pipe crimped, the roar became a hiss, then stopped. It might still be leaking, but it wasn't flooding the room with gas any more. And it would have to do; I had other things to worry about.

I tried to pick up the bomb, cradling it in my arms. It was too heavy, and even with two good legs I wouldn't be able to carry it. I set it up on its narrow edge and tried to drag it but there was nothing to hold on to. I hopped into the hallway on my good leg, looking for something, anything. I pulled open the airing cupboard. Towels, sheets, blankets. I grabbed a blanket and unfurled it as I hopped back into the sitting room. I spread it on the floor, tipped the bomb onto it and dragged, pushing with my good leg and balancing on the other.

It was hard going, but I dragged the unwieldy box, inches at a time, into the hallway. The door to the landing was straight ahead, but should I drag it out there? People might be trying to get out and, assuming I could get it down the stairs, I would only succeed in getting the bomb to where the people were. I grabbed the other end of the blanket and dragged it into the bedroom.

The windows in the bedroom were large and swung outward like the windows in the sitting room. There were two of them, with a double bed situated between them. Oak bedside tables sat on either side of the bed, beneath the windows. I pulled the nearest one out of the way and opened the window wide. I stood the bomb on edge and inched it up the wall, gouging the plaster, until it was balancing on the window sill. C4 is a very stable explosive; you can kick it, drop it, throw it against a wall or even shoot it and it won't explode, so tipping it out the window shouldn't cause it to go off. But the fall might jar the timer, and that might make it explode, and there might be families in the lower flats.

The snow and sleet had turned to rain now, so the ground would be soft. Still, I didn't want to take any chances; I took the blanket, wrapped it around the bomb and inched it out the window. The weight of the device strained against the fabric and I struggled to keep a grip as I lowered it, like a baby in a cradle, as far as I could. When it was dangling below the first floor window and threatening to pull me out with it, I released one end of the blanket and let the bomb tumble out. The sudden release of weight and my own survival instincts caused me to fling backward onto the bedroom floor, the blanket still gripped in my hand. I cringed, waiting for the explosion.

Nothing happened.

I opened my eyes, crawled back to the window and looked into the darkness below. The bomb had hit the soft soil, rolled a bit on its narrow edge and was now lying on its side just a dozen feet from the building. The area in back of the flats was quiet and empty, but a commotion was building at the front. I heard voices and distant sirens. If the bomb was as powerful as Carl claimed, it would tear the ground floor flats apart. People in the courtyard or still in the flats could be hurt, maybe killed; I needed to move the bomb. I looked at my watch. Seven minutes left, give or take, left.

I tied the blanket to the bedpost, threw back the duvet and ripped the sheet off the mattress. With the blanket attached to the sheet, I had a rope that reached almost to the ground. I lowered it out the window, tested the knot and climbed out.

Sliding down the makeshift rope wasn't hard, but stopping was. I slipped off the end and landed hard on the wet ground, my leg screaming in pain. I rolled over and stood up, limping towards the bomb, before I realised what I had done.

I had no way of dragging the device and it was too heavy to lift. I hauled it upright, standing it on its narrow edge, then I pushed and rolled it onto the next edge, grimacing as it thunked to earth. I rolled it again, and again and, like a big square tyre, wheeling it away from the building. I was judging whether I had enough time to get it into the trees when I heard a shout. "Police! You're under arrest!"

I turned and saw Special PC Alex Marsh running towards me. I let the bomb fall and jumped aside. She anticipated my move and we tumbled to the ground.

The last thing I needed was a charge of assaulting an officer levelled at me, but this was my erstwhile friend. Did a catfight count as resisting arrest? There was no time to debate it, and Alex wasn't in the mood for catching up. I broke her hold and hobbled upright, trying to get away.

She grabbed for my shoulder. I blocked her arm and pushed her away. She blocked me and grabbed again. We stood facing one another, swinging our arms and blocking each blow like Mr Miaghi and the Karate Kid playing wax-on, wax-off. Then she went for her Captor spray. I grabbed her wrist, twisted it away and tried to push her over with my free hand. She grabbed my arm and twisted and we stood, puffing and grunting with the strain, Alex hampered by her heavy police gear, me hamstrung by my wounded leg, neither of us daring to let the other go.

"Officer needs assistance," she shouted.

"Alex, quit it."

I felt her grip ease. I did the same. "Rachel?"

"Yes," I said. "Now help me. We haven't much time."

Without explanation, I grabbed an edge of the bomb. Alex continued to stare, dumbfounded.

"Hurry. We only got about two minutes left."

"What are you talking about?"

"This is a bomb. We have to get rid of it."

She hesitated. "Rachel, really—"

"Alex, you've got to trust me on this one; there's about twenty pounds of C4 in this thing, courtesy of the people who really did blow up Keymer View Court. Do you want to help me get rid of it or are you going to stand there and let it blow us up?"

"Shit," she said, grabbing a side.

Together we lifted, grunting under the strain. My leg shrieked and threatened to buckle. I shut out the pain and found it could support me just enough to allow a hobbling step with my good leg.

"Where are we taking it?"

I had only wanted to get it as far away as I could, but together we could move it faster and another idea came to mind. "The pill box. This way."

Around the side of the building, two police officers charged towards us.

"Get back!" Alex shouted. "There's a bomb. Get everyone out. Now!"

The officers skidded to a halt and ran back around the building. We shuffled through the break in the trees to where the dark hulk of the reinforced concrete structure stood, already decked out in red, white and blue bunting. Alex tried to lead us towards the door.

"No," I said. "The door is locked . . . go around front . . . the gun port."

She nodded, not wasting breath with conversation. We edged around the pill box and hoisted the box by inches until it was level with the gun port on the front wall. We coxed a corner of the bomb into the opening and pushed. The metal box ground against the edges of the concrete. We pushed harder, it moved further.

"How much time do we have?"

We pushed again. It was halfway through now.

"I don't know. Not much."

Another push. Closer.

"Listen," I said. "At Keymer View Court there's a work shop . . . the two men in there, they did this . . . I have them tied up."

I grunted against the strain; the bomb slid forward another inch.

"Kevin Sawyer is behind it . . . he's flying into Gatwick from Fuerteventura tomorrow at five o'clock . . . he'll be carrying a suitcase with a million euros in it."

"Why are you telling me this?"

We pushed again. It was nearly there. "Because I'm going to push this through or die trying and you're going to get away and arrest Sawyer."

Another push, another inch.

"Don't be such a dope."

"Someone has to finish this. And you have more to live for than I do."

We steadied ourselves and pushed in unison. The bomb slid further into the hole.

"Stop talking like that."

"It's true." I started to cry, blurring my vision, making my efforts less effective. Then I got mad at myself, for crying, for losing control, for making such a hash of something so simple. "My life's a mess."

She said nothing. I swiped at my eyes and pushed along with her. "Alex, go."

She braced herself and gave a karate yell as her body arched and tensed with effort. I pushed and strained, my muscles searing, my legs throbbing. I screamed along with her, but merely from pain. The box slipped forward and fell with a clunk onto the concrete floor, echoing in the empty chamber.

"Run," Alex shouted.

I hadn't the strength, but she pulled me with her. We managed a dozen shuffling steps before the blast knocked us down.

We pitched forward onto the damp earth with Alex on top of me. A tongue of flame shot from the gun port like dragon's breath, shattering the plate glass windows of the furniture showroom on the far side of the street. A smaller glow lit up the back where Martin's steel door bowed but held. The pillbox expanded like a puffed toad, its walls flexing, the roof arching. Cracks appeared, glowing red, as the structure threatened to burst and shower us with chunks of concrete. Then the roar subsided and the pillbox eased into its original shape, as if exhaling.

The eerie silence that followed was punctuated with the sound of stones dropping. First one, then another, then more and more as the pillbox collapsed in on itself until there was nothing left but a pile of smoking rubble festooned in a tangle of red, white and blue.

"Are you all right?"

Alex's voice sounded as if she was under water. I tested my limbs. "I think so."

"Then get moving. But keep out of sight."

"I thought I was under arrest?"

She smiled and eased off of me. "Take the offer before I change my mind." She knelt next to me and helped me into a sitting position. "But tell me," she said. "What happened at Keymer View Court?"

"Ask PCSO Harris. He was on duty the morning after, when I visited the scene. I think he has my camera with the photos in it."

She stood up then and hobbled towards Bishops Court, waving her arms at the officers racing around the building. "Keep back. It's too dangerous."

After a surreptitious glance behind her, she went forward, distracting her comrades.

I rolled onto my hands and knees, hurting in places I hadn't known existed, and crawled into the cover of the trees, moving through the shadows in the opposite direction.

Chapter 28

WEDNESDAY MORNING, THE REAL Remembrance Day, was bright and sunny with the crisp tang of autumn in the air. It was enough to entice me outside to see how I fit into the world. I left my house for the second time in four days, waving to Dee—who watched me like a mother sending her first born off on her inaugural trip to school—got into my shiny, pristine car and drove to Horsham. My leg still throbbed at times, but I no longer had a noticeable limp and the rest of my body was slowly forgiving me for what I had put it through.

After the bomb, I had crawled the perimeter of Bishops Court, unobserved as police cars, emergency vehicles and half the population of West Sussex gathered around the ruins of the pillbox. The riskiest part was the walk back to my car, which was lengthy and agonising. I kept to side streets where foot traffic was minimal. To lessen the risk of discovery, I pulled off my wig and gloves and stuffed them into my bodysuit, arranged around my waist so that anyone seeing me would think I was just another jogger so eager to shed the extra pounds around her middle that she had done herself an injury. It also didn't hurt that there was little chance of running into a police officer or being spotted by a patrol car.

By the time I got to my car I was soaked through and shivering, but the sleet and snow were all gone. Once my car started and the engine stopped shrieking, I backed onto the now deserted road and headed for home.

It was midnight by the time I staggered, drenched and seeping blood from half a dozen places, through my back door and into my kitchen. I had barely had enough time to peel off my bodysuit and hide it before Dee pounced, and for once I was glad to have her. I explained my wounds away, as well as the state of my car, by telling her I had had an accident and she spent the remainder of the weekend fluttering back and forth between her house and mine, nursing me while the twins were napping or otherwise engaged. She clucked and cooed and patched me up and tried to insist on taking me to hospital. I told her I would be fine and slept until noon on Sunday when she knocked on my door to bring me soup and a tuna sandwich.

On Monday, she had Nigel take my car to a garage and get it fixed. I think they felt responsible for my accident, and I felt a little guilty about not dispelling that thought, but I hoped it might keep them from trying something like that again.

Stephen had the good grace to disappear. Dee told me he had put in for a transfer and was moving to Leeds. Whether she thought that would cheer me up or not, I don't know. All I know is that I wasn't bothered one way or the other. I wasn't depressed about Stephen; I was hiding in my house, avoiding contact with the outside world while I waited for the knock on my door. On Tuesday, just after noon, it came.

I was still in my dressing gown, reading a forgettable novel and enjoying the company of a Chilean Sauvignon Blanc when Alex arrived. She had texted early Sunday morning, or late Saturday night, depending on your lifestyle, to check on me and to tell me she would be visiting, but she had sent it to Nadia's phone and I hadn't thought to check it for messages. As it turned out, her message was the single, personal contact among the many hundreds of texts from reporters and journalists, so I wouldn't have found it anyway. But I was glad to see her, and glad to see they had sent her to bring me in. It was an odd relief, like the feeling long time fugitives have when the law catches up with them. She was even out of uniform.

It wasn't until we were seated inside and she had made herself a cup of tea that I began to understand she was not there to arrest me. In fact, I was out of the frame, as she put it. She was the only person who could make a connection between Rachel Davenport and Nadia Penric, and she wasn't talking. The police were unable to trace the true identity of the person who rented the garage and they were still looking for a dark Ford Escort; they had failed to get the registration number.

Then she pulled a half-dozen folded bits of newspaper from her handbag.

"Nadia Martyred Saving Children" was the headline from the local rag. "Night, Night, Nadia" was the headline on *The Echo*; "Nadia, We Hardly Knew Ye" said *The Gazette*; "Why the Cops Hated Nadia" from *The Daily News*.

I scanned the articles, stopping occasionally to wipe tears from my eyes.

The gist of it was that Nadia martyred herself by dragging the bomb into the pillbox and was disintegrated in the blast. The outpouring of public grief had been amazing, and then the photos of Carl and Derek digging in the back of Keymer View Court surfaced, proving her innocence once and for all.

"So PCSO Harris did take my camera?"

Alex stuffed the news articles back into her handbag and pulled out my camera. "I convinced him to come clean. He said he thought it was just a camera someone lost and once he realised what it was he freaked and didn't know what to do. He was more than relieved to give me the camera in return for my promise to not dob him in."

"So how did the photos get in the papers?"

She shrugged. "I don't know; someone must have leaked them."

I made us a late lunch; a sumptuous feast of fish fingers and chips. I even dressed for the occasion, the first time since Sunday I'd been out of my dressing gown and PJs. While we ate, she filled me in on what I'd missed.

Sawyer had been picked up on his way through customs, along with his attaché case. Derek and Carl were in custody and—as Alex quaintly phrased it—Carl had rolled on Derek, Derek had rolled on Sawyer and Sawyer had rolled on his syndicate connections and the local councillors who were on their payroll. And Jazziah Halder was already gaining media attention and corporate backing in his efforts to start an outreach program to help wean young offenders away from a life of crime.

During our easy conversation, I noticed how light I felt; it was the same feeling I'd had on my first day in Fuerteventura, but without the cloud of my impending return looming on the horizon. Now, the skies were clear.

"What are you smiling about?" Alex asked, stuffing another ketchup-soaked French fry into her mouth.

"Is it true? I'm no longer a fugitive?"

She nodded. "And I think it would be best to keep it that way."

After the meal and the washing up, Alex helped me go through the house to collect anything that might link me to Nadia. We gathered the bodysuit, shoes, gloves, wigs, make-up and utility belt and went through the clothes I'd stuffed in the boot of the Golf. We put it all in a box and drove in Alex's car to where the Escort was parked, still unmolested, on the side street in Maidenbower. I rented another storage unit at a different location, in my own name this time, and parked the Escort inside. It would be safe there; once the excitement blew over, I could decide what to do with it.

By then it was getting dark and we drove to a secluded place on the Downs for our own, private and belated bonfire night. When the fire was roaring, I threw everything into it, one item at a time. The last thing I threw in was the figurine of Wonder Woman. It lay for a few moments on top of the glowing coals, then melted into a red, white and blue pool, and disappeared.

"No more living the double life," Alex said.

I smiled, but then remembered my whole life was a lie.

"What is it?"

I sighed. "There's something else."

She looked at me, her face impassive and non-judgmental in the flickering firelight. This had nothing to do with being on the wrong side of the law; it was simply a question of trust. I looked at her and decided she was trustworthy. "I'm not really Rachel Davenport, or at least, not just Rachel Davenport, the unemployed, ex-superhero. I'm still living a secret life."

Her eyes studied my face. "I thought so," she said.

My smile returned. "It feels good, not having secrets."

Alex looked into the fire, strangely pensive. "We all have secrets," she said.

Out of habit, I left my car at the park and ride and took the bus into town, feeling as if I were bunking off of work. It was twenty minutes to eleven and I wanted to be at the pillbox for the two minute silence; my way of saying a final farewell to Nadia. I walked down the Bishopric and passed The Pedaller. The shop front had been replaced and a new security gate put in place. I gazed though the glass. Malcolm and Robin were both there, both looking my way. My heart constricted, then eased and settled like a cold lump in my stomach when I realised they were looking at me as if I was a stranger, which I was.

I moved on and pulled Nadia's phone from my handbag. It was the only thing I hadn't burned; I was hoping it would ring. It never did.

The pillbox, or the site where the pillbox used to be, was ahead of me. I had been hoping for some private time, but a crowd was gathering. Many of them, heedless of the blue and white crime scene tape and orange health and safety barriers, had placed flowers on the mountain of bouquets already obscuring the pile of rubble; some were crying, all were reverently hushed. I arrived and mixed in, keeping to myself as the throng buzzed and hummed around me. More people arrived, a news van pulled up, a police car idled nearby. At the stroke of eleven, everyone fell silent.

We stood together, heads bowed, joined in our mourning for those who sacrificed all for the sake of others. I glanced around at the crowd, surprised by the turn out. Sanjay and his family were huddled together, the mother gripping Sanjay in a protective hug, and nearby I recognised several residents of Keymer View Court. Howard and Maggie were there, as well, along with Chantelle. The news crew from the van, microphones in hand and cameras on shoulders, were also silent and bowed, but continued edging towards the rear of the crowd where a pair of PCs stood on either side of Jazziah Halder. Carl was there, too, but unguarded, meaning he must have been granted bail.

There was also someone I didn't see. I bowed my head and tried to put it out of my mind. That was not what I had come for; I was here for Nadia. I was going to miss her, but in actuality she didn't die, she was in me, where she belonged all the time.

When the two minutes ended, the crowd dispersed in solemn silence. A gaggle of girls moved forward; I recognised a few of them as the party girls from town. They stretched far up the pile and tossed a Nadia tee shirt, a handful of buttons and even a couple pair of knickers on the top. They landed next to the crowning flower arrangement: a cross of white roses bearing the inscription "I am Nadia."

I turned away and, in the ebbing crowd, caught sight of a group of people—two men and a woman—walking slowly away. I recognized the woman as Christine, but the men walking with her, both wearing sport jackets, did not look like the Malcolm and Robin I had just seen in the shop. If it hadn't been for the blonde ponytail on the taller of the two I would have thought they were someone else. I smiled; Christine must have made them smarten up for the occasion. Somehow, that thought brought me peace.

There were only a few people at the scene now. Among them were the police and Halder, who was being interviewed by the news crew. Nadia's legacy lives on.

One other person lingered near the barriers, taking an inordinate amount of interest in the rubble. It was Martin. He noticed me standing there and looked my way. We exchanged nods. I looked back to the pile of flowers. "I'm sorry about this, Mr Palmer," I said, wondering if he knew what I was apologising for.

"I'm not," he said. "I was looking forward to the ceremony, it's true, but I am so proud that my efforts—our efforts— allowed this Vickers machine gun pillbox to be used for the

231

defence of our countrymen. I'm just so sorry this brave woman had to sacrifice herself to save those people."

He pulled a hanky from his pocket and dabbed his eyes. "She disintegrated in the blast, you know," he said when he composed himself. "Such a brave and selfless act."

I nodded. The police weren't daft enough to believe that, but they allowed everyone else to think it, hoping it would draw Nadia into exposing herself. Good plan, but it wasn't going to work. And at least they were allowing Nadia a good send off.

Martin came and stood next to me, still looking towards the pile of rubble. "I'm sorry I fired you," he said.

"I deserved it."

"No, I overreacted. We'd just been burgled, and I was upset and, well, you can have your job back if you want it. I heard about your accident. You can take sick leave for your missed days."

I stared at the flowers marking Nadia's grave. "That would be nice. Thank you, Mr Palmer."

"You can start back Monday. Take the week to get yourself better."

He walked away then, without a word, his head bowed, looking like a man in a funeral procession. I was about to move when my phone rang. I reached in my handbag. It was Nadia's phone.

All Nadia had received so far were texts that had gone unanswered. Dead people don't respond to messages, and they don't answer the phone. I looked at the number; I didn't recognise it. I took a chance.

"Hello?"

Silence. Oh great, I thought, here we go again. Then a voice.

"It's you?"

"Yes," I said. "So you finally decided to call. Nothing like keeping a girl waiting."

More silence.

"I was afraid you wouldn't answer. I wouldn't have been able to face that. The papers all said . . . I looked for you half the night after the police let me go. I didn't know what to do."

"Well. I'm fine. Is that all you wanted to know?"

"Yes. Well, no. Am I going to see you again? Without you trying to get us both killed, I mean."

I waited to make him think I was considering it. "When?"

"Well, I don't know, I suppose—"

"Costa Coffee, West Street, ten minutes," I said.

"Well, sure, I—"

"If you're busy, we could make it another time."

"No. No, I'll be there. Will I recognise you?"

"Don't worry, I'll recognise you. By the way, nice sport jacket."

"How did you—"

"I'm a superhero, remember?"

I hung up, smiling.

It was taking a chance. Did I trust him enough? I removed my glasses and tossed them on the pile of flowers. They landed near the base of the cross. It was as fitting a memorial as I could think of. I turned and walked back towards town.

About the Author

Michael Harling is originally from upstate New York. He moved to Britain in 2002 and is the author of *Postcards From Across the Pond*, *More Postcards From Across the Pond* and *Postcards From Ireland*, as well as The Talisman series. He currently lives in Sussex.

Lindenwald Press
Sussex, United Kingdom

Printed in Great Britain
by Amazon

57075308R00138